Y054934

` ıuld be returned
ּtampeᵈ '

D1341708

Okay Then That's Great

By Susannah Wise:

This Fragile Earth

Okay Then
That's Great

Susannah Wise

First published in Great Britain in 2022 by Gollancz
an imprint of The Orion Publishing Group Ltd
Carmelite House, 50 Victoria Embankment
London EC4Y 0DZ

An Hachette UK Company

1 3 5 7 9 10 8 6 4 2

A CIP catalogue record for this book is
available from the British Library.

ISBN (Hardback) 978 1 473 23237 2
ISBN (Export Trade Paperback) 978 1 473 23238 9
ISBN (eBook) 978 1 473 23240 2
ISBN (Audio) 978 1 473 23241 9

Typeset by Deltatype Ltd, Birkenhead, Merseyside

Printed in Great Britain by Clays Ltd, Elcograph S.p.A

www.gollancz.co.uk

For Chloe, Caro, Fritha, Lou, Rachel, and Nikki:
women I love, gone too soon.

Chapter 1

I'm standing in the booze aisle of Waitrose on Essex Road, when I see my dead sister. It's my third sighting in as many months. As I stare at a wall of indecipherable rums, there's a familiar sound that makes my head flick up, as one might for a fire alarm, or more appropriately in this instance for something resplendent, the peal of church bells perhaps. This particular noise is objectively prosaic yet, to my ears, entirely gorgeous. It's the sound of Perdita clearing her throat.

There she is not twenty feet away, studying the label on a bottle of white from the refrigerator section. I see her nose wrinkle as she puts the bottle back on its shelf. She looks at her watch and closes the fridge door. My feet are already moving me towards her, but she's turning her back and walking in the opposite direction to the tills at the far end. My mouth opens to call her name, but it's as though I have something jammed inside. I rush at her, telling myself that this time it'll be different. She won't disappear before I reach her. She won't.

Here she *is*, right up close.

Closer.

She's faster than me. She's wearing a pale grey cardigan that billows as she hurries away and chic black leggings, and I'm unable to connect this person with the Perdita I knew, who was a slouch, as I still am.

In a flash, she's rounded the corner and disappeared. My heart. No, no, no.

I race after her, but she's gone – just poof into thin air.

My sister. My twin. My Perdita.

I lean against a shelf, head in hands, to catch my breath. I can smell her perfume. Grapefruity.

It *had* to be her. Didn't it?

I almost glide to the till to pay for my stuff. I'm crying but I don't feel sad. I have no idea what it is I feel.

'And then she disappeared,' I say.

'Again,' Schlap says.

'Exactly. Though the previous sightings have been from further away.'

'Tell me about them.'

'Okay, um, again? I've told you already. The first was when she came out of Pure Gym on Essex Road just as I was passing, remember?'

Schlap doesn't.

'She was wearing red Lycra and carrying some sort of juice. I ran after her, then she just ... wasn't there any more. It was as though she'd dematerialised. The second time, I was wandering through Hackney by the canal. You and I discussed this in our very first session.'

Schlap nods. I'm not sure if this means 'carry on' or 'stop there, I remember now'.

'I saw her ahead, walking up one of those steep ramps they have on the towpath where the locks are. I followed her. When I reached the crest, that was it – gone. I wasn't even convinced then that she truly resembled Perds, it was more a sense of her, an essence. But, well, *three* times? Each time she's looked the same age as I am now. That's confusing, isn't it? If she's a ghost, why hasn't she remained seventeen?'

Schlapoberstein says nothing. I hear the ticking of the wall clock.

'Do you think I'm going mad?'

'I'd be interested to know,' my shrink begins, carefully, 'if *you* think you're going mad.'

He's always interested. I try to imagine him saying, '*Tell me, lady.*'

'I don't know. And the throat-clearing thing she did? When we were young, Perdita would do that before an exam or running a race – events that would cause her adrenaline levels to rise. I don't think she was even aware of it.'

In truth, this used to irritate me, but I don't suppose this is currently relevant.

'Can I ask, do you enjoy these sightings?'

'Enjoy isn't the right word. More: marvel at. But it's only marvellous if she's real, isn't it? Not if she's a figment of my mind.'

Schlap removes his glasses, cleans them on his jumper and replaces them on his nose. 'You say you were in the Waitrose alcohol aisle at 10 a.m. Do you drink frequently?'

'Yes, but not in the morning! I wasn't *drunk*. Jesus. I didn't even get the rum I came for. I forgot it in the confusion.'

'Rum?'

I flap my hands dismissively. 'The twins have asked for Caribbean punch at their party.'

'The twins ... ?'

'Um. Blythe and Sylvia?'

He looks at me blankly. Why is he forgetting everything? He forgot my name yesterday.

'Schlap! My twin daughters! They're turning eighteen next weekend, remember? Ben and I are throwing them a big party? And it's a deal because that's the same age, you know' – I take a breath – 'that Perdita died.'

'Yes.' He smiles kindly.

'I took a pause just then; it isn't because I'm sad. I mean, I *am*, obviously, but not like that.'

'Like what?'

'Just to say her name.'

We begin a staring contest. I look away first.

There's a painting of a large white mouse, or perhaps a small white rat, on the wall; in five months of coming here, I've never noticed.

'I'm thinking, Marnie,' he says, 'about symbols. About the sightings of your sister as symbolic. As a sort of living mandala.'

'A ... ? Symbolic? Of what?'

Schlap beams beatifically. 'You've described your job, your poetry, as "immature".'

I'm becoming hot under the armpits. 'Well, not immature, per se. The official pigeonhole for my style is contemporary, whatever that means. Poetry really shouldn't be classified, but that's how the publisher marketed it first time round.' All those years ago. Oh, God. 'I'm probably not contemporary any more. I'm vintage. Maturity is relative. You likely think of me as a child.'

'Is that what I think?'

'No. Sorry.'

'Why are you sorry? I'm not upset.'

'OK. Sorry. Oops.' I laugh. Schlap doesn't. 'My dad tells me off for apologising.'

'He tells you off.'

Schlap's wearing a signet ring. Do Jews have coats of arms?

4

Pretty sure Dad's ancestors didn't. I think of Perdita in Waitrose, her grey cardi.

'Do you believe in multiple universes, quantum entanglement, that kind of thing?'

His eyebrows go up. 'Do you?'

'I don't know. If it's good enough for the world's best physicists ...'

He nods. '... then it's good enough for you?'

'You talk an awful lot for an analyst,' I say, though this is the opposite of what he does.

'I do?'

'I thought you were supposed to be mostly silent?'

'Would you like me to be silent?'

'Not really.'

'Okay then.'

There is the sound of drilling outside. The soft part of my elbows are itchy, but I try not to scratch.

'Why does thinking about symbols make you ask about my work? Can we not talk about writing. I've a meeting with Veronica tomorrow morning. The only symbols here point either to quantum entanglement, or to my suffering from some sort of mental illness. Neither of these options make me sound particularly well, do they?'

'Veronica?'

Oh, bloody hell. 'She's my *editor*. Remember? I've talked about her *so* many times. At Euclid, my publishing house?' He obviously doesn't. I stare at my fingernails. They're dirty. They always are. I can't work out why. 'How can Perdita be a mandala?'

'Well, could she be a subconscious representation of the missing divine? And/or a distraction from pain.'

'The ... what? I don't think so. I don't need divine – I've

got science and death, and that's enough to be going on with, but if you're interested in my subconscious, you might want to hear about last night's dream. It was a new one.'

I love telling Schlap about my dreams. He never yawns or looks away or says things like, 'Other people's dreams are so *complicated*.'

'If you like.'

I wipe my face with the back of my sleeve. 'In it, I had a penis. A large one.'

The long hand moves to eleven forty-five on the wall clock. An extended silence, in which Schlap's face doesn't twitch, not even the corners of his mouth.

'And what happened with your penis?'

'Nothing. It was just *there*. When I say large, bigger than normal is what I mean. That's no judgement, by the way, about men with small ones. The size might not be relevant, but I wanted to tell you in case it was. And it was circumcised. A woman with a penis.' I'd like to stop saying the word 'penis' now.

In truth, it wasn't strictly a dream, more of a daydream – one I've entertained many times in the past.

'Is your father circumcised?' Schlap is saying.

In my head, my father climbs into his morning shower, his shrivelled member no bigger than a flesh-coloured Jelly Tot. 'Uh, yes. But the dream wasn't about my dad's, er ...' I feel a little green. 'It was about me; my willy.'

'And your son?'

Dad is out of the shower and stepping onto the bathmat, patting Blenheim Bouquet across his fresh-shaven face.

'For religious reasons,' I say, hoping this non sequitur can row us into a conversational delta.

I wasn't thinking at all when I suggested this. I'd prefer now to be back discussing Perdita, my poems, the mandala.

'Your son is circumcised for religious reasons?'

'No, sorry, my dad. I'm an atheist. My son is intact, so to speak.' I laugh in case intact is incorrect terminology. 'As are my daughters. Because we're not in Somalia.' My words echo in my head. 'I'm so sorry. Female circumcision is not a joke.'

Schlap's face remains expressionless. He's not to be trusted. Analysts don't miss a trick – seventy-five pounds for forty-five minutes works out at roughly one pound sixty-six per minute. He could at least crack a smile.

'And if nothing happened, then what did you *want* to do with your penis?' he asks.

'Put it inside someone.'

'A man?'

'Gross. No, a woman.'

'A man would be gross, but not a woman.'

Always the rhetorical question. I long to shrug but don't in case Schlap thinks I'm a self-hating Jew.

'Inside your sister?' he suggests.

'Oh my God, are you crazy?'

He crosses his legs the other way. One of his suede shoes makes a brushing sound against the rug.

'Have you ever used a strapped-on penis?' he asks.

I laugh again. It's sort of a snigger. He's in his eighties. His eyes narrow slightly. He might be offended, though he'd probably say that's my projection.

'The correct name is strap-on, and that's a very personal question, Schlap.' I raise an eyebrow, show my teeth, aiming for complicity between us, for a feeling that together we're winning.

'You flirt when you're embarrassed.'

'I ... ? No.' Bit optimistic, given his age.

'*I* ... ?' he says.

'Hmm? I? You? What?'

This is the equivalent of intellectual origami.

'You said, *I*,' says Schlap, 'after which you self-censored. I'd be interested to know what that thought was. Would you like to finish?'

'Not really. Let's stick to facts. I had a dream: in it, I had a penis.'

His head is nodding. 'So you say. Interesting.'

'Is it? The dream was sort of sexy. I woke, took the dog out, picked up his poo, brushed my teeth, had breakfast, got the kids off to school, went to Waitrose, saw my sister, which I feel is the most *important* part of our talk here today. After our session, I'll be visiting my ageing parents, returning home, hanging out washing, emptying the dishwasher, shopping for the week's food. I might get five minutes to stare at my computer. I might not.'

'You like to stick to facts,' Schlapoberstein says matter-of-factly.

The clock does its on-the-hour chime. My eyes flick up. Midday: good.

'When you're not busy with domestic chores,' he adds.

Technically, it's the end of our session, but he's not making any finishing-up movements. He pins me to my seat with his analyst's gaze.

'Could your sister's apparition be an escape from the mundanity of life?'

As a reflex, my hand fiddles in my bag for my purse. 'Oh,' I say, nodding at the clock, 'it's time.'

'It is?'

'You must have other clients waiting.'

'Must I?' Schlapoberstein breaks a smile. He's saved it for when I'm leaving. 'Patience.'

'Yes, sorry. I have a tendency to hurry.'

'No. *Patients*, not clients. My visitors; they're patients.'

'Ah, course. Ben always corrects me on that. Our kids think it's funny.'

I know Schlap knows I made up that last bit.

'That I get it wrong,' I say eventually. 'Look, you're probably hungry. For lunch. I know I am.' I sound ridiculous. I pull out a wad of notes and count them messily in front of him.

It's not that I don't wish to talk about Perdita with him, I really do. It's just that under pressure I can't stop making jokes. I don't know why.

'I have a suggestion for you,' he says.

'Oh. That's. What is it?'

'Have you ever made a list of all the things you love about your sister?'

'No.'

'I'd like you to have a go.'

I give him the side-eye. 'Why?'

'Keep an open mind.'

I try to stand. The chair is one of those ergonomic ones. It takes two attempts before I'm on my feet. Schlap remains as is. He recrosses his legs. I long to warn him about damage to his spine. I place the money as quietly as I can on the table beside his chair.

'Goodbye,' I almost whisper, not sure why.

'Goodbye, Katherine.'

'Marnie.'

'I beg your pardon?'

'My name. It's Marnie.'

'So it is.' He blinks at his mistake.

'Who's Katherine?'

'No idea. See you tomorrow, same time.'

I leave his room and pass the curtained area where the next client possibly waits. Someone has changed the flowers in the hall: red roses, where irises had been the day before.

A second after stepping out of the double doors into Harley Street, I'm on the phone to Ben. I'm not going to tell him about seeing Perdita. My sister and I would always share secrets. Keeping it to myself for the moment is my way of honouring that. Besides, when I reported the previous two sightings, Ben didn't believe me. My own partner. How awful is that. None of my family did.

'How was the sesh?' he says in place of hello, which I like.

'He called me Katherine.'

'So?'

'It's not my name.' My bag drags on my shoulder. I can't remember what's in it.

'Right.'

'Don't you think that's odd? I mean, the eminence; his books and all that.'

'You did say you needed an old-school shrink who looked like a Jewish Father Christmas. A little synapse failure goes with the territory, surely.'

This makes me smile. 'But the name-forgetting thing is just weird and out of character. He's forgetting loads. Is that old person stuff, or Freudian transference? It's not very professional.'

Ben makes a funny noise at the other end.

'What? Don't scoff at a laywoman. You think it's something else?'

'No. Soz. Dropped the cashews. They were in that mini Tupperware, the one without the lid. You were saying?'

'You're like this with your own clients – I mean patients – aren't you? Not really listening.'

'I'll admit I occasionally fall asleep when they're in the room.'

His mouth is full. 'But they don't realise, you know, because the chaise faces the big window.'

I pass a woman with two crazed white poodles on retractable leads. 'The *chaise*? You told me you'd ditched that relic.'

'When?'

'Six months ago.'

'Did I?' he says. 'I must have changed my mind. It's a classical tool for extracting truths.'

'It acts as a sort of psychological dentist.'

'Exactly.' Ben giggles. 'It encourages clients to relax.'

'And you too, apparently.' The poodles are yapping irritatingly close to my ear. 'You know, Schlap asked me to make a list of all the things I loved about Perds.'

'Sounds nice.'

'*Nice?*'

'Sensible. Helpful. Appropriate.'

His lack of engagement propels me to blurt, 'It happened again.'

'What did?'

'I saw Perd—'

'What's that barking noise? I'm busy drafting chapter ten, Marns. Hang on a tic, the kettle's boiled. Be right back.'

The sound of Ben's socked feet on flexing wooden floorboards, moving away from the microphone. The kitchen cabinet is opening. The scraping of a cup on marble. Gurgling water.

The poodles are running round and round their owner, winding her legs in nylon like Houdini. I wait for Ben to return to our conversation. He's left the phone face down on the table, I can tell. His feet are on the move again, travelling further off.

'Ben?'

A door slams in the background.

I pull the phone away from my ear and call into the screen. 'Ben? I'm still here, for God's sake. I saw Perds again! I saw her in—'

The faint tinkling of pee on ceramic.

I know he hasn't done it on purpose.

'Tell me about what happened with Perdita,' I say to myself in an approximation of Ben's voice. Then I reply in my own, 'Thank you, Ben, I will. I'll tell you later,' and click off.

Ben is writing an analytical, yet highly commercial, self-help book entitled *How to Stay in a Partnership*, by Dr B. Hopkiss. I really miss my sister.

The Toyota waits patiently for me in its bay in the NCP beneath Cavendish Square. I pip the key fob thingy and climb in. I set off to Mum and Dad's, the car's motor doing whatever hybrid engines do – sort of hum – and pray for a smooth run up the A1 while I think about how on earth I'm going to compile Schlap's list.

It's nose-to-tail Audi Q5s as I coast into St Albans. Something about this place sends my stomach to my feet. I sit in line, staring at the Fat Faces and the White Stuffs, and mull over my session: a woman in possession of a penis, even in a waking dream, must surely be suffering from deep sexual dysfunction. It's no wonder Ben and I are simply cohabiting. I wouldn't marry me, either.

I wish I were a more traditional sort of female, one with less *yang*; the sort who pushes a Bugaboo into LK Bennett on St Albans high street to buy nude patent platform courts.

I google 'mandala' and wonder again exactly what Schlap was driving at. I can accept – just – my sightings of Perdita as a distraction from pain. But Perdita as a mandala – a symbol? Of what? She was my other half. Simple. Grief doesn't get better with age. In that respect it's not anything like cheese.

My phone bleeps. It's a text from Faaris Agarwal at Bethnal Green Working Men's Club, with whom I've had, so far, a fruitful glyphic relationship but am yet to meet in person:

> Could we chat about your girls' party sometime today?
> Caterers need to finalise details. Party in nine days; we
> respectfully remind you we haven't yet received payment in
> full.

I chuck the phone on the passenger seat. Perdita and I were meant to share our joint eighteenth at the same venue. History repeating itself, I know, but my girls specifically asked to stage it there. I think they were trying to honour her, acknowledge my loss, that sort of thing. I was so touched I couldn't say no. I'll nudge Ben about the money later.

There's a woman on the pavement waving at me through the passenger window. She's trapped in a teal-coloured synthetic skirt suit and black heels, the regulation uniform for Foxtons at the end of the road. She'll probably have a green Mini parked round the corner with one of those vanilla-scented button fresheners on the dash. She's smiling but it's more of a gurn.

I sense a longing to escape behind her intimidating row of clenched white teeth. Or maybe that's another projection. Since I started seeing Schlap, life has become like a series of exhausting Agatha Christie novellas. Nothing is as it seems; every event, every action, leads to a rabbit hole of hidden motives and subverted desires *of my own*. She could just need the loo.

She's still waving. I don't know her. I look the other way.

The high street clock clanks to 1.30 p.m. I'm fifteen minutes late. My mother will be sighing over spoiled baguettes. The

13

traffic's bad; it's her fault in the first place for moving here. I was never late when they lived in Kentish Town.

The suited woman is now pointing at the front of the Prius. I don't think her bob suits her. She looks like Richard III and makes me think of Nicola Barker at Torriano Primary. Nicola's recent following of me on Instagram coincided with her second marriage and subsequent assault of photos. I wrote 'pretty lady' in the comments section. I'd wanted to write 'pretty woman' to mark myself as feminist, but thought it might be wrongly interpreted owing to the film.

I lower the glass. 'Do we know each other?'

'Your front light isn't working.' Her voice is surprisingly deep.

'Oh, right. Thanks,' I say, 'but it's daytime.'

'Yes,' she says, 'but for later.'

I wave goodbye as I sail through the lights, piqued that she's appropriated my 'but' as adjunct to ordinary syntax. I read it as a subconscious act of aggression. Or perhaps it's unconscious. I get the two muddled.

My phone rings. It's my mother. I check for police before wedging it between chest and chin.

'I'll be there in five, Ma.'

'The baguettes are going hard.'

I bought my father a bread maker for his birthday, though only Mum uses it; he still prefers to make loaves by hand. As well as the spoiled 'truncheons', there will be smelly unpasteurised cheese, cherry tomatoes and possibly some elderflower cordial from the Saturday market. My dad cooks all the time, especially at weekends, when his friends make the pilgrimage from London to eat like kings. Afterwards, they receive signed copies of his latest recipe book, *Around the Med with Diabetes*. It's sold surprisingly well.

I'm stuck at yet another set of lights. Teal-coloured Richard III has caught up with the crawling traffic and is about to make her second pass of the Prius. She catches my eye in the rear-view mirror, smiles shyly and looks away.

I'd lay bets she's not aspiring to own a penis. I imagine her at the end of the day letting herself into her flat on the outskirts of town, throwing her jacket across the sofa, sitting down in front of *The Voice* with two girlfriends and a Pinot Grigio. She'll have a boyfriend called Ant; they'll have sex mostly doggy style, all of which makes me sound snobby, though in truth I'm sad and envious about these imagined facts and can't quite fathom why. I notice a small green stain on the side of her skirt. Maybe she likes to roll in grass.

Mum's calling again. 'Have you passed Rymans yet?'

'Yes. I'll be there soon.'

'Your father's blood sugar is low. I had to give him a glass of juice.'

'Feed him! Don't wait for me.'

'God waits at our table, Marnie.'

'Ha. Perhaps because He's tried your baguettes.'

She huffs, but without force.'You've deliberately misinter-preted what I meant. God hears you.'

'No He doesn't, Mum, because He doesn't exist.'

'Hurry up,' she says.

I can't remember the last time my mother was angry. I carry the anger for both of us. This is proof, I tell my parents, of the non-existence of God: if He were real, He'd have distributed the rage more evenly.

I pass the cathedral and wind my way along Fishpool Street onto St Michael's Street. My parents' house is strikingly beautiful; a hotchpotch of Victorian brickwork with Georgian windows. The previous owners painted the plasterwork a vintage off-white with sills, door surround and guttering a dirty fawn gloss. If this sounds disgusting, it really works. Every time I turn into the snub driveway, I understand why my parents live here.

With a mother's sixth sense – or perhaps because the Prius is pinging following my premature decoupling of the seat belt – she awaits me at the door, boobs in inverse proportion to her height, like a sexy Mrs Tiggywinkle. Covering her torso, which is robed in white, is an apron: 'It's called DIET because all the other four-letter words were taken'. My dad bought it for her.

'Your front light isn't working,' she says by way of greeting.

I remind myself not to mention my most recent sighting of Perdita. My mother didn't handle it well the first time. Or the second. I thought she was going to throw a pot at me across the living room, and not in the artistic sense. She's a ceramicist.

I'm pulled into an embrace. She smells of Roquefort and the moonstones dangling from her ears are cold against my jaw.

'You've been using that Aveda curly stuff again,' she says through a mouthful of my hair. 'Patchouli.'

I extract my face from her jewellery. 'Does that mean you like the way I smell, or you don't?'

'Umm ...' Her forehead wrinkles. She looks into space. It takes her an inordinate amount of time to consider such a simple question. 'I don't know. It reminds me of my pre pre-Alpha course days.'

'*Pre*-pre? That's confusing; before-before your rebirth?' My gaze wanders. 'Sort of like what came before the Big Bang?'

There's another new statue in the front garden.

'St Michael,' my mother says, excitement in her voice as she follows my line of sight. 'The church auctioned him off. He fell from that lone gravestone on the little patch of non-consecrated ground when they dug the grave up to get to the Roman amphora.'

'What Roman amphora?'

'Didn't you know? Relic of Verulamium. Worth a fortune. It's gone to The British Museum. Some old dear – actually he's our age and a friend, but seems *so* old comparatively – found it with his metal detector. Traces of iron ore in the paint. That's what set the detector off. He'd bought himself a new one: very expensive, *terribly* sensitive. Queen gave him a commendation at Buckingham Palace.'

'Why are you talking like an army major?'

'What? Don't be silly.'

'Yes. Giving me headlines. Like that.'

I hear my father clashing plates in the kitchen. My mother smiles and gently steers me into the house and down the hall, its long white walls unfurling.

'Jack!' she trills. 'She's here!'

We hit the enormous kitchen. I breathe in. The sun pools yellow light on the parquet.

'The cavalry!' exclaims Dad, beaming.

He's pulling apart a chicory heart with his bare hands; this is about as manly as it gets around here. He used to be an actor, very well known, but turned away from it when Perdita died. The death of a child can do that to a person. I've read this in numerous books about grief. Better to reinvent oneself, live a new life rather than remain inside the old one.

I touch my fingers to a windowpane; it feels warm. An untraceable melancholia lands in my stomach.

I plonk down a bottle of pink fizz on the worktop. 'Happy anniversary, parents mine.'

'I'm making lunch,' says my dad, who enjoys stating the obvious, 'as a gift for your precious mother.'

Love heats my chest. I walk towards my father with my arms wide. He farts, grins.

'Pardon me.'

I give him a squeeze. He also smells of Roquefort. He holds up a jam jar of vinaigrette. The olive oil sloshes gold in the sunlight.

'Can I put garlic in?' he says. 'Planning on snogging anyone later?'

'Don't be disgusting.' I think of Ben tapping away at his laptop.

'Sylvia's coming to stay on Saturday,' says my mother beadily. She pours elderflower cordial into three glasses.

'She is?' My daughters keep secrets from me. For girls of seventeen, they're unusually keen on spending the weekend with their grandparents. 'Just Sylvia? Blythe not coming, too?'

'Blythe said something about a nightclub.' Dad chuckles softly.

'It beats me why Blythe isn't coming here, too,' my mother complains.

'Twins don't have to do everything together,' I say.

Mum's face drops. 'Yes. Thank you, Marnie.'

'Blythe also mentioned a boyfriend,' Dad adds.

'Did she now?' I pop the cork on the fizz.

'I told her to save herself till she's married.' My mother removes her apron and folds it into an asymmetrical shape. Underneath, she's wearing some sort of tunic.

'For God's sake, Ma. She's seventeen. You were at it hammer and tongs at that age.'

'That's different. It was the sixties – I was artsy and yet to meet God. Blythe is entirely scientific: it's a different beast. She already enjoys our Sunday service very much.'

'Science is not a beast.' I can't think of anything cutting. 'Also, Ma, what *are* you wearing? You look like a monk.'

She doesn't seem offended, more surprised that I don't know who she's channelling. 'Today, I'm Nico in *The Inner Scar*.'

'Who? I hope you're not planning to wear that to the girls' party?'

'Course not. I've got something else up my sleeve.' She taps her nose and grins, then says under her breath, 'Can't believe she doesn't know who Nico is.'

'The point is, Patricia' – my father steers us deftly away from these conversational rocks while steering us towards the table – 'Marnie's daughters are off her hands this weekend.'

The possibility of two kids out of the house on Saturday night glistens like a jewel just out of reach. Now, if I could also palm off our thirteen year-old, Stan, Ben and I might have dinner alone, in peace. Twenty years and three almost grown-up children later, I'm still optimistically searching for any opportunity to secure my other half's attention.

A selection of coloured bowls appears on the long kitchen table.

'Chicory, pear and Roquefort,' explains my father with pride. 'Tomato with basil. Panzanella. Olive and orzo. Wild boar salami. Prosciutto crudo. Goat's cheese and your mother's yet-to-become famous baguettes straight out of the maker.'

It looks delicious, and very middle class. 'Are we feeding the five thousand?'

My mother's face darkens. '*And the tongue is a fire, a world of unrighteousness.*'

My dad makes the sound of a buzzer.

'St Albans West?' Mum now in her best University Challenge voice.

'James 3:6?' offers Dad.

I put my head in my hands.

Mum gives a tinkling laugh. 'Correct! St Albans – ten points.'

'No,' says my father, deflating. 'It's five points. Only the starter's worth ten.'

My will is fading. 'Can we eat?' My phone rings. 'Sorry.' I feel my parents bristle as I pull the mobile from my bag: an unknown number. 'Might be Stan's school.'

'But it's the summer holidays,' she counters.

'They're doing academic workshops, I told you. Better take it.' I slink off to the hall, cradling the phone beneath my chin. 'Hallo?'

'Katherine?' says a voice.

It's Schlap.

'It's Marnie.'

There's a pause.

'Who?' Schap asks.

'You've dialled the wrong number, Schlap.'

'Who's Marnie?' He sounds scared.

'I'm your client. Patient. You saw me earlier, just before lunch. Remember?'

'I did?'

'Yes.' I try not to panic. 'We talked about my ... never mind. I've been seeing you for five months? Twice a week to begin with, then five times a week more recently? Which has been expensive – I've borrowed money from Ben to pay for it, which I fully intend to pay back, by the way – and also rather time-consuming. But worth it. I'm not saying I don't love coming, because I do. I think it's helping.'

There is silence at the other end. I'm not sure if this is as a result of my verbal diarrhoea or because he's still in the dark.

'I'm in my late forties. Average looks. Dark hair.'

The blowing noise is Schlap releasing breath. 'Marnie, of course it's you! Yes. I've muddled the number. I was trying to call someone else.'

'Katherine.'

'What?'

This is both awful and ridiculous.

'When I answered the phone you said Katherine. That was who, *whom*, you were trying to call. Wasn't it?'

'Marnie!' My mother's soft tone carries into the hall. 'Lunch is getting warm.'

I sigh. 'Schlap, I've got to go. I'll see you tomorrow, 11 a.m.'

'Look forward to it,' he says cheerily. 'We could perhaps address your feelings about money.'

The line goes dead before I can answer. I make my way back to the kitchen.

My father points at his already full mouth. 'You know how I get. Didn't fancy passing out in the goat's cheese.'

'Of course,' I say. 'Sorry for the delay.'

I sit at the table. My parents' Ercol dining chairs are beautiful but, once seated, like rods against one's buttocks. I take off my sweater and slide it beneath me.

My mother raises an eyebrow. 'Who was on the phone?'

'My shrink.'

She makes a little noise like a hiccup. My father spoons delicious things onto my plate.

'What did he want?' she says. 'You've only just walked out of his office, haven't you?'

I take a forkful of ham; it melts on my tongue.

'He dialled a wrong number. He seemed a bit confused, to be honest.'

My father lays down his cutlery in mock alarm, '*To be honest. Marnie. You, of all people.*'

'All right, calm down. We can't all be Baudelaire. Ham is amazing, by the way.'

The image of Perdita hurrying away from me in the

supermarket is in my head again and the area around my heart is jumping.

'You give me such a hard time over church,' says my mother, smiling.

'What does that mean? This chicory salad is better than ever, Dad.'

'Blessings,' says my father. 'The poetry of food is my business, but you're the real poet.'

And my mother says, 'Well, *analysis*,' at the same time.

I, too, now smell of Roquefort. I pour a large glass of pink bubbles and down it in one. I pour another. My mother's not done yet.

'Analysis, therapy, whatever; we all know it's the modern religion. It's no different from Christianity, except that yours costs a fortune. Loving God is free.' She pulls a piece of pork gristle from her mouth and wraps it carefully in her napkin. 'And one thing I can tell you—'

'Only one?' The bubbles allow me a satisfying belch.

'God *never* dials a wrong number.' She lays her napkin on the table.

The gristle glistens pearly white and plastic-looking, like something the dog might bring up. She watches as I pour a third glass of fizz.

'Aren't you driving?'

'Shame for it to go to waste,' I say. 'Anyway, the car's electric; doesn't count.'

'It will when you're lying face down across the A1.'

'Happy anniversary!' I finish my glass with a flourish.

Mum and Dad exchange glances.

★

By the time I get home, it's 4 p.m. and Stan is traipsing up the path behind me. He waits dejectedly on the front doorstep, rucksack hanging from his elbow as I find my key.

'Good day at summer school?' I ask.

He grunts, which is Stan for affirmative, and pushes past me into the hall. He smells of school and teenage hormones.

He scowls. 'Why does your breath reek of beer?'

The dog lurches at my jeans. I push him down.

'I don't *reek* of beer.' It isn't actually a lie.

Stan stomps up to his room.

'Anyway,' I call after him, 'how do you know what beer smells like?'

'Because I'm thirteen. You also reek of blue cheese.' His door slams.

I climb the stairs, the dog in my wake licking my fingers as if they were sausages. I stand in front of my son's closed door.

'I thought you were going to Trey's this afternoon. Get off me, Parker.'

Stan's muffled voice just about reaches me.

'I've come home to play with Trey.'

'Is he in there with you?'

His door opens suddenly.

'Mum,' he says. 'I'm playing *Fortnite*. Trey's console is at his house. Mine is here. It's a multi-player game.'

'So, let me get this straight – in order to have a play date—'

'*Play* date? I'm not five.'

'In order to hang out with Trey, you have to be in your separate homes?'

Stan stares. 'You've only just noticed? Good to know you've been paying attention.'

'You're back later than I thought!' Ben's shout carries down from the top floor.

'You're here!' I shout back unnecessarily.

'I'm having a poo!'

'Ugh, Dad!' Stan's door slams again.

'My mother gave me a coffee' – I aim my voice in the direction of the bathroom in case Stan thinks I'm still addressing him – 'and made me lie on the sofa for thirty minutes before she let me leave their house.'

'Right,' says Ben.

I study the picture on the landing; the one with the funny cylinder shapes, sketched in charcoal by Ben's artist aunt, Esther. All I see when I look at it are penises. Penii? Penes? The dog whines. I look down. He's bent in half to clean himself.

I make my way downstairs thinking about Schlap, about his muddled memory, and wonder if he's aware it's going. How terrified I'd feel if I were him, if my brain was letting me down, playing host to a dark magician, an enemy.

My mobile rings. Please let it not be Schlap. I pull it from my bag. It's Blythe.

'You at home?' is her greeting.

I notice Ben has left his fencing foil in the hall. The rubber safety stopper at its tip has frayed.

'Yes, I am. How are you?'

I'm in the kitchen now. I open the back door. Parker bounds gratefully into the garden.

'D'you know where my history book is, the orange one: *The Glorious Revolution*? That one. Have you seen it?'

'I haven't. How was school study today?'

'Right. Thanks.' She calls off.

On the table, my laptop is open and asleep, the screen black and disappointed-looking, as though it's long ago given up waiting for me to work at it. The dog is scratching outside the door. I let him back in, sit down in front of my computer and hit the space bar, but all that's in my head are the words: *Veronica tomorrow, Veronica tomorrow.*

The poem I began five months ago but still haven't finished glows bathetically in the digital blue light, the cursor flashing at the end of the word 'govern': it's not rhyming. I'm not even sure what it's about. Nominally words disappearing from a sheaf of paper, but any idiot could tell that's not really it. Since I saw Perdita that first time outside Pure Gym back in May, nothing has really made sense, as if seeing her has robbed me of my right to express myself.

Beneath the table, the dog settles on my feet.

I cast my eyes balefully left to right across each line before switching fonts to Chalkboard to make myself laugh. I'm procrastinating, but only because I know I'll be interrupted in about two minutes.

Sure enough, the phone rings.

'Me again,' says Blythe. 'I forgot to say, please could we put Pantea on the list for the party. And also, give Parker a kiss from me.'

'You can give him a kiss yourself in a minute when you're home.'

There's sudden discomfort in the area of my crotch. I hope I'm not getting thrush.

'*Mum.* I'm not coming home till much later.'

'Why not?'

'Because I'm looking for my history book, I just told you. Is your memory going?'

'You didn't tell me that. You said—'

'It doesn't *matter.*' She hangs up.

I return to my computer. I thought she and Sylvia had fallen out with Pantea.

Ben lurches into the kitchen, glasses pushed up on top of his head, giving himself an unintentional cowlick.

'Is there anything to eat? I'm starving.'

He sweeps past me, brushing my lips with the tips of his fingers, which sounds sexy but isn't. He likes to fiddle with a ball of Blu-Tack while he's writing. He says it helps him think.

I stare at the dog. The dog stares back.

Ben opens a cupboard. His head disappears inside.

I close the laptop and get to my feet. 'I think there's some lasagne I can reheat for you in the fridge.'

'Where are the cashews?'

'You ate them. When you were on the phone to me earlier.'

'I did?' He pulls his head out.

'Yes! What's wrong with everyone today? By the way, the twins are out on Saturday night, according to my dad.'

'Your *dad*? How is he now the High Priest of their social calendar?'

The dog yawns.

'Dunno. We might want to think about pushing Stan out for a sleepover,' I say. 'Then we could go out together. Just us. There's something I need to talk to you about.'

'Mmm? Don't use the downstairs loo; it's broken again.' He wanders from the room, a bruised banana midway to his mouth.

Once he's gone, I remember I've forgotten to tell him about the money for the party.

It is later and somehow, I've managed to corral my entire family round the kitchen table for dinner. I've rustled up tofu stir-fry, which unfortunately Ben hates, but the twins are in a vegan phase and it was the only appropriate foodstuff in the fridge.

Everyone chews valiantly, eyes streaming, noses blowing, because I accidentally added too much chilli thinking it was the mild kind and not the kind that blows your head off. Stan is picking through his bowl, fork hanging limply from his left hand, hooking out the onions and scraping them from the tines to the tabletop. I tell him to stop. He tosses them to Parker instead.

'Don't do that!' yells Blythe. 'Dogs can't eat onions!'

'Is there anything I *can* do?' he yells back, pushing his fringe out of his face.

Sylvia shushes him and Stan says, 'Anyway, Parker likes them: look.'

It's true – the dog is gobbling up Stan's offerings, licking his chops and lifting his head for more. I wonder about the chilli and its effect on animals.

Ben pulls a hanky from his jeans and mops his brow. He catches me looking and gives a martyred smile.

'Mmm. Great, Marns.'

'You're welcome.' I turn to the twins, who are simultaneously texting on their phones. 'Are you writing to each other? No devices at the table, please.' They put them away. 'So,' I say, 'tell me all about your study days at summer school.'

'What would you like to know?' Sylvia asks reasonably.

'Well.'

What *would* I like to know? How was lunch? I know the answer to that one already. What did you learn? Boring. How does school compare to when Perdita and I were young, perhaps, but that's far too generalised, and anyway, I've asked this before. Plus, it's not really school per se, it's summer school, which is surely something different. Really, I just want to feel a connection to my children, of any sort. They seem far away from me tonight, as if they're in another house entirely.

Stan says, 'Mum, did you breastfeed us?'

'I certainly did.' The intimacy of his inquiry makes me flush with pleasure.

27

Blythe snorts and Sylvia looks up from her bowl. At least now I don't have to answer my daughter's question of what I want to learn from her about school.

'For about nine months I breastfed each one of you.' I'm warming to my subject. 'It was far tougher with the twins, of course.' I really don't give my kids the credit they deserve. 'On one breast I had—'

'Right.' Stan cuts me off. He tosses another forkful of onions at Parker, who is now panting. 'It's just, we're doing a project on animal teats in science.'

'That's nice.'

I look to my girls for assistance – they're usually on it at the slightest hint of anti-feminist rhetoric – but Sylvia is busy with her food and Blythe is staring at me with faint disgust.

'What?' I demand.

'It's just ...' Her lips curls back.

'Boobs like two tangerines in a sock?' chuckles Ben, shovelling stir-fry down his gullet as Blythe bursts out laughing.

'That's so wrong, Dad!' She's in hysterics.

Parker laps frantically at his water bowl.

'I beg your pardon?' I turn my body towards my partner with affected melodrama, reminding myself of my mother.

'Like two pitta breads?' Stan chips in, obliging Ben's misogynistic moment.

I'm not even offended. I mean I should be, but I can't be bothered. Also, the image of my boobs like pitta breads *is* quite funny.

'Thank you, ladies and gentlemen. I'd like it to be known that I'm still a respectable D cup.'

Stan looks traumatised. 'What's a D cup?'

'Moving on,' I say. 'What about other aspects of science?'

I'm thinking about my day. All three children look up. Stan asks what I mean.

'Well, do you,' I begin airily, 'study quantum mechanics, for instance?'

The kids are blank-faced. I quickly mention 'Many-Worlds Interpretation' and ensure my intonation goes up at the end, so they know I require an answer. There's a silence during which the only sound is Parker's laboured breathing.

'Er. That's university-level stuff, Mum,' says Blythe. 'Dad?'

'Huh?' Ben looks up suddenly, as if caught doing something he shouldn't. 'What's that?'

Blythe rolls her eyes. 'Many-Worlds Interpretation.'

Ben looks blank.

'Quantum entanglement,' she presses. 'Know it?'

'*Know* it?'

I've lived with Ben long enough to realise that when he stresses a word in order to make the other person look stupid, he's playing for time.

'Wouldn't say I *know* it. I'm *familiar* with the concept. Why?'

Blythe shrugs and lifts her chin at me. 'She's asking.'

'*She?*' I say in the same tone Ben said *know*. 'Thanks a bunch.'

Ben pulls a single strand of long hair from his mouth. I forgot to tie mine back while cooking. He tries to shake it from his finger, but it just entwines itself further, like Captain Haddock and the sticking plaster in *The Calculus Affair*.

'Why d'you want to know about quantum entanglement, Marns? Seen another UFO?'

My cheeks burn. It's true: I did once claim I'd seen a flying saucer while on a writing retreat in Suffolk.

'Forget it.'

I can't tell him about meeting Perdita in Waitrose in front of the kids because I haven't mentioned any of my sightings to them thus far. The omission was on the pretext of preventing anxiety, but really it was in case the kids sniffed that their mother was nuts. I dip my face towards my bowl and shove in some broccoli.

Things I Loved About My Sister: Part 1

This is the start of my list, Schlap.

The first thing I'm going to write about is going to sound insignificant and facile. It might be an odd way to begin, but it's my list, so.

She loved Caramac chocolate bars. My sister. Perdita. So did I. We both did.

I can't remember why we were so obsessed with them; I can't stand the things now. A thin rectangle of beige plasticky, toffee-tasting 'chocolate' wrapped in red paper and labelled in yellow cursive, it had the texture of a sweetened trainer insole. We once wrote, as a pair, to Jimmy Savile (or 'Jim'll' as we genuinely used to think he was called), when he was still a national hero, ha what a joke, to ask if we could bathe in a huge vat of melted Caramac. He didn't reply.

Every day on our way home from school, we'd walk to the only corner shop on Regent's Street and buy a packet of Quavers and a Caramac each, an afternoon snack that made up for the generously portioned yet increasingly bizarre packed lunches assembled by Dad. Seriously, Tartex sandwiches – a revolting vegetable paste in a tube – were the norm.

One summer, on the tube journey home, Perds instructed us to sit on our Caramacs. She said it was a proven fact that chocolate tasted better when warm. Something scientific, to do with the aroma accentuating in the gas phase.

Unfortunately, I'd already opened mine and eaten a piece, so by the time we reached Kentish Town, the melting resulted in a very stained and sticky Northern Line seat and a skirt covered in what looked like a bad bout of food poisoning.

Without missing a beat, Perdita shrugged off her blazer and wrapped it round my waist, just like that. I had no idea what she was doing.

And this is the best part, *she didn't even tell me* I had a dirty backside – just insisted she was hot and I should carry the blazer for her as she had an aching shoulder. She knew, you see, how mortified I'd have been if I'd had to march home in the knowledge that I'd shown my mucky butt to members of the public.

Like I said, it may sound trivial now, but these things are of the utmost significance when young.

Chapter 2

I walk up the steps to Schlap's home the following morning. The iron-riveted black front door is ajar. I push my way in and wait on the faded Persian rug. I'm early so I stand there like an uninvited guest.

There's no one around. It's cool in the wide hall and hallowed as a church. I hear the shuffling of papers from somewhere deep inside the house.

I edge forwards until I'm standing at the bottom of the staircase, following the lacquered banister with my eyes. It curves steeply upwards for six glorious flights, finishing in a domed skylight. But my neck isn't what it was and overcome by vertigo, I steady myself on the newel post, which feels so shiny I can't help myself – I lean forwards to give it a sniff. It smells of piano keys.

More shuffling of papers. Then a soft *plafff* as if a whole sheaf has fallen from table height and fanned out across a carpet.

'Ohhh!'

A woman's voice. She's not English, I deduce from that one exclamation. Australian maybe. Schlap's wife?

'Hello?' I creep forwards.

The paper-shuffling ceases. I round the corner into the waiting area. The same red roses sit in the vase on the walnut table.

Here hangs the faded pink curtain; William Morris print, all blooms, leaves and curling vines. It's probably been here since the 1980s. I can tell someone is already waiting behind it, because there's the shadow of a shoe on the carpet.

And also, an actual shoe. It's an E.M. Forster sort of shoe: brown leather with tassels and a low heel. There's a wad of collapsed yellowish papers strewn on the rug. One page of manuscript sticks out halfway between the curtain and the rest of the room. It's inked with spidery black writing. I try to nudge the sheet back to its owner with my trainer, but the paper just curls like a wave at one end and refuses to budge. I've now left a rubbery black mark in the corner.

'Oh, God, sorry about the stain.'

Silence from the other side.

I wonder what to do next. Surely two people aren't permitted to wait next to one another. That would be a breach of confidence, wouldn't it? Or have I got that wrong? Is it possible that Schlap has muddled the dates and that two of us are now expecting to see Schlap *at the same time*?

There's a heavily varnished wooden chair with pale silk upholstery against the wall, so I plop my bottom down. Whoever is behind the arras, so to speak, must at some point reveal themselves.

Themself? I've always been hopeless at grammar.

Two delicate white hands attached to delicate white wrists, which are, in turn – at the risk of making the owner sound like a chocolate truffle – enrobed in burgundy velvet bell sleeves, busy themselves collecting the papers.

'Jesus H. Christ,' says the voice.

I instantly like her.

'Need some help?' I say, risking a second silent rebuffal.

'I'm all right, thank you.' The word thank sounds like think.

A Kiwi. A Kiwi who is now talking to me, at least.

She picks up the last piece of paper – the one I've soiled with my adidas. I hear her tut. I look at my watch: two minutes until my session.

Perhaps she's the patient of somebody else. It's possible there are other shrinks practising here. Though Schlap did say he was the only person operating under this roof, that he owns the building and lives on the top three floors. Which means this person is ... who, exactly?

One of the woman's hands appears halfway up the end of the curtain, which is swept open.

'Gosh,' I say.

She's dressed in a burgundy velvet overcoat, white frilled Edwardian shirt and a thick calf-length charcoal wool skirt with fabric buttons up the front. She has brown bobbed hair, a penetrating gaze and a chunky fringe that, unlike the Foxtons Richard III in St Albans high street, really suits her. I calculate she's ten years younger than me.

Something about her makes me adrenal. It could be the sheer eccentricity of her attire. Here's the sort of woman who may well have had thoughts of owning a penis.

She peels her eyes from my face and turns to collect her stitched bag from the bench against the back wall of the curtained area.

'*Room with a Pew*,' I say.

The woman turns with a scowl. 'Beg pardon?' She stuffs her manuscript into her bag.

'Sorry. *Room with a* Pew?' I'm drawn inexorably to repeat it, though the joke is a car driving slowly towards a wall.

'I heard the first time. I don't understand.'

'Right. Yes. *Room with a View*, but there's a bench there so, *Room with a* ... E.M Forster: you know, because of your

34

clothes? Sorry, that sounds rude. You look amazing, by the way.'

'Oh. Thank you.'

She looks down at herself as if surprised she's wearing anything at all, then moves over to the flowers in the vase. She rubs one of the red petals between thumb and forefinger, a faraway look in her eyes. Perhaps she's just finished an enlightening session with Schlap. Perhaps her mind is processing it all.

'Amazing roses,' I say, trampling over her contemplation. 'Such brilliant red.'

She nods. 'I always have them in my house. As if they've been dipped in wine and left to dry.'

'What a fabulous description.' Her words are ringing bells in my head. 'Is it your own or someone else's?'

She looks me in the eye. 'My own.'

'Would you mind if I borrow it? I'm a writer. A poet.'

I say borrow, but really it would be more like stealing; it's not something I can give back once used.

'I'm afraid I would, darling,' she says.

Bit funny calling me darling when we've only just met.

'I'm also a writer,' she adds.

'What a coincidence that we both see Schlap.'

She gives me a funny look. Her feet are on the move again, backwards this time.

'What's your name?' I ask.

'Katherine.'

She heads swiftly out of the waiting area into the main hall towards the front door.

Of course! Katherine: Schlap's patient. She's already had her appointment.

'Schlap mentioned you yesterday.' I skip into the hall after her. 'Wait a sec!'

35

'I'm afraid I can't. Circumstances beyond my control force me to leave immediately.'

'I'm Marnie!' I yell at her departing back.

I stand on the Persian rug, breathless. That was Katherine. That was the woman with whom Schlap keeps muddling me up, and it's no wonder: we're both writers, we both have brown hair and we're not a million miles apart in age.

The little brass bell rings in Schlap's room. Time.

He's looking particularly dapper today in a brown wool suit, fluffy white hair slicked back like an otter. He sits in his usual chair, agitating the carpet with his brogues, and I worry that his habits are already beginning to grate. What will happen when we've been seeing one another for five years? Will it become like a marriage, when even the other person's breathing is cause for irritation?

He gives me what passes for a smile: an analyst's smile, kind but chilly.

I dump my bag on the floor next to the ergonomic chair and flop into the seat. It's not really a flopping sort of chair, though, and my body lurches backwards in its deep curve. I rearrange myself as elegantly as possible and come to rest with my hands in my lap.

I've come to learn that we're supposed to observe a respectful silence at the commencement of each session, as if gathering our thoughts mindfully and not rushing into things willy-nilly.

And to be clear, I don't intend to bring the word 'willy' anywhere near Schlap today.

I count five seconds. When I can stand it no longer, I say, 'Morning,' in a faux Cockney accent.

'Good morning,' Schlap replies in his own voice.

'I've just met Katherine in the hall.'

'Who?'

I get a closing feeling in my throat. 'Katherine. In the waiting area.' I'm going to speak slowly and clearly. 'Yesterday, you called me Katherine a couple of times; once in our session and once when you dialled my mobile by accident hoping to speak to a person of that name. Remember?'

He frowns. 'Oh?'

'Do you have a client, I mean patient, called Katherine?'

'No.'

'A daughter? Your wife?'

Schlap's head is shaking no.

'She's a writer,' I persist. 'Ringing bells? Wears funny clothes? Carries a manuscript?'

Then, 'Perhaps it was Katherine Mansfield you thought you saw. Perhaps another ghost.' He chuckles. 'This used to be her house, you know.'

'Yes, I've seen the blue plaque on the wall outside. How is this relevant?'

'She went to the same school as you, on this very street.' His eyes are two black raisins. 'Interesting.'

'What is?'

'That you had an imagined encounter with Mansfield.'

'It wasn't imagined.'

'Do you think *she* could be a symbol?'

'Another one?' I swallow. 'This woman wasn't a symbol.' I feel strange because I've just remembered the description she gave of the roses – dipped in wine and left to dry – is from a short story, *Carnation*, by exactly her: *Katherine Mansfield*! 'I'm not crazy. She really was there. You mentioned a Katherine twice yesterday. You've forgotten, but I can promise you you did. She was real.'

Schlap smiles kindly. 'All right, Marnie. I'll have a think about that. Maybe it's my mistake. Maybe I do have a patient called Katherine. Perhaps I know her by another name.'

'Like what?'

'I don't know. A nickname? A diminutive?'

But you called me Katherine, not a diminutive of Katherine, I want to say, but it's not his fault his memory's going and that a woman of his acquaintance – probably a patient – has a Mansfield fixation, likes to dress up as Mansfield and pass off Mansfield's observations as her own. I mean, this is an assumption I've made based entirely on the fact that she's here in this building, most probably seeing Schlap rather than just standing in the hall talking about flowers, and is therefore more likely to be a kook. And it's not Schlap's fault he's temporarily forgotten who she is. I don't want to embarrass anyone. I wait another second or so to see if he'll remember we're supposed to be discussing the 'money aspect' of our sessions, but ... no.

'I had the nightmare again last night,' I say.

'With the penis?'

'No. That wasn't a nightmare. The other one.' Please don't let him have forgotten.

'Would you like to tell me about it?'

I sigh. 'The Purgatory one, where everything is blackness.' How can Schlap have let go of it? It's analysis dynamite: I repeat to him this dream, about the dark place in which I'm completely alone and terrified because I don't know where I am but can hear Perdita talking from some other side. As if I'm trapped in a black hole with invisible curving walls. 'I think it was a result of my sighting yesterday.'

'Perhaps,' he says.

If you're wondering why I'd spend Ben's good money on an analyst who frequently forgets things, the reason is simple: Schlap feels like home. He's warm and caring and has kind eyes. He carries within him five months' worth of my thoughts and feelings, even if he can't recall them all the time, and I have neither the energy nor the inclination to change to someone else. Also, he's a good person. I trust him.

'You mentioned the word Purgatory,' he begins again. 'Which I find interesting. Why do you think your parents became "born again" after Perdita's death? Why not some other religion? Buddhism, for example.'

'I don't *know*.' I'm being childish. 'Because they were miserable and they just happened to live next to a church? Dad was a lapsed Jew. I mean, he didn't care. They just wanted to feel better. Feel less.'

'Yes. But they could have converted to something else.'

'Also, they didn't become born again directly after – not until about four months later. It felt soon, though. Time bends, doesn't it, when there's grief around you.'

It's funny we haven't covered this stuff in the past. I can't remember what we've talked about, truly. I think it was mainly the writing, or lack of it, and sundry cold hard facts of present day life.

Schlap is nodding, as if he knows what I meant about time bending, as if he's experienced a grief of his own. Perhaps he's lost his wife. Poor Schlap. I look for a wedding ring. There's some sagging in the webs of skin between his fingers.

'... together?' Schlap has asked me something.

I swim past his mystery question. 'For example, Islam was too far away from who my parents already were, I suppose. Buddhism was probably too complicated, what with its ideas around acceptance and karmic rebirth.' I hear my words after they've left my mouth and sigh heavily. 'Do you know, I'm sick of my inability to take things seriously, even in my head. It's irritating to others.'

He regards me, unblinking.

'People always think I'm being flip,' I continue. 'Or it's

hidden anger or something, but it's just a coping mechanism.'

Shlap nods.

'I suffer from a facetious inner child who screams to be free. Life's essentially boring, unfulfilling and lonely.' At least I'm being honest now. 'I think the goal of this facile voice is just to add colour. I mean, my intention is to charm, but it mostly backfires. If I were a man, I don't think anyone would mind my flipness so much – that isn't a word – flippancy? It's affecting my success with work. I don't take myself seriously, so how can anyone else take me seriously? But life shouldn't *be* serious.'

'You find life boring, unfulfilling and lonely.'

He says it like it's an unwanted parcel that's flopped through his letter box. He's missed the point.

'You've missed the point.'

'What *is* the point?' He lifts his bottom from the seat and pulls his trousers out at the knees.

'There isn't one.' I choke on my own saliva. 'Life has no point.' I start to cry, because what I've said is true. The only point of life is that death is at the end of it, and sometimes in the middle, or if you're very unlucky, at the beginning. 'And I've started making your list and it's really *hard*. Oh, God, and now I have to go and meet Veronica.'

'And Veronica is ...?' Schlap says.

I'm waiting on the oversized Chesterfield in Euclid's sterile reception area experiencing that weird tingling, burning feeling in my crotch again, but it's too public here to do anything about it.

For reassurance, I gently pat the sofa. I think this sort of furniture is supposed to be effortlessly trendy, but the effect is one of aesthetic self-consciousness. The faint smell of dead cow is rising from the leather and I'm forced to perch in the very centre of the centre to avoid the popped springs either side. I wonder if—

'Marnie!'

An exclamation mark floats hopefully at the end of my name. Veronica has sneakily approached from behind, as if she knew a full-frontal greeting would send me running for the hills.

My neck twists awkwardly. 'Howdy.'

She kisses me on both cheeks, a greeting that leaves me feeling silly for my nerves.

'Shall we go through?'

Her arm goes out in the direction of her office. The office that's waiting for us through a maze of glass cubicles.

'Yep.'

I follow close at Veronica's heels. My editor's hips sway gently as she moves. It makes me wonder about her home life. She's head-to-toe turquoise, with matching turquoise nail varnish and eyeshadow, which is brave and possibly a bit mad. We sweep past a variety of youngish intelligent-looking people in glasses, some of whom I recognise but who don't seem to recognise me. Veronica stops in the open-plan corridor, if 'open-plan corridor' were a thing that could exist, and does another arm gesture towards her glass box.

'After you,' she says.

I head towards the door, so clean and shiny I'm barely able to decipher which side to push.

Once in, I sit on a curving woollen armchair. So far, today mostly seems to have consisted of lowering myself into unfriendly furniture while feeling edgy.

'Well ...' Veronica puts her turquoise bottom on the seat opposite me. 'How *are* you?'

'I. Am. Good. How are you?'

'I'm well, thanks.'

There's a little pause in which it feels like we're both sinking.

'Why so blue?' I say.

She shakes her head. 'Sorry?'

'It was a joke, because ...' I point at her skirt.

Her expression is unchanging.

'Is there ... ?' She makes a little circling movement with her hand.

'Is there ... ?'

'Anything? On paper?'

'Veronica, I'm going to be honest. I haven't got any poems for you. I'm sorry.'

She takes a breath and looks at me with sad eyes. 'You know, I understand. But we're three months past the deadline, Marns.'

'I know we're past the ...' I study the floor. 'I'm trying. The words just don't want to come out.'

'The problem is,' she sighs, 'I know you, and I love you, and I'm happy to wait till the cows come home, but The Others upstairs are antsy. We've only clung on to you at my insistence.'

'Oh, God, I *know*. You've been so patient and so lovely.'

'They're on my case, you see, so I have to be on yours.'

'How far exactly are they on your case?'

'They're threatening to cancel publication,' she says, carefully. 'Unless you deliver all twenty-seven poems within the next week.'

I jump a length out of my seat before gravity takes me down again. 'A *week*? But I haven't written one poem in five months! Not even one!'

'Therein lies the problem.'

We stare at one another.

'I guess I need to pull my finger out.'

'I guess you do.'

I hang my head. 'I'm so shit.'

'You're certainly not shit.'

Someone's knocking outside her office. It's one of the young people in glasses.

'So sorry, Marnie, I have a meeting to go to.' Veronica is rising from her seat. 'Can we check in again in a day or so?'

'Of course.'

She takes both of my hands. 'Just remember, I believe in you.'

'That means a lot,' I say and walk towards the glass door with as much dignity as I can muster. My sister is coming towards me from the other side.

Perdita. Perdita is here in the office with me. I feel sick and happy and sad and like screaming all at the same time.

A wave travels through my body before I realise it's my own reflection.

I head to meet Sylvia for lunch because their school summer workshop is on a day's hiatus while the teachers have staff training. Blythe has decided to use this afternoon to visit Claire's Accessories to buy hairbands, apparently. The twins are supposed to be prepping for some new post A-level qualification which, if they pass, will count towards their university application, but their revision thus far mostly consists of cooking fancy dishes at my parents' house.

I've let Sylvia pick the venue. She's chosen Govinda's vegetarian restaurant on Soho Street. I make a vow not to think about Veronica's ultimatum till later. I'm not going to panic.

I walk along Oxford Street avoiding the tourists, trying not to feel old as I catch sight of myself, once again reflected back at me from the shop windows. I feel even older as I look beyond my own face to the girlish mannequins with their frozen slender bodies and pointed toes. Three of them in a line are attached to metal poles supporting plastic torsos, which seems a strangely violent means of suspension; the impression is of butterflies, pinned and desperate to fly.

My mind returns to pretend Mansfield, her alter ego, imagining her past, her cuckoo act of resurrecting a long-dead author, how she came into being. I tick off a mental list of possible ailments: depression, a breakdown certainly, bipolarism, narcissism, personality disorder. I'm impressed with my list of diagnoses, which is professional and sounds a lot like something Ben might draw up. I'm longing to meet her again to probe further. The fleeting fear that I might have seen a ghost is swept away when I remember my dirty trainer print on her manuscript papers.

Behind me in the glass, a woman with dark hair is swinging along on the opposite side of the street. I'm confused after what's just happened at Veronica's office and tell myself that it's my reflection I'm looking at, but there's a large Jaeger bag dangling from her elbow, which I'm not holding. And how could it possibly be my reflection, on the other side of the street?

Cortisol engulfs me, like pins and needles in each cell.

I make a sharp turn and skid across the road, dodging in and out of buses, but when I reach the opposite curb, the woman has gone. I say 'the woman'. I'm sure it was Perds. No messing this time, not a distraction from pain. I know her walk. My sister. I know the way she ... but wait, *Jaeger?* Really? My sister would never have been seen dead in Jaeger.

She'd never have been seen dead. That's what she is. Dead. It wasn't her. *Unless she's on another plane of existence ...*

The problem with Many-Worlds Interpretation is that in it, time isn't linear. Everything happens at the same moment, in a sort of 360-degree fashion, no past, present or future. Or think of it another way: it's like millions of wriggling strings

– life paths – criss-crossing one another. Once you jump onto a different string, you can never return to the one you were on before – it'll have moved too far away or changed course completely – and *this* will mean everyone existing along your new string, with no idea you're a fresh version of your former self, will consider you bonkers. This may be the issue I am facing now.

I hit my fist on my head three times: a) I'm not going mad, b) I'm not going mad, and c) I am *not*-going-mad.

Govinda's is warm and fragrant and full of people who look like they're about to watch documentaries at cinemas that serve artisan popcorn in little paper bags. The walls are pink and sweating and condensation pools in the sills. I think about all the water-borne germs permeating the air until I see Sylvia, already here and sitting in the corner in her denim jacket, waving to me. I make my way over, pushing past the counter where people queue for food. The long dining tables are hidden beneath silver thali trays, each one dotted with splodges of green and beige: spinach, okra, daal. My mouth waters.

'Mum!'

'Love!'

Sylvia leaps to kiss me. In a curious mirroring of the greeting between my own mother and me the previous day, the small gold studs in my ears press hard against her cheekbone and I smell her shampoo.

'You've been using my Aveda products,' I say.

The scent of it's nice; I don't know why Mum couldn't decide if she was a fan.

'Mine ran out,' Sylvia says. 'Dad told me it would be okay. He practically forced me. How are you? How was Slap? You know there's a Daunt's bookshop on Marylebone High Street? Well, can we go after? Nana says she's got another new dress

45

for our birthday party. I don't want her doing any of her impersonations – I just want her to come as herself.'

My heart sinks. 'Has she mentioned who she will be yet?'

'She said either Bette Davis in *All About Eve*, or Barbara Streisand in her flowing trouser suit from *Meet The Parents*.'

'Oh.'

'She's excited, Mum.'

Sylvia seems to see me for the first time since I arrived. Her expression changes.

'You all right? You look sort of pale.'

As I said, I haven't reported any of my Perdita sightings to my children. It's for the best, but it kills me.

'I'm fine.'

'How was your meeting with Veronica?'

'Tell you later. Let's get in line for food. I'm starving.'

I stand behind my daughter in the lunch queue and love her silently. Her dark hair hangs in a ponytail between her shoulder blades, the ends curling in a tight C. There are green nickel ring stains around three of her fingers, a testament to her predilection for Camden Market jewellery. I see the outline of her legs through the thin material of her long summer dress. Blythe and she are very different from the other living women in our family: both taller by at least two inches, broader too, with handsome shoulders and long, slender feet.

Sometimes when I look at them both, I wonder how they came out of me. The person Sylvia most resembles is Perdita. Not the build – Perds and I were identical, of course, just like Sylvia and Blythe are. It's more the quality of breath, by which I mean that Perdita and Sylvia both sigh a lot, not from boredom or frustration, but more an acute sense of life passing, an ability to see time moving. It's endearing.

46

Was endearing. *Sighed* a lot. I must stop talking about my sister as if she's still here.

Perdita's dead.

I say these words to myself a great deal to test if it still hurts.

Though not if she's in a quantum—

Sylvia turns to me, empty tray in hand.

'Oh. Forgot to say. Blythe and I were thinking we don't really need a birthday *cake* at the party, if that's okay? Bit babyish.'

I resist the urge to smile.

'We were thinking more: vegan custard doughnuts,' she suggests.

'Doughnuts?'

'Yeah.'

'Custard?'

'That's what I said. Custard is just *it* right now. But vegan.'

'K. *It* vegan custard. No problem.'

She hugs me. 'Okaythenthat'sgreat.'

Last minute that same evening, I head into town to the theatre to meet my parents. Their friends from St Albans – he of metal detector fame and discoverer of Roman amphoras, plus wife – had bought four tickets for *The Comedy of Errors* at the Gielgud. The couple have now, apparently, been struck down by food poisoning, and their spare tickets have devolved, through various other elderly suburban couples, to Ben and me. Ben, of course, is too busy; it's his special night for writing his book, so I alone am playing third wheel to what's now my parents' date night.

They're waiting for me in the foyer by the time I arrive, sipping wine and chatting to three people. I assume they're actors from Dad's professional days, because the two men are in cravats and the woman is in a trench coat. Mum has dressed in

47

sparkly silver leggings and an oversized Aran jumper with a fox dancing its way across her front. Dad just looks normal.

Over the actressy woman's shoulder, Dad spots me and grins. 'Marnie!'

I sidle up and shake hands as Dad says, unnecessarily, 'my daughter' about fifty times, then leans to one side, plucks a large glass of wine from a wooden shelf running along the wall and hands it to me.

'You'll need it,' he whispers as Mum starts a story about how when I was small I wasn't remotely interested in Dad's career and would talk loudly in the wings every time he was on stage.

I have no memory of this, but it's interesting that she doesn't include Perdita in the telling. My sister must have been there, too, chatting away. Unless she wasn't. Unless she stood there obediently silent, while I ruined it for everyone. It's possible.

I sigh and look around the foyer at the other theatregoers. I wish suddenly I was at home watching reality TV with the girls while Stan grunts at his Nintendo Switch.

Three hours of Shakespeare? I don't mind reading it, but why people insist on performing his plays over and over, as if there weren't about a million other fresher, more relevant voices today, is beyond me.

The three-minute bell rings. Mum and Dad say goodbye to Dad's acting buddies and we make our way into the auditorium. We squeeze past several pairs of legs to reach our seats and I'm hot and thirsty before we've even settled ourselves.

The seating plan goes Mum, Dad, then me. Dad's hand immediately spiders to Mum's knee. She does this shimmy thing with her shoulders and giggles.

She leans across Dad and says, 'You know, this has had *terribly* good reviews, Marnie.'

Dad scrunches his eyes. He's chewing and there's a strong smell of rose about him.

'Is that Turkish delight?' I whisper.

His shoulders go up and he says 'Yes,' like he's five years old.

I hit him on the bicep. 'You know that's not good for your diabetes.'

He looks at me beseechingly. 'Special occasion.'

I rest my head on his shoulder. 'Luckily, I love you.'

Mum, who is straining to remove her coat from behind the back of the person in the seat ahead of her, turns and sees me leaning on Dad and frowns, so I sit up straight.

The lights go down. I scooch low, preparing myself.

As it turns out, the production isn't too bad. The actors are, in general, good, apart from one young actress who has an ingratiating manner and insists on sending her lines up at the end into a question, as if she's Australian. The play is about Dromio and Dromio, slave twins separated at birth. Don't ask who gives their identical twin sons the same names; massive fail on Shakespeare's part, in my opinion. They become mixed up in a case of mistaken identity with their masters, and everyone believes they're going mad, which I relate to on many levels.

The interval comes and the lights go up. My dad sighs and mentions his prostate and Mum says she needs another drink. I spend the majority of the allotted twenty minutes worrying about whether in fact quantum entanglement means I could actually be Perdita and she could be me – an idea sparked by a line in the play – and so listen to very little my parents say as we neck as much alcohol as possible.

After Dad has peed, Mum says she needs to go, too, and then only just makes it back in time for the start of the second half. The music starts, and she announces that the queue for the ladies was like the starving lining up for Jesus and his loaves and fishes, and someone in the row beside her tells her to shush.

Mum turns to them and rudely demands, 'What?'

Dad hisses, 'Patricia!' Mum pipes down after that.

The play's plot gets messier after this, or maybe it just seems that way owing to the amount of wine I've consumed. There are people being imprisoned and wives coming out of the woodwork to save everyone, but by the end, everyone is married to the right person and the twin slaves are reunited with their masters.

As we applaud, I think to myself that remaining as slaves probably isn't *that* happy an ending for the twin protagonists and that Shakespeare could have done with a good editor – someone like Veronica, for example. She has a hawk-eye for overwriting and an over-convoluted plot and she'd certainly have nixed the dual-names issue. Mum seems happy, though, leaping to her feet and shouting 'Bravo!' so that everyone around us turns to look at her instead of the actors taking a bow at the front.

Dad says 'Very good,' as we get up from our seats and Mum asks loudly if he's going to go to stage door to congratulate everyone, but he says he's too tired. She runs her hand along his cheek in a sensual way that makes me feel vaguely sick.

We part ways outside. Mum lets me know she'll be coming over to my house very early in the morning to collect a specific item of cookware and I think to myself that her visit will put the kibosh on any flow I might have been hoping for with my writing.

Then I head towards the tube feeling supernaturally hungry.

It's Friday, the next morning and, after an enormous fry-up at 7 a.m., I've been hunched over my laptop, digging my fists into my forehead, but it's no good. Every time I put words down,

I think of the play, the madness of mixed-up twins. I see Perds in my mind's eye – at the supermarket, on Oxford Street, Essex Road, Hackney – and I delete whatever crap it is I've written.

What does it *mean*? Perhaps nothing: an insignificant mystery event, objectively meaningless.

But doesn't everything have meaning? In which case, why did I tell Schlap that life had no point?

I throw my arms onto the keyboard. There are no words this morning. Life is an amorphous mass, constantly remoulding itself. How anyone is expected to keep up is beyond me.

My mother drops round as promised at 8 a.m. to borrow my special Iranian rice cooker. She turns up in cream jodhpurs and a cravat. She also carries a walking cane in one hand like a theatrical prop.

'Good grief,' I say.

She flinches.

'Are you going riding?' I ask.

'Don't be silly. I'm channelling Jeremy Irons and Meryl Streep, and there's nothing wrong with *that*.'

She pushes past me and looks around the hall for Ben, who is her favourite person, not counting blood relations, but her timing is poor; he's walking Parker.

'Nothing wrong at all,' I agree. '*Out of Africa* meets – what exactly? – *Reversal of Fortune*?'

She shrugs and wanders into the kitchen. 'Eclecticism is a gift. Don't let your mind become locked. Your father and I like to mix things up. No shilly-shallying. He's doing Art Malik in *The Jewel in the Crown* today. I told him he should have done himself in *Calder*, but he said he would be recognised dressed as himself and that that would be boring and narcissistic.'

'Weird,' I say, but under my breath because my mother has excellent selective hearing.

'Oh,' she says, as she spots my laptop on the table. 'Trying to write?'

I've placed the rice cooker on the kitchen worktop in advance. Mum gets jittery if she turns up and thinks I've forgotten the purpose of her visit.

'*There* she is.' She lays a gentle palm on the cooker lid as if it were a virgin ship about to launch. 'Lovely, lovely Tahdig. Your father's going to do his recipe with green herbs, turmeric and cardamon.'

It almost sounds sexy the way she says it.

'It's for the church fair on Sunday. To serve with that new Israeli couple's shakshuka. You are coming?'

The question is a pointless frivolity on her part: my attendance is a fait accompli. Israeli Christians and dishes that sound like something from a catering competition – so blooms the eclectic beauty of the St Michaels Summer Fair in St Albans year on year. Endless rows of home-made soaps smelling of rancid oil and knitted mice in miniature clothing. There will be no getting out of the fair. It's my one consolation to the Holy One per annum.

'Of course I'm coming. I'm looking forward to it.'

I smile at Mum's mouth rather than her eyes because, like her hearing, she has acute sensitivity in the presence of bullshit.

'Lovely.' She picks up the cooker and cradles it in her arms.

I take a breath. 'Mum. I need to tell you something.'

'Yes?'

The cooker goes down again and she stares at me hopefully.

'I think I saw Perdita again. I was in—'

My mother holds the walking cane in front of her like one of Ben's fencing foils.

'No! No, no, no.'

It's as if she's King Lear.

'*How* many times?' she cries.

'Fine. How about this: I saw Veronica yesterday and I've been given seven – no, *six* – days to complete twenty-seven poems or they're going to pull the book.'

'Oh, Marnie.'

Her face softens and I think she might be about to put her arms around me, which would be nice.

'I told you all those years ago with your first collection not to go with Euclid. They have a questionable reputation.'

I grit my teeth. 'Sylv says you've bought another dress for the party.'

'Oh, change of subject. And?'

'And who are you going to go as? Barb or Bette, because I don't think channelling Barb in that particular movie is going to give out the right message at an eighteenth, if you don't mind my saying.'

My mother frowns, snorts, then throws her head back and *laughs*. She's like the British weather system with her constant changes of mood.

Stan walks in in his pyjamas.

'Why haven't you left for school yet?' my mother and I say in unison.

How did I not know he was still at home?

'Hmm.' He shakes his head and falls into a chair.

I can smell his feet from here.

'Don't feel good. Temperature 'n' all that.'

'Poor little…' My mother puts her hand to his forehead, as if that would make any bloody difference. She nods and hurries to fill the kettle, tapping the rice cooker with her cane on the way for good luck. 'He doesn't feel hot, but I'll make him a Lemsip just in case. Where's your thermometer?'

'We're all out of Lemsip,' I say. 'Stan, do you by any chance have a test at your workshop today?'

My son obviously thinks he can hide in plain sight. Our house is big. I don't know how we ever afforded it on one analyst's wage and the sales from fourteen copies of my poems.

'Huh?' He looks at me with big eyes.

'Mum,' I say. 'Stan's got a case of maths-itis. He's off to workshop *immediately*.' I turn to him. 'Aren't you?'

'God, Mum,' he moans, 'you always spoil everything.' He flumps past. 'I just want *one* day to relax. Like grown-ups get.'

'Stanley.' My mother sticks out one black riding boot, barring his way. '*The Lord will not hold him guiltless that taketh his name in vain.*'

Stan looks at the boot.

'Mum.' I can't resist. 'In this house, I'm afraid the Lord does hold us guiltless because we're constantly throwing His name about and He's given up.'

My mother shakes her head. She's still smiling. I don't know how she does that.

'My darling daughter, you're letting life pass you by and you don't even realise.'

'I'm sorry?'

'Since you started seeing that shrink.'

'I started seeing that shrink because I started seeing Per ... Because I stopped being able to write.'

'Exactly.' She gestures skywards with the cane. 'You're creatively impotent for a reason.'

'Cheers.'

'We're powerless in the face of God, but there are ways in which we can take control of our world, should we so choose.' She glares meaningfully from under her fringe.

'Okay. What's actually happening here?'

'You tell me.'

'I have no idea, but it's extremely left field.'

'That's the best field.'

And just like that, Mum is back to herself and the moment has gone. Whoever she thinks I am, she's welcome. Life may be passing me by, and I may be temporarily ... *impotent*, but I am okay, relatively speaking.

I sniff the air. 'Stan, you might want to take a shower before you depart. And what do you mean, grown-ups spend their days relaxing? What in heaven's name are you talking about?'

He's in the doorway clinging to the doorframe, laughing softly to himself, like a character in a Tennessee Williams play.

'You and Dad do absolutely nothing all day. Just hang around the house drinking beer and stuff, as if you didn't even know you're alive.'

'Are you on drugs?'

'Huh?'

'We do *not* hang around all day. I'm *working*.' I point at my laptop. 'Thirteen is too young for an existential crisis. And what's your sudden obsession with beer?'

'Oh, *I* know,' says my mother. 'He's been reading *The Catcher in the Rye* again. Haven't you, Stanny?'

Stan points at the rice cooker back in my mother's arms. 'Parker chewed the plug on that cooker and it doesn't work any more. Just like the car and the downstairs loo and everything else in this house. Who are we even, anyway? We're *nothing*, cosmically speaking. Bye, Nana.' He blows her a kiss and leaves.

'Puberty,' I mouth to Mum.

A second later, there's Stan's howl from the hall.

'Everything all right?'

'Dad's bloody fencing foil was sticking out of the cupboard!

55

I've spiked my toe. No wonder Nana wears riding boots when she comes here.'

My mother and I look at one another. We can't help it; we start to laugh. Then she stops abruptly.

'What are you doing standing there, Marnie? There's no time to lose. Sit down and get scribbling.'

Things I Loved About My Sister: Part 2

When I was nine, I had a phase in which I enjoyed nothing more than filling the bath with warm water and climbing in fully clothed. I found this completely hilarious. Perds never joined in because she was sensible and she knew it drove our parents mad, especially Mum.

One summer's day, I ran the bath for this exact purpose but became distracted, ran out to play and forgot all about it until there was a scream from Mum, who had been getting quietly stoned in the living room. Water was pouring through the ceiling rose onto the brand-new kelim rug Dad brought back from his latest shoot in Istanbul. Mum, red-faced and furious, demanded to know which one of us had done this. There was silence as I stared at the sodden rug, and Mum and Perds stared at me. I couldn't think of a single excuse as to why I'd dreamed of doing such an idiotic thing. I deserved whatever punishment was coming my way.

Then I heard Perds' voice.

'It was me,' she said. 'I ran it 'specially for Marns' eczema. A cool bath. Her skin's really bad in the heat. Show her, Marns.'

I wasn't going to argue. My sister was saving my arse.

She had the dust allergy, I had the eczema, which seemed fair in the way of things. Dutifully, I held out my inner arms.

Perds said, 'I put in a *ton* of Aveeno.'

Mum totally bought it. I was off the hook.

Later that night, I gave my sister all the Drumstick lollies left in my trick-or-treat bucket from the previous year. She hadn't asked for anything in return, but I felt she deserved a reward.

When I looked in my treat bucket again a few days later, the lollies were back. She'd only taken one and returned the rest.

That's how she was: kind and expert at managing her expectations. I think a lot about this, about how she was the superior twin. Not that I was bad or anything, but just that maybe it would have been better for everyone if it was her who had lived.

Chapter 3

It's 9.52 a.m., an hour since my mother left my house with the rice cooker. Ben and I are waiting outside the gift shop Flying Tiger on Oxford Street, trying to get a head start on the twins' birthday knick-knacks before he goes to work to sort out other people's problems and I go to Schlap's to have my own problems sorted.

After Mum left, of course I managed zero words on my laptop. What with getting Stan off to workshop and having to wash Parker following a very muddy walk with Ben, there was barely time to get dressed properly, let alone make art. I now carry a deep sense of failure. The only thing I console myself with is that if we are indeed all existing in a multiverse kind of world, somewhere, somehow, another me wrote twenty-six poems this morning and delivered them to Veronica on time.

Behind the locked doors of Flying Tiger, delightfully youthful members of staff are standing around the till chatting and looking at their phones. Every now and then, one or other of them glances up, stares at us, then continues with their conversation.

It's warm already and Ben and I are both fanning ourselves with our hands. He's flicking through some notes from last night, scrawled onto A4 paper.

'I don't know why you don't store your work on your phone, as well,' I say. 'That way, you can a) read it, and b) won't lose it.'

'Unless I lose my phone,' he mutters, eyes still fixed on the paper.

'Well,' I huff. 'Obviously.'

'Or the phone breaks.'

'*Okay*.' I turn away to signal my irritation, but he's not looking at me, so the gesture is pointless.

A guy with green hair and a stud in one eyebrow comes to unlock the doors.

'Hey,' he says. 'Welcome! You're keen.'

'Yeah,' I say as Ben breezes past, still staring at his notes. 'It's our daughters' birthdays soon and we need to get going on some—'

'Great,' says the guy, turning away, skipping back to the till.

I pick up a basket and stand next to Ben, who has come to a halt several metres in front of the entrance, head in his papers.

I'm unsure where to start, there are so many amazing colourful sparkly things to look at, then I notice that like all fabulous Scandi shops, they've helpfully marked arrows on the floor every two metres saying 'this way please' so customers can navigate the snaking layout.

I follow these arrows, imagining a parallel world in which people are only allowed to stand on each one and move forwards onto the next once the person in front has also moved, like automatons. No one in your personal space, no jostling: bonus. But also, no personal contact, no non-sexual touch, no platonic intimacy. It would be horrid. Thank God, *that's* never going to happen.

'Benny.' I nudge him with my elbow. 'Enough already with the work.'

'Sorry.' He folds the papers into his jacket pocket and follows me along the designated route.

It's all such glorious tat. Nothing so fanciful existed when Perdita and I were the twins' age. In preparation for our party, Mum and Dad went to Woolworths, which was great in its own way but mainly consisted of bags of penny sweets. When the party didn't happen, the bags were left untouched in the spare room for almost a year, the unmistakable odour of synthetic strawberry leaking through the gap at the bottom of the door.

'This is nice.' Ben picks up a small china ornament of a robin holding a twig.

'Ooh, yes,' I say, pleased that Ben is now engaged in the task. 'Sylvia particularly would love that.'

He picks up a potato peeler that also acts as about five other things. 'This is more Blythe.'

The observation is accurate and makes me laugh. We put both items in our basket and continue. I'm trying to decide which colour writing paper the girls might like, when Ben's phone bleeps several times. He walks ahead, looking at it.

'Who was that?' I say once I've caught up with him.

'Davina.' He squashes the phone back in his pocket.

My stomach does a little jump. 'Davina?'

'Analyst at the practice? She wants to know if I can take on her referral because she's overloaded.'

He becomes very involved with looking at inflatable mini drinks holders intended for people with hot tubs, or those who presumably like to sip cocktails in the bath.

'Oh, sorry, just you said it like I should know who she is and you've never mentioned her before so ...'

Ben puts down the packet of inflatable holders sharply and looks at me.

'Davina is seventy. And a lesbian.'

'Sorry.'

'It's fine.' He throws in a marble chopping board, which weighs a ton, and a cocktail shaker. 'These are for us.' He's smiling, but he must see something in my expression because his smile dies, and he says, 'Everything okay with Schlap? The sessions are helping?'

'Yes, everything's going okay. Why would you ask that?'

It's so rare for Ben to be engaged enough to notice my state of mind that I've immediately cornered myself into a defensive position from which I can't return, instead of welcoming this chance to be honest, to talk things through.

'No reason.' He shrugs, giving up on me, walking away like everyone else in this bloody shop. 'You've just been unusually jumpy recently.'

For the second time in as many minutes, I run to catch him up. 'And?'

'Well, the sessions are pricey and I was wondering to what extent they're helping.'

'Not as pricey as yours!' The cold hand of shame and the equally hot hand of rage creep their way down the back of my T-shirt. 'How does one quantify *how much* it's helping, anyway? You do realise he's given me a reduction since I switched to five days a week?'

'Calm down. I know.'

Ben studies a row of colourful rubber phone cases hanging on the wall. He's maddeningly unflustered.

'It's fine. Forget I said anything,' he mutters.

I stand next to him, staring angrily, unseeing, at the cases.

'What?' he says.

I turn to him. He's still not looking at me.

'I just think it's insensitive of you to bring up the money

issue, B, then tell me to forget it. We both know I don't make as much as you. It's humiliating.'

Ben's gaze moves from the cases to, oddly, my thighs.

'I'll pay you back.' I'm irritating even to my own ears. 'I'd love to be able to afford it myself.'

'Marnie, it's not about the money, I promise. I just want to make sure you're getting the best treatment possible.'

'I am.'

We move on to a pile of flat-pack wooden marble runs.

'Stan would like these,' I offer in an attempt to make peace.

Ben snorts. 'About ten years ago.' He picks one up, shakes it and puts it down again. 'Are those Blythe's pedal pushers you're wearing?'

'They're *my* pedal pushers. That Blythe borrows all the time!'

I stalk away towards the fingerless-gloves section, annoyed with Ben all over again and furious with myself for being me.

Schlap regards me from his chair. He seems puzzled, forlorn. I'm pretty sure this isn't my projection but reality.

'Marnie. I have something important to say.'

'Okay. So do I.' I see his face fall. 'But after you.'

Schlap nods. 'Thank you. It'll involve a break with protocol, but I'm afraid in this case there's no alternative.'

I giggle.

His eyebrows move together, and I know my reaction has caused irritation.

'So sorry,' I explain. 'It's not funny, I'm just nervous.'

'Not a problem.' He adjusts the collar on his shirt.

There goes the infernal sound of his shoes scuffing the carpet.

'It's my professional responsibility to give you some news. I hope you won't mind if I preface it by saying I spent the night deliberating the correct manner in which to let each of my

62

patients know this information, followed by a lengthy phone consultation with my supervisor early this morning.'

'Okay, long sentence.'

He's being terribly formal all of a sudden. My heart beats faster. What if it's something to do with me, with Perdita, or my Many-Worlds theory or—

'I had a recent appointment at a clinic here on Harley Street.' He pauses. 'It turns out I'm suffering a condition that causes memory loss and confusion.' He looks at the ceiling. 'Can't quite remember its name. It's the result of my having had what's termed a "silent stroke". The blasted thing occurred a few weeks ago. I had no idea it had happened. Damaged part of my prefrontal cortex. I went for a routine check yesterday afternoon and' – he waves two fingers – 'hey presto.'

'I'm so very sorry to hear that.'

There follows an almighty silence in which I sense Schlap *analysing my response*. He is, if nothing else, professional to the last. What if he's about to end our sessions forever? I really don't want that to happen; I like him and trust him, and he has too much of my life contained within that head of his. Or at least, he did before the stroke. I search frantically for the right words.

'Is it permanent, your condition? Do you have a prognosis?'

As his eyes flick from my face towards the white mouse painting, I fear these two questions aren't entirely appropriate.

'They don't seem sure,' he begins. 'I should be able to continue living a relatively normal life, caring for myself and so on for the foreseeable future, but it may affect my work: an occasional compromise in lucidity, and my memory, of course. Then again, it may not. I'm not duty-bound to retire.'

Thank God.

We both look at the mouse painting now. There's a man

contained within it. I hadn't spotted him last time. He's standing at the front door of a tiny cottage far away in the background, his hand held out to the rodent in the foreground. There's a spaniel at the man's feet. The man is wearing green corduroy trousers and a flat cap. A rifle rests against the doorframe. There's something in his open palm, a lure for the mouse, per-haps cheese. A signature sits at the bottom right-hand corner: a name I can't read from here – it looks like *Daniel* and then a long surname beginning with S. *Schlapoberstein?*

Schlap interlaces his fingers in his lap and gives me a lopsided smile.

'That said, I would like to offer all of my patients the chance to transfer to a different therapist, should they wish. I can recommend a number of highly respected people in the field.'

'Would you like me to move? I mean, would that be easier for you, sort of better if I made that decision instead of you?' I'm not going to cry.

He sits forwards in his chair. 'Not at all. I'm hoping you'll stay. Here, as my patient.'

'Oh. Okay. Good.'

'But my condition may affect our work together and I wish to unburden you of any sense of loyalty.'

'But I like coming here.'

He's the only person who can bear to listen while I give reign to my irritating inner monologue. That's what the price of a session gets you: unconditional friendship.

His head lowers and he pins me to my seat with his gaze. 'A sense of loyalty,' he continues, picking up his previous thread. 'Or perhaps a sense of pity.'

'Schlap, of course I don't pity you.' That doesn't sound right. 'I mean, I do, but not in a bad way. I'm just so sorry for your loss.' Worse. 'Not sorry for your loss, but ...'

'It's fine, Marnie.' His lips curl at the corners. 'I got your name right, at least.'

He giggles. I have to look away.

I suddenly have an unadulterated window into his core; the pride concealed behind the Father Christmas exterior. I see the young man he must once have been, his vaulting ambition, his achievements and failures, his female conquests, sexual and emotional. I wonder if he ever anticipated this coming to pass, this older grey-haired version of himself. Death creeping in, his body, previously at full beam, suddenly on the wane. His mind retreating imperceptibly at first, then all at once perceptibly in the confirmed diagnosis of another medical professional working on the very street where Schlap earns his living.

'I appreciate your words,' he says, eventually.

Another of our silences.

Finally, he nods at the clock. 'If you'd genuinely like to stay—'

'I would.'

'Shall we continue post-haste? We've already taken up far too much time talking about me. I shan't count the minutes already passed as our session. The session will start' – he looks at the clock again – '*now*.'

'Um. Yep. Great. Let's go.'

He settles back into his leather chair and regards me blankly, the chatty gentleman of the last few minutes gone. He's deliberately signalling a return to professional analysis, but there seems now to be three of us in the room: me, Schlap and the other more jovial Schlap, which makes the transition hard.

'You start,' I offer.

I regard him from the corner of my eye. I no longer feel like talking about Veronica. My creative constipation is a trifle in comparison to his news.

'I was thinking, Marnie, perhaps you might like to read some of your poetry out loud. It could be from your old collection. Would that be all right?'

He's never asked me this before. I'm unseated.

'But ... why?'

'Please, sit down. Because we've been talking about symbols. I haven't heard any of your poems in the five months you've been in attendance here. I'd be interested to hear your words.'

'It's ... I don't know any off by heart.'

He regards me neutrally.

'When are we going to talk about my list?' I ask.

'List?'

'You know, the *list*. You asked me to make a list of things I loved about Perds.'

'Ah, so I did. And how have you managed so far?'

'I have two entries.'

His eyebrows rise towards his hairline.

'There's been a lot going on.'

'I see.' He nods, sagely. 'Shall we wait, then, until there are more?'

'Okay. How many?'

'Four? They don't have to be long – just a sentence or two will suffice.'

I smile to show I understand.

'Now, please ...' He gestures with his hand. 'Your poem?'

'But I ...'

I know how to retrieve my work – it's in a digital folder. I give in and pick up my phone.

'Excellent.' He rubs his hands together. I'm touched by his enthusiasm.

I scroll through the phone. I want to choose one that doesn't expose too much. He might hate it, might lose respect for me, my sessions dismissed like my writing as the mediocre musings of a substandard mind.

'Are you *sure* you want to hear one?'

'Absolutely.'

'Right, here goes. It doesn't have a title.'

> *our skin is ruined*
> *in the rain*
> *this clifftop afternoon flooded by heavy brown shadows*
> *and the lazy winter light*
> *a little way beyond*
> *wind licks rust*
> *from our delirious hair*
> *it drives your dress across my face*
> *until I become your paisley windsock*
> *and your arms rest across your nearly naked body.*

I keep my head down. I can't bear to see the disappointment on his face.

'Thank you, Marnie. How did you feel reading that?'

'Scared.'

'How so?'

Duh. 'In case you didn't like it.'

'It's important to you that I like it,' he says.

'Obviously.'

'Do you wish to talk about why you chose that particular poem? What symbols you think it holds?'

'No.' I feel suddenly exasperated. He will keep banging on about symbols. 'I wrote it when I was nineteen. It's sentimental and not terribly accomplished, but it was about my sister and there's nothing people love so much as an author's tragic backstory. Well, that and brilliant writing. And celebrity cookbooks. I wish to talk about something else.'

'All right.'

'I wish to talk about how unfair it is being a woman, viz creating – making creative works, like this one. How it's easier for men.'

I'm not sure where this has come from. Schlap isn't, either. His nose wrinkles.

'Yes?'

'First, obvious, but the world is completely weighted in men's favour. They get better job opportunities, better pay, more respect. They can create whatever they want without an agenda due solely to their not possessing a pudendum.' I pause. 'On top of which, in the rest of their life, they have little to no danger of sexual predation on the streets, no periods, don't have to squeeze a human watermelon out their fanny if they want offspring, don't have to take time out whilst raising said watermelon into a fully functioning human being only to return to work and find their childless peers have overtaken them. They have less societal expectations of "good" be-haviour. They're allowed to let hair stay on their body, smell of sweat, fart, burp, get fat, grow old without adverts and editorial campaigns covertly encouraging them to put needles in their face or poison in their hair.' I'm breathing fast. I stare at the rat painting. 'After years of rotten periods, you don't have to have a *menopause*, which goes on for years and which doctors and everyone around you use as an explanation for everything that's wrong in your life or with your health, and for which there's no remedy. Unless you want to swallow hormones, which I do, but they're all 'one-size-fits-all' and hormones don't. Fit all, I mean. There should be provision for individual womens' endocrine systems. It's all set up for men: everything. You even get to pee standing up, for God's sake, *wherever* you like.'

'And you would like a penis,' he says at last, without judgement.

68

I leap from my ergonomic chair. 'Yes! If I had a penis, I wouldn't *be* here. I'd be out *doing* stuff, writing my poems, *achieving*, making babies at forty-nine, pushing into everything. Men don't even have to think about this — they get it all for free.

'I keep worrying I need to be more feminine, but in truth, it's the opposite — I need to be more like a man. According to my mother, I'm creatively impotent. Ergo, I need a metaphorical cock.' I hear another Marnie inside telling me to calm down, stop talking shit, go back to discussing normal things, like my dead sister. 'And who *is* that?' I'm pointing at the man in the rat picture now. 'I mean, what is he even doing there with his flat cap and his silly gun? What is *that* a symbol of?'

'My son painted it,' says Schlap.

'Your son painted that?' I feel my cheeks redden. 'You have a son?'

'Had.'

'What?'

'Dashiell. He died.'

'When?'

'Twenty-one years ago.'

'How old was he?'

'Forty.'

'But ... how?'

I lost my twin a few days before we turned eighteen and it was the worst thing that ever happened to me, but to lose a child ... I don't think I'd still be functioning. I think I'd have died myself.

'The post-mortem said a catastrophic aortic aneurysm.' Schlap looks uncomfortable. 'No one could have prevented it. He was an artist.'

I burst into tears. 'Do you still see him?'

'Of course I don't see him, he's dead. It's okay, Marnie,' Schlap says in a soothing voice. 'It's in the past. It's gone. It's okay.'

Our Friday session has ended. I've managed to stop weeping and have apologised for the death of his son, as if I somehow had a hand in it, which is ridiculous, but Schlap has batted this away with a flick of his hand. I've apologised, too, for shouting earlier, but he said it was okay, he'd seen worse. Now, I'm wondering what kind of worse.

I think of his other patients: the Mansfield impersonator, for example. She has baggage. Schlap has given me his affable wave as I've walked out of the office and has assured me that we'll see one another the following Tuesday. I've corrected him with Monday and the other less formal Schlap makes a cameo appearance and he accepts his mistake with a humorous chuckle.

He's lost his son – I don't know how the muscles on his face still turn his mouth up like that.

I've emerged onto Harley Street. I'm hot and my armpits are wet with sweat. The sun is beating on the pavement and the air smells inexplicably of Dettol.

I think about my outburst, what I said about women. I feel bad for shooting off at Schlap, but I meant it all. It was a relief, in truth, to say it aloud with force.

That's when I see her: not my sister, the Mansfield impersonator. In front of my old school. Strictly speaking, it's her school, too – the real Mansfield, I mean – about a hundred years before me. I'm on the opposite side of the road as she hoves into view round the corner of Queen Anne Street. She marches swiftly by the creamy-white pillars of the school in the direction of Schlap's house, passing the exact spot where the bad thing happened to Perdita, in the same clothes she was wearing yesterday. People's heads are turning as she passes. Her burgundy velvet coat streams out behind her. The only change to her appearance is her hair, tied back in what looks to be, from this distance, a tortoiseshell clip.

'Hey!' I shout.

She's on a mission. Or perhaps she's late.

'Katherine!' I'm waving.

She comes to a standstill. Her head goes left, right.

'Over here!' Still waving.

She scowls.

She seems unwilling to budge from her current position, so I dodge in front of a black cab and run to join her on the opposite pavement. I stand directly in front of her.

'Sorry,' I say. 'Waving, not drowning.'

'Beg pardon?'

'Beg' sounds like 'big'. Her accent is a thing of beauty.

'It's me,' I say. 'From yesterday. At Schlap's house? We met in the waiting area.'

'Oh?'

'Marnie.' I point to myself.

'I remember,' she says, but her eyes say she really doesn't.

I begin to wonder if she, too, has memory problems. That would be a disaster for Schlap. That would be the blind leading the blind.

'What are you up to?'

'On my way home. To collect some papers. Late for a meeting.'

'Something nice?' I should mind my own business. 'Do you live round here?'

'Just up there.' She points in the direction of Schlap's.

'Lucky,' I say. 'So convenient: no wonder you chose Schlap as your shrink.'

'My ... ?' Her brown eyes blaze into mine.

All of a sudden, I want to write a poem about her: I have to. This is such an amazing feeling, I feel heat gather in my pelvis and wonder if I'm about to wet myself.

'Would you mind very much if we saw one another again? Would you be interested in going for a coffee one day?' My throat tightens as I wait for her answer.

'Yes, very well.' She pronounces it 'yis' and then laughs freely. 'Yes, why not?'

'Fab.' I reach for my phone. 'Do you have a mobile number or ... ?'

'A? No.' She gives me an odd look.

'Right.'

I'm about to suggest committing a time to our diaries, when she says, 'Though I do pass here each day at around this hour.' She points behind her to the pillars of the school. 'Right by my old school.'

She can't *actually* have gone to the same place? How likely would that be: the real Mansfield, myself *and* the Mansfield pretender all attending the same school?

'Next time I shan't be in such a rush,' she continues. 'You could just hail me on the street. I'd rather like that; leave it to fate. I know a little place on Marylebone Lane where we can go.' She lowers her voice. Her eyes twinkle. 'They sell cheroots.'

'Cigars. Good.' I'm not sure if she's joking.

'See you tomorrow, then.' She sweeps her coat from around her ankles and hurries away.

I watch her leave. I remember that tomorrow is Saturday and so of course I won't see her then.

★

I trundle home and stare at my computer for a further hour. I try to entice words from my fingers by reminding myself of the feeling I had with Katherine on the street, the *desire* to write about her, so connected to the desire to get to know her better. I manage one solitary line: you crease me. It's a start.

How does Perdita just disappear like that whenever I run after her? If she is a ghost, I haven't actually seen her dematerialise, as such. And why would she be a ghost who is the *same age* as me, as I've mentioned to Schlap? Why wouldn't she still be seventeen?

I suck on my pen and make a decision. I *will* get to the bottom of this. By myself. I will not consider myself a victim. I will think like a man. This will probably involve penetrating something.

Saturday evening arrives and Stan does, as per my wish, disappear to his friend Trey's, and Ben and I get my much longed-for night to ourselves. We clop along to the Vietnamese on Upper Street. I spend a great deal of time slurping noodles, splashing pho broth over my T-shirt, trying not to itch my elbows, which are annoyingly red and raw, tentatively relating my last two sightings of Perdita at long last. Ben doesn't seem overly surprised, which is a relief. He responds by saying how interesting and asking me what I think these appearances symbolise.

I tell him of Veronica's new deadline, discuss Schlap and fake Mansfield, and go through the gifts we collected in Flying Tiger for the twins' upcoming eighteenth.

He wears a look of absent-minded concern through most of it and does a lot of nodding. He doesn't notice my shoddy table manners. I know he's immersed in thinking about his book. He runs his hands through his hair in that self-conscious way men do when they're having an affair, though I don't imagine Ben's having anything, he really is just thinking about his book. I feel more envious than offended.

His comments at the end of my conversational monologue are that I should consider myself lucky to have such an honest analyst in Schlap. At least he knows he's going dotty – most just grow old and crackers and carry on practicing without even noticing. And don't worry about Perdita – plenty of perfectly normal people see dead relatives. And regard a deadline as optimism in its most potent form. I quite like that last part. After this, he looks at my elbows and refers casually to the perimenopause.

We come to pay. Ben's forgotten his wallet, which is usual, and I realise I've also forgotten mine, which isn't. There's an awful moment while the waiter clears our bowls and we stare at one another across the detritus of chopsticks and puddles of broth. The waiter finally departs for the kitchen and Ben leans over the table.

'This is embarrassing.'

'The washing-up beckons.'

He rises, pushing his chair out behind him. 'Stay here. I'll sprint back to the house.'

'*Sprint*? What are you: Usain Bolt? It took half an hour for us to walk here.'

'Fine. What do you suggest?'

'Let's do a runner. It's what Katherine would do.'

'Katherine? Katherine who? What's got into you? No way.'

'For God's sake, Ben! What have I just been talking about? Fake Katherine fucking Mansfield.'

'Oh, her,' he says.

'Benny, the food wasn't amazing and it's only' – I refer to the bill – 'twenty-four quid. C'mon, live a little.'

Ben looks at me like I've completely lost my mind, which I

suppose in a way I have; I'm channelling a woman pretending to be a dead author from the 1900s.

'That's completely unethical,' he says.

Before he can protest further, I collect my coat from the back of my seat and stand. I stride confidently to the door and step into the humid evening. People are smoking outside the pub next door. The sky is yet to go black. I inhale deeply: it's the smell of fags – delicious. I don't wait for Ben. I set off at a stride along Upper Street, pretending to be Katherine on her march past our old school. I know what I've done is unethical and I don't fucking care.

A few seconds later, Ben catches up, out of breath.

'Oh my God! Marnie, you nutjob. Run!'

'Run?'

'They're on to us!'

I look over my shoulder. Several hundred metres behind, our waiter is searching the pavement, one hand clapped to his forehead. He spots us and his arm goes into the air.

'Hey!'

Ben and I take off along the street, whipping past the brightly lit bars and restaurants, my coat flapping against my heels. I really don't need a coat tonight; it's far too warm. I've worn it deliberately in homage to my new acquaintance.

We run and run until we've gone at least a mile along the Essex Road, out of puff and danger.

'Oh my God.' Ben turns to me. 'That was terrifying.' His eyes are shining.

'Let's do it again sometime.' I throw my arms around his neck, practising a new word in my head, imagining how it will sound. '*Darling!*'

Ben steps backwards. 'Why are you calling me that?'

'I don't know.'

He looks hurt. 'It's not you,' he says. 'It doesn't sound like you. It sounds affected.'

'Okay. Sorry.'

He stares at the sky for a minute and I wonder if he's about to cry, but all he says is, 'Interesting.'

'What is?'

'Significant others approaching midlife in a state of creative constipation. The sudden actions, severally, totally out of character, after two decades of cohabitation. I may inadvertently have stumbled on a new section for the penultimate chapter of my book.'

'Fuck off.'

Things I Loved About My Sister: Part 3

She was an atheist, like me – and Mum and Dad, of course, back in the day.

Chapter 4

I arrive at St Albans station at midday on Sunday on the pretext of putting my head in at the church summer fair but really to pick Sylvia up from my parents' house after her sleepover. She'll have been dragged to the service this morning and I don't want her consolidating any of my mother's more outlandish Christian ideals. I'm attempting to rescue her from the clutches of the Lord. I want my daughters to feel I'm 'there for them'.

I've travelled here on the train because the Prius is in the garage following Ben's inexplicable decision to replace the car's broken front light himself. I don't know what he was thinking. He's an appalling mechanic.

It doesn't matter, anyway – I like travelling by train. Trains mean getting to study back gardens. This is one of my favourite pastimes: semi-private parts of other people's lives laid bare. Observing the startling frequency of un-netted trampolines, I try but fail to compose a fresh line of the nascent 'crease me' poem and eat my way through a whole packet of strawberry Fruitella. Four and a half days until the bell tolls on my career and I've managed no more than three words. I tell myself I'm beyond caring.

Walking down the high street, I keep an eye out for signs of my sister but instead spy female Richard III again. She's in mufti, this being a Sunday. I suppose even Foxtons has to close sometimes. She's coming out of LK Bennett in a pair of spanking nude patent courts. There's a man on her arm. It's probably Ant. He's older than I'd pictured in my head.

She gives me a funny look as we pass. I'm not sure if she recognises me, or if she simply thinks I'm a woman in a mess. I'm wearing a pair of Ben's old jogging shorts, which are baggy around the waist, and Stan's blue-and-white striped football socks, and there are muddy paw prints on my bare legs, courtesy of Parker. In the armpits of my purplish silk top – purportedly Stan's choice for my birthday, though I know it was the girls who picked it – sweat has stained wide crescents.

I lift my chin in defiance. It's a sunny Sunday. She's busy; I'm busy. Richard III may have helmet hair, feminine shoes and a great boyfriend, but I'm picking up my daughter. I've produced three children from my vagina. And I have my own job, albeit on hiatus. This woman is my sister-in-arms.

'Ant?' I call once I'm safely past, to see if I've guessed correctly, but the man doesn't turn round.

When I reach my parents' house and ring the bell, no one answers. I check my watch: twelve fifteen. Church is long finished. My folks and Sylvia should definitely be home by now. I peer through the letter box. A shaft of sunlight from the kitchen breaks up the shadows at the end of the hall. All is quiet.

It's hot and sticky. Too hot for grief. I stare at Dad's handwritten laminated card stating, 'Rose Family' beneath the bell surround, pushing away thoughts of Perdita. I think instead of Schlap's son, which is no help at all, and ring the bell a second time.

'Hello?' My voice echoes up the stone staircase. They can't *all* have had a fall?

I take out my key. I could have used it to let myself in straight away, but I like them to know I respect their privacy. Just in case they're on the lav, or getting changed or, God forbid – like one fatal Saturday morning when Perds and I were thirteen and popped back to pick up our forgotten travel cards – having sex on the living room daybed.

I push the door open and stride down the hall to the kitchen. There's a squeaking sound coming from somewhere in the garden. The kiln shed. Of course, that's where they'll be. My mother will be *creating*. Lucky Mum, good for her. No impotency on her part.

I head out of the back door, pushing my way through the drooping wisteria to cross the lawn, which is more of a field, really. The grass is sere and snapped; Dad has been unable to work the Flymo since the onset of carpal tunnel. Mum blames his condition on years of grinding their oversized pepper mill.

The squeaking noise increases its frequency. My mother's potter's wheel lacks oil on its pedal joints, but she refuses to let anyone tamper with it. The squeak, she says, is a sort of a ceramicists' metronome, helping her to gauge its speed, thus improving her throwing.

I hear voices as I close in. Inside, it smells of my father's evil apple home brew. My dad and Sylvia look up guiltily. They're crowded over my mother like some mini satanic cabal as she sits at the wheel fashioning beautiful things from lumps of mud. Dad, bizarrely, is wearing a white linen suit and a panama and looks like the man from Del Monte's suburban cousin.

'Mum!' says Sylvia.

She comes to kiss me. She smells of bacon, toast and ... *cider*.

'Marns, just in time!' yells my mother, her body bent low over the wheel, forearms around the pot as if she's riding a particularly difficult horse at the Grand National. 'I'm crafting ...' She peddles furiously, the red clay rising like a phoenix

79

from the spinning circular plate, the squeaks joining into an ear-rending sostenuto. 'A last-minute planter for the raffle.'

'It's going to be first prize,' my father shouts, pink cheeks beaming. 'Because the original intended first prize failed to materialise.'

'The planter won't be ready in time, will it?' I shout back over the wailing wheel. 'It hasn't been slipped yet, has it. Or even fired.'

Dad gives me a look. His lips make the shape of my name. I can't interpolate any of what follows.

'Say again?'

'iPad!' he yells, drawing a rectangle shape in the air with his hands. 'First prize was supposed to be an iPad. We were let down.'

'Oh!'

The enormous pot is almost thrown. My mother puts the finishing touches to the rim with a flourish of her index and middle fingers, winds a cheese wire from her pocket around her hands and carefully slices the base of the pot from the metal wheel plate. Her torso and arms are streaked with red. The wheel grinds to a halt.

The sound of two wood pigeons drift through the slatted cedar shed. A lawnmower buzzes in the distance.

'You look great, Mum.' Sylvia points at my shorts. There's no trace of sarcasm in her voice so I assume she means it.

My parents say nothing: they're staring at the pot as if they've just birthed a third child.

I watch as my dad struggles to the worktop with the fresh wet pot on the slender metal wheel plate. 'Need any help?'

'No!' squeals my mother. 'No one is to touch it apart from your father. The Lord will protect.'

I push air out of my mouth. 'The Lord will protect what? What does that actually mean?'

'*So do not fear, for I am with you; do not be dismayed, for I am your God.*'

My dad does his *University Challenge* buzzer noise. He dumps the plate on the worktop and tries to nudge it away from the edge. Mum's watching him like a hawk. My dad is undeterred.

'Isaiah ... umm, hang on ... don't tell me.'

'I'm going to have to hurry you.' Sylvia giggles.

'Ladies and gentlemen.' Mum looks at her watch. 'We've no time for *University Challenge*. Come. We're to stand by our stalls.'

Sylvia and I trundle out of the shed after my parents, Dad saying, 'Your amphora's looking good, Patricia. Beautiful ostrich motif, just like the original.'

An amphora *just like the original*. No wonder Mum's hurrying it through for today's fete. It's a vanity project, a replica of the one recently discovered by their theatre-going friend, that brought him his invitation to Buckingham Palace. Despite being firmly anti-royalist, Mum has always longed for Her Majesty's commendation.

We enter the kitchen. Sylvia's dressed smartly, I notice now. I think it's one of my mother's shirts she's wearing.

'How was it?' I whisper in her ear.

'Really lovely,' she says. 'Grandpa made his vegan pasta specially and afterwards we watched *The Shining* and after that we played Scrabble for ages because Nana said she wouldn't sleep with her head full of those creepy twins. My final score was 762.'

'I meant church this morning.'

'Oh, that. Yeah, great.' Her eyes dart away.

We watch as my parents pull a large empty platter from the cupboard.

'You smell of alcohol.'

'What?'

'Have you been drinking?'

'Don't be an idiot, Mum.'

My mother and father are cooing over the rice cooker as Dad tips the rice upside down on the platter.

'Smells *so* glorious, angel,' Mum's saying with a glance at my legs. 'Thank goodness you got it working again after Marnie's wretched dog chewed *another* of their implements.'

'Mum,' I say. 'Why does Sylvia smell of booze? You didn't get her drunk on home brew last night?'

My mother throws her head back. 'Never mind that. Come and smell these herbs, Marns. It's like a head shop in here!'

'Fragrant.' Dad nods.

'*Mum!*' My voice has risen considerably. 'Did you let Sylvia drink Dad's home brew? It's too strong.'

I've no idea why I'm reacting like this; I really don't care if she drinks it, but something doesn't feel right here and I'm mandating my 'man' thing by throwing out penetrating questions.

'Oh, Marnie.' My mother's shoulders rise. 'Don't be dramatic.'

'Ha. That's rich.'

'*How sharper than a serpent's tooth is an ungrateful child,*' she says, quoting King Lear.

'I rest my case.' I appeal to Dad, but he shrugs helplessly.

Perdita drank Dad's genuine apple cider home brew once when she was fifteen and threw up all over my bed in the middle of the night. I'm dying to remind Mum of this, but it would be a leap into the abyss: like fight club, the only rule in this house is that we don't talk about Perdita, not since my parents converted to Alpha, anyway. The gift their faith has granted them is the right to silence.

Dad has covered the rice cake with cling film and lowers the platter, rice and all, into a huge cylindrical Tupperware. He steps around the table, a loving hand coming to rest on my shoulder.

'Love, we didn't get her drunk on home brew.'

Not to be outdone, Mum comes to take my face in her hands. Given that she's still covered in clay, it's not ideal, but I appreciate the gesture.

'What's all the fuss, sweet pea? Come, let's go have shak-shuka!'

She says shakshuka like she's saying tequila, clapping her hands and executing a little step ball change. They're definitely hiding something.

'To the church!' Dad holds out an imaginary sword.

My eyes narrow.

'Don't worry, Mum.' Sylvia throws her arms around my neck as we all squeeze through the front door. 'It's going to be fun.'

'Are you going as a Red Indian?' Mum's addressing me.

'Sorry?'

'The streaks on your cheeks?' She makes a 'wah-wah' sound, palm to mouth.

'We say Native American now, Nana. You know that.' With a tut, Sylvia produces a tissue from her pocket. She wipes my face clean with spit as if she were my mother and not the other way around. 'That's better. It was clay, Mum. Don't worry, it's all going to be fine.'

I'm not sure what she means when she says that.

We enter the churchyard en masse. It's a *hive of activity*, which isn't a phrase I habitually use but feels right to employ while in St Albans. Speakers on long poles blare Abba classics. There are so many trestle tables draped in white cloths and covered in sweetly misshapen home-made goods that my spirits lift. I try to imagine what my Katherine Mansfield impersonator would make of it all.

Dad disappears inside the church with Sylvia to help set up his food stall. Mum makes a beeline for Vicar Pete, who is chatting to a woman with meaty arms.

'Patricia!' the vicar is saying to my mother. 'Just look at Sandy's candles!'

My mother leans over to inspect the candles and her boobs touch the vicar's elbow. The vicar discreetly moves away, which is reassuring. He puts his hands together and bows to the women, then wanders off to greet a man selling metal detectors.

The vicar and the metal detector salesman huddle, heads touching. They appear to be studying one of the models on show, but every so often, they look up and over at me. At least, I think it's me they're looking at: I'm prone to slabs of paranoia, which Schlap has assured me is just another form of narcissism, so it might not be me they're talking about at all. I glance over my shoulder, see no one and walk instead in their direction, hoping to catch the gist of their discussion. Perhaps they're Masons.

I'm intercepted by a teenage girl dressed, inexplicably, as a milkmaid.

'Care to buy any local milk?' She points behind her to a stall full of dairy produce.

'*Local* milk?' I look around. 'How local?'

The girl shrugs. 'Dunno. It's for the church.'

I smile at her. 'I'm all good for milk, but thanks.'

I'm having a strangely out-of-body experience standing outside a church in the boiling heat with a fifteen-year-old in fancy dress, as if I'm staring at someone else's dream. I picture

Perdita rising out of one of the graves like something from a horror film.

Except she isn't buried here. She isn't buried anywhere. Her ashes were scattered. Pieces of her are all over the world: after the funeral, Mum thought it would be a good idea to divide large portions of my sister into white plastic bags, distributing her to her friends, asking that she be left in places of significance to their friendship.

That was before my parents' conversion. I wonder if Mum regrets giving her away now.

I'm not sure what my parents have done with their bag of ashes. My portion is still in my underwear drawer. I like to talk to her when I'm getting dressed. I think Perdita would enjoy this if she knew.

Words brew at the edges of my brain: 'the spine of my ...' I know instantly they form part of the next line of my 'crease me' poem.

There's a loud clanging from inside the church, the music halts and everyone in the churchyard shushes.

'One-two, one-two,' comes a young male voice on the tannoy. Some deafening microphone-tapping. 'Hi, everyone! Welcome to the annual St Albans summer fete! Good to see such a healthy turnout. Sorry to interrupt your preparations. Before we open, I want to invite you all inside for a special surprise. If you could make your way in now, that would be marvellous.'

'I thought the welcoming was your job?' I call to Vicar Pete, but he and his detectorist friend have disappeared.

People are filing into the church like sheep. I follow.

Inside, it smells of cake and warm cream. More laden trestles line the walls either side. Someone is selling a Magimix, I notice. A handsome dark-haired man in his twenties with a healthy-looking East London beard is manning the mic. He stands on a dais beside the font, rolling up the sleeves on his white shirt at the elbows, as if he's about to take part in a boxing match.

'Welcome, welcome!' He leans into the mic, addressing the people gathered half a metre below him. The stained-glass windows are throwing pretty colours onto the stone floor. 'I'm Stelan. Many of you know me already.' He smiles. 'I'm group leader of the Alpha Course here. I'm so glad the congregation of St Michaels, the Alphas and our visitors can be here to witness a very special moment on a very special day.'

Low laughter from the parishioners. I feel like I'm at a party where the rules haven't been explained. I crane my neck to locate my parents and Sylvia, but there are too many heads blocking my view. Vicar Pete steps like a magician's assistant from behind Stelan.

The vicar has changed his outfit. In place of his black trousers and V-neck jumper, he's now in white ceremonial robes. He must be roasting. I've no idea what's about to happen except that Sylvia is going to be involved, because she's just appeared behind him, like the smallest doll in a Russian matryoshka. She looks nervous or shy, or both. A couple of young men flank her. They look nervous, too.

Stelan plucks the mic from its stand, hops off the dais and hands it to Vicar Pete. I get a sinking feeling in the pit of my stomach.

Things I Loved About My Sister: Part 4

When we were fourteen, my sister and I developed an obsession with horror films. This was unwise, because

I was terrified of them. One could argue that being terrified was the point, but the difference with me was that I couldn't let it go once the film had finished. I'd spend nights lying awake staring at the ceiling, resisting the urge to check under the bed or look in the wardrobe until fear got the better of me and I'd pad around our bedroom in the small hours, trying to keep us all alive.

I never wanted to wake Perdita because a) I didn't feel it was fair to keep both of us up, and b) I felt ashamed. But wake invariably she did. She'd call me to her, tuck me in beside her, hold me close and sing me to sleep, actually sing to me, like a good mother does with her baby.

I think she sometimes sang A-ha because of the high bits, but mostly it would just be a tune she'd made up.

Chapter 5

I'm drumming my fingers on the kitchen table in my parents' house. A crestfallen Mum and Dad are seated opposite. Sylvia is out of earshot at the top of the house running herself a shower and changing out of her baptism outfit.

'Carol and Graham were thrilled with your amphora, darling. They said they're going to plant the pampas in it,' says Dad.

The golden evening light dances on top of his grey curls, giving him a cherubic appearance. He reaches for the tray of tea and his home-made lemon drizzle cake, offering up the teapot as an apology.

'Top-up, Marns?' he whispers.

I have a sudden throwback to when Perdita was alive, when we were kids, when my dad was Emmaus Calder in the programme *Calder* and a bit of a celebrity, when we still lived in Kentish Town. My parents had a room painted entirely brown and decorated with those mirrored Indian cushions. An endless procession of handsome men who all looked like Terence Stamp – one of them probably was Terence Stamp – would sit around smoking pot and discussing the ashram in Puna, demanding from Dad when the veggie tagine would be ready. After the tagine, they'd all drink tea out of the teapot and eat cake, like maiden aunts, except with bloodshot eyes. I miss those days.

'What I don't understand,' I say, breaking through my own tangled thoughts, 'is why no one *told* me.'

Three quarters of an hour ago, I had to stand and watch as Sylvia was baptised, or christened, whatever being inducted into the Christian Church is called now. It went on forever. I'd forgotten how long-winded religion can be. At the end, Vicar Pete had taken my daughter's shoulders in his hands and kissed her roundly on both cheeks as if she were his dearest parish-ioner, and I'd experienced a stab of something that felt much like envy. With water dripping from her hair onto her shirt after her dip in the font, Sylvia's eyes had searched the crowd until she'd found me. I'd smiled at her, nodded, indicating I was giving her my blessing, which I wasn't.

Never have I felt so betrayed: why did nobody, not one of my own flesh and blood, come to me in advance to let me know, to *warn* me, that this would be happening? I understand now why Sylvia was wearing my mother's shirt and why she'd smelled of booze this morning – she'd taken the sacrament. She'd been *practicing*.

Now, my mother rests her hands on the dining table, palms up. 'Poppet, we knew you'd object. I'm sorry we kept it from you, but Sylvia was worried. You and Ben are so intolerant of faith.'

'We're not,' I say.

My mother looks to the heavens. '*And he said to them, why are you afraid? Do you still have no faith?*'

'Mark 4:40,' says my dad automatically. 'And,' he adds, 'with respect, Marnie, it's really not your business which mast Sylvia chooses to pin her colours to.'

'I'm sorry, but I know that,' I say.

'Don't apologise,' Mum says. 'It's passive aggressive.'

I reach for the biggest slice of cake and stuff it in my mouth.

'Why are you so upset?' Dad continues over the sound of my chewing. 'There's room in the world for all creeds.'

They glare at me, the weight of their eyes like stones on my shoulders. Why *am* I so upset?

'Sylvia's my responsibility until next week, when she becomes an adult. I just ... I don't want her to choose any particular one faith.' Then I add, 'Yet,' at the end to prevent Mum's tears. 'I want her to rely on herself. She took the sacrament this morning, didn't she?'

'I like rice paper,' comes a soft voice from the door.

Sylvia's standing there wrapped in a towel, her skin perfect. She reminds me so much of my sister.

The spine of my ... favourite book.

That's the end of the second line of my poem! After months of mental block, these few words, like delicate spring shoots, are all of a sudden here, at this most inappropriate of moments. More words pool at the front of my brain, like sticks in a dam. They jostle for attention. I stand quickly.

'Need some air.'

I stalk out to the garden and dial Schlap's home number on my mobile. It's supposed to be for emergencies. It trills four times before he picks up.

'Five six zero three?'

He sounds sleepy.

'Schlap? It's Marnie.' I hold my breath in case he doesn't remember me.

'Marnie. Is everything all right?'

'Not really. Sorry to call you on a Sunday, but I need your help. My daughter has just been christened.'

'Yes?'

'Well, Ben and I are militant atheists. No one told us this was going to happen. I'm so angry.'

'Interesting. It sounds as if you might be feeling shame at your own reaction.'

I stare at the apple trees. 'Not shame, I'm *cross*. We both know there can be no God if He takes young people away in the prime of life.'

I hold my breath in case I've gone too far.

'Yes. I see,' says Schlap, after a moment. To my relief, he doesn't seem upset. 'And how do you think a practising Christian would respond to what you've just said?'

Exasperating.

'Marnie, are you still there?'

'They'd say it was God's will, that He doesn't interfere, just observes. And that success in life is measured by being able to keep one's faith even in the hardest, most testing moments.' Inexplicably, I'm back to my sudden stab of envy in the church. 'Isn't having a faith a fundamental weakness of character?'

There's a long pause at the other end of the line.

'Is that what you think?' he says.

'Yes. My daughter's displaying what I take to be signs of abject stupidity.'

Perhaps I do feel shame. That Sylvia's weakness is my doing. That I've epigenetically handed the trauma of loss on to the next generation and that loving God is her only way of dealing with it.

Schlap's not saying anything again. I wonder if he's going to charge me for this session.

And then it strikes me that what's most upsetting to me isn't Sylvia's making a choice to be part of a creed I set no store in, nor that she didn't tell me, but that she didn't ask my *permission*. But I've no right to demand this from her — she's a free, autonomous young adult woman – nearly. The only thing I may allow myself is a small dollop of parental disappointment.

'*Everything in life that we really accept undergoes a change,*' Schlap intones eventually. '*So suffering must become Love. That is the mystery.*'

I'm suddenly alert. 'What? What did you just say?'

'*Everything in life that we really—*'

'Yes. That. Why would you say that? Do you know who wrote that?'

Schlap says calmly, 'No, though I assume from your reaction you're about to tell me.'

'Katherine Mansfield. It's a quote from Katherine Mansfield.' I don't even know how I know this: probably from my history A-level dissertation, which was ... *all* about her in the context of the rise of feminism through the twentieth century. How have I not remembered this until now? 'That's so weird.'

'Is it weird that I used Mansfield's words? She's very famous.'

'Yes, it is,' I say, avoiding the fallen apples as I stomp across the grass. 'Because I saw her. *In your house.*'

'Marnie, you're not drunk, are you?'

'Of course not.'

'Good.' His voice moves away from the mouthpiece. 'Well, we can continue this conversation on Monday. Is there anything else?'

'Oh.' I take a second. 'Yeah, there is one other thing. I've come up with a couple of lines for a new poem. That's good, isn't it?'

'That's very good.' The doorbell goes at his end. 'I'm sorry,' he says. 'I have to go.'

'Where?'

'We'll talk more in our session tomorrow. We'll consider your sightings of Katherine Mansfield and what she presages.'

'Presages?' Sounds ominous. I hear him fiddling with a zip, a woman's voice calling – '*Hello?*' – from a distance.

'Schlap?' I say.

'Yes?'

'You still there?'

'Yes.'

'Good. Sorry. Thanks for listening.'

'You're welcome.'

'Have a nice—'

But he's hung up.

What was the title of my dissertation about Mansfield? I wrack my brains but can't recall.

I rejoin my parents and newly Christian daughter in the kitchen. Life gets weirder every second. I want to think of a better word, but 'weird' is the best I can come up with at the moment.

'*So suffering must become Love.*' I realise I like that.

Sylvia and I sit opposite one another as the train whizzes past the tiny gardens at the edges of satellite towns.

My daughter stares out of the greasy window, fingers distracted and rolling one over the other in her lap. She's back in her own dry clothes, wafts of my mother's lemon-scented shower gel drifting towards me.

'I'm not cross,' I say. 'Just a little taken aback.'

'I heard what you said to Nana and Grandpa. You're upset with them and now they're upset because of it.'

It's true – only my father came to the door to say goodbye.

'It's not their fault I got christened today,' she says. 'I mean, it's not *that* bad, is it? Not like I'm taking drugs or stealing cars.'

'Of course not.'

'Or doing a runner from a restaurant without paying for a

meal, which would be a criminal act. Have you thought about the loss of earnings for the people who work there?'

I lean forwards in my seat. 'Excuse me?'

'Blythe texted this morning. She said she came back early from her sleepover, and you and Dad hadn't noticed she was home and were discussing it in the kitchen at 7 a.m. You were laughing.' She shakes her head and says under her breath, 'Too much saki.'

My arms fold across my chest. 'Can we change the subject? Can we talk about your party for a moment?'

'Only if you promise to go back and pay the bill.'

'Fine,' I say, thoroughly shamed again. 'I'll do it.'

Her face lights up. 'Good. Now, the vicar has offered—'

'You've invited Vicar Pete to your birthday?' What is *wrong* with my daughter?

'We've invited all members of the church.'

'*What?*'

She's silent as the train pulls into a station. People pile in, claiming the spare seats, carrying with them clots of hot summer air. Energy trails crackle inches behind each one of them, vibrating at a unique frequency.

What does that even mean? God, I'm hormonal.

'Blythe wants her friend to do a DJ set.'

'She does? Which friend? Not Pantea?'

'No. Pantea's not invited. Another ... friend.'

She's looking shifty again. It must be someone Blythe fancies. I don't mention that Pantea is – according to Blythe – definitely invited.

'I'm sorry I disappointed you today,' she says. She lets out a couple of her inimitable sighs. I see Perds in my head, at the same age.

'Oh, love,' I say. 'You could never disappoint me. Never.' This isn't strictly true.

'It's perfectly normal to have things we want to hide out of shame,' she says. 'I brought my stuff into the light and held it up to God. You should try.' She gets out of her seat and comes to sit beside me, resting her hands in my lap.

What kind of stuff does she have to hide? She lives one of the most blessed lives in existence. I mean, literally, she wants for nothing.

'Love conquers all, Mum,' she says. 'That's all there is: love. Why fight it?'

Suffering must become love. But love cannot conquer death. *That* is the real mystery.

In the weeks following I stare out the window and think about the past. Perdita's death, my brain went funny. I'd always had thoughts in an episodic sort of way, events in life occurring in one long line. After she died though, things started happening all over the place, all at once, in no particular order. My dad would say 'what Marns and I did yesterday' and I'd think, no, we haven't done that yet, or vice versa. No one except me seemed to notice. They were all too busy being sad themselves.

What should have been our eighteenth party celebrations passed unmarked. I received a hastily penned card from my parents and a stuffed teddy, as if I'd just turned six.

Then there was the funeral. It was kind of okay, in a terrible sort of way, because there was so much to think about. Everyone was coming in saying how sorry they were, and we were all encouraged to be brave and noble. Mum and Dad chose to have it in a church for ceremonial reasons, I think. There were drinks afterwards among the graves, which was just awful. Everyone had run out of 'sorry's by this time and stood around, in that very English way, looking uncomfortable and drinking too much.

Mum and Dad hardly spoke for around two months after that – or at least that's how it seemed to me. As I said, my grasp of time wasn't too hot back then. On top of which, they were so taken up with grief, they said yes to just about anything. *Can I have chocolate for dinner?* Yes. *Can I smoke a joint in the house?* Course. *Can I skip school on Friday?* Yes, yes and yes. I needed boundaries, routine, but instead I received the most middle-class form of neglect. I was so profoundly lonely it's hard to remember it.

Then Mum started acting out of character: up at night, sleeping all day. In her defence, she was probably on some super-strong medication. A few months in, on the advice of our GP in Kentish Town, she began attending a weekly grief counselling group at the local church. She'd come home saying nice things about God and angels in the sky and forgiveness and how Perdita was in good hands. This was remarkable only in that she'd never had any truck with religion until that point.

Dad went along with it for a while, sometimes rolling his eyes at me, or smiling conspiratorially – as though that would make it any better – but then he started going with her and the two of them would both come home repeating the stuff. The only plus side of all this was that once Mum found God, she stopped acting strangely and, apart from her conversion, went back to being her old self.

Meanwhile, the school sent me to the in-house counsellor 'to help process my feelings'.

The counsellor was a well-meaning woman, not particularly talented, about thirty years old, and Spanish. In our first session, I told her that since Perds had died, I'd become very afraid of the dark. An hour later, she asked me why I was afraid of the dog. Our relationship didn't last long.

In September, I cancelled my place at Bristol to study English, much to everyone's dismay, and instead locked myself in our shared bedroom, curled up at one end of Perds' bed and began writing poetry. I didn't realise at the time, but I'd inadvertently struck upon the one thing that was capable of pulling me out of the deep hole I'd fallen into. Several weeks of scribbling later, I woke and felt ... nothing. Not great or anything like it, but able to function. This was a triumph of sorts. I'd healed the widest part of my wound with words.

Dad's friend – a publisher – came over one day and asked to see my work. He pronounced it remarkable and I landed gratefully on what was to become, or so I allowed myself to hope at the time, my career. My first collection, *Gone*, all about my sister, was a critical success. I was described as 'one to watch' by several broadsheets. The whole ego thing was an excellent distraction from pain.

A couple of years after the first collection was published, I wrote another. Veronica liked it very much, but the men in suits at Euclid – the ones she still refers to as The Others – felt it lacked the power of the first and the poems never reached publication. So often it's the story *behind* the writing that makes it a success. I fought hard against disillusionment, but I'd lost confidence. And anyway, how can life flow with such devastation? Of course, I wasn't healed. The pain returned. Not worse than before, just, the same.

Does one collection of poems equal a career? No, it does not. It's Ben who makes the money in our house. In the intervening years, I've scraped myself off the floor, taught various private classes, held numerous minor posts on the faculties of universities, contributed articles about poetry to newspapers and magazines, and generally cobbled a few pennies together from two pamphlets and other bits and bobs. Veronica, and Euclid in general, have been unusually patient and understanding, and I'm extraordinarily grateful to them. Which makes it all the more difficult now, because I really do *not* want to let them down.

My children have been the biggest healer. Time resumed its linear trajectory once I had the twins.

Our train hoots, and another passing hoots in return, startling this expositional monologue from my head.

It wasn't until I started seeing Perds again this year that all this came up, like effluent floating to the surface of a lake. Almost as if I'd been involved in some sort of brainwashing programme early on, which had allowed me to get on with life, but only for a limited number of years. Now time is all over the place again, and I don't like it. Not one bit.

I look at Sylvia, her body swaying slightly with the gentle motion of the train, and wish for her, silently, never to lose someone too soon, never to feel that pain.

My daughter catches me looking and smiles. I smile back. She turns away again and I turn, too, staring out at the glass office blocks and new-build homes and defunct sidings and small back gardens containing trampolines without nets.

We arrive home. Ben's in our garden dressed in full fencing regalia. He's practicing his moves on Stan, who's shielding his torso behind an enormous cardboard box and holding a separate foil with a straight arm in front of him.

Parker jumps at Stan's feet. Blythe sits in a garden chair in the 'sunny corner' doing her homework, laptop on knees, books and papers spread across the small table. She acknowledges our return with a wave of her hand but without looking up.

'Balestra lunge!' Ben's out of breath, the tip of his foil carving shapes in the air. 'Parry carte. You'd riposte, Stano.'

'You want me to riposte?' Stan flourishes the second foil.

'Whoa. No, don't *do* it! "Would" – conditional tense. Safety first. The tip's gone. Six. Feint. Sept. Octave.' Ben spots us and removes his helmet. 'Oh, hi. Good sleepover, Sylv? How was the fete?'

'Sylvia's a Christian,' I say, my voice even. 'She's been baptised by Vicar Pete.'

Blythe's head raises from the computer screen.

Stan frees himself from the cardboard box. 'What? Sly!' He lets the foil drop to the floor.

'Please don't call me Sly,' Sylvia says with dignity.

'Sly!' Stan repeats.

'Stanley,' chides Blythe.

'Stop arguing, everyone.' Ben waves his foil in the air.

Blythe rises from her seat and walks towards her brother. 'Stan, look. Everyone's an atheist these days. Think outside your little box.' She flicks the cardboard, then the side of Stan's head, and goes to stand united beside her twin. 'I'm going to be christened the weekend after our party. Come if you want. Or don't. I don't care.'

'You are?' Sylvia's head turns.

'*Et tu*, Brute?' says Stan, who is studying *Julius Caesar* at school.

'Wait a minute.' Sylvia shushes everyone. 'Blythe, you said you weren't going to. You said—'

'I changed my mind.' Blythe shrugs.

'But why didn't you tell me?' Sylvia's voice rises.

I want to say *Now you know how it feels, young lady*, but that would be mean.

Sylvia takes a step to one side, putting distance between her and her sister.

'Why didn't you convert with me this weekend, then? Do Nana and Grandpa know?'

'Not yet. I spoke to Vicar Pete and ... What's wrong?' Blythe huffs defensively. 'I wanted us to have our own experiences, Sylv. I didn't want to steal your thunder, or you mine.'

'Whatever.' Sylvia stomps into the house.

'She'll get over it.' Stan's nodding, patting Blythe's arm.

There's the sudden return of the strong burning in my groin. It's not an infection sort of a feeling, more the sensation I had when pregnant with Stan; his fingers would point downwards inside my womb, right into my pelvis and the top of my vagina, as if he wanted to dig his way out. The midwife joked that was probably exactly what he was doing. Today is the worst the pain's been. I clutch my running shorts and double over. Blythe puts a hand on my back.

And then it's gone and I feel normal again.

'Period,' I say in response to my daughter's raised brows. 'Perimenopause. Who knows?'

She nods. 'Our wombs are our darkest mystery.'

'Yuk.' Stan wrinkles his nose.

'Oh, grow up,' she snaps.

'The laws of physics remain constant,' says Stan. 'I can't grow any faster than I am already.'

He walks off into the house with a straight back. We watch him leave.

'You can in a quantum world!' Blythe calls after him.

'So, you're a Christian, too, Blythe?' Ben says as he wriggles out of his white fencing jacket.

I look for a tell, a clue to what he's really thinking, but none comes.

'What do you think has prompted your conversion?' he asks.

Blythe looks at the sky. 'Oh, Dad, *please*. I'm not one of your patients.'

Ben sighs. 'Look, what you do with your life is your decision. I just want to make sure that you're clear about your choices.'

'Okaythenthat'sgreat.'

My daughters are always using this expression. I've no idea where they get it from. I find it inordinately irritating.

Blythe spins on her heel and hurries inside. Parker trots after her.

I watch Ben sliding the foils back into a black protective bag, a complex series of knobs and curves to their pistol-grip handles. It's like he's zipping up corpses.

'Well, I think that went well.' He's grinning.

'It's not funny.'

The pain in my groin returns. I fold in half again.

'Marns, you sure you're okay?'

'Yes. Yeah. It's nothing.'

I'm traipsing back down to the Vietnamese on Upper Street with an envelope of money and my tail between my legs. Luckily, the restaurant is open on a Sunday and the waiter from yesterday is working. His eyebrows half rise in recognition as I walk through the door.

'You?' he says in an understandably frosty way.

'I'm so sorry,' I begin, handing him the envelope.

Several diners nearby look up from their food.

'We accidentally came out without cash last night. It was entirely my fault. I encouraged my partner to run away because I've made this new friend and I thought she ...'

I look at his face. He's not remotely interested. I muster what dignity I have left.

'Well. That's the full money we owe, plus a large tip for the inconvenience.' Even I'm able to detect the obsequious whiff in my tone. 'Like I said, please accept my heartfelt apologies.'

'No problem.'

He turns his back on me and walks to the till while I wait.

I realise he isn't coming back and leave the restaurant, the tuts of clientele following me out.

I walk home, gritting my teeth at how desperately middle-class I am. How middle-class my life, my preoccupations and my actions. I don't want to be all self-loathing about this, because not only is it not helpful, but it's also in itself highly middle class. I mean, it's not my fault, but it does warrant acknowledgement. So I'm noting it, here today, wandering along Essex Road on this hot afternoon without my envelope of money.

That evening while my three children are on the sofa, plugged into their screens, headphones on, Ben, minus headphones, is similarly plugged into an analyst's non-fiction book, *Dream, Death, and the Self*, by J.J. Valberg. No prizes for guessing what *that's* about. Meanwhile, I lounge idly on the 1970s pouf inherited from Mum and Dad when they moved from Kentish Town to St Albans and wonder if anyone would notice if I got up, walked out of the front door and never came back.

They'd realise at some point, of course; say, when breakfast didn't turn up, or for Ben, perhaps, in the middle of the night, when I wasn't poking him to stop snoring. Otherwise, I think my absence could pass unremarked for some time, possibly twelve whole hours. I don't feel particularly sad about this. The way I'd describe it is more ... resigned.

If Perdita were here, she'd know instantly if I'd left the house, even if she wasn't in the same room as me: twin's instinct. I'm betting Sylvia and Blythe have the same unique ability. Though no doubt, my girls, with their new-found faith, would never feel unappreciated or invisible because God would be with them at all times, would see them even if no one else was taking much notice. No fear for them of disappearing, of not being appreciated, of heading towards death because – guess what? – He would be waiting for them on the other side.

Ben clears his throat, turns another page of his book and pushes his reading glasses up his nose. I take in his Swedish army shirt, a bottle green that makes him look like a particularly stylish gardener. He's had it since before we met. For a shrink, he's pretty handsome. In my limited experience, analysts aren't known for their looks, don't ask me why. Possibly, like the less prepossessing actor described as having 'a good face for radio', analysts are born with faces fit for hearing trauma. But not Ben. Some of his patients must have a crush on him. If I were one of them, this would make it almost impossible to reveal anything negative about myself. It makes me glad I'm seeing Schlap, who is of course beautiful in his own way but towards whom I have no sexual feelings whatsoever.

Ben's eyes flick up and catch me staring. 'All right?'

'Yep.'

'Bored? Why don't you read a book?'

This is the sort of thing my dad said to me when I was little. I do feel a bit like Ben's child right now, sat at his feet on our silly leather pouf.

'I'm quite enjoying studying you,' I reply.

He looks pleased for a second, then suspicious.

'Have I got something on my face?'

'No.'

He half-laughs and shakes his head and goes back to his book, but he reads in a self-conscious way now, aware of me looking, and I bet that none of Valberg's theorising is actually going in.

Ben was thirty and I was twenty-seven when we met. It

seemed that he was enough ahead in years to be vaguely mysterious and certainly more knowledgeable. He was a little absent even then – an attribute that enhanced his air of mystery until I discovered that the real puzzle was how he always managed to be thinking about something other than me in my presence. I wouldn't call him a man of hidden shallows, exactly, but for someone highly educated, someone intellectual, he certainly wasn't, on further inspection, *complex*.

Mum had dragged me to a birthday party for her friend, Ruth, in a large house in Camden. Ruth's son, and Ben, had been training together at The Tavistock. I'd walked into the living room to find the two men standing there, Ben attractive in a young presenter of a culture programme sort of a way, Ruth's son friendly faced and horse-toothed. They were huddled in a corner with four or five undernourished women in badly tailored skirts and hair that looked like they'd had their fingers jammed into plug sockets. I later discovered that this was standard uniform for novice analysts in the late nineties, the theory being that when you're dealing with the mad, your sartorial choices shouldn't be the priority. Ruth's son had been in estate agents' shoes, and jeans that were tight on his bum and flared at the ankle. Ben was also in jeans, but better ones, and the same green Swedish shirt he has on now, and he had long legs and big hands and was laughing at something one of the skirted women was saying. It was probably an analyst's joke – there are thousands. None of them are funny.

I didn't manage to speak to him until an hour later, when we bumped into one another in the kitchen and I said, 'There's pickled onions over there.'

To which Ben replied, 'Yes, you've been eating them, haven't you?'

I said, 'No.'

And he said, 'Well, your breath smells a bit funny, then.'

I'd been both mortified and pissed off. And he'd had to come over later and apologise and explain that it was a joke and my breath smelled just fine, and he'd only been trying to make me laugh because, like me, he'd been nervous in my presence. I said I had no *idea* why anyone would feel nervous around me, thank you, and it was okay, and he said no need to thank him, people often found him hard to read. Then he'd asked me out.

Now, this story feels like someone else's memory that's been implanted in my brain. Sometimes the past can be like that.

Since then, over twenty years, we've made babies, bought and sold a flat and latterly, a house, and yet great portions of his life are still a mystery, and not in a good way. His job, by its very nature, is largely hidden from me, his few friends separate from mine. I don't mind. At least no one could accuse us of being codependent. It's just, do I *know* this man?

I have one of those moments, popular in '70's films, when the leading actor realises they've had the wool pulled over their eyes for the previous however-many minutes, and the camera crashes in on their face at the same time as the background gets further away.

Could Ben be experiencing multiple worlds, like me? Could he, in fact, not be my Ben at all, but a Ben from another dimension?

His phone beeps a text. He picks it up, squints at the screen and puts it down again.

'Who's that?' I ask, feeling dizzy.

'Hmm?'

'Text. Who is it?'

'Oh. No one.' His head is already back in the Valberg.

'*No* one?'

'One of those PPI things. Shh.'

I watch him for a minute longer. Secrets. All couples have secrets from one another. Sometimes – so the magazines say – this can be a good thing. I'm not so sure.

I look at the kids. Stan's laughing at something on his Switch. Blythe's scrolling through a thread on Snapchat with Sylvia.

I glance at the bookshelf, where my first collection, its simple blue spine, sits modestly amongst a sea of other titles, *Gone* by Marnie Rose. That is me. I wrote that.

My eyes flick to the ceiling. I pretend I'm on the clifftop in Dorset where I wrote the poem that's in the collection, the one I read aloud to Schlap, about Perdita.

Later, I go to say goodnight to my children in their respective bedrooms. They usually retire way later than me, but this evening, for some reason I'm awake and seize the opportunity to visit them one by one. I want to kiss them, of course, tuck them in like I used to, read them a story and stroke their heads, but this is out of the question. These days, they need nothing more from me than food, shelter and the occasional tenner.

Stan's sitting up in bed reading a *Deadpool* comic while simultaneously listening to music on his headphones, nodding in time to the beat.

'Night,' I say.

He doesn't hear me.

I wave and he eventually looks up and nods peremptorily, like he works in accounts and I'm his secretary going on lunch.

When I open Blythe's door, her head is bent low over her desk, her fingers flying across her laptop keyboard. The glow from the anglepoise directly above her makes her hair shine like chestnuts. I'm so proud of her: her vitality, her strength. Barring the occasional trip to Claire's Accessories, she's such a bright, diligent student. Seeing her so focused, I try to edge out of the room without disturbing her flow, but she catches me in her peripheral vision and says, 'Okay, Mum?' without looking up.

'I'm fine,' I say, pleased she cares enough to ask. 'Sorry to disturb – I just came to say night.'

'No, it's fine.' She hits the space bar and slams the laptop lid down. 'It's eleven. I'm done.'

'What work was it?' I don't know why I ask. I literally have no clue about science.

'Just physics stuff,' she says, wisely choosing to leave it there.

It's amazing that one twin can be a maths genius and the other all arts. I imagine my womb must have been like Willy Wonka's chocolate factory, with all variety of elements waiting to be taken up by the incumbent parasites Ben and I created. On cue, my crotch begins to throb again. I make a mental note to call my gynaecologist in the morning.

'D'you need anything?' Blythe says after a second.

'No,' I say. 'Just fancied a chat.'

I wonder if now would be a good time to tell my daughters about Perdita. To explain to them what's happening in my life. Of all people, I feel they with their new-found spirituality might understand.

But then, of course, they're my children. It's neither fair nor responsible to burden them with my troubles.

The door opens further and in walks Sylvia.

'Blythe, have you got something to say?'

Blythe's eyes narrow. 'Have *I* got something to say?'

'Yes. Like, "I'm sorry about planning to convert without telling you".'

Blythe makes a perfunctory noise.

'Fine.' Sylvia gives a martyred shrug 'I'll turn the other cheek and come to your baptism, K?'

I'm impressed.

'We'll see,' says Blythe grumpily.

'For goodness' sake!' Sylvia turns to me. 'Mum? Aren't you going to say something?'

I hold my hands up. 'Don't involve me. This is your argument to sort out between you.'

She sighs with weary acceptance. 'Have you got any of that lavender roll-on stuff left?'

'Are you having trouble sleeping, darling?'

Sylvia's eyes flick to her sister briefly then to me and I know she's weighing up whether or not to tell me something they've agreed to keep quiet, because this is exactly the look Perdita and I used to share during such moments.

'Well?' I prompt.

She shifts uncomfortably onto the other foot. 'Blythe and I watched *The Exorcist* the other night and images from it are keeping me awake.'

'Right,' I say, wondering how annoyed to pretend to be. 'Well, that was foolish, wasn't it?'

Blythe faux coughs and says, 'Hypocrite,' under her breath.

This means I must have told them my sister and I watched *The Exorcist* at the same age. I don't remember doing that.

'How about you guys sleep in the same room until the images have ... dissipated. You know it's not real.'

'It's based on a true story,' Blythe asserts.

'It isn't. Well, not in the way they make out in the film.'

'How d'you know?' Sylvia's eyes are like dinner plates.

I long to give her a hug.

'I just do.'

I'm not going to tell them I checked only a few months ago on Wikipedia after I had a nightmare about a girl who could turn herself inside out like the one in the film, and wanted to reassure myself that that particular part hadn't actually happened in the real-life version.

I raise my hands again, signalling peace. I'm not entirely sure this is how it comes over, though, because Sylvia instantly asks me if I'm all right and Blythe says, 'What are you doing? We're not at Pilates.'

I sit on Blythe's bed and decide to come clean.

'Look. When we ... when I watched *The Exorcist*, I was younger than you by some years and I was *so* scared.'

Blythe leans back in her chair. 'You've told us about five times.'

'Oh.'

I know what I haven't told them: that I found the crucifix masturbation scene erotic. I haven't told a soul this, not even Ben. For an analyst, he's disappointingly traditional around the subject of sex. I haven't discussed my penis envy with him for the same reason.

My phallic obsession is precisely the sort of thing I could tell my mother – she loves to pathologise – but no child wants to talk sexual stuff with their parents.

The girls are now engaged in a chat about homework. I think about them as babies, lying in their matching Moses baskets next to my side of the bed. Mum gave me the blankets she used for Perdita and me, hand-knitted wool, one in purple, one in red. Blythe had reflux and would only sleep on her front. She puked constantly over the purple one until it smelled permanently of rancid milk. And they both cried an awful lot. I was exhausted and irritable, and Ben and I didn't have sex for a year, but they were so adorable with their little almond eyes blinking up at me in the middle of the night, I forgave them anything.

Now, their bedrooms are full of books on critical literature and the action of single-celled organisms, and they're Christians and probably love boys – or girls – I have no knowledge of.

I become aware of the silence. Blythe and Sylvia are wearing that look of gentle pity – the one I employ when my mother bangs on about God. Sylvia has pulled a chain hanging at her neck from beneath her jumper and is fingering the cross dangling at its end. I try not to think about the actress Linda Blair.

'Well,' I say, standing and stretching my sides to see if I can make my crotch pain go away. 'It's been real.'

Blythe says, 'Mum.'

'Yes?'

'*It's been real*? Just be yourself, it's fine.'

Things I Loved About my Sister: Part 5

She didn't have one armpit that smelled more unpleasant than the other.

If you're wondering what I'm talking about or think I'm joking, or trivialising, or are struggling to understand the syntax of the above, let me explain: I've always had one armpit that, when it sweats, smells distinctly more awful than the other. It's the right armpit, in case you need to know which – and it's a total bastard.

The problem didn't begin until puberty. I wasn't a small child with freak body odour. And actually, even as a teenager, I didn't smell *that* bad. I mean, Mum does like to remind me how, when I was fourteen, like Stan, I used to walk into the kitchen in the morning before school and my hormones would be detectable from over one and a half metres in distance, but that was Mum, so she was probably making it up. The problem has progressed as I've aged, staining my T-shirts and causing embarrassment. Like everything else, life likes to hit you when you're down.

Perdita didn't ever smell. She really didn't – except briefly at the age of seven when we both had a phase of wearing the perfume 4711 bought for us at the airport by Dad on his return from the Middle East; he'd been playing Jesus in some American series. So even as a child, she smelled fragrant, not sweaty. She was fresh and breezy in every way.

How was this possible when I was such a stink bomb and we were twins? How had I alone inherited the malodourous gene? It really got me down.

At sixteen, I came home on a particularly hot day to find Perdita waiting for me in the downstairs loo. This was bizarre in itself, but events took a stranger turn when she presented me with a folder of research on the various health benefits of perspiration. It seemed that sweating didn't just release toxins, but also provided a whole raft of other medical advantages, the likes of which I shan't list here as this isn't the point.

The point is that this is what Perdita's love looked like: spending most of her Saturday afternoon in Kentish Town library reading up on the subject of armpits for the sole purpose of her twin feeling better about herself.

Chapter 6

I'm woken on Monday morning by a warm, swollen feeling between my legs, as if someone has stuffed hot rolls into a balloon and left them near my thighs in the bed: unfamiliar, but not unpleasant. I lie on my right side facing the wall, unwilling to move, listening to Ben's timpani of snores. I must be getting cystitis, after all, and it's not even from sex, and it's three days till my deadline. Great.

Ben turns, his body pressing into me, the hairs on his chest tickling my back.

Something is happening in my groin. The warm rolls feeling is changing, morphing into something bigger, something solid. I put my hand down for a quick check.

Okay, it feels like I have an erect penis and two small testicles attached to my body.

I lift the covers and stare into the murk, holding fast to whatever it is that's mistakenly stuck itself to my pelvic area in the night. It definitely feels familiar in my hand, but more peculiarly, I feel the sensation of my hand from the perspective of whatever the solid thing is, as though it were also a part of me instead of just a foreign object. I sit up in bed and throw the covers onto Ben's side.

I'm greeted by a skin-coloured hard, uncircumcised, warm

and breathtakingly *large* cock, its eye winking at me in the daylight. My hand flies to my mouth.

I will not scream. I can't breathe. I'm going to faint.

My next instinct is to hide myself from Ben as if I've done something wrong, as if it's my fault, but he's still wrapped in the duvet, fast asleep.

Secrets. This is how secrets happen in a relationship. They grow from shame.

I push the thing this way and that, examining the skin where it protrudes from my mons Veneris. The testicles rest between my thighs, pink-purple and wrinkled as passion fruit. My fingers search frantically beneath the balls for my vagina. It's still there, hidden, shy, eclipsed by this new ... thing.

I'm still for a moment. Must. Gather. Myself.

What *is* going on? I wished to be more like a man, more yang, didn't I. I look over at Ben again, touch his shoulder lightly so as not to wake him. He feels sweaty, his skin blushing white then pink under my fingers. I bite my cheek. It hurts.

Someone's playing a trick. A practical joke. Perhaps Ben, having spoken to Schlap, has drugged me in the night as aversion therapy.

I place my finger in my mouth and dab it onto one of many bitten areas; there's blood.

I agitate my eyes beneath my knuckles. When I look down again, all of my new body parts are still there. No seams. No glue. No tricks.

The clock blinks 7.55 a.m. Amazing that time appears to be going along its merry way when I'm obviously having a breakdown. Or, a more surreal but potential alternative, I've been transported to *another* parallel universe and am existing on a similar, yet entirely different, plane.

I'd like to insert a caveat here, in case anyone believes that

I'm transphobic. I wholly support and endorse any individual's choices, sexual or otherwise. In my instance however, the change I've undergone has been entirely unplanned and poorly rendered.

I need a pee. I climb silently out of bed, my hands shaking like autumn leaves. My feet touch the carpet. I stand, legs wobbling, and look down. There he – or she – or it – is, standing proud, helpfully pointing me in the direction of the loo upstairs. I can feel the weight, volume and circumference of my new balls. They're heavy. So much heft. How do men do it?

I wrap a dressing gown tightly round myself and head for the door. I check for any sign of the kids. Parker is stirring downstairs, his metal tag clinking against his collar. I pad along the hall, purposefully averting my eyes from Ben's aunt's phallic cylinders painting, and make my way up the stairs towards the bathroom. I close and lock the door behind me and throw the dressing gown from my body. I stare into the mirror above the bath.

Good grief. I hang on to the sink for support.

My penis is enormous, pointing at my reflection accusingly, out of proportion to the rest of my frame. I'm a freak show. I turn round for a rear view. I appear entirely normal from this angle.

Okay. Breathe.

My condition could be temporary.

'Mum?'

Sylvia. I spin round. My phallus stares back at me from the mirror.

'Why have you locked the door? I need to pee.'

What if my voice has deepened? I clear my throat and hum; the notes float in my usual mezzo. I replace my dressing gown and secure the belt about my midriff. I check the mirror again:

nothing visible below my waist except the erection. I need to siphon. Then the thing will ... deflate.

'Just on the loo,' I offer.

My voice is normal. Good. I make my way over to the toilet and sit.

My penis points directly at the loo seat. If pee is to travel out of the end, it'll surely spray everywhere, soak everything. I push it down with my hand, not easy when it's stiff, and angle it towards the toilet bowl. There's no time. I'm desperate. I have to let go, allow nature – whatever that means any more, everything is upside down – to do its thing. Pee gushes. Sweet relief.

But it seems to be pouring from both orifices *at the same time* – my new genitalia ... and my vagina. My body lurches towards the carpet. I stop myself just in time; Sylvia's waiting.

I finish up, dab toilet paper around my crotch and check myself again. The dressing gown sits smooth now against my legs.

I unlock the door. Sylvia's standing with her back to the hall wall, one leg tucked under her like a flamingo.

'Morning.'

She's always so chirpy at this time. It's not natural for a girl her age.

'Morning,' I squeak and rush past her, downstairs to my bedroom.

Ben's stirring, hair sticking outwards at angles and flopping onto his forehead. He sits up blearily.

'B?' I loosen the belt around my waist and let the dressing gown hang open. 'Look at this. *Look*.'

My mouth isn't working correctly. I barely form the words.

'Time is it?' He twists sideways to squint at the alarm on the bedside table. 'Shit! Shittitty-shitty-shit – eight already?' He leaps out and flings on the unofficial analysts' uniform he's laid carefully over his chair last night. 'Shiiit.'

'*Ben!*'

He's pulling on his shoes.

'Look at me!'

He hurries past. 'You look lovely.'

He's gone, kissing me on both cheeks, hurrying upstairs.

'*Ben!*' I follow, dressing gown gaping. 'It's an emergency!'

He stops. 'Is anyone dying?'

'No, but—'

He's on the move again.

'No time, sweetheart! Brush my teeth. Mrs Falcon in thirty minutes. Need to scan refresher notes.'

Stan's waiting in his pyjamas outside the bathroom, hands clasped protectively at his crotch. I know how he feels. I snatch the dressing gown around myself.

'There's a queue, Dad.'

My son's voice is always croaky in the morning.

'For God's sake. Blythe, hurry up in there!' Ben turns to me. 'When is that infernal plumber coming to fix the downstairs loo?'

'Wait! A! Minute!' Blythe yells from behind the door.

'How long will it take, woman?' This is Stan.

'Stanley! You are *not* to play the misogynist,' says Ben. Then, 'Sod it.' He races down two flights of stairs to the ground floor.

I run after him, my cock and balls swinging uncomfortably between my legs.

'Ben, we need to talk!'

Parker, tail wagging, waits at the foot of the stairs with his usual greeting, front paws on my shoulders, nose wiggling. His head dips into my groin area. He sniffs.

'Get off!'

I swipe him aside and trail after Ben, who's on his way to the kitchen to collect his one posh coat.

'And again: *Ben!*'

Ben shrugs the coat over his shoulders, turns on his heel and retraces his steps through the hall, stopping briefly at the front door.

'Marnie, I'm sorry, but whatever it is, it'll have to wait. Wish me luck with Falcon.'

'Good luck.'

'Love you.'

He slams the door behind him. Parker stares at me dolefully.

Then I wake up.

I know.

This sounds like something one might read in a weakly plotted book, something an author might write in response to some critical notes, say, from their editor or agent, fearful that a novel about a woman with a penis might not sell well, but I assure you, this is not the case. I'm not in a book. This is honestly what happens. My life is a collection of clichés. I wake up.

Ben's still sleeping beside me, the house is in silence and I am penis-free. I leap out of bed. I almost skip up the stairs to the loo, coasting through the morning routine, a big grin across my face.

Perhaps I didn't really want a penis, after all. My cis female fantasy might be over. Simple as that. Who needs analysis? One nightmare can do all the work for you.

The only peculiar aspect of it all is that every other detail of the real-life morning is exactly as it had been in my dream: Ben being late for Mrs Falcon, the kids outside the loo and so on.

I provide my children with a semblance of breakfast, me on one side of the kitchen worktop lost in thought and they on the other, munching cereal and toast. Sylvia's still preoccupied with ignoring Blythe and Blythe with pretending she doesn't care. I call the hospital and speak to the secretary of my hero gynaecologist Dr Riba, with whom I'm on first-name terms after three children and equivalent episiotomies, to make an appointment for a few days' time. I do check my crotch a few times just to make sure, but no one seems to notice.

Other than that, it's business as usual.

I'm taking the tube to my session with Schlap. I'm eager to share my lucid dream-slash-nightmare with him and to hear his thoughts.

It's hot. Sweat is sliding off my palms as I cling to the train's jiggly plastic handle. Staying upright is tricky. I'm wearing a voluminous summer dress – I'm not sure why, as it makes me look like I'm pregnant. Beneath the dress I'm sporting my Calvin Klein dotty orange knickers. What would it be like if I'd failed to wake from the dream, if I really *had* had a penis? I'd have had to wear Ben's boxers.

It's 10 a.m., the train is crowded, commuters squashed millimetres apart, eyes on the floor or staring out of the window at the blackness, anywhere but at one another.

These people are *normal*, in so much as they aren't, to my knowledge, dreaming of alternative genitalia, seeing dead people or living under a bone-crushing creative deadline.

Bodies sway and press against one another as the train moves through the tunnel. Out of politeness, I try to keep my distance from the older woman beside me. Her bum is butting up against me. No one likes being touched on the tube, not even me.

Euston. The train empties.

'Excuse me.' My female neighbour nods her chin towards the sliding doors.

I try to move back, allow her space to exit, but we're boxed in. She edges past me, the recorded tube voice instructing anyone who cares that the last set of doors won't open. Her entire backside makes contact with my body. For some unknown reason, I concave my bottom away from her.

The woman's head flicks round. 'Did I step on your toe? I'm so sorry.'

'No. Nope. No, no, you didn't.'

I watch her leave, the double doors beeping closed behind her as if it were solely she for whom they were waiting open, and the tube moves off again. I have no idea why I did that.

Heat is rising on the pavements of Harley Street, along with a vortex of brick dust thrown up from the endless Central London building works, stirred afresh at the middle of the road with the passing of each hansom cab.

That's not right – all of that's bad syntax and feels breathless. And maybe it's 'London cab' or 'black cab'. Whatever. It's dusty; there are taxis.

Nearly there now. Not far to Schlap's.

Between the rows of Georgian buildings, a fat runway of blue sky interrupted by a solitary fluffy cloud, shaped like a cloud. If this sounds affected, it's because I'm deliberately apportioning floral literary interpretations to banalities to take my mind away from the runnels of sweat tracking my thighs. For the millionth time, I wish I had more grace. I wonder what Schlap will make of my penis dream.

Perhaps he's right: there is no Perdita. And Mansfield is genuinely just a crazy impersonator. Perhaps this *is* all about symbols. I'm not sure which option, real or imagined, is the more terrifying.

I press the buzzer and wonder who it is who always buzzes

me in. It can't be Schlap – he's in session. I make my way into the hall.

I walk through to the waiting area. There are no flowers today, just an empty vase. The place is unoccupied, the William Morris curtain drawn back, an invitation to sit on the wooden pew against the wall. I lower myself carefully. Plonking isn't an option in this dress. And anyway, no one needs to hear about my post-birthing Stage 1 bladder prolapse. No one. This is the last time I'm going to mention it.

The sound of Schlap's door opening. Flat-footed steps towards the waiting room. Someone rounds the corner.

I'm on my feet, dragging the curtain on its rail. I don't want anyone to see me here, more to save their embarrassment than mine.

I'm hidden but wrestling the temptation to peep, to check if it's fake Katherine. I put an eye to the slit where the curtain joins itself. I feel like Norman Bates.

Standing with his back to me, a man, head bent. There's a symphony of little beeps as he fiddles with his mobile. His proportions strikingly remind me of Schlap: short legs, chunky football of a head with ears like mug handles. Same stooped shoulders. More hair than Schlap, though, and far younger.

It can't be Schlap's son, because he's dead. Each time I remember this, my stomach lurches. It's less about triggering thoughts of Perdita and more that I feel sure we'd have got on, his son and me – got on very well, maybe even loved one another. I'm not sure where this idea has sprung from.

What if he has two sons and this is the remaining living one? No, he'd have mentioned it ...

I watch as the man puts his phone to his ear. Schlap's nephew, perhaps ... In which case he wouldn't have just been in for a session.

'Yo, P?' he says, which jolts me backwards from my peep-hole.

His voice is nice. Sort of smooth, reassuring, but '*yo*' is jarring vernacular for someone his age.

I listen to the clink of loose change as his other hand fidgets inside his trouser pocket.

'Time will you be back?' He scuffs his suede brogues against the Persian rug.

That's a giveaway. He *has* to be Schlap's relative.

What if he *is* Schlap's other son? What if we laid eyes on one another and instantly felt as if we'd found the part of ourselves we'd always been missing? We'd stare into each other's eyes all day and night because—

A Charlie Brown voice at the other end of the line.

'Hmm. Mmm. Swans.' He's nodding. 'So, the twins are okay with that?'

The *twins*? A coincidence. I wonder if he has boys or girls. I settle on boys – begin a separate daydream about his boy twins dating my girl twins. But then his phone call ends and he leaves, and I'm back to me and ...

> *I wonder how men do it?*
> *It must be hard for them ...*

No. Terrible. I scratch the lines from my brain and sigh. I long to get very, very drunk.

Schlap's bell rings. I take a breath, steel myself and walk in.

'Good morning, Marnie.'

Formal, as if I hadn't spoken to him at home only yesterday.

The room smells pleasantly of cloves. It could be his aftershave, or maybe the aftershave of the man on the phone in the waiting room.

I lower myself into the ergonomic chair. I wait the pre-requisite minute while Schlap stares at my nose.

'I'm going to tell you about a very realistic and, some might say, extremely *enlightening* lucid dream I had this morning,' I begin. 'And I'd like you to tell me what it truly means. But first, apologies for the delicate question, you don't happen to have another living son, do you?'

He doesn't look upset, which is a relief.

'No. Why do you ask?'

'No reason.'

I register the vague press of disappointment against my sternum. We wouldn't have felt like we'd found the other half of ourselves, anyway, Schlap's non-existent living son and me. That was a childish fantasy. That feeling was the one I shared with my sister. And she's gone.

'Marnie?'

'Yes. Okay. My dream: it's a tad embarrassing.'

'Are you all right?' He sits forwards. 'Something serious?'

'Not sure.'

'I'm worried about you.'

He's *worried* about me.

'Why? No one else is. Ben's not worried.'

'Ben?'

Oh my God. 'My partner. He's a therapist. An analyst like you, remember?'

'Yes, yes, very good.'

What's the point of it all when Schlap can't even remember my significant other?

'I'm going to be honest,' I say. 'I'm worried about *you*, Schlap. So that means we're both worrying. About one another. That's not great, is it?'

'Would you like to talk more about this?'

'No. I wouldn't like to talk about this. I wanted you to tell me what my dream meant, but now I'm not so sure. I want ...' What do I want? 'Would you like to come to the pub with me?'

'Would I ... ?' Schlap's eyes open wide. 'That would be far from appropriate.'

'A few drinks? Don't you ever just long to make it all go away?'

Schlap fingers some papers on the side table beside him, then says thoughtfully, 'Have you considered that you might be depressed?'

'I'm not *depressed*. I don't lie in bed all day with the curtains drawn. I'm really busy and there's a *lot* of opportunity and hope in my life. I'm ...'

I get to my feet, spread my legs in a haka stance and to both our surprise, I let out a long, deep primal scream. It's a monumental release, yet at the same time I know how ridiculous it is. It's as if I'm outside myself watching a documentary about someone having troubles.

Schlap is on his feet now, sprightlier than I'd imagined.

'What are you doing?'

His tone of controlled panic vibrates in my ribcage.

'Marnie! You can't shout like that in here without warning. There are other people in this building.'

'Are there? Who?' I sway my hips side to side, which is probably a little obscene given the position of my feet. 'You're forgetting everything, but you won't forget this.' I have *no* idea what I'm doing. I walk to the door, laughing wildly. 'The day you went to the pub with a—'

His hands motion me to the door. 'It's time for you to leave.'

'Just listen.'

'There is a line!' he bellows.

The door to his office shuts in my face.

I swelter on the corner of Mansfield Mews and Harley Street for twenty minutes. I'm shaking, wondering if I ought to try again – go back to Schlap's office, apologise, beg to be seen.

I'm outraged at myself. How could I have behaved like that? What was I *thinking*? I'd imagined I was waking us both up in some vague way. But that wasn't it: what I was truly doing was shaming. Shaming him for his illness and me for being out of control. Ironically.

Schlap doesn't need rescuing. It's me who needs help. It's becoming increasingly clear that I've lost my grip.

And now, here I am, alone on Harley Street. A bald guy in a Hawaiian shirt is shouting at a traffic warden.

I've just listened to a voicemail from the man making the twins' birthday custard doughnuts for their party; would the girls prefer eighteen candles or thirty-six? And where is he to put them, anyway: maybe just one candle on one single dough-nut to keep it simple. It makes me want to throw the phone in the gutter.

Oh, how I long to see Perdita. I will her to walk past.

Schlap could refuse to see me again or feel compelled to report me to his supervisor. Or after seeking advice, he could recommend a psychiatrist. Medication. I have an irrational fear of mental health medication. Ben, inadvertently, has passed on too much information about the side effects.

From behind, a breeze and someone wafts past. It's fake Katherine Mansfield trailing patchouli as she heads onto Harley Street in the direction of Schlap's house. I run to catch her up. My hands clamp onto her shoulders. I spin her round.

'What are you doing?'

She's ducking away, my approach too sudden, but I'm in no mood to let go.

Sit on my hands for you.

These words flow into my consciousness just before she says, 'Oh.'

I think she recognises me, because she breaks a smile.

'Marnie.'

I'm tingling pleasantly, as if I've been connected to a mild electric current, all previous moments' thoughts of shame and fear gone, just like that.

'Yes! It's me!' I'm breathing hard. 'Sorry if I shocked you. You walk so fast.'

She's dressed in the same garb. Doesn't she have any other clothes? It doesn't matter – she smells fantastic.

'I always walk fast,' she says. 'There's so much to fit in. What are you doing? Do you feel like that coffee?'

'Oh, *yes*,' I say. 'I might pass on the cheroot, though.'

She laughs. 'Another victim to pusillanimity, my dear Watson. Come, let us go.'

She links her arm through mine and we begin to walk.

'I love Conan Doyle, don't you?' she continues. 'So fresh, so modern.'

She leads me to Queen Anne Street and on towards Marylebone Lane, my feet barely touching the ground. This is almost the best thing that could have happened right now.

'A coffee, please,' Katherine is saying to the woman serving us. 'From your finest percolator, if you don't mind.' She winks, but only at me.

The waitress wrinkles her nose. 'Uh, the coffee is from the machine. Okay? Proper fresh. Better than a percolator.'

'As you wish,' says Katherine. 'Just be sure it's your finest.'

The waitress shrugs and disappears up the narrow stairs. Katherine has brought me to a dank, overlit basement café on a corner of Marylebone Lane. It's not the smartest establishment I've visited, but it does have a charm of its own. The only other person present is an ancient man with a yellowing beard reading the *Financial Times* and drinking tea through a straw. In my head, I revisit my haka moment in Schlap's office and feel like dying.

'Interesting place.' I stare at the peeling woodchip walls. 'Come here often?'

'Oh yes.' A nod of her head. 'I'm a regular. It's here that they sell the cheroots. You know, so few places do these days. And also that funny brown drink, Coca-Cola – have you tried it?'

In spite of everything, I giggle. 'A few times.'

She puts her hands over mine on the table's damp Formica. Her fingers are cool. I get that feeling again, like electric currents travelling through me. She feels it, too; I can tell by her face. Her eyes meet mine. Goosebumps pop up along my arms.

'You have such soft skin,' she says.

'Thanks.' Heat spreads across my body and my crotch begins to throb once more. If I had a penis, it would be stirring. 'So do you.'

The waitress returns with a tray of drinks.

'Black Americano for you.' She places a mug of steaming coffee in front of me. 'And our finest for you, my dear.'

Katherine's drink is a tall glass with a silver holder. Inside is the milkiest coffee you've ever seen. Katherine reaches for the curved handle. One of her velvet bell sleeves trails in the frothy top, trickling beige liquid across the table.

'Do beg your pardon.' Katherine grins at the waitress.

'Don't worry, dear.' The waitress pulls out a cloth and leans across to wipe up.

'Weird that they don't seem to know you here,' I say to Katherine. 'You being a regular and all.'

'Oh, they know me.' She taps the waitress on the arm. 'Don't you, Mona?'

The waitress frowns, finishes wiping and goes up the stairs.

'My name's not Mona, but if it makes you happy, then yes.'

Katherine's volume rises, 'And could we sample one of your cheroots, please?'

The ancient man looks up briefly from his paper.

Katherine laughs. 'She's a card, Mona. We have this routine going.' There's a silence. 'What's going on in your life, Marnie?'

'Not much.'

She studies my hair.

'I find you fascinating,' she says. 'You seem to be under the illusion there's a headshrinker living in my house.'

She touches my cheek with the tips of her fingers. It tickles.

'It's as if you've come from a different era. What year do you believe us to be in?'

I tell her the correct date. I look at the stains on the wall, smell the chip fat and know that I'm right where I've always been.

Unless ...

'Interesting,' she says.

Why does everyone always say *interesting* after I've spoken?

'I'd love to write a poem about you,' she whispers.

'That's exactly what I thought when I met you!' My voice has gone all high. 'But I ...'

'Yes?'

I'm not yet ready to tell her about my writing constipation, my deadline. I'm scared it'll reduce me in her eyes.

'My daughters are converting to Christianity,' I blurt instead. 'Well, technically, they both already have. They're Christians.'

Katherine squints. 'Is that a problem?'

'I don't know.' I must restock my conversational armoury. 'What perfume are you wearing? It's really good.'

Her eyes grow round. 'I'm thrilled you like it. It's made by dear lonely monks in Italy.'

The waitress reappears and gives the old man his bill.

'Mona, the cheroot?' Katherine prompts.

'Cheroots are off.' Not-Mona stomps up the stairs again.

Katherine sighs. She studies each of my features in turn, beginning with my eyes, then moving to the tip of my nose, which makes the skin between my eyebrows fizz pleasantly.

'Tell me something you've never told anyone else,' she says.

Now she's staring at my mouth. It's stupidly erotic.

'I thought I actually had a penis this morning.' I can't help it; the words just come out. 'I mean, it was a dream, but a terrifying one, and when I woke, I was so relieved I didn't have one. Then I had all these awful thoughts about whether or not my terror meant I was a latent transphobe. But I'm not. It's just… I've had this fantasy secretly for a while, and the 'reality' felt so different, but I think only because I wasn't prepared for it. The worst part is that now I kind of miss it – not the fantasy, the actual dream penis. Is this hard to follow? Does it sound puerile? It's not meant to.'

This might have been at the root of my shouting in Schlap's office – a subconscious frustration that people might not take my fantasy seriously and an even deeper desire for my phallus to be real.

Katherine's mouth is curling slowly, her eyes creasing. 'Yes, hard to follow. But not at all puerile. Not at *all*. In fact, I'd say more thrilling. Maybe you could lift your dress and show me. I can tell you if it really *was* a dream.'

'Um. No. No need.'

No shaming. And not with this woman I barely know.

'But how can you be sure if you don't have any witnesses? *Risk! Risk anything!*' Her volume rises.

I say shush in my head.

'*Care no more for the opinions of others, for those voices,*' she proclaims.

The old man looks up from counting change for his tea.

'*Do the hardest thing on Earth for you.*' Why won't she stop? '*Act for yourself. Face the truth.*'

I recognise these lines: yet more quotes from the real Mansfield. I used this extract in my A-level history dissertation as an example of her very particular brand of feminism.

Her eyes are challenging me. I can't resist.

'Okay,' I say. Fuck it. 'I *shall* show you. Don't get excited though – there's nothing there. And not here in the café. I'm not going into a dingy basement café toilet with you, for example.'

'Fine. Can you wait until this evening?' she says, fiddling with the top button on her white frill shirt.

There's a pretty ginger freckle on her right collarbone.

'You can come by my house around seven,' she offers. 'Drink vodka for some Russian courage before *la grand revelation.*'

Vodka. Of course she drinks vodka.

'There won't be a *grand revelation* because there-is-nothing-there. It's a subconscious des—'

She giggles. 'We just want to give your ferret a run.'

'My ... what? Now who's being puerile? I'll show you my ... pants and you can confirm there's no bulge, and we can have a drink and then I'll go home.'

One of her eyebrows rises. 'Whatever you say.'

The old man has paid. He begins a laboured ascent of the stairs.

'Give me your address,' I say.

She laughs again. 'Why, you silly! You go into my home every day at eleven in the morning. Upstairs, third-floor apartment. It says Kass on the buzzer.'

She stands, shrugs on her coat, blows me a kiss.

'Would you mind getting this? I've left my purse at home.' She rolls her eyes. 'Ugh. Back now through the streets I go, Marnie, through the London crowds, the pilgrims straining forwards to nowhere.'

I sit in the empty café and stare at my half-drunk Americano cooling in its mug. Not-Mona returns with cloth and tray and busies herself wiping up the detritus of this most unusual of coffee mornings.

'Your friend,' she says, shaking her head. 'She's crazy. She thinks smoking a cigar in a café is allowed. Poof. Mona! My name is Amina.' She gives me a look. 'You're normal, dear. You should spend time with normal people.'

But I'm not normal. I'm going round to a stranger's flat this evening to show my pants. Maybe that is normal? My hand goes to my crotch.

I have an open mind towards people in general, but when it comes to myself, my mind closes. Why is that? How is it that I'm kinder and more tolerant of others?

Before I leave, I case the entire joint to check if Perdita might be hiding here, sat at a table behind a pillar – things are so strange at present, it doesn't seem an impossibility – before handing Lately-Mona, Presently-Amina a ten-pound note at the counter on my way out and hope I have neither under nor hugely overpaid.

The pavement beyond the café door is in shadow. I cool in the overhang of the old buildings and work out how I'll explain my evening sojourn with Katherine to Ben. It's Monday. Ben has evening clients and won't be home until nine tonight. My narrative will involve lying to him later.

It's midday. I'm jumpy. Then, inexplicably, I begin to cry. I blow my nose on a crumpled tissue from my bag, then wander round the corner to Marylebone High Street to grab some sushi. I'm suddenly ravenous. My phone rings.

My mother. She'll only keep ringing, convince herself something terrible has happened if I let it go to voicemail. I swipe the screen.

'Marns?' she says.

'Yes, Ma. It's my phone. Who else would it be?'

'Something's happened.'

My heart bumps. 'Is it Dad?'

The traffic is building, expensive cars flying past inches from my knees.

'No, don't be silly. You're father's fine. It's Vicar Peter.'

'Why is that silly? What's wrong with the vicar: have you finally committed ceramicide?'

'Cerami ... ? What *are* you talking about? He's had a fall.'

'Oh. Sorry,' I say. 'Traffic this end. That's awful. Is he all right?'

A monster Volvo, all shine and leather interior, slows beside me in the line, waiting to turn right. It's puffing out exhaust.

'No, he isn't all right. He tripped on the scarf I was wearing while we were doing morning prayers. Damaged his cruciate.'

'Your *scarf?*' My voice is rising, my emotions drawn inexorably into her drama by years of family conditioning. 'How's that possible? How long is it?'

'It's a Tom Baker in *Doctor Who* scarf.'

'Why would you wear a ... oh, for God's sake.' My mum wafting around the house trailing reams of multicoloured wool on this sweltering day ... 'Where's Dad? I'm sorry about Pete—'

'*Peter.*'

'Peter, but what's the purpose of your call?'

The Volvo waits beside me, engine still rumbling, stinking of diesel. The back of the driver's head indicates a woman with long dark hair, just like Perdita's. There's someone in the back seat: from the height I'd say a child, maybe eleven or twelve years old.

'He's been ordered complete bedrest. He'll be staying with us for a while.'

'Okay.'

'In your old bedroom.'

'What? Why?'

'It's the biggest and it has the best view. Anyway, *you're* never in it.'

She's testy.

'I'm sure he'd appreciate a visit if you're passing.' She coughs and calls away from the speaker, 'What's that? Got to go, darling.'

She rings off.

I stare stupidly at my phone, the way they do in TV shows, as if my mother were living inside it. I'm hardly ever 'just passing' St Albans.

The woman in the Volvo is turning to the person in the rear, her hand out. She's offering something: a sweet, a tissue. As she turns back, I get to see the child is actually a dog, its ears straight up and swivelling like satellite dishes. I also get a proper look at the woman's face.

It's Perdita.

The car moves off, turns right.

'Hey!' I give chase. 'Wait!'

The car accelerates into the distance. I don't catch all the number plate. It's PR or K something something, something something, then an X.

I'm standing in the road. Behind me, another car honks. I jump out of the way.

What was it? PR or K something.

Perdita again. It looked like her. My sister. My Perdita.

Something, something something, then an X.

I make my way to Regent's Park. I sit on a bench in the sun.

Perdita. My sister. It looked like Perdita.

My fists bunch and dig into the wooden slats, the pain satisfying.

It couldn't be Perdita. Nothing in my life works. I'm losing my marbles.

I see Veronica shaking her head at me. Schlap, my mother, too.

When I glance at my watch, forty-five minutes have passed without my even noticing.

Things I Loved About My Sister: Part 6

I fear that a lot, if not all, of these excerpts for things I loved about my sister must sound terribly childish, but when you think that she only lived to be seventeen and eleven twelfths, you can, I hope, understand why my memories of her almost entirely lack maturity.

The inverse of this is that even though we were young, my sister always made me feel grown-up. In my head, at least. The conversations, the ideas we shared, felt solid somehow – not the ramblings of two kids but the linear and gravitas-laden theories of a pair of budding philosophers. She never laughed at my dreams or told me I was stupid. (Okay, once she did, when I was six and I cut the hair of her only Sindy doll so Sindy could have an affair with Barbie. At that age, I felt only short hair could justify the blossoming of Sindy and Barbie's amorous union, which is interesting to me now, especially in the light of my lucid dream).

Perdita still carries a lot of my childhood secrets. Not literally, because she's gone, of course. What I mean is, she's taken them to the grave with her. I can't remember what these secrets were, they were almost certainly of no importance in any objective sense, but I know she honoured them, never told a soul.

Chapter 7

A silver Volvo XC90.

I should be writing, but instead I've googled the car's make and model as soon as I've reached home. P then an R or a K then X at the end – like doing the crossword. If not her, then someone who looked *exactly* like her. Seven seats in the car signalled a large family.

The chances of a doppelganger are more likely than my sister's resurrection, though sure, it's a mighty coincidence, a doppelganger idling next to me like that, which leads me back to that woman actually *being my sister.*

It had to be her. All right, it *could* have been.

I don't know what to do with this information.

Is this the fourth or fifth sighting, or the sixth?

Meanwhile, twenty-six poems are waiting to be written in three days.

Twenty-six.

There are too many numbers floating around my interior world right now.

Later, I stand outside Schlap's building staring at his third-floor windows.

The sun is glowing a soft orange yellow, the sky a deeper

blue. Odd being in this place at this time meeting Katherine, the prospect of vodka and pulling up my dress fast approaching. Unsurprisingly, I'm nervous.

I'm not sure where today has gone. I seem to have floated through the last hours with numb bones, spending the day mostly alone and preoccupied by the aforementioned googling, managing only a poor collection of conversational banalities with the kids on their return from summer school.

With Ben still at work, I left the three of them in the kitchen making a mess of their dinner and headed back out on my bicycle to Harley Street. I felt like cycling this evening. I'd hoped the fresh air would clear my head.

Now, I step up to the big black doors and study the series of bells, bottom to top:

Practice rooms
J. Schlapoberstein
Kass
J. Schlapoberstein

How have I not noticed these names before? And also, how is Schlap living both above *and* below Katherine? Perhaps she's his daughter – a delusional bastard child, locked out of sight like the first Mrs Rochester.

I ring the buzzer marked Kass, step back and wait.

I hear the creak and bang of a heavy door opening then closing high up inside the building. The sound of footsteps descending.

I do a quick mental check-in: I'm waiting on the threshold of my analyst's house, which turns out not to be solely his home at all but also the home of a dead author who attended my school, or someone who's impersonating her and could be a relative of Schlap's.

And there's a person in the world who looks like my sister. Or *is* my sister.

The door opens.

'Hello, stranger.' Katherine smiles lazily. She steps to one side to let me in.

She's gorgeous, dressed in an aubergine velvet smoking jacket, ruffled white shirt, black evening trousers and neat black patent brogues. Her hair is greased back and parted to one side. I work hard not to stare, though I've a suspicion staring is exactly the reaction she's aiming for.

'Great outfit.'

'Thank you.'

Katherine's in charge here, in her home environment, and I'm a lamb to the slaughter.

'How are you?' I squeak.

'Good. You're not going to stand on the doorstep all night, are you?'

I step into the hall. Schlap won't be in his practice rooms but upstairs making dinner or whatever old men who live alone do in the evenings. We ascend the wide carpeted staircase to the first floor. I'm not going to tell her about seeing Perds. That information is mine alone.

I come to a halt.

'What's the matter? Attack of the jellies?'

'It's just ...'

I'm terrified in case we bump into Schlap. He may feel obliged to call the police. Also, what am I *doing* here, turning up to show a stranger my underwear?

'Is there anyone else in the building tonight, do you know?'

She giggles. 'Don't worry. It's just me, myself and I.'

She moves to stand on the step above me. My eyes are now level with her breasts: they're fulsome. I smell her perfume.

'And you, now you're here,' she adds.

She swivels on her heel and takes the stairs two at a time. She runs on the uncarpeted edge closest to the banisters, as I used to at school, her brogues click-clacking on the stone. I can hardly keep up.

We arrive at the third floor. I'm panting.

She raises an eyebrow and sashays through the open door to her apartment.

'Follow me.'

The interior hallway is small and square with carmine walls. Colourful paintings hang salon-style: Native Americans in feathered war bonnets and ceremonial dress standing in a line, a wide expanse of yellow-dusted American prairie lands, abstract graphic designs of what look to be mandalas. I can't stop staring.

'Who did these?' I ask.

'Fabulous, aren't they? My friend Dotty painted them. Dorothy Brett? Heard of her?' she says.

'Er. Yes. They're prints?'

'No, originals.'

She's pulling my leg, and I don't say that Dorothy Brett died in the seventies so it's unlikely they're still friends, because I saw my dead sister today in an estate car, so what do I know?

Katherine inserts one hand jauntily into the pocket of her smoking jacket. 'She moved to New Mexico some time ago; now, we never see one another. It's just letters, letters, letters.' She sighs, opens another door and disappears. 'Drink?' The sound of her patent brogues moving across wooden boards.

'Yes, please.'

The empty vase from Schlap's waiting area sits on the floor beside a large wooden bucket of umbrellas just inside the front door. I follow Katherine into the next room.

It's a large high-ceilinged drawing room with three sash

windows open to the street below. A couple of electric ceiling fans provide the only breeze. Katherine isn't here but there are sounds of tinkering from another room: the clink of glasses, the glugging of liquid from a bottle.

'Vodka all right?'

Her voice resonates. The kitchen must have tiled walls.

'It's all I've got, I'm afraid. I have a girl come every Monday, but she fell ill this week and I've not had a chance to get to the market.'

'Vodka's great.'

A couple of standing lamps with red tasselled shades are on in one corner, lending half of the room a soft pink glow. Books line shelves either side of the marble fireplace. On top of the mantle, a sepia photograph of a man in period garb and another of a baby from what looks to be the late nineteenth century, all fat cheeks and sporting a white dress-cum-overall. It's airy in here, but also warm and inviting.

'Make yourself comfortable,' Katherine is saying. 'You might need a few stiffeners to relax before the big reveal.'

I sink into one of two blue linen sofas and let my back curl until it meets the cushions at the rear. The sofa is deep and my feet are off the ground like a child. The sound of traffic echoes against the buildings opposite, comforting in its ordinariness.

This isn't so bad. I'll just knock back my drink, lift my dress and beat a hasty exit. I'll be home before Ben. No lying required.

A plaster sculpture of a naked woman, arms lifted above her head in a gesture of fluid abandon, stands nearly a metre tall on a low coffee table to my right. Her hair is coiled around her head like a crown, small lifted breasts, a torso of sinuous elegance; I wonder who she is.

Katherine comes back with tumblers clinking with ice. She

hands me a glass, lemon slice floating at the top, the liquid almost overflowing.

'Vodka and Indian tonic.' She sits on the second sofa facing me. 'Keep the mozzies off.' She winks. 'Bottoms up!' She takes an enormous slug of her drink.

I have a sip of mine and nearly choke.

'You all right?'

'Just, interesting dilution ratio.'

'It's meant to put hairs on your chest.' She giggles.

I point at the dancing statue. 'Not you, is it?'

She laughs again. She laughs a lot, I've noticed.

'It's of my friend Nina Hamnett, by my dear late friend Henri.'

'Your late friend? I'm sorry.'

Her face clouds and she stares at the sky through the window.

'The war has taken so many.'

'The? In Syria? Or ... ?'

She turns to me. 'With the Jerries, darling. You must have lost at least one person.'

'Um ...'

'And to the pandemic.'

'The pandemic? What pandemic?'

She tosses her head. 'Why, the Spanish flu. Don't tell me you don't know at least thirty people who've gone. All that's left is to laugh, fuck and get drunk.' And with that, she downs her entire glass, lemon and all, then gets to her feet, chewing the rind. 'Another?'

'I haven't even finished ...'

But she's gone.

I have a funny feeling in my pants. It must have been when she said the word 'fuck'. I stand up. Something feels different. I'm not sure what.

'Everything okay?' Katherine calls from the other room.

'Yeah. Yep.' I return to the sofa and resume my position. Things have gone quiet. 'Katherine?'

I rise and head to find her. It's suddenly stifling in here. I long for a cold shower.

The kitchen is empty. It's small and painted a sunny yellow with Persian patterned tiles around the sink. A set of folding-leaf doors make up the far wall. They are closed. I hear movement on the other side.

'Katherine?'

'Wait a minute!' An up-and-down cadence to her voice. 'Just slipping into something more comfortable.'

The doors concertina open. Katherine stands half a metre from me, arms stretched sideways at shoulder height, as if she's about to take off. She's in a floor-length pink silk shift tied at the waist. It's beautiful but looks night-timey. Perhaps it's a dressing gown. Her feet are bare.

'Well, don't just stand there gawping! What do you think?'

'You look ... nice.'

This is hardly adequate, but her mouth opens into a smile. I've never noticed her teeth before. Perhaps she's never shown them to me. They're surprisingly white and even.

'Listen, I've—' I begin.

'This is my bedroom.'

Her voice rides over mine, her arm waving at the room. She says, '*thess*' instead of '*this*' because of her accent. Then she giggles as if we were teenagers at a sleepover.

'Listen—'

'In a *minute*.'

Behind her head on the back wall, an open sash, beneath which is a small double bed covered with a blue-and-rose patchwork bedspread. Alongside are two metal bedside tables and two reading lamps with small pinkish shades. Her smoking jacket and other clothes are puddled on the floor, like the skin shed by a snake. The room looks girlish and old-fashioned. I think of my sister, wonder if she'd have had such a room had she lived, and suddenly want very much to lie down on that bed and go to sleep.

'Are you all right?' She comes towards me.

I stare at the floor. Her fingers rest on my collarbone.

'I ...'

She looks down at my crotch area through my dress.

'Oh, my goodness,' she whispers, eyes growing.

'What?'

I put my hand down to check and nearly fall over. I have an erection. I mean, I have a penis with an erection, my dress tented out. I back away, as if in doing so I can put distance between myself and it, but it comes with me, of course, until I'm flush with the folding doors.

Katherine approaches once again and exhales a long, warm, ethanol-infused breath across my face. A shiver runs from the top of my head right down to my toes and my cock rises further. The feeling is actually amazing. Somewhere outside, a car honks its horn.

Katherine pulls my face up to meet hers and leans forwards to kiss me softly on the mouth. I've never kissed a woman before. Her lips are pillows, her skin soft, hairless. It feels like falling.

She draws away and cups my cheek in her hand. Her brown eyes pierce and warm me. If this is a dream, so far it's one of the best I've had.

She drags me gently across the room until I'm at the edge of her bed and moves towards me, her whole body pushing into mine. I feel her curves, her hair through her thin silk shift, the hard bone of her pubis pressing against my thigh. One of her hands drops out of sight. She grips my swollen cock through my dress.

'Oh, that's *really* there, all right.'

I can no longer think. All sensation is in my crotch. Who cares what is, or isn't, real? Someone could bring a live tiger into the room right now and I wouldn't budge. I try to think about Ben, remind myself that this is adultery, but I'm helpless in the face of this burning.

Katherine tugs at the cord on her gown and the silk slides from her shoulders to the floor. She's wearing nothing underneath. She's slim with rounded edges and magnificent breasts.

I turn, trying to put space between us; I need a second to think before this intense feeling – it's almost painful – juggernauts me further into danger.

'I just wanted you to tell me if it was there or not.' My voice is so weak it makes her laugh.

'Your turn.'

She whips my dress over my head as if she's done this a thousand times before – perhaps she has. We stand semi-naked before one another, her eyes on my crotch.

'Well, would you get a look at that.'

Another fact from my A-level dissertation floods my synapses: *gonorrhoea*. Katherine Mansfield was famously promiscuous.

My erection deflates.

Katherine's eyes glitter at me in the pink light. 'What's wrong? Not up to the job?'

'No, I ...'

But this isn't the real Katherine, is it? This is a fake version, one unlikely to have a venereal disease. And I'm probably dreaming. It hardly seems the time to ask.

'Suck it.'

She's thrusting one pink nipple at my mouth. My penis

engorges. I fling my head forwards, led on by a spirit from another world, Eros perhaps – it's the only one I can think of right now – taking her breast in my mouth, licking and sucking. She moans, grips my shoulders – she's surprisingly strong – then drops backwards, pulling me with her onto the bed. I'm lying directly on top of her, her skin warm and smelling of rose oil.

'Fuck me, Marnie,' she says, ripping off my pants. 'Put your cock in me.'

'Okay.'

In an ideal world, *okay* wasn't what I'd have said at a time like this, but there it was: *okay*. I couldn't unsay it.

I take my cock in my hand just like I've seen men do and rub it up against her. She spits on her hand and wets my tip. It feels out-of-this-world good. I nudge myself through her hair to her vagina. She's so wet. Is this what I feel like to Ben? I prop myself on my arms and lean forwards, concentrating my energy in my pelvis, and push inside her.

Oh, wow. This is *incredible*. I love this dream. I love being a man – or a woman with male sex organs. I'm wrapped up in her warm, wet inside. My cock is so big I'm surprised it hasn't exploded. It feels like it's cocooned in a hot, wet mouth.

Why do people write about sex in red and pink? This feeling is so ... *yellow*. I'm making a lot of noise, grunting and things, my elbows aching from bearing my full weight.

Then I'm yelling, 'Oh, God!'

She's gripping my back with her fingers, her legs around my bottom and saying, 'Yes! Yes! That's it!'

I come in a shuddering, pumping mess. Liquid spurts from the end of my cock right up inside her.

I saw my sister again today, my Perdita. I will it to be real. I loved her so.

I collapse onto Katherine, my face beaded with sweat, and

bury myself in her neck. That was quick, I think, and fall instantly asleep.

When I wake, Katherine is sitting naked, smoking a cheroot in an armchair facing the bed and studying my face. I put my hand down to my crotch. It's still there. I drag myself up to sit.

'Am I awake, for real? I thought it would have gone by now.'

'What would have gone?' she says. 'You went out cold. Hope you haven't made me pregnant.'

I'm surprised by the pleasure, the liberation, I feel that I'm still here, wherever 'here' is.

'I'm producing sperm?'

'Nah. I was joking. I smelled it.' She waggles two fingers at me. 'Odourless. Not sperm at all. Probably more urine, something like that.'

We glare at one another for a moment. I see the corners of her mouth twitching and we start to giggle. I fall back onto the pillow and look at the ceiling.

'That was mind-blowing,' I say. 'Did you come?'

'Oh yes.'

I glance at her. I can't tell if she's lying. I remember something.

'What about Ida Baker?' I ask.

Katherine leans her chin heavily on her palm.

'What about her?'

'Well, isn't she here, your lover? Living with you, on and off?'

'We're on hiatus.'

My legs seem to have lost all power. My cock feels sticky and also, there's something that feels like an actual *sticker* attached to the tip. I throw the blankets off: sure enough, a small rectangular piece of paper is plastered to its end. It's white and waxed, with thin red piping at the edges and typed writing at its centre. It looks exactly like the message from a fortune cookie. I peel it away from my penis carefully – the action really hurts – and hold the paper up to the light.

> Could we change our attitude, we should not only see life differently, but life itself would come to be different.
>
> Katherine Mansfield

I stare at her sitting there, insouciant.

'Oh, the paper,' she says, head shaking. 'Don't worry about that. Happens every time.'

'Every time what?'

'I have sex.'

'Even with Ida?'

'Don't keep mentioning her, Marnie, please, it's bad manners.'

'But what does it mean? Where does the paper come from?'

She shrugs. 'Somewhere in my pipes. I don't know. Cervix? It may be a side effect of the medication for my illness.'

'Your illness?' I feel myself pale. 'Gonorrhoea?'

'Gonorr ... ? How dare you.'

'Sorry.'

'Tuberculosis.'

'Right.'

'Though there's good news on that score; I haven't coughed in months. I think it might have been the trip to Switzerland with John.'

'Do you mean Jacob? Schlapoberstein?'

Now her eyes narrow. 'Middleton Murry. My husband.'

Her husband – of course.

146

She gestures to the paper. 'Keep it. It might come in useful one day.'

She takes it from my fingers and slips it into the pocket of my dress, which is folded over the back of the armchair. I don't remember putting it there. She stands above me, staring at my crotch.

'Jesus, Marnie. We should tell a newspaper or something. We could make a fortune.'

'I don't want to do that, actually, if you don't mind.'

'I'm going to fix us both another drink.' She exits through the folded doors to the kitchen.

Katherine is shaking me awake. She has two drinks balanced in her other hand.

'I can hear your mind whirring,' she says loudly.

I bolt upright. 'Did I fall asleep a second time when you left the room?'

'A second time? What are you talking about?'

I look at my naked body. No penis. Just the old me, back with the sex organs I was born with. The back of my brain starts to prickle with pins and needles.

'It's gone.' I allow myself to fall back on the bed.

'What's gone? What are you talking about?' She hands me an iced vodka and comes to lie next to me.

I take a healthy glug this time. It's delicious.

'Did we have sex?'

'We *made love*, Marnie, yes. It must have been very poor for you to have forgotten already.'

'No!' I say, so vigorously that some of the liquid in my glass tips on the bed. 'You were brilliant. So, we had sex, I mean made love, without my having a ... penis?'

'Goodness.' She pulls her chin in. 'Sexual relations between two women do not, to my knowledge, involve nor *need* a penis.' She lies down next to me and throws something long, blue and penis-shaped to the floor. 'Don't need *that* any more. Were you not satisfied? You sounded satisfied.'

'No, I ...' I'm so confused. 'I thought I had a ...'

She sighs. 'I know. You told me in the café. Remember? And we established you didn't forty minutes ago.'

'No, I don't remember. What happened after that?'

She snorts. 'It's no wonder you're seeing a headshrinker.'

For once, I'm all out of ideas, except the knowledge that Katherine is right: it's no wonder I'm seeing Schlap. My mind is a soup.

'Tell me one of your poems,' she says.

I feel myself freeze despite the heat in the room.

'Why don't you tell me one of yours?'

'Can't,' she says.

I turn my head to her. She has a lovely profile. Her eyebrows seem to have been drawn on – maybe they are.

'Why not?'

'Copyright.'

I laugh. 'I'm not putting you into print. I'm lying here next to you, just you and me and no one else, asking you to say a poem out loud.'

'I asked first. You tell me yours. Do it.' Her face meets mine. Those liquid eyes.

I think for a second and find an old one stuffed into a corner of my mind. While I say it, I keep my eyes firmly fixed on the ceiling.

> *Grandma's hands had nothing*
> *On yours. Fluidity to*
> *Solid things. I melt.*

Silence. I begin to worry she's fallen asleep.

Her voice cuts through the room.

'A not-quite haiku? For someone you loved?'

'Yes.' I'm pleased, but I still can't look at her.

'A man?'

'My sister,' I say. 'I was listening to a lot of Bill Withers at the time.'

She kisses my shoulder. 'Who's Bill Withers?'

'Never mind.'

I get to my feet and dress myself, trying but failing to get my head around my latest hallucinatory narcoleptic episode and going forward, what this might mean for me in terms of sexual orientation. I stand in my bra and pants and put my hands on my hips.

'Isn't it tiring, pretending to be her?'

'What do you mean?' She's startled. 'Who?'

'I've got to go.'

'So soon?' she says.

'It's late. My family will be waiting.'

I struggle through the kitchen, the buttons on my dress stuck over the widest part of my head, effectively rendering me blind, my shoes in one hand. I feel about for my bag in the darkening living room.

'What happened to your sister?'

Slowly now, I undo several buttons, pull my dress over my head and refasten each one. Katherine is standing in the doorway to the kitchen, the pink shift covering her body, an arm draped above her head.

'How do you know about that?' It feels like my voice is coming from underwater.

'You told me,' she says. 'In the café.'

'No. I didn't.'

'You did,' she insists.

Perhaps she's right – everything is such a muddle.

'Tell me what happened. Please?'

I find my way to the red hall. I'm extremely drunk, I realise.

'I haven't time,' I slur.

Katherine follows me. It's airless here, the traffic outside distant, echoey. The paintings loom from the walls.

'She was run over. Okay?' I say these awful words, but it sounds like someone else speaking. 'It was a hit-and-run outside our school, right here on Harley Street. In the summer holidays. Just before our joint birthday in August. We never found the person who did it. No CCTV in those days.'

'I'm very sorry,' she says. Her forehead bunches.

'Thanks.'

'What's CCTV?'

'Forget it.'

'How old were you?'

'About to turn eighteen.' I make to leave. 'We'd just finished our A levels. We were going to share a birthday party.'

I pull Katherine's heavy apartment door open, shoes still in hand, and step out onto the carpeted landing back into Schlap's world, welcoming the sudden gust of cool air. The carpet runner feels soft under foot.

'Marnie,' Katherine says.

She puts her thumb gently on the skin between my eyebrows. So many words, tiny one-syllable poems, push hard against the pressure of her hand.

'She wasn't even supposed to be there,' I'm saying. 'She'd borrowed my stupid camera for her A-level photography project and I forced her to make a special trip back to school to collect it so we could use it at our party.'

'It wasn't your fault,' Katherine whispers.

I shake my head free.

'It wasn't,' she insists.

'Thank you for a special evening.'

I walk heavily down the stairs, holding fast to the banister, watching my bare feet alternating until I reach the ground floor.

I had a penis, then it was gone. I had a sister and then she was gone, too. Only one was a dream.

Katherine calls after me, 'I lost my brother, you know, in the war? His photo is on the mantel. I miss him every day. Dear Leslie. Dear Chummie.'

I slip my shoes on. I step onto the street. The front door bangs closed behind me.

> By the remembered stream my brother stands
> Waiting for me with berries in his hands ...
> 'These are my body. Sister, take and eat.'

Katherine's voice from above, loud, full of feeling. 'I want to see you again soon!' She's leaning dangerously out of her living room window and she's half-laughing and half-crying, arms waving. 'Never regret, Marnie! Never look back!'

I hop off the bicycle outside my house. The ride has sobered me up. It's nearly midnight. The words that gathered as Katherine had lain her hand across my forehead are expanding like paper flowers in water. They're almost itchy. I long to get them out.

Our Prius has returned. Ben must have collected it from the mechanic. It looks shiny in the dark, the moon reflecting off its newly fixed front light, its freshly waxed exterior. The kids are presumably in their bedrooms, their reading lights burning halos through the blinds across the windows. I let myself in and try to be quiet. I don't want to speak to anyone. Ben will have to be faced in the morning. Tomorrow is his day at home for writing. I'm not sure I can lie to him.

Parker is turning circles in the hallway, tail whipping against the wall. He yawns and whines at the same time. I put my fingers to my lips, pad through to the kitchen and let him out into the back garden. I let him back in, settle him in his basket and sit at my laptop.

> It's a terrible thing, electric light.
> This lake is so flat it is a continuation of my eye.
> Later tonight, in a windowless room
> it will come to seem a physical impossibility.
> The glare of the bulb,
> All of us exposed, fresh in our undergarments, like chickens or
>   children.
> This liquid horizon, which never existed at all.

The words make me whole again, filling the gaps in my body where the feelings escape. This is better than ... okay, not better than sex, but as good as.

Katherine. Katherine has done this. Or rather, my cock in Katherine has. Or rather, me *imagining* my cock in Katherine. She's lost a sibling, too. She's written poems for him. She knows exactly how I feel.

I work fast. It wouldn't do to be surprised by anyone from upstairs. I bash out the lines, read them through once and fire them off in an email to Veronica without even a spellcheck. There, that ought to keep her quiet for a day or two.

I close the laptop and creep silently up the stairs.

Please, God, let no one need the bathroom, or a sandwich, or to tell me about the latest twist in the book they're reading. I reach my bedroom. So far, so good.

I've written a poem. Good good good.

The bedroom door is shut. Ben could be asleep. Make it so.

I steel myself, turn the handle. The room is empty, the bed undisturbed. He must be in his study writing. He's not usually a night owl. I decide I'll climb into bed and pretend to be sleeping.

I change out of my clothes and fling them on a chair, then scrabble around in the chest of drawers looking for a T-shirt big enough to sleep in. Instead, I unearth my maternal grand-mother's floor-length cotton nightdress, preserved as a keepsake, a legacy for my children's children. I slide it over my head. It's tiny.

I climb into our massive bed in the little nightie, lie down and pull the covers up to my chin.

I've written a poem. I've had sex with Katherine. I've seen my sister alive again.

Though was it her, *really*?

My heart is pumping too fast for sleep.

Each animal has a set number of heartbeats, Ben told me once. The heart works like a woman's eggs – the full set of which are inside her ovaries before that little girl is even born. Though unlike the eggs, each animal's heartbeat in each species has the exact same number before it pegs out. How weird is that? I mustn't get too stressed. I don't want my heart to beat out too quickly. I don't want to die.

I wake in the night from another dream, one in which I'm sprinting to the top of a red canyon, exactly like those one might see in photographs of Australia. The gusting wind brings my hair into my mouth, but I don't care. The ridge is hot and wild. Schlap and Ben, Sylvia, Blythe, Stan, my mum and dad are waiting for me. Parker pants at Stan's feet. We're each of us completely naked, our skins vulnerable against the blue sky. My family is united, solid as pillars of salt.

I throw my arms wide, push my sternum out, lift my chin to the sun. My cock is back again. It raises itself, as if it knows it won't belong to me much longer.

All thoughts are gone, save one: time is nothing.

My mouth opens, 'Here I am!' My voice flings itself against the rock face far away and returns: '... *I am!*' I laugh to hear it.

An open-topped jeep skids to a halt behind us. In the driver's seat, Katherine. She leaps onto the scorched earth, scarf around her head to keep the fine red dust at bay.

I look down – 100 metres beneath my penis, and then my toes, the land spins.

All at once, there's Perdita right beside me, as if by magic. I can't say her name but I reach out my hand. She steps closer. She's wearing our school uniform. It is far too small for the woman she is now.

When her hand's safely in mine, she says, 'Marnie!' and giggles. 'You're so old!'

I watch her as she looks out over the canyon.

A lone vulture wheels in the thermals.

I wake. It's still night. I sit, wipe sweat from my hairline.

Ben isn't in bed. Nor has he been at any point this evening – his pillow is undented, the duvet still neatly in place on his side. I peer at the alarm clock: 4.35 a.m. I turn my attention to his chair – his work clothes aren't there. In fact, none of his clothes are.

I check my phone. No messages.

I climb from the bed and go upstairs to his study. It's difficult to ascend each tread because Granny's nightie is so restrictive. The room is in darkness, Ben's computer is off. A doorstop of papers – handwritten notes – lie at one side of his desk. I flick on the desktop lamp.

Outline notes for *The Descent into Madness*: a talk at CERN.
I look again at the writing. The hand isn't Ben's.

Shaking, I scoop up the papers and rifle through: 'Modernism through soma', 'The future of AI in mental health diagnostics', 'Heisaku Kosawa', 'My father's works'. I have no idea what any of these mean, except that modernism is an art movement and Heisaku Kosawa is possibly Japanese.

Who's written these and why does Ben have them here?

Adrenaline is making my legs light. I close the door to his study, return to the desk and switch on his computer, guiltily.

The screen lights up. Something beside the little password box in the centre catches my eye: D's Mac.

That's not right. It usually reads: B's Mac. I take a step back to refocus, in case it's my failing eyes muddling the letters. It isn't.

I know the passcode because I heard Ben telling Stan just the other day: *Flèche*.

I tap the letters into the keyboard. The screen wobbles. I repeat. It wobbles. I'll be locked out in a minute and Ben will know I've been here.

Or D will.

I study the glow from the anglepoise lamp, how it falls on the desk like it knows something.

People thought Galileo mad when he said the Earth was round. Could I have jumped into yet another quantum realm?

I make my way back to bed and lie beneath the covers, scared and holding my crotch like a nervous child.

Things I Loved About My Sister: Part 7

She always let me copy her homework.

Chapter 8

I wake with the alarm. Ben still isn't in bed. I go downstairs. To my relief and annoyance, I find him fast asleep on the sofa, one leg out at a 45-degree angle, supported by the pouf.

I shake him awake. 'What are you doing?'

He rubs his eyes. 'Time?' I hear his tongue unstick itself from the roof of his mouth.

'Where have you *been*? I was worried.'

'Out.'

Not only is this rude, but it's also wildly out of character.

I push his leg to one side and perch on the edge of the pouf. 'Out where?'

'That work thing, remember?'

'Nope.'

Upstairs, the kids are moving about.

'I texted last night. Said we were going on somewhere else. Didn't you get it?'

'No, funnily enough.' Have I checked my phone since leaving Katherine's last night? I'm not sure I have. 'Who's D?'

Ben, who tells me frequently that he has a mind like an Exocet missile, sits up and stares at my face. 'What are you wearing?'

'Granny's nightie.'

'Why?'

'I don't *know*. Don't change the subject. Who's D?'

Ben gives me his what-the-hell-are-you-talking-about-look.

'On your computer,' I hiss, because Stan's now doing his usual flump downstairs. 'It said "D's Mac", not "B's Mac". And also, some odd handwritten sheets with research that isn't yours.'

Ben's eyes have narrowed to slits.

'I looked last night. When you were out late. I was worried.' I drop my gaze.

'I see.' He offers only these two words. I can't believe it.

'So, come on, who's D?'

Stan, presumably hearing voices, sticks his head round the door, says 'uh, Granny's nightie?' then disappears to the kitchen.

'Marnie.' Ben's tone is grave, despite his hangover. 'I think you might need help.'

'What d'you mean, help? Around the house?'

'You know I don't mean that. For your ... mind.'

My heart feels like it growing swollen and angry. 'You don't believe me? Fine. Go and look in your study.'

He sighs wearily, shaking his head as he leaves the room.

I sit in the empty living room listening to the sound of Stan crunching Coco Pops in the kitchen.

'Like I said.' Ben is back already. 'It's my computer, Marns, no "D", no handwritten papers. Everything's normal.'

'No, I ...' My throat tightens and I get to my feet, as though standing will make me somehow more credible. 'But it was there last night!'

'You go and look!' he says, turning his back on me as he beats a second retreat up the stairs. 'Marns, truly, we need to talk through some of this.'

I get that lumpy throat feeling that comes just before I'm about to cry.

'That's ironic, given you never have time to talk to me about anything else,' I say knowing he can't hear me.

I'm so unimportant to him, he can't even bother to stick around to tell me I'm mad. No one believes a bloody word I say.

'I have to go to work,' he calls down. 'But we can discuss it later. K?'

He's back down, fully dressed, before I've even moved from my spot in the living room.

The kids sense something's up. My clumsy attempts at fudging the details over breakfast do nothing to allay their suspicions. Once they've left for school workshop, I shower and dress. It's 10 a.m. I'm dazed from lack of sleep and, well ... everything. I try to run a brush through my hair, which is desperately dry these days.

I'm growing old. I can no longer rely on my body to do what I ask. Even my hair is disobedient.

My phone rings: it's Veronica. I answer with the brush suspended halfway through my knots.

'Veronica?'

'Marnie?'

'Yeah?'

'I received your poem.'

My heart starts to pound. 'What d'you think?'

I hear people typing and photocopying in the background.

There's a brief unbearable pause before she says, 'I think it's *incredible*. I mean, *outstanding* work.'

'Really? You're not just saying that?'

'Yep.' Her voice lowers in volume. 'Listen, this collection could be the one.'

'The one what?'

'That clinches you the laureateship.'

'The ... ? Veronica, have you lost your mind?'

'I'm serious. If you keep up this standard, we could be in with a shout.' Her voice moves away from the speaker. 'What's that? Coming!'

'But—'

'Marnie, got to go. Come by the office on Tuesday. And keep *writing* – twenty-five to go. Brilliant work.' She rings off.

I suddenly wonder who exactly it was who came up with the decision that I'm required to write such a specific number of poems, and why. Why not forty, sixty or however many I want? I don't remember at any point having a conversation with Veronica about costings or printing or any other reason, and I'm thinking: was this a self-imposed amount? I mean, is this the number I promised her in a fit of enthusiasm and editor-pleasing one day and I've forgotten?

I stand in my bedroom, hairbrush hanging at my cheek, and look at myself in the mirror.

The *laureateship*? Veronica must be losing her grip, too. She *was* wearing a disturbing amount of blue when we last met. Perhaps this is what happens to all women *d'un certain âge*. This thought calms me.

'Where's your picture gone?'

I'm in Schlap's office staring at the wall where his son's painting had, until today, hung.

'What?'

'I thought you had a painting of a mouse with a man in a house – hey, that rhymes – the man who is really you, standing in the background, hanging up there?'

Schlap shakes his head. 'I don't recall such a painting.'

At least he's agreed to see me. He hasn't alluded to my sudden ejection from his office yesterday. God, that feels a lifetime ago.

I, in turn, have yet to make mention of last night's incident with Katherine, or that I'm convinced I saw Perdita again, or any of the other landmines exploding in my life right now.

There was no sign of Katherine at Schlap's when I arrived today except, back on its plinth in the waiting area and now overstuffed with scented pastel sweet peas, was the empty vase that I'd seen on the floor in her hall last night. The strangest part is that her name label was still on the buzzer: Kass.

I need this session. Ben thinks I require help, more of it, whatever that means: pills, probably, but I need Schlap to tell me Ben's wrong. Then I need to seek out Perdita, or her doppelganger.

PR or K, something something, something something, then an X: how difficult can it be?

My cortisol levels must be off the charts. I think again about my heart pumping out all of my remaining beats and take a long, slow breath in, then out.

'Okay,' I say. 'Is it possible that you could imagine something, really imagine it, see it, touch it – a bunch of notes, say, written by a stranger instead of your partner, a computer that appears to have been taken over by a hacker – but when your partner looks the next morning, the notes could no longer be there, the computer normal, even though these things were definitely genuinely *there* the night before?'

Schlap also breathes deeply in and out – perhaps it's contagious – and says, 'Are we back to your quantum entanglement theory?'

'Maybe.' I chew my nail.

He crosses his legs. 'Have you heard of cognitive bias?'

'Not really. What is it?'

Ben mentioned these words in passing regarding a patient once.

'In layman's terms, it's a systematic error in thinking that encompasses a great many different ways in which the mind makes erroneous assumptions based on previous memories or beliefs.'

'Uh-huh.' I have only the vaguest grasp what he means.

'I'd say your brain is telling you one thing, but the reality is *possibly* something different. This isn't your fault – it's your brain's way of processing trauma.'

That old chestnut. I hate how everyone dismisses me because I suffered a loss, as if this one event sums me up, my entire identity.

'But if your brain tells you something, that *is* your reality, isn't it? I mean, that's how reality works: it's subjective. I agree that at the moment, my reality may seem to be out of synch with other peoples', but that doesn't make theirs right and mine wrong.'

He nods.

'What if I'm objectively correct?'

'Do you think you are?'

'It's a possibility, is all I'm saying.' I think of something. 'You know I've now compiled seven sections for my list of things I loved about my sister.'

'Would you care to share them?'

I love that he always allows our conversation to go wherever I choose to take it.

'Not yet.'

PR or K something something, something something, then an X.

The *laureateship*. What was Veronica *thinking*? I'm not going to win a writing accolade for two measly collections over twenty years.

'Are you okay?' he prompts.

'Yeah. Why?'

'You seem distracted.'

This makes me laugh out loud. But laughing out loud isn't the correct response to 'you seem distracted' and serves only to make me look more crazed, more distracted.

'Would you care to interpret another dream?' I say, switching subjects again.

'If you'd like me to.' He sneaks a quick glance at the clock.

'It's a dream of symbols.'

I relate my dream of the red canyon to Schlap in great detail. I watch his face carefully. He nods, one ear turned sideways on, as if straining to catch every word. I end with the bit about the vulture in the thermals, after which I lean back in the ergonomic chair.

'Shall we start at the end, with the vulture?' He says 'we', but really he means me.

'All right.'

I'm convinced I spy a rectangle of lighter paint in the exact spot where the mouse picture used to hang. I wonder if Schlap's lying when he says he doesn't remember it.

The *laureateship*?

'The vulture could mean danger circling, threatening to carry any one of us off at any moment?' I offer.

Cognitive bias, my arse. Ben *and* Schlap believe me to be mad.

'Yes.'

And if the multiverse theory *is* correct, how does one know one's dreams aren't also an expression of it?

'And we were all naked, so …'

More nodding from Schlap.

'We're exposed?' I continue. 'No secret hiding places?'

'And you had your penis again, Katherine,' says Schlap.

'Marnie.' I feel my face redden with frustration. 'It's Marnie.'

'Marnie, I'm so sorry.'

'I did have my ... Can I ask you something?' I say, my words clipped. 'Do you have a friend or relative living here with you? A woman?'

'Absolutely not,' Schlap says without hesitation.

'So, who's Kass?'

'Kass?'

'A buzzer outside says Kass. And you're *still* calling me Katherine.'

He smiles. 'Marnie. That name stub has been there for a hundred years. It belonged to Katherine Mansfield, a person with whom you seem temporarily preoccupied, during her time living in this building. Kass was one of her many diminutives.'

'I know that.'

'It's a piece of history right here at my front door.'

'Okay. So, does *anyone* live on your third floor?'

'Not to my knowledge. Or, just a moment ...'

His face strains for something. I pray we might be getting somewhere.

'Nope. It's gone. I assure you, I live alone.'

'Right.' I'm disappointed and confused, but so, it seems, is Schlap. 'One last thing: do you happen to live on two separate floors in this building?'

'Do I ... ?'

'You have two name tags for buzzers under your name on the front door. One below the name Kass and one above it.'

'Ah.' He smiles broadly. 'Yes! Now that I *can* explain. I've had a lease on this entire building under the De Walden estate for some years. That lower nameplate is a hangover from the eighties, when I rented out the first floor to a dentist, but he asked for my name to sit there instead of his own because he'd had a stalker since university and his wife at the time insisted he protect himself.'

'Okay.' I wasn't expecting that.

'I know.' He does his foot-scuffing thing on the rug. 'You've reminded me that I must change it. Thank you.'

He shakes his head as if willing more information to fall into his lap. Forlorn, he looks up at me and I know he's forgotten my bloody name again.

I massage my brows with my fingers. '*Marnie.*'

'Marnie, yes. Would you like to read one of your poems?'

'Another one?' I've no fight left. 'Sure.'

I drag my phone from my pocket and scroll, unseeing, through my emails until I find the right folder.

It's empty. Prickles spread across my whole body.

'Someone's wiped my work. My old work and my new ... oh, God.'

Pages and pages of blank screen. Is this another episode of ... cognitive bias? I scroll until I reach a solitary poem at the bottom of the file. It's in an unusual font.

'Look, there's only one,' I croak, showing Schlap the phone. 'Just one, see?'

He pulls his glasses onto his nose and peers at the screen.

'You can see there's just one there, correct?'

'Yes.'

'That means that this is *real*. Would you agree?' This is happening. Ben can go fuck himself.

Veronica has my latest poem on her email. If it has gone from my phone, it's okay, not to panic, she'll have it somewhere – and my old ones, of course. Heart be slow. I also have twenty-five more that haven't been written yet, which isn't okay but is, in context, lucky.

I read out loud from the screen:

Across the red sky two birds flying,
Flying with drooping wings.
Silent and solitary their ominous flight.
All day the triumphant sun with yellow banners
Warred and warred with the earth, and when she yielded
Stabbed her heart, gathered her blood in a chalice,
Spilling it over the evening sky.
When the dark plumaged birds go flying, flying,
Quiet lies the earth wrapt in her mournful shadow,
Her sightless eyes turned to the red sky
And the restlessly seeking birds.

I'm calm. I place my phone carefully on the little table next to the ergonomic chair.

'So,' says Schlap.

'It's brilliant. I didn't write it.'

'Say again?'

'That poem. It's not mine.'

He sits forwards. 'Whose is it, then?'

'Mansfield's.'

He nods. 'Interesting. It's awfully redolent of your dream at the red canyon, wouldn't you agree?'

I stare at my hands.

The wall clock tings.

'Goodness. I'm sorry, Marnie, our time is up.'

I make a noise like a groan but more staccato. 'Cognitive bias. Aren't you supposed to take that seriously as my analyst?'

Schlap stands. 'Cognitive bias is most often a harmless temporary affliction. I do understand your partner has concerns. But ultimately, it'll be me who decides, from a professional standpoint, if you're a danger to yourself. And in my learned opinion, you aren't. Now, I'm so sorry, but I have another patient.'

'A danger to myself? Like suicide?'

He drops his chin.

'Is your next patient Katherine?'

'Who?'

Dear oh dear. 'You know, *Mansfield*. Her ... impersonator.'

The one I slept with last night using my imaginary penis on the third floor of your house.

'Marnie,' Schlap says firmly. 'Our time is up. We'll continue this in our session tomorrow.'

He rings the little bell imperiously and I leave the room.

I was originally going to Bethnal Green Working Men's Club after my Schlap session to talk to the man named Faaris about alcoholic punch for the twins' party, but of course I'm not. I'm standing holding on to some railings along Harley Street.

Where's my poetry? Who has wiped my emails? Or is all this because I'm cognitively biased?

The older poems will still be on my computer at home.

And they *are* in a book, that printed hard copy with the blue spine that we have on our shelf.

What if it's no longer there? Or what if it is there, but in my madness, I think it isn't?

I take out my phone for a second trawl. Nothing.

I dial Veronica's direct line.

'Veronica's phone?' A stranger.

I assume it's a woman, because the person has an unnaturally high voice, as if something's compressing her larynx.

'Hi, it's Marnie. Is Veronica there, please?'

'No, I'm afraid Veronica isn't in today.'

'But I just spoke to her in the office an hour ago.'

'No, you couldn't have. She's visiting her niece in Margate for a few days. She left last night.'

'What? Why would she do that? Look, whoever you are, I'm sorry, but my poems have ...'

I'm not even sure Veronica would believe me.

The voice says, 'You still there? Can I help?'

'I was wondering if you could check on a poem that I sent over yesterday. It'll be under Marnie Rose in Veronica's inbox. It begins, "*it's a terrible thing*". By the way, who am I talking to?'

'Pantea. I'm filling in for Veronica while she's away.'

There's tapping of keys.

'How funny my daughters have a friend called Pantea well sometimes they're friends you know how it is with teenage girls I've not met you before.' I say it just like that, no full stops.

The voice of Pantea says, 'Okay, Marnie. I've found your poem, "*Across the red sky two birds flying*", that one?'

I grab the finial of the railing. It's cold and surprisingly sharp.

'That's ... It's Katherine Mansfield's.'

'So it is,' says Pantea. 'It's very good.'

She sounds amused.

'I'll just ...'

I ring off and focus on the middle distance. My mouth is open.

Ben thinks I'm mad, I believe myself to be on another quantum plane, and Schlap says what's happening to me is harmless and temporary. My poems are gone and I'm seeing things that aren't there.

Sod this. I dial 999.

'Emergency. Which service do you require?'

'Um ...'

'Hello? Which service?'

'Police, please.'

I only have to wait two seconds.

'Police. What's the address of the emergency?'

'It's not an emergency. Well, it is to me. I saw my dead sister alive and I'm trying to trace the number plate of her car.'

There's a brief pause before the person says, 'I need to make you aware that prank calls are a criminal offence and carry a fine.'

I'm too shocked to respond.

Then the voice says, 'I'm going to terminate this conversation now.'

The line goes dead. A fine? I call straight back. It's a different voice.

'Emergency services, which ser—'

'Police!'

'Police. What's the address of the emergency?'

'Someone at your end cut me off. I've written some poems that have disappeared, as well as my sister, and things are appearing and disappearing all over the place and everything is completely weird.'

'I need to make you aware that prank—'

'This isn't a prank call!'

The voice becomes horribly gentle. 'Love, I think you might be better placed calling Samaritans in the first instance and then calling us back once you've spoken to them. Okay? Putting you through now.'

There's a connecting sound and a ringing tone at the other end.

'Samaritans?'

I put the phone down. The emergency services person, Ben and Schlap are all wrong. This stuff is *real*. I wander towards Marylebone High Street in case the Volvo is passing again today.

There's a new voice message on my phone. It's from my mother requesting my immediate presence in St Albans. My dad has had to go to London for a meeting with a food photo-grapher and she's all alone. She needs to pop out to the shops but can't leave poor incapacitated Vicar Pete by himself in case he needs the toilet or similar. Could I come over? She's sorry to ask.

I call Mum back. A male voice answers.

'Rose residence.'

'Vicar Pete?'

'Yes. That you, Patricia?'

'No, it's Marnie. Is everything okay?'

'Yes, quite all right.' The line crackles. 'She couldn't get golden stew.'

'What golden stew? What d'you mean?'

'She. Couldn't. Get. Hold. Of. You.'

I wince, even though he can't see me. 'I'm awfully sorry.'

'Your dad's out and I think she was hoping for a helping hand, but honestly, I'm quite—'

'No, no ...' I order myself not to go to St Albans for a man who's telling me he's perfectly fine alone. 'Don't worry, I'll be there soon.'

'Ah,' the vicar says. 'Not necessary but thank you ever so much.'

I wheel round and start towards Cavendish Square NCP. Thank goodness I brought the car; it's almost as if I knew this was going to happen.

I mustn't mention the Volvo to Mum. She'll go nuts. If I tell her, I'll have to tell her about Ben's fears for my mental health and the poems and everything else. It'll all tumble out because I'm incapable of hiding things from her.

I try to think about something else – anything except all of that, my phallus or my heartbeats.

A poem comes to my mind – a little star twinkling in the

middle of the dark. It demands to be written. I pull onto the hard shoulder – very dangerous – grab my notebook from my bag and scribble. Sweet relief. I don't know where the words have come from, or what they relate to. Sometimes it's like that. Sometimes things just are.

The vicar greets me at my parents' door wearing beige cargo pants, a green cashmere V-neck and holding a crutch, and I wonder why on earth Mum imagined he needed babysitting when he can clearly get around the house by himself. I almost don't recognise him out of his cassock or whatever it's called as I struggle from the Prius in another random dress I threw on this morning. My armpits are leaking.

The vicar thanks me again for the inconvenience and I say no inconvenience, which is a lie. He asks me if I'd prefer to leave - I've probably got much more important things to be getting on with. This is true, I do, but he has such a lovely welcoming face and I'm desperate not to get straight back in the car, so I tell him I'd prefer to stay. He smiles. I smile back.

'Well.' He looks over my shoulder. 'Come on in, then.'

I've just written another poem. Good – twenty-four more to go. Or is it twenty-five, now that last one has gone AWOL?

I go after him along the hall to the kitchen. He *is* terribly slow on that crutch. Maybe it's just as well I'm here.

A large bowl of chickpeas soaking in water is on the worktop next to a fresh loaf of my mother's bread, a long, skinny salami still in its paper label, and a small figurine sculpted in clay, slipped and fired the colour of burnished bronze. It's a naked woman with her arms above her head and looks just like Nina Hamnett. I stare at it.

It *is* Nina Hamnett.

'Did Mum buy this?' I ask.

'No, I think she made it herself. Why?'

'No reason.'

But there is a reason. I just need to work out what.

Through the double doors, the garden beckons. Once I've settled Pete, I'll lie in the grass and stare at the sky for a while, maybe make shapes from the clouds.

'So lovely out there,' I say, turning to the vicar, but the room is empty.

I must have been staring through the doors for far longer than I'd imagined.

There are footsteps in my parents' room directly above. Vicar Pete is hobbling between the bedroom and the en suite.

I recheck my phone for anything from Ben and search again for my poems folder, then move to the kettle, fill it from the tap, light the gas on one of my dad's many oven rings and wait resolutely for the water to boil.

Tea seems the right thing to make when someone is injured. I'm not sure what else I'm supposed to be doing to help, anyway.

Fresh coffee! That'll be even better. Caffeine will be my friend, as well as Peter's. I need to stay sharp, and it may give him a little more facility on that crutch.

I fetch Dad's coffee grinder and funnel beans into the top. My body vibrates pleasingly as I switch the grinder on and hold fast to its lid. I screw my eyes at the din. The grinder stops. I brew the coffee and pour it into two of Mum's blue glazed cups, risk a tad of milk with no sugar for the vicar and walk into the hall.

By the stairs, I pause to sniff my wrist. I've always found the scent of my own skin comforting, especially in the summer, apart from my armpits, obviously, particularly the right one. In doing so, I manage to tip half of the vicar's coffee down my dress. It's not too hot, but it makes an awful mess.

My mind hooks on the inadvertent rhyme of 'dress' and 'mess', and my brain begins a little merry-go-round of similar-sounding words, which feels a little ... crazy.

Then I castigate myself for a bad choice of clothing today, and then a bit more for being unkind to myself for calling myself crazy.

'Can't get the blasted thing to flush.' Vicar Pete's voice is distorted, as if he's bending or upside down.

'I've made you a coffee, Pete.'

I'm not sure he's heard me. I climb the stairs, reaching the door to my parents' bedroom, which is closed, and turn the handle slowly. Perhaps he's fallen.

The bedroom is empty. There's the rustle of clothing, the plink of Mum's home-made soap dish against the sink. Silently, I push my head round the corner of the open bathroom door. I don't know why I don't announce myself, but I don't.

Pete's body is listing like the Leaning Tower of Pisa as he supports himself on a crutch. He's struggling to refasten the Velcro on his shoe. His pate is shiny and conker brown and vulnerable-looking like a baby's, and I have to resist the urge to tiptoe over and give him a hug.

'Golly, Marnie!' He straightens.

I think he might be blushing.

'I'm so sorry. I did call out. I've made us coffee. Yours is only half full because I spilt some on myself. Can I help you with your shoes?'

Vicar Pete smiles and takes the cup from me, cradling it in both hands as if he's freezing and this is the only thing that could possibly warm him.

He takes a sip and his lip curls back like Parker's. 'Mmm.'

I crouch in front of him to do up his shoes, then stand up and step back again. There's an awkward pause.

'Thank you.' He places the cup on the side of the bath. 'Um. Anything specific you need in here?'

'Nope.'

'Oh.' He looks around the bathroom. 'Anything I can help you with?'

'Not really.'

I pick a bottle of shampoo from a shelf and put it down again. I take a sip of my coffee. It's like someone's melted the road. My top lip sticks itself to my teeth.

'There is one thing.' I swallow. 'We could talk about it in the kitchen, if you'd prefer.'

He smiles. 'Here is just fine with me.'

'Okay.' I scratch at a small rough patch at my elbow. 'I've been thinking. How do you catch a faith?'

'How do you ... ?'

'Catch one. Is it like flu? How does it work?'

He laughs. 'I wouldn't put it quite like that. It's not an affliction.'

A noise erupts from my mouth, a sort of raspberry, as though I think he's talking nonsense, which isn't the case at all. I'm thirsty for his knowledge, his experience.

Pete could be my mentor, in addition to Schlap. Schlap's brain is failing and everything in my life is seriously off-message, so I could do with at least two of them. No one believes what's happening to me, but the vicar might. He has to, if he believes in God, surely. He could provide the shining light I need to navigate my ship that's veered, let's face it, way off course.

I'm worryingly D-minus with my metaphors these days, but I don't think he'll be able to help me with that.

'Do you ever worry that being religious is just cognitive bias?'

'Just . . what?'

'Cognitive bias. It's like a form of madness, but harmless and temporary.'

He has the generosity not to look affronted. 'Goodness, no. A faith is a blessing. But ... honestly? It's not easy. Every day is a battle against one's own doubting mind. Even more so when ...' His eyes fill with worry.

'Yes?'

'When you've suffered a tragedy in your life, as you have, your family has.' He makes himself as comfortable as he can on the edge of the bath. 'How can there be a God, you may ask, when He or She has taken away the thing you love most?'

'I ask myself that. I asked my shrink that just the other day.'

The sound of the leaves on the chestnut tree outside the bathroom window as they brush against the glass turns my head to the side. When I look back, the vicar is studying me.

'Is there something else you'd like to ask?'

'Oh. Er. I guess I wanted to know, do you believe in re-incarnation?'

He smiles. 'Well, that's more a principle of some other religions, reincarnation.'

'What about Jesus at Easter?'

'That was for three days only and isn't considered reincarnation, as such. I suppose I believe that *elements* of those we love may be passed down to others who come after.'

Epigenetics, I think in my head. That's what that is. That's not the same thing at all.

'And do you believe in alternative universes? The Many-Worlds Interpretation?'

'I don't believe in that,' he chuckles. 'That's more of a science fiction conceit, isn't it?'

'No,' I say with more authority than I feel. 'In fact, the Interpretation is something espoused by the lion's share of physicists today.'

I'll keep plucking this fact from my intellectual arsenal. Stan read it to me from his *1082 Amazing Facts You Won't Believe* book.

'Okay, then, how can you be sure that you're not imagining God? How do you know He's real?'

'I don't.'

It's like the sun has come out in my head. 'What?'

The vicar turns his palms to the sky. 'It's all about trust.'

'Trust?'

'In yourself. And a higher power.'

Trust myself? How can I trust myself when everyone warns me not to?

'Are you ready, is the question?' continues the vicar. 'Are you *brave* enough?'

'Brave? That's a little cryptic. Bravery, like many things, is subjective. I was hoping for something more black-and-white, in all honesty,' I say.

The front door bangs. 'Hellooo?'

It's my mother. Oh, fabulous. Fabulous timing.

'Peter? Everything okay?' She's at the base of the stairs. 'Did you manage a movement? Did Marnie come?'

'It's fine, Patricia!' Vicar Pete calls down. 'Marnie's here, with me. Everything's under control.'

When he says it, I almost believe it to be true.

'Wonderful!' she calls back. 'The shepherd tending his flock, even in his own hour of need.'

The vicar and I look at one another.

'Go down to her,' he urges. 'I don't need help, but your mother might.' He winks.

It makes me giggle.

'Marnie, I have faith in you,' he asserts. 'You'll see.'

'Thank you so much.' I pick up my cup. 'For the chat. And sorry about the coffee. I think I put too many beans in.'

As I leave, he says, 'You know, it *is* all a matter of interpretation, as you say. There's nothing truly black-and-white about any aspect of life, Marnie.' I think I spy love in his eyes.

'Except nuns and zebras,' I quip unnecessarily, as I leave.

I make my way back to the kitchen despairing that my natural reflex is always to render fatuous the sincere.

My mother's resting dramatically against the central island, weighed down by Waitrose bags for life. There are chiffon scarves flying, a long floral dress, her face half hidden beneath a large straw sunhat. She looks up, spots me and hastens in my direction, throwing her arms apart as if we haven't seen one another in twenty years.

'Here you are! Thank *goodness*.' Her body presses into mine. She pulls away, grips my shoulders and stares at my face. Her eyes are telling me something. 'Everything okay? What were you and Peter chatting about?'

'Not much.' Then straight away I say, 'Mum, I saw Perdita in a Volvo XC90 on Marylebone High Street.'

My mother's arms drop. It's as if I've hit her. Her mouth opens but nothing comes out.

'Mum?'

'Oh, Marnie. I've asked you so many—'

'But I did!'

She turns away, unable to bear the sight of me or something. 'What good that shrink is doing you, heaven *only* knows.'

I feel myself tipping, lurching sideways, one hand reaching for the worktop. It's as if I'm on a Waltzer at a funfair. The entire bowl of swollen chickpeas goes over, water and all.

My mother yells, 'Watch out!'

The vicar enters. He tuts and fetches a J-cloth.

'I'm so sorry,' I say.

My mother's on her hands and knees, the rim of her straw hat doing a little dance as she mops at the mess I've caused.

'We won't mention these sightings again, okay? We've been *through* this. And that's your father's Moroccan-style hummus down the Swanee.'

'There are different hummus styles?' the vicar whispers as we stare at the top of Mum's hat.

'It's not my fault I'm seeing Perdita!' I say, but when Mum doesn't respond I scrabble for a way to make it up to her. 'Mum, I love your outfit,' I gabble. 'It's so—'

'Judith Bliss.' She's scrubs more violently at the floor.

'Who?' says the vicar.

'*Hay Fever*?' my mother and I chorus.

'Noël *Coward*, Peter,' says Mum. She sounds cross. 'Do keep up.'

'Well, pardon me,' Pete says mildly.

He puts his hand on my arm. It feels nice there, steady.

Mum finishes her cleaning and stands. She eyeballs the two of us.

'What's going on?'

'What?' I say. 'Nothing's going on. What d'you mean?'

'What do *I* mean? I'm worried about you.'

'Me?' I look at Peter.

'Of course, you! Why ever would I be worried about the vicar?' She gestures at Peter as if he's on television and not in the room at all.

'I don't know! Because he's hurt his leg?' I will her to make some hummus, sculpt a figurine, anything, but just leave me alone.

My mother's voice goes awfully low. 'You know, Marnie, the start of the menopause can do terrible things to your mind, as well as your body. I can pray for you, if you—'

'I don't need you to *pray* for me.' This is embarrassing. 'I'm still having periods!'

But praying is exactly what I'd like her to do right now: Mum and Pete. I'd pray, too, if I had a faith. Pray and pray and pray for life to go back to ... whatever it was before. A long time ago. When I was little.

Mum's tapping her hand on her thigh.

Pete's voice pipes up instead.

'Now, how about Judith Bliss taking a perambulation of her late-blooming azalea beds? I couldn't help noticing from your bathroom window that some animal had been digging in them.'

I hug him in my mind.

Mum's head swivels to the double doors. 'Really? For goodness' *sake*! I've had your father out there peeing on the earth every morning and it *still* doesn't scare the foxes.' She storms out onto the grass. 'I think the insulin dilutes his urine.'

The vicar and I watch as she marches straight over to the azaleas.

'Oh, arse!' she's yelling. 'Oh, bum-bugger!'

I turn to Pete. 'I'm so sorry.'

'Don't be silly.'

His hand rests, now, on my shoulder. If I wait a little longer, perhaps it'll end up on my head.

'Have you ever had the sensation you have another body part?' I ask tentatively.

'Another ... ?'

'Like another organ, say, belonging to the opposite sex or something.'

'Oh?'

OK THEN THAT'S GREAT

The vicar smiles uncertainly and removes his hand. I immediately regret saying anything.

'I can't say I have. Have you?'

'All my hard work down the ...' Mum's bending suddenly to peer at the ground. 'Hang on! This isn't a *fox*. Something's buried here! Come and see.'

The vicar and I fight our way through the wisteria.

'Where?' The vicar calls to her.

'Jesus Christmas.' Mum's outstretched arm ends in one bony index finger. 'There!'

We arrive at the site. A small area of earth has been dug over. Something dull and circular pokes from beneath.

My mother's saying, 'Goodness me!' and 'Under the azaleas!'

'What is it?' Peter's peering.

'It's another amphora,' says Mum. 'I feel sure of it. Look at that shape. That's the lip. How extraordinary.'

She seems entirely captivated by the concept of treasure.

'Spade, Peter! No, wait, you're crippled and don't know where it is. I'll get it.' She runs to the shed.

The vicar and I exchange glances. I give the soil a rudimentary turn with my toe. There are squashed flower heads everywhere. Mum returns with the spade and two trowels.

'Ladies and gents,' she announces in a breathy voice. 'Time to dig.'

My knees sink to the earth. I prod the ground with a trowel. Mum's treading on the edge of the spade with her espadrille. She's getting properly angry with it.

We dig and poke, during which time Vicar Pete, humouring her, uncovers a little more of what is indeed beginning to look very much like a large jug. He's bent deep at the waist and I worry about his knee. We're all pouring with sweat. I hear my mother's breath growing steadily shallower.

179

'Faster!' Mum commands, as if the jug were about to get up and run away.

I look up. The vicar's eyes meet mine once more for the briefest of seconds. *I'm brave enough*, I try to tell him.

There's a dull thud.

'I've hit the bottom!' says Mum.

'Righto.' Vicar Pete plays along, getting as busy as he can with the trowel, given his injury, scraping and pulling layers of soil from whatever lies beneath. 'Well, well, what do you know? It *is* a jug.' His head is low and twisted sideways. 'Funny shape, though. Bit of pink colour here. A great deal of black. It's enormous.'

'An amphora?' says Mum. 'I told you! We've found a second Roman amphora! Think of their faces at the church. Hurry! Dig it up, then! Let's have a proper look.'

It doesn't take long to free the thing from its burial place. The vicar has to lower himself carefully onto his bottom next to me, wrap his arms around the jug's middle, and sort of rock it out.

'Careful! And your leg!' says Mum.

What if Mum's right and it really *is* an ancient relic? It's buried in the oddest place, but perhaps that sort of thing happens when the land is cultivated or turned into pretty gardens.

We all stare. The jug is covered in earth and of indeterminate age.

'Be careful with the lid. Don't remove it or you'll damage it.'

'Oops.' The lid slides off in the vicar's hand. 'Sorry. Too late.' His face goes into the mouth of the amphora. 'Oh, boy!' he says. 'Oh boy, oh boy.'

'What?' says Mum. 'Don't keep us in suspense.'

'Something. I don't know. It's too dark to see.' He puts his forearm inside the jug.

'Wait!' Mum squeals. 'That's a potential priceless artefact, a piece of history. Shouldn't you use gloves?' She hurries towards the kitchen. 'I'll get the Marigolds.'

'Looks an awful lot like the jug your mother threw for the fete,' Vicar Pete whispers.

I nod in assent, get to my feet, and help the vicar up too. Who could have buried mum's planter here?

The phone starts ringing inside the house.

Mum comes back with some yellow rubber gloves.

'I'm going to ignore that call,' she says. 'There are more important things going on here.'

The vicar dons the Marigolds. I try not to giggle.

'Let's see, shall we?' He gives me another wink and plunges his arm back into the pot.

Something catches my eye by the kiln shed. I swear I see the shadowy outline of my sister pass behind the curtain at the window. Her silhouette suggests she's in a long dress, not unlike mine. When I look again, she's gone.

Trust, I tell myself. *Trust* yourself. *Have faith.*

The first thing to come out of the pot is a solitary coin of beaten gold. It's the size of a ten pence piece, its edges uneven. It glistens in the sun, throwing circles of light onto the trunks of the fruit trees.

'Most extraordinary!' breathes Vicar Pete. He holds the coin near his face and his expression changes. 'Good Lord! It looks like a solidus of Arcadius, identical to the ones found among the St Alban's hoard! And it hasn't even tarnished. But ... this is almost impossible.' He steps towards Mum, eyes glistening. 'If it's genuine, this coin signals that whatever else is inside here was of great value to the person who buried it. But how would it end up in your planter from the raffle?'

Mum's nose wrinkles. 'My planter from the raffle? What are

you talking about? Don't be ridiculous.' She's as mad as I am.

Vicar Pete flicks me another glance, shrugs and his nose goes back into the amphora. 'There's a roll of papers, too.'

'Better be careful,' cautions Mum.

The house phone is ringing again.

The vicar pulls out a thick scroll held together with twine. The pages don't look very ancient. They look altogether modern – as in, from right now. He frowns and pulls one end of the twine gently and the pages flop open: white A4. Perhaps at last Mum will accept what Pete has been trying to tell her: no treasure here. There's typed words on the top sheet. He flips through the entire sheaf like a bank teller. 'A hoard of ... poems?'

'Roman poems; *fascinating*,' says my mother, the idiot.

'Patricia. Look at the paper.' Vicar Pete's tone suggests he's talking to a child. 'These are not Roman poems. I'm afraid this is a very elaborate hoax.'

'*Really?* Good Lord.' Mum sighs and crumples a little, then looks cross, then perks up suddenly. 'Hoax or otherwise, it's still a *remarkable* mystery that this jug came to be in my garden. Read one out.'

I pinch myself to check this is happening.

The vicar takes a breath.

> *On Hampstead Heath*
> *that bench beneath the bower*
> *with the Pollock bird shit art*
> *clear view to the Shard*
> *(Or at least: a shard of the Shard),*
> *St. Paul's etc etc.*
> *is where I choose to sit.*
> *Could be where ley lines meet perhaps*

I get that magnets feeling.
The rats scurrying the cement path
at my feet,
busy being disgusting,
mistaken for squirrels.
Down the slope the racetrack,
over-marshalled these days.
The runners, like me, abandoned it.
All down to greed and corruption,
Sorry.
Instead, we must pace ourselves across the sere grass,
risk the tics.
Supposed to be meditating,
instead, I close my eyes,
pink skin lids,
drink in the sun.
Later, gin and tonic.

He looks up from the paper. 'It's not *terribly* good, is it?'

'My poem!' I yell. 'It's my poem! But ... I wrote that on my way here, not an hour ago. Hang on.'

I make to go into the house to retrieve my bag, to show them my notebook, but change my mind at the last minute and instead try to snatch the poems from the vicar's hands. My mum is too quick, though, and whips them out of reach.

'Slow down, Marnie,' the vicar says. 'There are a lot more poems within this scroll. Are they all yours?'

'If Mum lets me look at them, I can tell you.'

My mother is stony-faced.

'Marnie?'

The house phone rings again.

'What is the meaning of this?'

The phone stops.

The two of them wait for my answer in the heavy summer heat.

Mum's eyes flick to the amphora and narrow. 'Peter, do you have a Handy Andy?'

'Andies,' I mutter, as Vicar Pete produces a cotton hanky from his pocket.

'What?' Mum snaps, taking the spotted piece of cloth from the vicar's hand.

'The brand.' I wish I'd kept my mouth shut. 'It's Handy *Andies*, plural.'

'And thus, an Andy when singular.' Mum is rubbing away the soil stuck on the pot. 'Pedantry, Marnie, is the eighth deadly sin.'

I look to Vicar Pete. He's frowning, no longer amused. A sense of dread descends on my head, heavy as a blanket.

'Mystery solved,' Mum says with satisfaction. 'This *is* my pot. My planter, as you suggested Vicar. From the fete. *Someone's* stolen it from Carol and Graham's pampas and fashioned a lid to go over it.' She glares at a point near my feet. 'Marnie.'

The phone starts to ring again.

'Explain this little April Fool.'

'An April Fool?' The vicar says to himself. 'In July?'

'It's ... I didn't. *No.* But my poems. How did they get in there?'

The ringing of the phone drills at my skull.

'I'd better answer that,' I say.

I escape to the house. I make it to the kitchen before I fall against the wooden chopping block, reminding myself again of my mother.

Of *course* I didn't put my poems in there. What am I, a magician? What could possibly be my motive? When have I ever been a practical joker? And where on earth would I have found a fake gold coin? I'm hurt my mother and Pete would even entertain this idea.

But who did put them there? How could someone have found their way into my bag and copied out that latest poem, and many others, in the short time I've been here? Not the vicar, that's preposterous. I can't imagine a single individual, except perhaps Katherine, who would find such a thing amusing. The phone rings on and on.

I feel my way to the hall table and lift the receiver with a sweating palm. 'Hello?'

'Mrs Rose?' An official-sounding woman.

'No, it's her daughter, Marnie. Who's this?'

'Ah, could I speak to your mum, please, Marnie?'

'Are you going to try to sell her something? Because if you are, she's not in.'

A short breath at the other end. 'I'm Stephanie: a nurse at UCH.'

I grip the receiver.

'I'm calling about your dad.'

I go suddenly cold. 'Is he okay?'

This is exactly how we found out about Perds. I was standing right next to this very phone, albeit in my parents' old house, when the hospital called.

'He had a funny turn at King's Cross station. A passer-by called an ambulance. He's going to be fine. He's diabetic, isn't he?'

'Yes.' I lean against the wall.

'The paramedics revived him and he's stable now.'

'He's conscious?'

'In and out. A bit disoriented. Perhaps you and your family

would like to come here. Fourth floor. Davis Ward.' She's about to put the phone down.

'Wait!' I say. 'He was in town for a meeting with a photographer about his recipe books. He finds work things terrifying these days. He always forgets to eat.'

'All right, Marnie. We'll see you soon.'

I stumble back outside. '*Mum!*'

But, somehow, my mother already knows, is on the move, knocking my shoulder in her rush to get inside the house.

'He forgot to eat again, didn't he?' She throws her keys into the rattan shopper on the worktop, a bunch of parsley sticking out of the top. 'Which hospital?'

'UCH. He's okay but disoriented, the nurse said.'

'I'll follow you,' Vicar Pete calls from the garden.

'Don't be silly! You can't drive with your leg in that state. Hold the fort,' my mother yells as we race to the front door.

On the drive, she stops, runs back inside and returns seconds later with the salami.

'What on earth are you doing?'

'It's kangaroo, his favourite. It'll help to orient him. I promised I'd buy one from Matthieu at the market.' She runs round to the passenger door of the Prius. 'You drive. I can't possibly concentrate.'

I turn on the engine and we pull out with the underwhelming silence of every electric car ever invented.

'Mum,' I say as we turn onto the road, 'I really, really need to talk to you. There are a lot of strange things going on for me at the moment and Ben thinks—'

'Not now, Marnie,' she says. 'I'm far too stressed.'

186

Things I Loved About My Sister: Part 8

She was the kind of person who shared things. For example, her secrets, or her maths assignments, or once, her chicken pox.

When we were fifteen, there was a girl in our class at school called Sal. Sal's mum was a meat eater and, despite her best efforts, her daughter wasn't. In an odd act of parental control, Sal's mum refused to let Sal take anything except meat or fish in her sandwiches for her packed lunch. Sal would sit at the table in the dining hall each day with tears in her eyes because she felt a) unseen by her mother and b) extremely hungry. Each lunchtime, Perdita would share her own vegetarian sandwiches with Sal: the ones Dad had made that morning – as long as they weren't Tartex, as that's disgusting, no one likes Tartex – the carrot sticks; the funny muesli bars. Even her mock chicken, which was her favourite item. She'd do it all discreetly, so no one would notice.

Perds never complained about being hungry or boasted about being generous or told anyone else in class, and not once did she ask to share my lunch or ask me to share mine with Sal instead. I mean, I never offered. Partly because I was a heavy meat eater myself, but also because I wasn't a sharer. And if I'm honest, Sal wasn't actually very nice, but that's not really the point. The thrust of this is that Perds *was* a sharer. She was simply marvellous in every way and that's not just sisterly bias, that's a fact.

Chapter 9

We're coasting down the M1. My mother, still in her Judith Bliss hat, is tapping her fingernails nervously against the glove compartment. She switches the radio on and immediately off again.

'Classic FM!' She shakes her head. 'Radio 3 is far superior.'

'I can't understand that modern stuff. It's spikey.'

'Don't be silly. It's music for *intelligent* people. I must say, I do like that you've started wearing dresses, Marns.'

'I put it on by accident.' I turn my thoughts to Dad.

I may have said the dad bit out loud, because my mother says, 'Darling, don't worry.' Then pats my hand.

Her fingers are freezing.

'It's going to be fine. Now, we're not going to talk about what just happened.' She waves the scroll of poems in my face. 'Though I have to say, I'm *flabbergasted*.'

I make to grab them with my free hand. 'Why have you brought those with you? Give them back! They're mine.'

'Hands on the wheel!' she screams, then: 'In a minute. We need distraction.'

She reclines her chair, which infuriates me, and chucks the scroll on the rear seats.

'Ask me something,' she says.

'What?'

'No, scratch that. I can't concentrate on questions.' She removes her straw hat and rotates the enormous brim between her chilly fingers. 'I don't know what Judith Bliss made of it, but this hat is *terribly* itchy. I'll be bald in a week.' She stares at the satnav. 'What does that say? *How* much longer?'

I do wish she'd stop talking in italics.

'Forty minutes.'

My mother sighs. 'Oh, Jack, Jack. You silly boy.'

We pass the Jewish delis as we glide along the edges of Hampstead Garden Suburb. I think of hot bagels and my mouth waters. Mum pulls out her mobile and stabs at the buttons. Parker has more dexterity.

She holds the phone to her ear. 'Hellooo?'

Her telephone voice is breathier than her normal one.

'Blythey?' she whispers into the mic. 'It's Nana.'

'Mum,' I say. 'Why are you calling the kids?'

She ignores me. 'Is Daddy there?'

I hear Blythe talking. My hands tense against the steering wheel.

'*What* time?' My mother turns to me. 'Blythe says Ben didn't come home last night until the wee hours of the morning. Did you know?'

'Mum, of course I knew. I live with him. And don't say wee. You're not Scottish.'

'But is everything all right? Why didn't you mention it?'

'I didn't think it was any of your concern. Also, we've been a bit preoccupied, you and me, what with the vicar's knee and Dad's illness and finding an ancient artefact that I apparently hid in your garden as a *joke*.'

My mother's lips purse and she turns her face into the phone again. 'Grandpa's had a bad turn. He's at UCL.'

189

'UC*H*!' I yell.

'UCH,' she echoes. 'We're on our way there. We're very shaken. I think you and Sylvia and Stanny had better come right away.'

Blythe says something and then my mother looks to me.

'Which ward? That parsley in my bag absolutely *reeks*, doesn't it. Organic, you see. Far more potent.'

'Fourth floor. Davis Ward.' My teeth are gritted.

'Fourth Floor, Davis Ward,' repeats my mother. 'Hurry, children. There's no time to lose. Your mother's very angry right now. We're all in shock. We'll talk about it later.'

'We aren't in shock!' I shout. 'And I'm not angry! It's all okay, Blythe!'

Nurse Stephanie is there to greet us at the double doors of the Davis Ward. She's smiling but in a way that's not too smiley, as if she shares our worries about Dad.

'He's doing well. Room five.'

My mother and I have hands wet with sterilising gel, so we just flick them in the air by way of greeting, like drama teachers.

The gel is awful for my eczema. I wipe the remaining liquid on my dress, feeling grateful we don't live in a world where we're forced to use such stuff every day.

Nurse Stephanie sets off at a lick down the hot-neon corridor, soft soles squeaking on the lino. She has wide hips and short legs, and her back looks strong from lifting all of those invalids.

'Why did you make the kids come, Mum?' I say as we follow Stephanie. 'There's absolutely no point.'

'Children should bear witness to the full tapestry of life,' she says. 'Not just its happy parts.'

'I'm going to tell them not to.'

When I take out my phone, there's no reception. They're probably already on the tube, anyway.

I peer in through open doors to the various rooms: a woman in a plastic armchair eating yoghurt, a man lying in bed hooked up to a ventilator, an ancient lady on a Zimmer frame calling, 'Nurse! Nurse!'

'In a minute, Irene!' Nurse Stephanie talks to us over her shoulder. 'Bless her. She should be in geriatrics, but they ran out of beds.'

'We're all living so long,' says my mother as we reach room five. 'It's not natural.'

I wonder if this makes her think about Perdita.

Stephanie pushes the door open. My father is semi-supine in the bed, arms out either side, palms up, as if in supplication to the cannulas, bags of saline and glucose dripping into his veins. He's the only patient in the room and his eyes are closed.

'Jack, your family's here!' Nurse Stephanie speaks loudly.

Dad's eyes flick open.

Stephanie turns to me. 'I'll leave you to it. Call if you need anything.'

'Thank you, dearest Stephanie,' says Mum.

'Hi, gang,' Dad croaks. He spots my mother's hat. 'Ah, Judith Bliss, I presume? Sorry about this.'

My mother's already on her knees at the side of the bed, salami in hand. She leans her head along his forearm. '*Darling.* I love you so.' She stands abruptly, producing the parsley from the rattan bag like a rabbit from a hat and placing the sprig upright in Dad's plastic drinking-water jug.

Dad watches her. 'And I love *you*.'

'Poor thing was wilting in the heat.' She primps the herbs into a circular shape, as one might a bunch of flowers.

'Unlike my love, forever cool.'

He got that bit right. You could freeze vodka with the temperature of her fingers.

'This salami smells divine. Kangaroo?' he asks.

'*Bien sûr.*'

I walk round to the far side of the bed and kiss his forehead. 'Hi, Dad. You had us worried back there.'

'You forgot your lunchtime latkes, silly billy,' Mum cuts over me. 'I found them in the fridge after you'd gone. I gave one to Peter.'

Dad perks up. 'Did he like it?'

'*Loved* it,' she says. 'Asked for another. The hummus has gone AWOL, I'm afraid, and Ben stayed out *all* night.'

My dad does a little jerk in the bed. 'Oh? Everything okay?'

'Ask Marnie. She lives with him.'

My parents' eyes train themselves on me.

I blink slowly, hoping that in doing so I can make this moment go away.

'He's just. Everything's fine. He's preoccupied with his book. Things have been strange lately.'

'You're telling *me*,' says my mother.

My dad makes a comforting tut. 'Stay calm, darling.' They start kissing.

I stare out of the window. The view is amazing. The Post Office Tower is right there.

I hear young voices in the corridor.

'It stinks of piss,' Stan is saying.

'Shh.' That's Sylvia. 'Room five. Here we are.'

The door opens and there stand my beauties. I say beauties – objectively speaking, Stan looks awful in saggy tracksuit bottoms, hair sticking out, gold headphones around his neck, but the girls look good.

'Grandpa! You're okay!' cry Sylvia and Blythe in unison.

They all cluster around Dad's bed, leaning too hard on the mattress, drowning him in kisses.

'Hi, Nana,' they say in turn, and finally, 'Mum.'

'The train said five minutes on the board, then it took *fifteen*,' Blythe complains.

'And it was full of Everton fans.'

Stan is almost shouting. I don't know why boys have such problems with volume.

Sylvia comes close to me. 'You okay, Mum? I overheard your conversation with Dad this morning.'

'Did you?' My voice is barely audible.

'About mental health and help for you.'

I sneak a glance at my mother. She hasn't heard.

'Sylv, one thing at a time. I suggest you and Blythe quit all this eavesdropping. Can we just deal with Grandpa?'

My mother's speaking in a deep voice. 'Perhaps you'd like to lead the prayer, Blythey?'

'*Mum*,' I say. 'Please.'

Blythe says, 'What? Mum, I *want* to.'

'Fine.'

Blythe, Sylvia, my mum and dad all close their eyes, clasp hands.

'Stan?' Mum says, free hand out. 'Joining us?'

'You're all right.'

He pretends to be as interested as I am in the Post Office Tower through the window.

'Dear God,' Blythe begins.

I study my feet.

'May Grandpa be wrapped up in Your love, found deep in Your everlasting wings, carried and kept, safe and cherished ...'

And then, as if driven by an exterior force, my palms are moving towards one another. I'm powerless to resist, even though I give it a go, pushing against the air in between as if they're two magnets that can repel one another, but it doesn't work. My hands continue to rise slowly, inexorably, towards my chest.

Instead of panicking, I say to myself, *I'm brave enough*. Vicar Pete would be proud.

My palms stick fast in a prayer shape. My eyes close. I try to think of nothing, but almost immediately, I'm begging God to return things to normal. A strong, hot surge is growing between my hands. It radiates along my arms, courses through my entire body. It's an entirely pleasant sensation. It's energy, I tell myself, nothing more, nothing less, but boy does it feel good.

Is this what a religious conversion looks like? Was it this way for Paul at Damascus? And for Vicar Pete, presumably not at Damascus but somewhere near St Albans?

What about Irene down the corridor – is she a believer? Does the thought of God sustain her in the long closing of her life? It would if I were in her slippers.

And perhaps, like me, everyone who doesn't believe secretly longs to.

There's a throbbing between my legs. I place my hand beneath my dress. It's back. Oh no, no, no.

I grip it tightly, willing it to go away, but instead it comes off in my hand, breaks off like a branch, painlessly. I'm holding my own penis, detached from my body, its anchor.

Beads of sweat form on my forehead and begin to track their way along my temples. Please, I pray, make this not be happening. I pull my hand – the one clasped around it – out from under my dress and open my eyes.

Nothing there. Fear courses through me. Could this be a test: God asking if I have faith?

'And please let everything be all right, *everywhere*.' Blythe's incantation echoes my own.

Stan's still staring at the view and hasn't spotted that one of my hands is in a classic prayer position, the other open-palmed and close to my face, my mouth gaping.

I glance around the room. The rest of my family innocent, heads bowed, hands linked. I don't want them to see me like this.

What if I'm not really here?

'And may the healing power of Christ breathe across your being now,' Blythe finishes.

I swivel my body to the window, pressing myself against the box radiator, which maddeningly seems to be on. The heat from its top vent is so intense, it scalds my skin. I squeal. My hands fly up.

'Marnie?' Mum's at my side. 'You've burned yourself?'

'No, no, I'm fine. Just struggling with …' I gesture at nothing.

My mother takes my hands. '*If we are faithless, He remains faithful – for He cannot deny Himself.*'

I struggle not to scream. 'I don't know what that means.'

My father raises his arms from the bed. 'Please. Ladies who I love.'

Nurse Stephanie makes another appearance, this time with a woman in a teal skirt suit, hair neatly bobbed in a helmet shape. I'm so confused, it takes me a moment to realise it's Foxton's Richard III.

'Jack Rose?' She gives the whole room a short smile. 'I'm Doctor Smythe. Spelled Smythe but pronounced Smith. I'm the consultant diabetician and endocrinologist on duty. How are you feeling?'

'Worried,' says my dad.

'This must be your family.'

We nod.

'So, Jack, there's really nothing to worry about. Your bloods all came back satisfactory. I think in a couple of hours, we'll be able to discharge you.'

The kids cheer.

My mother is saying, 'Oh, thank God!' and 'Nine lives,' to my dad, who's looking distinctly chipper.

I pat him on the back. 'Hurrah.'

Doctor Smythe's eyes narrow as her gaze reaches me. 'We've met?'

'Thought you worked for Foxtons?' I murmur.

'Sorry?' Doctor Smythe-pronounced-Smith shakes her head inside her hair that doesn't move.

'The estate agent?'

My mother says, 'Marnie.'

I hastily erase Ant, the Pinot Grigio and Saturday night with friends from Doctor Smythe's life and replace it with Proust, simnel cake and weekends on call at UCH operating dialysis machinery with her husband, Ivor, also a doctor.

'You live in St Albans,' I say. 'You informed me my front light wasn't working a few days ago. On the high street? I drive a silver Prius. I thought you worked at Foxton's because of your ... Never mind.'

'Ah,' is her response.

After a pause, my mother says in a tiny voice, 'We live in St Albans.'

No one in the hot hospital room knows what to say next. Stan scratches his head. Doctor Smythe eyeballs me. I stare back.

She breaks first. 'Jack, you've had Type two ...' She consults a file of notes in her arms. 'For five years.'

'Yes,' says my dad with a sigh. 'The perils of craft services.'

Doctor Smythe's expression says she's in the dark.

Mum says, 'The catering tables on set when you're filming? Where you help yourself all day. They're very good and should carry a health warning. Jack was once a famous actor.'

'I write recipe books now,' adds Dad. 'Perhaps you've heard of one: *The Live-Long Diabetic Cookbook*. Or: *Sweet As A Nut*.'

'Oh, that was a *lovely* trip!' says Mum. 'The Burusho in Hunza have many *stunning* ceramics.'

'*Around the Med with Diabetes*. That's the latest one, out now.' Dad looks hopefully at the doctor.

I will her to say yes, of course she's seen it, or 'that sounds interesting', anything.

'I've not heard of them,' she says at last, taking a step away from the bed. 'Perhaps we can get you in for a chat to calibrate your meds in a week or so. I'll get Steph to book it in. Nice to meet you, Jack. Glad you're on the mend.' She turns to Nurse Stephanie. 'Shall we move on?'

'Would you care to take some St Albans market parsley with you, Doctor?' Dad nods at the plastic drinking jug. 'Local, lovely, fresh.'

'I'm all good for parsley, thank you.'

'Kangaroo salami?'

'Thank you, no.'

The doctor revolves on one nude patent court heel and follows an apologetic-looking Nurse Stephanie to the door.

'*Mum?*' says Stan once they're out of earshot.

'What?'

'All that stuff about estate agents. It was embarrassing.'

My mother smiles tightly. 'Never mind that.'

Her hand goes into the rattan shopper and out comes the scroll of poems. She must have sneaked them back into her bag when I was parking. She slaps them on the wheely table at the end of Dad's bed.

'Wait until she tells you about her little practical joke with my planter.'

A couple of hours have passed and Dad has been discharged, with his parsley and salami.

When we eventually reach the revolving doors by the exit, Mum remembers she's forgotten her Judith Bliss hat and we have to wait another twenty minutes while she reascends to collect it. She returns and hands my poems back with a dark look. My parents are going to take a taxi to St Albans as there isn't enough room in my car for all of us.

I'm forced to make a great song and dance to my children in the car park about not putting the poems and a gold coin in the planter or burying the wretched thing in the ground.

The children and I glide the Prius home. My palms are still fizzing from the praying.

'But how did your poems get into the pot?' Stan asks for about the fiftieth time from the back seat.

'She doesn't know, stupid,' Blythe answers, opening the passenger window. 'She's already told you.'

'Thank you, Blythe,' I say, even though she's called Stan stupid. 'I promise, Stan, the burial of my work in Nana's raffle planter has absolutely nothing to do with me.' I feel the children's full attention, bright like headlights, upon me.

A text bleeps on my phone as it charges in its satnav holder. Blythe has already leaned in to read it.

'It might be Dad,' Sylvia declares from behind.

'Who's Kass?' Blythe asks.

I nearly crash the car. 'Sorry?'

'"*Marnie, I'm using modern technology*", exclamation mark,'

Blythe reads out loud. '"*Isn't it wonderful*", question mark. "*I must see you again. Kass. Z.*" I think she means X.'

'Yes, probably,' I manage.

'So?' Blythe isn't going to let it go.

'So, she's an old friend from school.'

The kids seem to swallow it. How the hell Katherine has acquired my number, I can't imagine.

We pull up outside our house. It's 5 p.m. and I'm exhausted. Sylvia takes her keys from the little bag over her shoulder as she climbs out of the car.

'Maybe Dad'll be home early today after his late one last night.'

I'm hopeful, too, though I don't say so.

Sylvia nudges the front door open and Parker bounds out, jumping at the kids, sniffing around my crotch.

'Dad?' My children bowl along the hall like marbles into different rooms.

'He's not here!' Blythe calls from the kitchen.

'Not here!' Sylvia from the living room.

'Nope!' yells Stan, exiting the broken downstairs bathroom.

They're searching for him as if we're in a game of Cluedo.

'I'm gonna go to my bedroom,' Stan yells.

The girls nod their agreement and they all bound up the stairs.

I slip my sandals off, let my feet cool on the hall tiles, rest my forehead against the wall. I close my eyes. The cylinder of rolled-up poems slips from my grasp and hits the floor with a thwack.

I've had enough now. I want to get off this fairground ride – it's making me sick.

The children move around heavily upstairs.

'Stanley, it stinks in here!' It's Blythe.

'Keep out, then.'

Parker is back at my feet, whining. His bottom is on my poems, a look of disappointment in his eyes. He points his nose dolefully at the front door.

'Missing someone? Me, too, old boy.'

He turns a circle and paws at the sheet of A4 nearest to his tail. It's the poem I wrote a few days ago, the one about words disappearing from a sheaf of paper. It looks finished, though I don't remember writing it in its entirety. When would I have done that – in my sleep? I drop to my knees and read softly as the dog waits beside me, mouth open. His breath is awful.

> *Here: this poem on paper,*
> *You read now hoping for something:*
> *Lift, transcendence, the text propelling you,*
> *Erasing your kingdom, the little you govern.*
> *It is what it is.*
> *And perhaps it's your eye, or a trick,*
> *Your brain losing mass,*
> *Its inevitable decay,*
> *But the letters are rising,*
> *Floating across this faithful curve,*
> *The Earth! The Earth!*
> *And you think: I know this, I know this,*
> *I've been here before.*

I ruffle Parker's ears. 'Is it mine?'

He gazes unblinking into my eyes and nudges his head at the paper. I need to read it again. I'm not sure it's any good.

When I glance down, the poem isn't there. The page is blank. I turn the sheet over. Blank on the other side.

I look at the dog. Perhaps he's magicked it away with his leg.

'Off.'

I shove him from the remaining sheets. My hands scramble through each one. All blank.

I'm not imagining it. The poems were definitely there, printed on the scroll. Mum and Vicar Pete were witness to them in Mum's garden earlier. Pete even read one out, for God's sake, and Stan was only moments ago asking after them in the car.

My poems have gone.

Again.

Perhaps God is teaching me a lesson. I never should have sent my sister back for my camera and He knows it.

I hurl the blank papers at the wall. The gesture exhausts me and I slump against the banisters, head in hands. When I look up, there are hundreds of tiny black flies floating in front of my face. I swat them away, but they won't leave. The light in the hall is murky.

I look again. They appear not to be flies at all. They're letters of the alphabet.

I put my hand out to touch them and meet nothing but air. I think to myself that this must be another of my hallucinations, my dreams, my alternate realities, and that it's beautiful in its own way, and then I relax a little and stare at them in wonder.

'*The letters are rising*' are the words I used in the poem. Is this about my work? Is it a message, a symbol? If so, perhaps all I have to do is decode it.

'Mum?' It's Sylvia from the top floor.

The letters vanish. Melt into thin air. I look around for them frantically.

'Mum, you okay?'

'Not really.' My voice is shaky.

'Are you hurt?'

'Not as such.'

I take out my phone and dial my own mother with a trembling hand.

She answers by reciting her entire mobile number with a question mark at the end.

'Ma, I've said before – there's no need to say the whole thing; it's a mobile. The person calling knows it's you.'

My mother sniffs. 'Why *exactly* are you calling? I'm busy with both your father and Peter recuperating in the house.'

'Oh, yes, sorry. How is Dad?'

'Getting better each passing hour. Peter's offered to cook dinner, bless him. Ben home yet?'

My jaw tightens. 'No. He's... at work.'

I hear my mother breathing and in the background the sound of frying. I picture her standing in the long hallway, much darker and cooler than my hall, in her Judith Bliss outfit. I picture the kitchen, the parquet soaking up the evening light. Peter will be cooking something – in the wrong pan, probably, according to Dad. The air will be rich with the smell of garlic. I remember suddenly why I felt such unlocatable melancholy as my hand came to rest against Mum's warm kitchen window days ago.

A game we played, my sister and me, one that we used to pass the time in the car on the endless journeys home after holidays in the UK. I can't remember the rules. The glass was always hot beneath my fingers as the car thrummed along the road. Strange that this has come to me now.

'Mum?' I say.

'Yes?'

'Love you.'

I hear her smile. 'I love you too, my sweet.'

'I'm ...' A tear trembles out of my eye and down my cheek.

Her voice softens. 'What is it, poppet?'

'I don't know. I'm scared.'

'That Ben came back late?'

'*No*. Other things.' I take a breath. 'I thought I had a penis.'

There's silence at the other end.

'Mum?' I whisper. 'You still there?'

'I'm still here.'

'Do you think I'm weird?'

'Of course not.' She exhales noisily into the phone. 'Though if you don't mind me saying, Marnie, I think now more than ever it would be wise that you open your arms to faith. To the possibility that the world doesn't start and end with your experience of it.'

I already know this to be true, but I don't tell her. I think about relating what happened to my hands at the hospital, the floating letters of the poem. I think about her reaction. Or lack of reaction. My tears dry up and go back inside.

'Mum! You'd better get up here!' It's Stan.

He's in my bedroom. I hear the girls' feet thundering from the top floor.

'I've got to go,' I say.

'But—'

I drag myself to my feet and gather the papers into a clump and put the phone in my pocket before mounting the stairs.

'*Mum!*'

Blythe's tone forces me into a different gear and I leap up the remaining steps. On the way to the bedroom, I pass something hanging on the wall of the landing that isn't quite right. There isn't time to think about it.

My children stand in front of my open closet. It's entirely empty, save for wooden hangers, dangling like collarbones from the rail.

Stan turns, hands on top of his head, like he used to when he was little.

'Everything's gone, Mum – everything of yours.'

Blythe turns to me accusingly. 'Another of your practical jokes?'

'No!' I say, but my voice is small and far away.

I look to my children helplessly, appealing to their trust, their faith in me, but I see in their eyes the truth. They think I'm lying.

'Would you say you've been having a hard time lately?'

This wasn't quite what I'd anticipated from the police. It's 7 p.m. and I'm at the kitchen table on speakerphone to one DI Marcus Brown. The kids are huddled in beside me, faces grave. I'm not sure if this is because of my missing clothes, or because I have insisted, against their wishes, that we involve the Met. In my defence, we've searched high and low for the clothes but can't find them anywhere in the house and called Ben multiple times to discover his phone permanently off, which is unusual in itself.

After a hesitant start on the part of the detective, he and I have been through all the usual stuff, like could any of us have loaned keys to strangers, could anyone have let themselves in and helped themselves to my property. Now, of course, we've alighted on the subject of my mental health.

Who would take my clothing? Not me, obviously: even if I have been having a hard time, am confused or depressed or cognitively biased, what on earth would my motive have been and where would I have hidden them? In an urn with my poems? I mean, *really*.

Ben will be home any minute. I don't think I can cope with more pitying looks.

I have for one brief second considered whether or not it could have been him who took them as a sort of test of my mental robustness but quickly dismiss this. I know I said all that stuff about secrets, but it's doubtful he'd stoop to such unconventional methodology.

So that leaves the kids, which is a hard no.

We're all in the kitchen drinking camomile tea, even Stan. Parker, who's cleaning himself at my feet, has taken a dislike to Marcus Brown and barks every time he hears his voice.

'I'm a poet and my partner, Ben, is a psychoanalyst,' I find myself explaining. 'He's been very busy. I've been dealing with some ...' I flick a glance at the kids. 'Emotional business, I suppose, but not to the extent that I've begun to steal my own clothing.'

'Right.' I hear Marcus scribbling.

Parker barks.

'Quiet,' Sylvia chides.

'It's just something we have to consider,' says Marcus apologetically, who has more perspicacity than I'd initially credited him with.

'It's something they have to *consider*,' Blythe says quietly, nudging my arm.

I'm not sure if it's because she agrees or disagrees.

'I'm going to be honest with you—' Marcus is speaking again.

'Please do.'

'At the end of the day, it's not really what we'd call a *priority*. With respect, Mrs Hopkiss—'

'Rose.'

'Your name is Rose?' says Marcus. 'Apologies. I thought it was Marnie.'

Parker barks.

'Shush.' Blythe taps the dog on the nose.

'My name *is* Marnie. Marnie Rose.' I raise my voice. 'Hopkiss is Ben's surname. We're not married.'

'Apologies for that, *Ms* Rose. To be fair, you may have to do some investigations of your own to begin with. Usually—'

Parker barks.

'Yes? You were going to say?' I prompt.

'Beg pardon?' Poor Marcus.

'You said *"usually"*,' I say, helpfully, 'before you stopped speaking.'

'Er. I don't. Oh, that's it. Your property will most likely turn up. One way or another. In a few days.'

'But, wait.' Blythe leans in towards the phone on the table. 'We've already told you: Mum's stuff has *gone*. Someone took it. Like, how would it just *turn up* again?'

Parker barks.

'Put him in the bloody garden,' I say. Then to the phone, 'Sorry. Not you – we're talking about our dog.'

'It's okay,' Marcus is saying. 'Well, you might have forgotten that your clothes are at the laundry, for example.'

'*All* of them? They're not.'

He sighs. 'We'll just have to wait a bit longer before we get involved in making an official missing property ...'

'Missing property *what*?' Blythe says under her breath.

Sylvia mutes the phone.

'Stop being mean, all of you. He's doing his best.' She turns to me. 'Thank him, Mum.'

She unmutes the phone and leans back in her chair, her hands wrapped around my mug that says '*Optimist*' in black italics except most of the letters are covered, so now it just reads '*mist*', which is strangely reflective of what's happening inside my head.

'Thank you, DI Marcus Brown,' I say.

'Not a problem. Keep in touch.'

The four of us sip tea while Parker whines at the back door, his nose smearing the glass.

'Does this mean we might miss our party?' Blythe asks miserably.

'What? No!' I say. 'Why would you think something like that? Why would losing some clothes mean your party won't happen?'

'Don't know.' Her head droops. 'Are you depressed, Mum?'

'*No.* I'm *fine.*' How many times? Jesus.

Stan pulls a face. 'You're not gonna kill yourself, are you?' He stands and pours the contents of his cup into Parker's food bowl before letting the dog in.

'The dog can't drink that!' Sylvia shrieks as Parker laps the tea.

Stan shrugs. 'Parker needs his moment of calm.'

'Enough.' I drain my cup, collect the empties and dump them in the sink. 'No plans to kill myself, thank you, Stan.'

Stan trips over his own shoes in the middle of the kitchen, Blythe locks the back door, Sylvia sighs like my sister and snaffles a yoghurt from the fridge.

I lean on the kitchen worktop. 'It'll all be okay in the morning. I'm sure my stuff will turn up.'

The kids ignore me and leave the room.

I stand in the empty kitchen staring through the back door at the darkening sky. All that greets me is my own reflection. I can't get away from myself. I hardly recognise the woman in front of me, anyway: wrinkled, confused. In the glass I spot my laptop on the table.

I go to it, search for my writing folder. It's not there. I smooth out the blank scroll of poems on the table next to the keyboard, which sends a storm of dust motes into the kitchen. I watch them dance in the beam of overhead light and think what a literary cliché the image is.

The magical letters I saw earlier could still be here, floating in this indeterminate ether. My clothes could be, too. And Perdita. *That's* not a cliché. The letters might not have been a symbol of my work at all, but a message that my sister is here, with me now.

I head into the living room, searching for my poetry collection. I look for its blue spine in the usual place on the shelf by the mantel, but it's not there. *Gone* has gone.

I think I almost expected it to be missing, am almost gratified that this, too, has disappeared. Somehow it makes sense. I shan't point its absence out to Ben. He might weaponise its as more proof of my mental fragility.

He's late again. Would I be bothered if it turned out he *is* having an affair? I'd have no right to be.

'Hi, Perds,' I whisper before turning off the lights and standing in the darkness, ears tuned for any messages from another world.

Parker's whiskers are tickling my knees. He stares hopefully at my face, awaiting instruction, bless him. His breathing is quicker than mine, which means his heart beats faster: he's four already and he's probably only got another seven years left. All those beats, taking him towards oblivion, to the place where Perds and the floating letters and maybe my clothes reside. I'm happy my sister will have the dog for company eventually. I stroke his head.

Parker trots off, along the hall and up the stairs. I feel my way after him in the dark. Before I reach my bedroom, I nearly trip over him on the landing. He paws at the wall, claws scraping with a sound that sets my teeth on edge.

'What, boy?' I flick on the landing light.

Ben's aunt's penis-cylinder painting has gone. In its place is Schlap's white mouse picture, the one previously in his practice room. This is what I noticed earlier, I realise, but didn't have time to absorb. A section of the painting appears to have changed: standing in front of the little house is an entirely different man. Gone is the likeness to Schlap in hunting garb. Instead, it's a much younger man with dark hair, stooped shoulders and short legs, wearing the hunting outfit, the same gun against the door with the same spaniel at his feet. He looks like the man on the phone in the waiting room at Schlap's house.

I take a step closer. The thing in the man's hands, which looked previously to be a lure for the mouse, cheese or whatever, is now a scroll of white papers just like my poems.

Schlap said his son painted this. I remember clearly reading the signature at the bottom right-hand corner: D. Schlapoberstein. D for Dashiell. Except now the signature reads: J. Schlapoberstein. J for Jacob.

Things I Loved About My Sister: Part 9

When we were twelve, we went through a phase of creating modern dance routines in our bedroom. Mostly, this would involve a few backbends, a couple of clumsy lifts and some hand gestures worthy of a 3 a.m. rave tent at Glastonbury. The exception to this was our robotics phase, in which we wore white gloves and a pair each of our Granny's sixties sunglasses complete with integrated sunblocking nose beaks.

The normal way of things was that after an hour or so of intense creativity, we'd holler down for Mum and Dad to act as the audience and they'd sit on the carpet while we pressed Play on the cassette deck. Sometimes we'd play Madonna, even though we hated her music, just to prove one could build something beautiful from a crap foundation.

Perds was a far better dancer than me – more elegant, lighter on her feet, suppler. This meant that often I'd play the man, crawling through her legs and arms as she valiantly maintained her crab, or trying to push her up onto my shoulders without planting my face in her crotch. In my defence, I was mostly the choreographer.

The day we attempted The Communards, 'Don't Leave Me This Way', we were both tired. I lay on my bed, sucking a large boiled sweet for energy, searching my brain for ideas. I stared out of the window as a river gull flew past and had a choreographic light-bulb moment. Unfortunately, my inspiration in this case was literal and I inhaled my sweet in its entirety, lodging it snugly in my gullet.

As I leaped off the bed, frantically waving my arms and pointing at my throat, Perdita didn't miss a beat. She came round behind me, no fuss, and performed an effective Heimlich manoeuvre, forcing the sweet out of my mouth and onto a shelf, where it stuck against my copy of *First Term at Malory Towers*.

How amazing is that? My sister saved my life. Actually saved my life. What other twelve-year-old do you know who would have the peace of mind to do such a thing?

Chapter 10

Contrary to my promise to the kids, things aren't okay in the morning.

Ben arrived home the previous evening around ten. I'd cross-examined him vigorously before remembering I'd forgotten he'd already told me he was going to be working late that night. My interrogation was followed by a brief, uncomfortable chat about the missing clothes while he'd readied himself for bed. Fatigued from his day, he'd been weary and impatient until, at my insistence, he'd finally opened my cupboard door and, *voila*, all of my clothes had been there again. I'd become panicked and Ben had become strangely solicitous, as if I were some dangerous psychopath, suggesting I should perhaps consider stopping my sessions with Schlap altogether and instead pay an immediate visit to a psychiatrist colleague of his. We hadn't spoken after that.

Both Ben and the children have already left by the time I wake, which is a relief: it's exhausting reassuring people I love that everything is fine. Plus, I have to go to Euclid today to explain the lost set of newest poems. Veronica won't be there. It'll be that woman on the phone: *Pantea*. Her name, brimming with exoticism, fills me with a sense of my own mediocrity.

Then I have an appointment at last to see Dr Riba, so she

can look at my fanny and reassure me everything's okay down there.

I check my cupboard. My clothes are all still present and correct. I pad back onto the landing and take another look at the mouse painting in the cold light of day. I say cold – it's extremely warm already and it's only 8.30 a.m.

The portrait is as it was last night, the central male figure different, younger. It definitely looks like the man from the waiting room. I think about ringing Ben's mobile or taking a photo and sending it to him as proof but decide against it.

I unhook the painting from the wall and put it on the floor. I'm going to take it to Schlap. This is how I'll begin our session. I'll hold it up in front of him and demand an explanation.

I drop Parker off with Ryan, our occasional dog walker. He answers his door, five dogs yapping at his feet, and takes hold of Parker's collar.

'Come on, old boy. We're going to have some fun.'

He gives me a funny look before closing the door behind him.

I wrap the mouse painting in a blanket and lug it to the Prius. Ben's black Leon Paul bag is already inside the boot; the fencing foils bag, the corpse bag. I unzip it. His pistol-grip handles are at the top, glistening. I zip up the bag again and slam the boot hard.

I try DI Marcus Brown to tell him my clothes are back, but he's not answering.

I text the number Katherine used:

How did you get my phone details?

I start the car. Silence as it glides away. So unsatisfying.

On Rosebery Avenue, my phone pips. A reply from Katherine:

A 'friend' gave it to me! Someone here you'd like to see! Come over!

For an esteemed author, she uses an awful lot of exclamation marks. I check there's no police nearby, then press the microphone icon. Dictating messages while driving isn't one of my specialities.

'I'm about to see my editor then to your house, comma, but first got to see Schlap, comma, my shrink, full stop.'

The text appears on the screen:

I'm about three to my end of her, then to your house, Bathurst to slap my shrink.

'For God's sake!'

Forgot to say, the screen types out.

'Delete message!' Katherine will have to wait.

The NCP under Cavendish Square is busy this morning. I drive round and round in the semi-darkness breathing noxious car fumes until a space becomes available. Cars queue right up against my bumper as I attempt to reverse in, wedging myself between a nasty bubble thing and a monster silver Volvo.

I pop the boot but can't open the driver's door. I scoot across to the passenger side, slide out sideways and make my way to the rear to retrieve the mouse painting, drag that out and crab-walk down the narrow gap between cars. I kick the front wheel of the Volvo for good measure. Another stupid XC90 in Central London.

Wait.

I study the number plate: PR16 TVX. It's hers. It's Perdita's, or the woman who looks like Perds. It has to be – it's even got her initials at the front. I push my head against the window on the driver's side, but the neon strip lighting of the garage means all I can see are yellow-white reflections.

I cup my hands around my face: cream leather interior. Satnav and phone clip on the dash and one of those coffee holders. Some CDs in the central compartment: *School of Rock's Greatest Hits*, *Sing-a-Long-a Sound of Music*, *The Best of Abba*. I'm not sure this is my sister's car. What happened to our shared love of Jimi Hendrix?

I move round to the rear. A couple of DVD players are embedded in the headrests of the front seats, which makes me tut. Why can't children just stare out of the window when they're going somewhere? Admittedly, there are no back gardens with trampolines to look at on a motorway, but there are fields and cows and other cars.

A graphic novel, *Manga Bible 2*, lies next to three empty Wotsits packets and a smattering of electric-orange crumbs that have rolled into the creases in the seats. I look in the boot, imagining the smell of synthetic cheese festering inside. The boot contains a red dog lead, a green umbrella, a cardboard box with the words 'The Wine Club' on the side and a large Fat Face bag. There's also, extraordinarily, a book entitled, *Penis Envy and Other Bad Feelings: The Emotional Costs of Everyday Life* by someone called Mari Ruti. The cover is baby pink with a butter knife pointing down towards an upside-down banana, so it looks like the book itself is feeling sad. I file the title in my brain for later.

There's nothing more to be done. I don't have time to wait for the return of the owner of the car, whoever they may be – my sister, my sister's doppelganger, the gay parents – they could be all day. My triumvirate appointments with, respectively, Pantea, Dr Riba and Schlap beckon. I pick up the mouse painting, exit the underground car park and stagger into Soho.

★

Once more, I'm in the reception area at Euclid. It's all quiet bustle and an air that people here are working at something fundamentally important, but I'm too preoccupied by my current reality to care much: the owner of the Volvo, who Katherine's friend might be, whether or not I'm currently dreaming.

Coming towards me with a smile on her face is a woman I've never met.

'Marnie.' She extends her hand.

I take it. It's not at all clammy.

'Lovely to meet you ... Pantea?'

'Indeed.' She frowns, puts her fingers to her lips and gestures at the office in general.

'Ah. Sorry.' I didn't think I was talking loudly.

She beckons for me to follow as she heads in the direction of Veronica's office.

I trip after her, the painting still in my arms.

'You're probably wondering who I am.' She stops and turns to face me.

What I'm wondering is if her voice is an affectation.

'Well—'

'I'm an on-call fill-in editor from an agency.'

'An agency? Like a temp agency? For *editors*?'

'Oh yes. Everything can be outsourced.' Pantea looks at her feet. She's wearing nude platform patent court shoes à la Doctor Smythe's. She taps her toes together lightly, like Dorothy from *The Wizard of Oz*. 'Even artists' – she looks up at me – 'can be substituted at the drop of a hat.'

'They can?'

'Mmm-hmm. There's always someone waiting to take the place of a creative mind who might have lost their way, whose best work may already be behind them, or who's no longer with us.'

'Sorry—'

'It turns out, women *can* have it all.' She points at her toes, taps her nose and her voice drops to a whisper. 'If we assume the *appearance* of normality.'

'I'm not sure I follow. What is "normality" anyway?'

'And one must never seek to make one's art funny. Ever. Patriarchy dictates that *literary* comedy is predominantly a masculine domain. Female authors and poets must confine their humour to a narrower spectrum. And even then they must be highly skilled to hit on target. People in the main won't find a strong, comic female literary voice cute – they'll find it childish and irritating.'

'They will?'

Pantea spins away and strides into Veronica's office. 'Also, not too much dialogue.'

I run after her, dump the painting against the glass and sit on the uncomfortable sofa. 'When's Veronica back?'

'Soon. Very soon.' She rests her hands in her lap and tilts her chin at me.

'My poem,' I say at last. 'The one I sent via email. Have you found it yet?'

She smiles. 'It'll turn up. Try not to worry.'

We regard one another. I miss Veronica. I miss her blue ensemble, her cosy manner.

Pantea adjusts one stray hair that's being blown repeatedly into her mouth by the vicious air con. 'There are but two days until your deadline.'

'Yup. Yup. No time to waste. I have, in fact, written three or four more, just so you know.'

Her expression changes. 'You have?'

Oh, God, but now they're *missing*. I do some mental gymnastics.

'I haven't emailed them to you in case they were also lost en route. I'll post them first class tomorrow.' But can I remember what it was exactly that I'd written? 'They should arrive here by six tomorrow evening ...' I quickly take into account the demands of the coming day. 'Or the morning after. I have some "lifemin" to catch up with. My clothes went missing, but now they're back.'

'Oh?' Her eyebrows rise. There's a silence. 'How old are you, Marnie?'

'I don't see how ... forty-nine.'

'Okay.' She taps her fingernails against the glass coffee table. 'I'm going to tell you something. And I say this as a *friend*: it gets better.'

'What does?'

She smiles again. So annoying.

'The change of life.'

I can't effing believe it. Is there a sign pasted across my forehead?

'I'm still having regular periods!'

'I've been where you are now,' she pushes on.

'I highly doubt that.'

'Think you're going mad? Things all weird? Can't sleep?'

'Yes, but—'

'It'll pass. Just hang in there.'

She does seem to know something about it, after all.

'Have you ever considered we might be living several realities at the same time?' I ask.

'Have I ... ?' She cocks her head to one side like Margaret Thatcher.

'You said women can have it all. Your statement could

217

be true. Quantum principles dictate that everything that *can* happen *will* happen, right? Could we therefore be living every possibility at once? And not be aware of it.'

'I suppose.' Pantea gives a short laugh. 'But your – admittedly most unique – question is a paradox. If we are, I'm not aware of such a thing and therefore can't provide you with an answer.'

She brushes her hands together. It's as if she's brushing the conversation away, then stands and smooths her skirt.

'I'll let Veronica know about the poems and ... your clothes when she returns tomorrow.'

'No need.' I stand, too. 'About the clothes, I mean. And, thanks. Your words: they're reassuring and entirely logical. Is your name Persian? You don't look Persian.'

'Oh no, I'm English. My parents were academics.'

She says it like it's a good thing.

Neither of us move.

'I'll see myself out.' I pick up the painting and leave for my next appointment.

I exist in a paradox, unable to settle, unable simply to sit down and *write*. I'm a middle-aged, middle-class woman, failing at life. And about this fact nobody, and I mean nobody – except me – truly cares. Even a complete stranger knows this. Pantea knows. She's been through it, whatever 'it' is.

'You have excellent pelvic tone. Maybe too excellent.'

'Too excellent?'

I'm lying on my back in lovely Dr Riba's examination room, legs spread beneath the glare of a white-hot lamp, a paper sheet covering my stomach and pubis, which I assume is meant to act as a barrier between us, patient and doctor. Somehow this differentiates the pornographic from the medical, though why I should need my own genitalia hidden from myself is something I've never understood.

'The inside of a vagina is like a wall,' Dr Riba explains.

'Is it?'

'Yes. The muscles are the bricks, the skin is the paint. Your bricks are fine, it's the paint that's beginning to slide.' She looks down at me and grins mischievously.

'I see.'

Dr Riba's head and fingers probe in the abyss. It's not an abyss, of course, it's my vagina, but I'm calling it that in my head for creative purposes, and to distract myself from the fact that what she's doing is actually quite uncomfortable.

'Mmm-hmm,' she says, withdrawing at last, pulling off her gloves and washing her hands thoroughly in the sink. 'Hypertonic. I see this a lot with females like you.'

'In what way like me?' I hope she's not going to mention the perimenopause.

'High-achieving alphas. Perfectionists.'

I almost laugh out loud. No one has ever called me high-achieving.

'It may just be a case of taking your foot off the gas,' she says.

'Not sure I can do that right now.'

'The good news ... You can put your clothes on.' She pulls back the blue curtain, which has been closed as per protocol, even though there's no one else in the room. 'The good news is that there's nothing really wrong with you: no infection, no "protuberance", as you'd feared. All fine.'

'That is good news.' I wipe the lube goop that doctors use for internal exams with a scratchy paper towel, put the towel in the bin and hurriedly dress myself. 'So, no sticky-out bits, no bits that shouldn't be there?'

Nothing that could look like a penis, I want to say as I come to sit opposite her at the desk.

'You have several skin tags, and your very low-grade cystocele and rectocele prolapses, of course.'

Of course.

'But they haven't worsened since I last saw you' – she looks down at her notes – 'two years ago. I suppose I could do a little stitch across your episiotomy scar under local, tidy you up, make you look more "pretty" down there, if you like?'

She smiles. I smile. We both know the cuteness of accepted language around this stuff is bollocks.

'But that may affect your nerve endings. You're still sexually active?'

I think about Katherine. About us licking and grinding and coming all over one another. 'Uh-huh.'

'Well. So, maybe we'll just leave things for now. Come back in a year for a follow-up.'

'Great,' I say, standing and picking up the painting that I'd leaned against the wall when I'd arrived.

Dr Riba comes round her desk to hold the door open for me. She's small and dainty and incredibly thin, with thick black hair that falls around her shoulders, and I suddenly wish I was her.

'A lot of women do experience vaginal laxity as they approach the menopause.'

I try not to sigh.

'If we were in Kerala,' she says, glancing at the painting but not referring to it in any way, 'I'd be sending you to an Ayurvedic hospital – a proper one, not one of those tourist places – for a month to do panchakarma, detox your body and de-stress. That would be my treatment plan.'

This sounds bliss and I tell her so.

'See if you can get over there some time. My sister can recommend some places. Let me know which one you're going to. I may even come with you.' She pats me affectionately on the arm.

I make my way to Schlap's house, trying to imagine what it would be like to spend a month chilling with Dr Riba at an Ayurvedic hospital in Kerala. How wonderful to forget everything, everyone, for just twenty-eight days. How wonderful to *relax*.

London is noisy today, as it is every day, and I'm unable to suspend my disbelief around this daydream.

There's a yell from above.

'Marnie!'

It's Katherine.

Once again, she's leaning dangerously far out of her window.

'Come up!' Her voice echoes off the buildings.

Passers-by are looking: a sweating 49-year-old woman in a kaftan holding a large canvas and a gravity-defying slightly younger New Zealand woman in period costume. I mime my intention to see her later by making a walking motion with two fingers of one hand.

'I'm coming down!' she bellows and disappears inside.

It's quarter to eleven; fifteen minutes before my session.

I look out at the street. Building dust, the sound of pile-driving in the distance. And Perdita walking past.

Her double.

Or her.

Right. Past. Me.

'Hey!' I yell.

She turns. It's *exactly* my sister, the very one I've been seeing all over everywhere, looking as she would if she'd lived until this day – my age, dark-haired, her face lined and still beautiful.

She looks right through me with a puzzled expression and walks on. I put the painting down and make to run after her, but trip over the blanket that's wrapped around it. By the time I right myself, Perdita's gone.

My knees are bruised. I pick myself up and sprint to the end of the block. She's nowhere. I sprint further. I call her name. Gone.

I return to Schlap's front step, feeling empty on the inside. The painting and blanket await me in a woollen puddle on the pavement.

The clack-clack-clack of feet on marble at the side of the stair runner and the front door opens.

'Oh, Kass.' My head goes into my hands. 'I'm so fucking confused. Ben's right: I'm mad. I've just seen my—'

'Get in here.'

Katherine hauls me inside with a furtive glance along the ground-floor corridor. She closes the front door behind me and chivvies me up the stairs.

'Wait,' I protest, but she shakes her head and jabs me in the small of my back to keep moving.

We reach her carmine hallway, stand in the tiny space, the painting between us.

'Something odd is happening,' she says, her face solemn.

'Tell me about it.' A headache is brewing. 'I saw Perdita again *just* now on this street.'

'Well, that's not all.' She drags me into the living room.

Ben's standing in the centre of the room. My mouth falls open.

'Why didn't you tell me your husband was Benny B. Rubinstein?' says Katherine.

'Who? Ben,' I walk towards him, the painting still in my

arms, and nearly impale him on its corner. 'What are you doing here?'

'Why didn't you tell me——' Katherine insists.

'For God's sake, be quiet for a minute, woman!' I bang the painting down. 'Ben. Have you been spying on me?'

'No,' says Ben mildly, so that the wind is momentarily taken from my sails.

Shortly after this, I'm furious.

'I came to pay a visit to Jacob Schlapoberstein, but *Katherine* here was on the stairs and insisted I come up for tea.'

He leans on the words 'insisted I come up' and I know that he's trying to tell me silently that she's crazy and is waiting for her to leave the room so he can tell me out loud.

'Why would you be visiting Schlap?' I say. 'You can't ask him questions about me, you know. That would be a breach of patient confidentiality.'

'Indeed,' Ben says, which infuriates me further.

'Right. Would one of you like to tell me what's going on?' I turn to Katherine. 'Kass, this is Ben Hopkiss. Not my husband, just FYI, but my *partner*.'

I turn back to Ben, 'See? You can see her: Katherine *Mansfield*, the author? Unlike the missing clothes and the funny name on your computer, which you tried to make me believe were figments of my mind.'

I turn back to Katherine. 'His surname isn't Rubinstein, Kass. Why are you calling him that?'

And back to Ben again. It's like watching tennis for my neck. 'Say something!'

'I came to see if Jacob could help me understand what's going on with you,' Ben says.

'What d'you mean, "going on with me"?'

His shoulders lift. I want to bash his head against the wall.

'Marns,' he says softly. 'The kids think it was you who took your clothes last night, that you hid them yourself. I think you might be a little paranoid. I know Schlap has had a stroke. His mind isn't in the best shape and I'm not sure that's helping anyone, particularly you.'

This is the full story. He doesn't trust me. He doesn't trust Schlap, either. He's checking up on both of us. And my children have lost faith in my veracity. I want to lie down and weep.

'It's none of your business.' There is no *way* I'm letting Ben take Schlap away from me.

'I think it is my business. We're all worried about you.'

'Oh. *Thank* you.' My whole family, gossiping behind my back. 'Do you know, a total stranger just told me that this is all happening because of my *menopause*.' I look over at Katherine, who seems to be smirking. 'Everyone keeps ignoring the fact that I'm still menstruating regularly. Why are you calling Ben "Rubinstein"?'

'Because that's his name, darling.' Katherine makes her way into the kitchen. 'He's the one who bought me the phone.'

Ben is shaking his head, whirring his finger around near his temple.

'I sent you the message,' Katherine trills. 'Tell her, Benny.'

'Yes, tell me, *Benny*.' I throw myself onto the sofa, arms folded.

Ben puts himself on the sofa opposite me. 'Marns,' he whispers. 'You must see she's bonkers? She's gaslighting you.'

'*Gaslighting?* Listen to yourself. We're not in a Hitchcock.'

'Why are you spending time here? She's not the real Mansfield. Who is she? Schlap's patient?'

'She's not Schlap's patient, for the umpteenth time. You imagine everyone's mad. She's the real McCoy: Katherine fucking *Mansfield*.'

Ben gives me a look.

'What?' I say and tense at the thought Katherine and he may have discussed the nature of our friendship. 'Don't look at me like that. Why aren't you at work? Why are you here, spying on me, sticking your nose into my life?'

He sighs. 'I just—'

'Okay, shut up about that. Who's Benny B. Rubinstein?'

'Benjamin B. Rubinstein was a famous analyst.'

'Right.'

'From the *nineteenth* century.' His lips purse. He does the finger whirring again. 'She's 24-carat nuts.'

From the kitchen, Katherine says, 'Bit early, but vodka, any-one?'

Then, from a long way downstairs, eleven delicate clock tings sound: time for my session. I can't miss it. I need answers as to how Schlap's painting came to be in my house.

Schlap's painting!

I leap up and throw the blanket off the picture. 'Wait! Ben! Look!'

Ben indicates it with a desultory lift of one leg. 'What's that?'

'A painting.'

'I can see it's a painting, idiot. Where did you get it?'

It's strangely comforting, him calling me idiot.

'In our *house*. It was on the wall where Auntie Esther's cylinder painting usually hangs.' I stand back, enjoying the moment.

'The phallic one?' he says.

'Yeah, that.' I hadn't realised he finds it phallic, too. 'This one here belongs to Schlap. Isn't that *weird*? It was in his practice room, then it appeared suddenly on our wall, then guess what? I saw Perds another time just now and here you are having tea or vodka or whatever with *Katherine*.'

The sulphurous smell of a match and scarves of strong-smelling cigar smoke float through the room.

'Sorry!' Katherine is saying. 'Have to puff when stressed.'

'Marnie.' Ben's sighs are deeper now. 'You didn't find this painting hanging on our wall.'

This is un-fucking-believable. 'Fine. Where was it, then?'

'I don't know! You could have just taken it from Schlap's wall yourself.'

Katherine comes into the living room pulling on her cheroot, glass in hand. 'You darlings don't happen to know if—'

'I didn't!' I shout, but I'm growing tired of this game.

I sit down again. Fine, let Ben not believe me. Let him think I'm doolally. I don't care.

Katherine makes a snorting noise and undoes the buttons on the neck of her ruffled shirt. She looks into her drink. 'Not enough danged lemon.' She exits the room again.

Ben and I stare at the empty space she's left behind, then at one another.

I step closer. 'B,' I whisper. 'Look at her. Look at all of her stuff.'

He casts his eyes about the room.

'I'm not imagining this,' I insist. 'She might be a nutter, but then why would Schlap be housing her here? I mean, come *on*, you have to agree it's strange.'

'You know it's rude to whisper,' Katherine calls.

Ben scratches his head. I dare to hope I might be getting somewhere, but then his digital watch peeps the hour. If I'm not downstairs in two minutes, Schlap will cancel our session and that will be that.

I lift the painting into my arms and say, with as much dignity as I can muster, 'And if you'll excuse me, I have to attend my appointment now.'

By the time I reach the little red hall, Katherine's at my side, her approach so stealthy as to be almost physically impossible.

'Wait a *minute*, will you?' she says, taking my face in her hands and leaning towards me.

She plants a kiss full on my lips. Liquid heat radiates from my pelvis down through my legs. Ben is just in the next room, but my mouth opens to let her in. Her tongue is hot and wet and tastes of cigar smoke, booze and lemons.

'Come back soon?' She presses her palm against my crotch. 'I've missed you.'

'I will.'

I drag myself across the threshold of the door to the main landing, the throbbing between my legs unbearable, and lurch downstairs to my session.

On the way, my phone rings: it's Marcus Brown, the policeman. I flick it to silent and go to wait behind the William Morris curtain for my session.

'This was on the wall in my house,' I announce.

I've adopted the power pose in the centre of Schlap's room because I hope it'll give me more heft. Schlap is currently on his feet too, weight on one hip. He's wearing his serious face, the one I get at the beginning of each session after the moment of silence.

'But I've never seen this painting before. Most curious.' He looks at me, mouth twitching.

'It's not *curious*, it's spooky.' I scowl. 'You've forgotten it was on your wall because of your stroke.' I jab a finger at the canvas. 'It's even got your signature on it, see? That wasn't there before. That means *you* are the artist. And it's an actual solid thing. It was in my home. Touch it.'

He does.

'Hard evidence,' I say, with a flourish of my hand for emphasis.

'How odd.' He runs a finger over the painting. It's as if he thinks it contains secret text in Braille. 'Forgive me, but whose signature do you imagine was here before mine?'

'Your son's!' I'm practically shouting. 'Dashiell's! And look, what's that in the man's hand? A scroll!'

'The significance being?'

I roll my eyes. 'They're my *poems!*'

'What makes you think that?'

'Because ...' I realise that I haven't told him about Mum's Roman amphora-slash-planter and my scroll and the disappearing letters. 'It doesn't matter. Just, it wasn't a scroll before, it was a lure for the mouse. Something on string.'

Schlap takes a step closer to me. He cups one hand around my elbow. 'Marnie, are you sure you didn't paint this yourself and add in my signature?'

I bite my lip. 'Even if I had the talent, which I don't, at what point in the last week do you imagine I've had time to paint an oil—'

'Acrylic.'

'At what point would I have had ... How do you know it's acrylic?'

Panic in his eyes, or perhaps I'm projecting because he's smiling straight afterwards.

'I did an art degree.'

'I didn't know that.'

His smile evolves, as if going to art college was something he'd enjoyed and was enjoying remembering.

'Yes. Before I trained as a therapist.'

'Three whole years at art school?'

He nods.

'In theory, then, you could have painted this and forgotten.'

'I suppose.'

'Have you ever heard of a book,' I ask, swerving subjects wildly, 'called *Penis Envy and Other Bad Feelings* by Mari Ruti?'

'*Penis Envy and* ... what?' Schlap's eyes widen at the turn in conversation.

My phone vibrates in the pocket of my dress.

I put my hand up. 'Hang on.'

The screen says it's Faaris from Bethnal Green Working Men's Club.

The twins' party. Good God, I'd almost completely forgotten.

'Need to get that?' Schlap asks.

'It's not important. Well, it is, but not right now. What was it I was saying?'

Schlap inhales expansively. 'Shall we sit for a moment?'

'No,' I say. But I'm exhausted. Sitting is exactly what my body wants and I find myself falling back into the ergonomic chair, arms limp. 'Ben's upstairs with ... doesn't matter.'

'Upstairs? Where?'

'The third floor. He's come to check up on me, apparently, but what he really wants is to talk to you about me and check up on *you* while he's at it.'

Schlap scuffs his shoes on the carpet. 'And Ben is ... ?'

'Oh, *God*.' I stare, unseeing, at the window for a moment. 'I need to make sense of all this.'

'Yes.'

'What it signifies.'

He shakes his head. 'You said "my poems" about the paper in the hand of the person in the painting. What makes you think these are *your* poems, Marnie? Could they be the poems of another person, for instance?'

'Whose?'

'Katherine Mansfield's?'

I blow air through my nostrils. 'Yes, well, that's *exactly* what's been happening, as it turns out. I found some of Katherine's poems in my own poems folder on my phone, remember? Everything that's mine is disappearing. The police are involved.'

His heavy lids disappear into their sockets. 'The police? For missing poems?'

'Not for that.'

'What, then? Has somebody died?'

'No. Well, actually, lots of people have died, haven't they, in the past, but that's not what I mean. Do you remember when I said I'd seen some writing on Ben's desk? Writing that wasn't his?'

'Um ...'

'You've forgotten, but I did. You said I had cognitive bias and it was harmless and temporary. But it's neither harmless nor temporary, as it turns out. Weird stuff keeps happening and no one believes me. Though perhaps Vicar Pete might if I told him, because he believes in God, and trusts himself.'

'I see.' Schlap looks at me doubtfully.

'And now Ben's upstairs having tea with *Kass*!'

'Who's Kass, in this context?'

My body sags further into the chair. 'I don't *know*.' My ears begin to ring. I get an idea. 'Schlap, who was the woman who came to your house last Sunday when we were on the phone? Was it a woman who dresses in old-fashioned clothes?'

He seems confused. 'You mean my voluntary visitor?'

'Your ... ?'

'A volunteer who visits old people. She comes every Sunday.'

'Because you're lonely?'

'Of course. We're all lonely.' He smiles. 'But, really, she

more just helps with shopping, cleaning, things like that. It's extremely generous of her to give up her time.'

'Yes.'

'But in case you were wondering, she doesn't wear antique clothes. She wears modern attire and her name isn't Kass, it's Doctor Smith. She's a very busy woman.'

He's got to be fucking kidding me. 'Doctor *Smith*? Pronounced Smith but spelled Smythe?'

'That's the one: Nellie Smythe.' He nods. 'Do you know her? She's a doctor, among other things. She always wears these lovely shoes.'

I rise from my seat. 'I ...'

But my body doesn't want to take me anywhere and I come to rest in a static position over the low table by my side, eye to eye with the box of tissues.

'Marnie.' Schlap's tone is gentle. He sighs like Ben did upstairs and stands and looks out of the long sash window. 'You mustn't worry.'

I can't believe he's offering platitudes. 'My kids need me. I'm sick of people feeling sorry for me all the time. None of this makes sense.'

'Which part of life made sense to you before?'

'Before what?'

'Well, before things changed to not making sense.'

I stare at his chest, at his gently drooping pecs beneath the cashmere jumper, trying desperately to untangle what it is he's getting at.

Did things make sense before they didn't make sense? *Really* make sense? Perdita's death, my parents' conversion – in truth, the actions and objectives of pretty much anyone who isn't me – have always been a mystery. The making sense part is entirely subjective, like Mum said. If I were to convert to Christianity properly, for example, God would suddenly exist and I could relax and kick back knowing He was in charge. I'd like that. That, in particular, would make a lot of sense right now.

'There's too much dialogue,' I say.

Schlap asks what I mean.

'If my life were novelised, Veronica would complain about all the talking. In fact, Pantea warned me against this very thing earlier. She's Veronica's stand-in editor. I know, I didn't realise they existed either. Life, like art, doesn't need talk – it needs *action*.'

'Is that what you think?' he says.

'Definitely.'

With a renewed sense of energy, I gather myself up, roll my shoulders back and take a breath.

There are so many things to do: return upstairs to Ben and Katherine, call Marcus Brown and tell him my clothes are back, attend to the organising of the kids' party, go back home to check if Auntie Esther's painting has rematerialised, as Ben seems convinced it will have. But, most importantly, I have to locate Perdita *and pin her down*.

This is a lot for one person to achieve, but I have faith. I trust myself. So.

The wall clock pings. Impossibly, it's twelve already.

'When do I get to read out my list of things I loved about my sister? I've a few now.'

'Good,' he says. 'Have you enjoyed committing them to paper?'

'Sort of. Why? Is that important?'

'Perhaps.' He puts his hands in his pockets.

Inexplicably, I reach over to give him a hug. He doesn't hug me back but, equally, he doesn't recoil in horror or push me away.

'Thank you,' I whisper into his bicep.

'What are you thanking me for?'

'I don't know. I just feel like I love you. Not in a sexy way, like a family member. Like Vicar Pete, maybe.' I pull away and he smiles.

'Would you mind very much leaving the painting here for now?'

'Sure,' I say. 'It's yours anyway.'

I walk out of his office with a heightened sense of optimism, which is, in context, bizarre. I briefly entertain the idea I might be bipolar – this is, I suspect, what Ben suspects – but only briefly, because there are other more *optimistic* things to be achieved today and I intend to fulfil them all.

When I return to the third-floor apartment, I find Ben gone and drag Katherine into her bedroom, where we roll around on top of one another fully clothed, rubbing and grinding our pelvises together. We come at the same time, but I have a funny sort of orgasm – sudden, too small, as if I've tripped over myself. Katherine's is much noisier and more drawn-out and mine feels inadequate by comparison. I fear I should reassure her in some way that it's not her: I'm older and more tired, and all the other stuff that comes with ageing. She doesn't seem to care, though. We're staring at each other when it happens, her eyes full of greedy enjoyment, her face shiny and hot.

'No "dick" this time?' she says as we lie next to one another afterwards.

I hear the smile in her voice.

She puts her fingers inside herself and pulls out another little piece of white paper. 'Here you go.'

'Again?'

'Every time. What does it say?'

233

I read:

It is of immense importance to learn to laugh at ourselves.
                                                    Katherine Mansfield

'What's the significance of that, do you think?' I ask.

'I really couldn't tell you.'

I lie there wondering about my occasional penis, my sexuality and where all this leaves me. How does one define such a thing? And does one have to? It's my reality that's fluid.

'I can laugh at myself,' I say finally. 'In fact, I don't take myself nearly seriously enough.' I place the paper carefully on the bedspread.

I'm weightless, springy. I could float up off the Earth at any moment. A burning heat is rising from my ankles and I feel my face reddening.

There's something I urgently need to do before I do all the other things I need to do. I climb off the bed.

'Where are you going?'

'Nowhere. The living room.'

'Why?'

But I'm already there. I sit down at Katherine's dining table and take a breath.

I'm primed, pregnant with words. It's *now*. From my bag I pull out the notebook with my 'Things I Love About Perdita' list in it and write twenty poems longhand, just like that – *twenty*. I'm writing so fast my hand can hardly keep up and I find myself having to flex my wrist every few minutes to relieve the cramp. A poem about love, a poem about death, about a painting. A poem about a lonely shrink, about a mad woman who thinks she's a famous author who truly turns out to be the author, after all. A poem about non-non-binary sexuality. The letters are barely legible but they're *there*! I'm in danger of repeating the jug analogy here, so let's just say each one pours out.

Katherine enters and demands to know what I'm doing, but I'm so focused, she has to ask three times, apparently.

'Marnie, that's amazing!' I feel her breath on my shoulder as she leans over me.

She sits and writes a poem of her own. She pushes it over to me. It's called 'Loneliness' and it's really good.

'Have it,' she says. 'You can say it's yours if you like.'

'Thanks, but no.'

She claps me on the back and snatches my notebook from my hands before I can stop her.

I watch nervously as she reads. She's frowning, head bent over the paper. She looks up.

'They're *quite* good. This one ...' She reads a poem aloud, goes back to the others. Her eyes narrow. 'You write a lot of love poetry.'

'I suppose. I hadn't thought of them like that.'

I wait for her to say more.

'You think love poetry's adolescent, don't you?' I ask when she doesn't. 'You think it's immature and reductive.'

'No!'

I love the way she says 'no'. It sounds like 'now'.

'If you want to experience profound immaturity, read my collection of short stories, *In A German Pension*.' She chuckles softly to herself. 'I was angry. About the miscarriage. Anger is a good engine for art, but in this instance, it wasn't the—'

'Whoa-whoa-whoa.' My pen flies out of my fingers and spins across the table. 'Miscarriage? Wait, yes, I remember you had one.'

She gives me the side-eye. 'What do you mean, you remember?'

How to explain that I spent six months at school writing 4,000 words on her, that she has her own page on Wikipedia?

'Now listen.' She moves the notepad back under my nose. 'I categorically do *not* think love poetry lacks maturity: John Donne, Keats, Manley Hopkins. Wonderful love poets, all.'

'Well, Manley Hopkins was mostly writing about God, so.'

'Does that not count?' Katherine does her one eyebrow rising thing. 'Man or woman?'

'What? Oh. In my poem? Man.'

She's nodding now, as if her head is heavy.

'I'm don't think I'm queer, Kass. If I were in possession of my dream penis all the time, I *might* be queer, but strictly speaking, that would make me something else, wouldn't it?'

'What would it make you?'

'I don't actually know.'

'It's all so terribly complicated.' She stretches like a cat.

'My kids don't think so.' I pick up my pen and get back to work.

After a few moments, she says, 'You know it's normal to have fallow periods. Take 1908: fifteen months of nothing on my return to London.'

'Oh? Heartbreak?'

'No, because I was just having *such* a good time.'

I manage about three words on paper before she interrupts me yet again.

'You're not writing comedic poems, are you?' She waggles a finger at me. 'No one cares for comedy, Marnie. Comedy isn't *literary*.'

'You sound like Pantea.'

'Who?'

'Never mind.' I think of something else. 'What about literary comedy writing if you're culturally Jewish?'

'Especially not then,' she asserts. 'Unless you're American. Or your primary subject matter is *being* Jewish. British Jewish comic prose, that isn't about Jews, doesn't win prizes. British people, in particular the English literary community, don't generally have ears attuned for the tone. Do you understand?'

I nod.

'Don't be droll in your authorial endeavours.' She takes my hands in hers. 'Just promise if you ever venture into novels, you'll never pen a funny one.'

'I promise,' I say.

'Write something where not a lot happens. Use words like liminal, inchoate and priapic. Then we're talking.'

'Okay.' I go back to my poems.

When I've finished, I carefully take a photo of each one on my phone and ping them to Veronica's email.

There. Done. I feel amazing.

Then, with his usual terrible timing, Ben calls on my mobile. I don't answer. He leaves me a message saying he's bought two loaves of cholla and a pat of unsalted butter from the deli next to the Conran shop, as well as some ricotta ravioli from Lina Stores for dinner later. These are my favourite foods but re-remind me of how middle-class we are and this makes me even more annoyed. Also, him sucking up to me is an admission he knows he was in the wrong, turning up at Schlap's like that.

As soon as I've put the phone down, he rings again. Perhaps he's had an accident.

'What?'

'Marns,' he says. 'Where are you?'

Let him suffer.

'Marns, you there?'

'I'm still at Katherine's.' All at once, I feel guilty. 'I thought you might have done me the honour of waiting, seeing as how you're *so desperate* to discuss my problems with my analyst.'

'Sorry. I've been out buying more things for the twins' party. I'm in session with patients all afternoon.'

'You have? Why?'

'Marnie, it's in two days.'

'I know that. I thought we'd got all the necessaries in Flying ... Never mind. I'm about to go to Bethnal Green to sort it out.'

The twins' party is in *two days*. Good grief. Faaris will be waiting for me at the Working Men's Club. I leap out of my seat and race to grab my coat while Katherine looks on in mild amusement.

'Don't worry, Ben.' I jam the phone between my ear and my cheek. 'I'll go directly to Bethnal Green.'

'Why are you talking like Samuel Pepys?' he says.

'Because I'm *busy*.' I chuck the phone in my bag and race along the landing.

'Well, see you later, then.' Katherine's voice echoes down the stairs after me.

Time hasn't been my friend. I haven't been careful. I've nearly let the girls' biggest birthday celebration slip through my fingers.

I keep both eyes out for Perdita on the run back to my car. When I reach the NCP, the Volvo has gone. Perhaps it was never there.

The Bethnal Green Working Men's Club has an imposing brick facade that looks more like a Victorian swimming baths than a place in which to drink beer. Someone has graffitied *Liberté, Egalité, Beyoncé* on the side wall.

I climb the steps to the entrance and wait inside a small

vestibule on red-and-white checked tiles near the ticket office and wonder how to get hold of Faaris. It's eerily silent.

Faaris knows I'm coming because I texted him on my way. I've only ever been here at night, when it's buzzing and pink lit like a womb and the bass moves through the fabric of the building like a heartbeat. I say 'ever been', but actually it's exactly three times that I've come here and only as a teenager. After Perdita's accident and our cancelled birthday party, I never returned. Being here now, with memories of the two of us going in and out of the swing doors in badly cut dungarees, peeing in the two sinks in the toilets, the smell of our watermelon lip gloss, makes me wonder if Ben and I are out of our minds holding the twins' party in the same venue. Somebody terrible once said it's 'how the light gets in', but I fear we may be opening old wounds rather than healing them.

Faaris appears, like Mr Benn, from a little door in the fake wood wall. He's round with melting brown irises, about seventy, and wearing a multicoloured scarf that looks a bit like Mum's *Doctor Who* one. He smiles when he sees me.

'Marnie?'

He's wheezy.

'Finally, you've come!'

His greeting carries so much warmth that I grin with pleasure. 'Good to meet you.'

I hold my hand out but instead of shaking it, he grasps it between both of his hands and looks right into my eyes. His palms are hot.

'Meet you? But you've been here before, isn't it?'

'Oh. A long time ago. When I was seventeen. It was lovely.' I add the last part in case he thinks I didn't enjoy myself.

'Seventeen?' he says. 'But ... no matter.' He heads off through the set of double doors to the main room. 'Come, follow me, please.' He's smiling over his shoulder. 'Though you know your way around, my dear: once you've been here, you never forget, isn't it?'

The main room is lit by neon strips and looks much smaller than it did in the past, in the dark. The bar is lonely with no one waiting at it and everything smells of lager. At the far end is the small stage, with the same pink heart that's always been there, picked out in light bulbs on the back wall. I think of Perdita, cheering all those years ago, when Victor/Victoria removed her sparkling jumpsuit to reveal pubic hair shaved in the shape of the CND symbol.

Faaris says, 'I won't take much of your time. We have yoga starting here in thirty minutes.'

'Yoga?'

'It's most popular. The women who like to practice connect to a deeper sense of their own reality.' He makes a prayer with his hands in front of his chest.

'Right,' I say, wondering if this is something I should be doing.

Faaris smiles impishly. 'And yoga keeps their bodies flexible, isn't it?'

I picture thirty female bodies in scant clothing sweating heavily in this windowless room.

'Do you have other stuff here? Meditation, prayer meetings and so on?'

He seems surprised by the question, then pleased.

'We do, Marnie. Why do you ask? Would you like to join one?'

He's remembered my name after just one mention. I feel like crying.

'Faaris? Please tell me to mind my own business, but are you a Buddhist?'

'I am.'

'So,' I say. 'You believe in reincarnation?'

'I do.' He sits on a chair as if he's a witness in court and me the barrister and looks at me.

'So, in Buddhism, someone who's died could come back as someone, or something, else. Correct?'

'Correct.'

'But what about them coming back as *themselves*, just on a different astral plane?'

'Ah, but you're talking about a ghost. This is different to reincarnation.'

'And do Buddhists believe in ghosts?'

He pats my hand. 'Not so much. We believe in the negation of self, my dear. The spirit needs nothing. Accept this and life will flow around all obstacles.'

I tuck his words into my mental Filofax to compare later with Vicar Pete's Christianity. Earth to earth, ashes to ashes; it's not dissimilar.

'Now ...' He springs from the chair with surprising verve – it must be all the yoga – and pops behind the bar. 'I'll show you a list of the food we've confirmed with the caterer and we'll settle on the drinks you asked for. Okay?'

'Great.'

'Your girls are looking forward to their party?'

'Definitely.' I wonder if that's true now, what with everything going on, their being *so worried* about me and all.

He leans across the counter and hands me a sheet of paper. I stare at the list: poached salmon, coronation chicken, potato salad, pickled onions.

I look up. 'Ooh. No. This isn't right.'

His chin drops to his chest and he regards me from beneath thick grey-black lashes. 'What is it that you mean?'

'I'm so sorry, but this menu is like a jubilee wedding celebration at the WI, not one for a teenager's birthday.' I wave the paper like a flag.

Faaris giggles. 'I know. The chef said to me on the phone that you must have meant it in an ironic way.'

'Um, no. I mean, I love irony, but I don't look for it in catering. I ordered dhal, a chicken curry, rice and okra and a vegan curry option. You recommended the chef – your cousin Samia. Right?'

'I know my cousin Samia, but I don't remember you wanting her cooking. And you said Pimm's. And you instructed them to make the cake in the shape of two swans and they've done as you asked.'

'*Swans*? I asked for doughnuts! With vegan custard! And beer! Everyone in my family hates Pimm's. You've muddled me up with someone else.' I feel the heat of embarrassment climbing up my neck. 'Faaris, so sorry, but we've got to resolve this misunderstanding. The party is in two days.'

He tuts. 'But how are we supposed to change it all now? This was agreed by you many months ago, with your deposit. I thought it was an ... original choice, as you're saying now, but everybody has their predilections. And, after all,' he chuckles, 'it *is* you who's paying. Have already paid, in fact.'

'Already paid?'

'Yes! Two days ago.' He looks at my face then laughs. 'You can pay again if you like.'

'Sorry,' I say. 'I don't remember doing that.'

Have I paid and not realised? Perhaps I have two personalities inside me, perhaps I'm schizophrenic.

Or perhaps I'm in another dimension.

I start to shake. 'I'm going home to check my account. I'll call you straight away.'

I leave him at the bar and stumble into the daylight.

Pimm's? Swans? Coronation chicken?

I jump into the Prius and speed home. I'll have to log in to my bank on my laptop because my phone won't let me do it without a bloody app. God knows what Ben will make of it all. Perhaps my bank account will have disappeared, too. And all of my money. All ten quid.

I think again about Veronica, her insane ambitions for my work, and am about to dictate a text to her via Siri, when I go cold.

I'm about three to my end of her, then to your house, Bathurst to slap my shrink.

That's not what I'd meant to say to Katherine. Siri misheard me. Is it possible that my ears, like Siri's, have made the same mistake whilst listening to Veronica on the phone? What if she never said, '*That clinches you the laureate?*' What if it was: '*The printers are going to love that,*' or similar?

I can't even call her to find out, because she's on bloody holiday.

I swear to God, I think I pass Richard III-slash-Consultant Smythe-slash-volunteer Nellie on the way home, waiting in her lovely shoes at a bus stop, but I'm unable to pull over and verify this because there's no time. There's never any time.

I park up and switch off the ignition, which in a Prius sounds basically the same as the ignition when it's on and means I'm denied the lovely moment of peace offered by the killing of a petrol engine.

I look at our house. It appears to be empty. I'm glad.

Our bedroom window is open. I swear I closed them all

before leaving this morning. Perhaps Ben came back before going to work.

One of the living room curtains is closed. This, I know, I did *not* do. I get a funny fizzing feeling at the nape of my neck.

I wish Parker were here, but he's with the dog walker. He'd at least try to lick an intruder to death.

I climb from the car, unlock the boot, take one of Ben's fencing foils out of its bag and let myself in carefully.

'Hello?' I call softly to the empty space.

I dump my keys on the side table in the hall and wander through to the kitchen, holding the foil, my skin electric. The pistol grip feels strangely familiar in my hands.

'Anybody in?'

There's my laptop, waiting for me as usual, lid open on the table. I approach it and press the space bar. The screen lights up:

Pimm's x 150
Coronation chicken x 120 (Sophie plus twelve friends veggie)
Mum's hummus sandwiches
Trifle x 100 portions (Eton mess for the others)
Call Faaris at BGWMC re closing time
Call Samia re swan cake (check gluten-free plus heart-shape
     curve is correct, not like on the sample!)

At the bottom of the page it says:

NB: Grandpa away filming but back by eleven. Must remember
     not to tell girls – his surprise.

I stare at this for a long time, hairs rising along my arms. Some-one typed this list. Someone who isn't me.

There's a noise upstairs, tuneless humming in a male register – not Ben's – then heavy footsteps clomp down from the top floor.

Oh, *God*.

I'm frozen in front of the laptop, the foil dangling from my hand as whoever it is galumphs down the next flight to the hall. This someone will provide the explanation for the missing clothes, Ben's computer and the painting. It's too nonchalant an approach for a genuine burglar. Whoever it is, we'll be face to face any second.

I scrabble for my phone, but my hands are unsteady and I can't get any purchase. Instead, I dive under the kitchen table – a stupid move, because I'm now at a significant height disadvantage – and hold my breath.

On the other hand, I have the element of surprise.

'Dum-di-dum.' Footsteps cease in the hall.

Sweat breaks out on my forehead. He's on the move again towards me.

I throw my palms together: *Dear God, please keep me safe from harm. Amen.*

But the interloper heads into the loo under the stairs. A moment later, the familiar male stop-start sound of pee as it hits the back of the bowl. The loo flushes. The door opens. I try to hold my breath, before realising I'm already holding it.

The intruder enters the kitchen, head bowed. Now, he's right in front of me.

It's the dark-haired man from Schlap's waiting room – the one who looks like a younger Schlap.

My mouth hangs open. The doorbell rings. The man does a U-turn and goes out to the hall again. I scan my own kitchen for a superior hiding place but find none.

'Oh, hi,' I hear him say.

A woman's voice. 'One dog, bit grubby. He's had a great time running about with the others.'

'Hopefully he'll sleep for the rest of the day.' The man laughs.

'Yeah. I'll invoice you later, Dashiell. Okay?'

'Great, thanks,' says the ... *Dashiell*? Schlap's dead son's name?

And a female dog walker with ... Parker? Where's Ryan?

And now I come to think of it, how is our downstairs loo working?

'Come on, Barley. In you come, you dirty mutt.'

Barley?

The garden.

In less than a second, I've raced out from under the table and through the back doors to hide among the flowers. The scritch-scratch of a dog's claws in the hallway.

Through the foliage, I have a narrow sliver of sight back to the house.

Parker enters the kitchen, nose aloft. He sniffs me out instantly and runs to join me, greeting me with his usual unreserved level of enthusiasm. I push down on his head while he licks my leg, and whisper for him to be quiet.

Dashiell is heading straight for my hiding place. I leap out, raise the foil and adopt a fencing stance.

'Goodness,' he says, not quite meeting my eye. Perhaps he's frightened, too. 'What are you doing out here?'

'Come any closer and I'll use this,' I say. 'Who are you? This is *my* house. My partner will be home any minute. Get out.'

The dog whines. Dashiell smiles a genuine smile, not the kind one might make if one had malign intentions.

'I'm not going to hurt you,' he says, still not looking fully at me. 'You may as well come inside.'

'Inside?' My voice is extremely high. 'I'm calling the police.' I try for my phone again, but my hand is properly trembling now.

'Okay.' He leaves me there and heads back into the house.

Parker gives me a look and trots after him.

I have the sensation I'm floating in space, like one of those astronauts without a tether.

I see Dashiell putting a bowl of water on the floor for the dog. 'Here you go.'

Could this man be a ghost? Schlap said Dashiell died when he was forty. And if he *is* a ghost, does he imagine he lives here? It would mean, for him, there's a strange woman in *his* house, and for me, well, I've seen him before in Schlap's waiting area.

Or have I jumped, yet again, to another quantum plane? If that's the case, why can't he see me?

I grip the foil tightly in my hands. Real or not, I'm going to put a stop to this right now.

I stride into the kitchen, affecting confidence. 'What are you doing here?' I wave my phone at him, my hands suddenly be-having themselves, and dial 999. 'What do you want? Do you have a message for me from the other side? Are you Schlap's son?'

Dashiell pulls out *his* mobile and also dials a number.

Now, a mobile isn't a particularly ghostly item. Furthermore, he's able to *touch* objects that I'm touching here, in my home: the dog bowl, the worktop et cetera.

'Calling the police, too?' I say, my voice clipped like a 1930's schoolteacher, goodness knows why. 'It's not a competition.' I raise the foil again.

Parker comes to sit on my feet.

'Sorry, buddy,' Dashiell says without looking up. 'I've just got to do this one thing and I'm all yours.'

247

The emergency line is ringing at the other end of my mobile.

Dashiell puts his back to me. 'P?' he's saying into his phone. 'Yo. When you . . . ? Oh, cool, five minutes. See you then.' He turns to face Parker and me. 'P will be home in five.'

'P?' I say. 'Who's P?'

'Emergency. Which service do you require?' says a woman in my ear.

'Police,' I whisper.

There's the bleeping sound of call waiting on my phone. I pull it away from my face: Faaris. Faaris from Bethnal Green is calling. He'll have to wait.

'Police. What's the address of the emergency?'

'It's 41 Larkspur Street, N1 5RD. There's an intruder in my house! Hurry!'

'Where are you now, ma'am?'

'In my kitchen.'

'Can you see the intruder?'

'Yes, he's right in front of me. He's been on his phone speaking to someone called P.'

'On his *phone*? Has he threatened you?'

'Not yet.'

'Try to leave the premises and if you can't, sit tight. We'll stay on the line.'

'No, don't stay on the line. I've got a foil in my hand. I need at least one hand free in case he does threaten me.'

'You have foil in your hand?' says the operator.

'No. *A* foil. Hurry up!'

'Is this a prank call? Please clarify what you mean by "a foil"?'

'A sword, but—'

'A *sword*?' There's some urgent murmuring in the background. 'A sword is an offensive weapon. Ma'am, I must ask you to remain where you are. We're on our way.' The call ends.

Great, now they think *I'm* the criminal.

Dashiell's response to all this is to do nothing. I brandish the foil afresh.

'Did you hear that? The police are on their way.'

Yes okay they're coming for us both, but Dashiell doesn't know that. Besides, once they arrive I can explain myself. Dashiell will have no such defence.

My phone rings: Faaris again.

Dashiell's phone rings. It's like standing in Carphone Warehouse.

'Dashiell Schlapoberstein speaking.' A pause. 'Mmm. Mmm.' He turns away. It sounds like work.

I answer my phone, keeping my eyes on Dashiell at all times.

'Faaris?'

'Marnie?'

It sounds urgent.

Dashiell is absorbed in conversation.

'What is it, Faaris?' I say. 'You'll have to be quick. I'm in a situation.'

'I checked our bank records when you left. Now, I know this is going to sound odd, but have you an identical twin?'

I nearly drop the phone. 'Had. She died.'

There's a drawing-in of breath at the other end.

'I'm so sorry. Maybe it is your cousin, then. She looked exactly like you when she came by. That's why I was so confused when you said you'd not been here since you were seventeen. I realised after you left that *she* was the one who paid for your daughters' party and not you. Perdita Rose is her name. She paid the full amount.'

'That isn't possible,' I say. 'That can't ...'

At that moment, the front door slams. Parker bounds out to the hall and Perdita's voice calls, 'I'm home!'

Things I Loved About My Sister: Part 10

As young children, I'd always longed for a kitten and Perds had always longed for a puppy. When we were thirteen, Mum and Dad finally capitulated and said we could choose one or the other, but not both.

Perds and I argued and argued about who would get the final word and, in the end, decided to toss a coin. Now, I had a special trick coin from a magic set I'd been given years before where both sides were heads and Perdita, fortunately, entirely seemed to have forgotten about it.

She and I sat at the table in the narrow kitchen in our old Kentish Town house, me with the double-headed coin clutched in my palm, not feeling remotely guilty, and Perds all innocent and none the wiser as I 'won' and got my wish. Perds was the most gracious of losers.

We chose a kitten from our neighbour who was giving away a whole litter for free – a sweet and goofy marmalade with massive ears we named Keith – and that was that.

In the two years that followed, I did get the occasional twinge when Keith wrecked yet another of Perdita's woollen jumpers or chewed through her shoes, but mostly I conveniently wiped my heinous deception from my mind.

Aged fifteen, Perdita and I decided it was time to spring-clean our room. Of course, these things have a way of coming back to bite you on the bum: she discovered my two-headed coin lurking in a drawer.

It took only three seconds for her to put two and two

together. She was understandably furious, threw the coin at my head and shouted at me to fuck off. I was contrite but would keep coming back into the bedroom, holding Keith up to her face, laying his little white sock paws on her cheek while saying, 'Look how cute I am,' in a kitten voice, which was no doubt monumentally annoying. But she was such a good sport that on the third go, she started laughing. Then I started laughing, too. Then Keith vomited on my feet and we *really* laughed.

And that was that: she never mentioned it again. She never brought it up in an argument or held it against me. Never.

Keith lived to be nineteen. Older than my sister. I think that might be why we have Parker. It's my way of saying sorry.

Chapter 11

My identical twin stands in front of me, in my kitchen doorway, looking old – well, my age – and still beautiful.

My mouth opens and closes but no sound comes out.

She's slim, in blue jeans and loafers and a stripy Breton top,
and my heart aches just to be able to say these words in my
head: Breton top, loafers. There's a pair of sunglasses pushed
up on her head. Her lips are wide and curling and her teeth
are straight and much whiter than mine. Her skin is dewy and
rosy at the cheeks and there's a pimple on her chin, which
she's tried to cover with make-up. She doesn't seem ghostly
but solid, real, and I don't feel at all scared.

I close my eyes. When I open them again, Perdita and
Dashiell are still there.

She hasn't spotted me standing in the corner because her
eyes are on the man who appears to be her partner in this other
world, and who, when the police arrive, is probably going to
be arrested.

Parker sits at my side, tongue lolling.

'Sorry, darling,' Perdita is saying, eyes crinkling.

She has crow's feet: they're very attractive.

'What was supposed to be a five-minute meeting with the
seven clients from Andorra went way over. One of them

downed a whole Chablis in half an hour. Who would have thought vultures involved so much boozing?'

Vultures? I do hope she works with birds. I'm not keen on the other option.

'Booze at lunch always sounds glamorous to me,' Dashiell laughs.

Why isn't he telling her about my phone call to the police?

'While I have your attention, Mrs Success, could you please explain what's happened to Dad's painting?'

'What?' She pushes her top lip up to meet her nose.

I remember that! I remember her doing exactly that – if she didn't believe you or thought what you'd said was silly.

'And it's *Ms* Success to you.'

This is *extraordinary*.

'Dad's painting has gone and there's some weird phallic charcoal drawing of cylinders in its place. Black frame, white paper.'

'Never seen it.'

'Odd. Must be one of Wills'. I'll check with him after school.'

The reappearance of Ben's aunt's painting. It's back in the house. This proves something. I don't know what.

Also: *Wills*. They have a son. He has a royal name.

Perdita runs her hands through her hair. 'Got to take a shower. Dreadfully sweaty in that meeting. Better look over my speech for tomorrow and final confirmations for Saturday with Faaris.'

It could be the same Faaris. Faaris and Perdita and I are connected across worlds. Or universes. She *is* alive in another dimension. She has to be.

Dashiell's saying, 'What time d'you have to be at the school tomoz?'

'Ten a.m. Big day.' She rolls her eyes. 'Speeches. The twins' party. Why does everything have to come at once? There's never enough time. I'd love to stand still, just for a moment.'

Those are my words. She's saying things I say.

'Also,' she continues, 'have you heard the rumour? About a sixth wave? Back into lockdown. Ugh.'

Dashiell looks aghast. He leans on the kitchen worktop. '*Again*? How's the country going to cope with another?'

'Yeah.' Perdita sighs hard and shakes her head. 'I mean, just a rumour at the moment, but better fish your mask out of the cupboard.'

Sixth wave? Mask? Lockdown? I have absolutely no idea what either of them are talking about.

Dashiell groans. 'Homeschooling? Jesus.' He fills the kettle. 'The twins will go nuts.'

'Don't mention it until we know,' Perds says.

The *twins*: that's who Dashiell was talking about on the phone in Schlap's waiting room. Not boys but girls, like my twins. Ethereal twin girls, similar to those in *The Shining*. I remember, too, Dashiell mentioned swans – of course, the *cake*!

Perdita's about to leave the room. This is my chance.

I step out of the corner into the middle of the kitchen, Parker close by my side. He's whining.

'Perds?' I say, suddenly shy. 'Perds? It's me. Are you a ghost or real? Or in another world? It's Marnie.'

Perdita stops moving and spins round towards me, arms wide. She's laughing, not looking at my face but somewhere around my knees.

'You're back!' she cries. 'I knew it was you. I knew you were here!'

I run towards her, to embrace my lovely shadow sister, but I've forgotten I'm holding the foil and, as my arms rise, the sword points right at her. Before I can stop myself, the foil has gone into her face, right through her and out the other side. I scream and fall backwards. The foil drops to the floor with a clatter.

'Barley!'

My sister's standing in exactly the same place, still with the big smile on her face, distinctly un-impaled and very much 'alive', whatever that means in this context. Parker jumps as high as her head and covers her in kisses.

'There you are, my boy!' Her arms go around the dog.

'Perds,' I say again.

How is something solid in my world simply ether in hers? She's busy fussing over Parker. I get to my feet.

'Perds!'

I shouted that. She looks up suddenly.

'What?'

'Over here!' I bellow, wave my arms.

'Hmm?' Dashiell is watching the kettle boil.

'Did you say something?' Perdita asks.

'Yes!' I yell. 'Over here!'

'No,' says Dashiell.

'Weird. I thought I heard someone calling my name,' Perdita says.

He turns to face her. 'Wasn't me.'

'It sounded like a woman.' She sighs. 'It sounded like Marns.'

'Because it *is* me!' I jump up and down. 'You're a ghost, Perds! Or from another world, I don't know which, but you don't realise we're in the same *room*! This is a once-in-a-lifetime experience and you have to wake up and see it, see me!'

I run to her, throw my arms around her neck properly this time, but still there's nothing but air. I close my eyes and stay like this, pretending we're truly hugging, holding my own elbows. It feels gorgeous and deeply lonely. This is what it would have been like if she'd stayed alive. This is what we could have done every single day.

God really does exist. He's brought her back just for me.

When I pull away, Perdita's eyes are closed and her head has inclined slightly, unknowingly resting in my embrace. She rubs her neck, fans her face, which is all red and cross-looking.

'Phoo, having another flush.'

'Sure it's not just the results of the lunchtime booze?' Dashiell says.

'Definitely not. Hormones. I'm hearing my sister's voice. Ha. It's all part of the change. The madness.'

You're not mad, Perds, I long to tell her. No madder than I.

I realise, with alarm, that I must call emergency services immediately and tell them not to come. Thank God the police no longer have the resources for rapid response. If there really had been a violent intruder, I might have been dead by now.

'You all right?' says Dashiell.

'Yeah,' Perdita and I say in unison.

'You're not mad,' he says, echoing my sentiments. 'You're lovely.'

'I miss her a lot today,' she says. I wonder where she thinks I've gone.

'Oh, baby,' he says.

Dashiell is the kind of man who tells his wife she's lovely and calls her baby. She *is* lovely. I want to swallow her whole.

'I don't want to embarrass the twins in front of their friends.' She walks into the hall, making a 'brr' shaking-it-off sound. 'Another lockdown, God. It'll kill the City. Going to take that shower.'

Her footsteps on the stairs. Parker and I follow. I don't really feel the treads beneath my feet; that's how high I am right now. I mustn't let my sister out of my sight.

She said a shower. I wonder if real water will come out of my taps. Perhaps there's a whole spectral universe of banal household items out there. I get tingles to think of it.

She reaches the bathroom door and slams it closed in my face, which feels rude, even though I understand why. I put my hand out to push it open.

My arm goes *right through the door.*

Now hang on. A moment ago, Dashiell and I were in the same room together, able to touch the same things, feel the same things. Then Perdita showed up. Now, I can't do either. Have I become the ghost? Is this how quantum physics works?

Perdita's in the shower. I'm going to watch her.

Parker's eyes follow my foot as it passes through the bathroom door. His head dips to one side and his ears prick up.

My phone rings. I pull my foot out from the door. No caller ID. It'll be the police. Oh, God, I've forgotten to call them.

'Hello?'

'Ma'am, are you still at the address? If you have the sword, I must ask you to put it down and step back. The car is less than two minutes away.'

'No. Wait. I thought there was an intruder in my house, but it turns out it's my brother-in-law.'

There's a pause on the other end of the line.

'Your *brother*-in-law?'

'Yes. I'd like to cancel the car, please. I'm very sorry.'

'We can't do that I'm afraid, my love.' Her voice has gone strangely gentle. 'You've mentioned you are in possession of an offensive weapon.'

'No!' I hiss. 'Your colleague got it wrong. I said, a *foil*: a fencing sword with a rubber tip that one doesn't need a license for. I was using it as a defence in case my brother-in-law was the burglar I originally imagined him to be. But he's not and

257

it's okay.' I can't resist adding, 'My sister's here now and she's having a shower.'

The woman breathes out. 'Do you know how many hours we waste fielding prank calls? They cost lives. You may receive a—'

I terminate the conversation and pray the police don't ring back. I don't deserve a fine.

The shower has been switched off. Perds has been too quick to wash and I've missed it. She throws the door open. She's wrapped in a towel. She walks right through me, which makes me feel hot and cold, and goes into the bedroom. *My* bedroom.

Parker and I stand in the doorway watching her dress. Her body's in great shape. Her boobs are firm. There are two creases either side of her back, where her ribs meet her waist. Her bottom has some pimples near her thighs. There's what appears to be a faint birthmark around her coccyx, which I don't remember when she was young, alive. Perhaps it's a scar.

She sneezes and says, 'Fucking dust.' It makes me smile.

My eyes fix on something sitting on the bedside table: the *Penis Envy* book by Mari Ruti. It's right there, bold as you like.

'You coming down, P?' Dashiell shouts.

'Yeah. Just a minute.' She looks up and catches Parker in the doorway. 'Hey!' she giggles. 'Stop staring. Go downstairs, Barley. Down. *Stairs.*'

She closes the door in my face. I'm left outside on the landing, Parker next to me. The door opens again.

'I said, down!'

I go downstairs. It's the only way Parker will do as he's told.

Dashiell is opening our snacks cupboard and bringing out the little Tupperware without the lid, which miraculously appears to have refilled itself with cashews. He tips a handful into his palm and throws them at his mouth. Parker sits at my feet. He places one paw delicately on my foot like a Regency lady.

My phone rings. It's Sylvia. I answer it freely and without hesitation.

'Yes, love?'

'Mum?' Sylvia says. 'Blythe says Pantea isn't coming to the party now because they've fallen out again.'

'Right.' I long to exist only in the event horizon of my daughters' cosy concerns.

'So, tell her it's not okay, Mum.'

I hear Blythe's voice arguing with her in the background. The dog barks.

'Hi, Parker!' she calls.

I stare down at Parker's large brown eyes.

'Quiet, Barley.' Dashiell has his mouth full of nuts. 'Oh, look, he's got his paw in the air!'

'Where are you?' I hear suspicion in Sylvia's voice.

'At home.'

'I heard voices.'

'It's the TV.'

'Okaythenthat'sgreat,' she says.

'*When* will you two stop running the words all together like that?' I snap.

There's a pause at the other end.

'Riiight. We'll see you back home after clubs. And then you can tell Blythe that Pantea *is* coming.'

'No! Don't come home after clubs!' The words are out before I can send them back.

'What? Why not?'

How to explain that Perdita will disappear once the kids arrive, that they'll tell me I'm imagining it, then become more worried?

'Just ... Go to the park or something for a bit, okay? Phone Stan and tell him to do the same. Come back after six.'

'I'm calling Dad.'

She hangs up before I can say she'd definitely better not do *that*.

The girls won't go to the park after clubs now, of course. Once they've phoned Ben – who, mercifully, is with patients until 5 p.m. – he'll agree I'm being weird, they'll race to pick up Stan and it won't be long before the whole family piles through our front door. My sister and Dashiell won't hang around once they arrive, of this I'm sure. I calculate I have max three hours before this happens.

Dashiell has finished the cashews. His head is in the fridge. I stand shoulder to shoulder with him and look inside: a half-empty bottle of Prosecco with a spoon in its neck, a jar of mayonnaise, three apples and something square wrapped in a white plastic bag.

'It's going to be takeaway tonight!' Dashiell yells.

'Okay!' Perdita shouts back.

My phone rings again. It's Ben: Sylvia must have caught him on a break. I don't answer. He couldn't possibly understand. He's never lost anyone, not even a grandparent.

I fold onto a kitchen chair, except of course I can't feel the chair beneath me at all. It's as if I'm floating in mid-air – an unnerving sensation. Parker drops to the floor and rolls on his back. I tickle his belly and his hind leg does that funny back-and-forth thing.

'Looks like it's you and me, old boy,' I whisper.

'Looks like Barley's got fleas again,' Dashiell says as Perdita comes back into the kitchen in a leopard-print onesie.

★

For the remainder of my time here, I sit – or rather, hover – in the kitchen marvelling at the comings and goings of my phantom twin and her husband, their feet continually passing through the fencing foil that lies on the floor, their brief companionable silences, their momentary exchanges: 'Hot again today,' or 'Can't believe it's four already,' or 'Taking the dog out in fifteen.'

I'm tense, primed for the arrival of my own family at any moment, yet dreaming of all the instances in which Perds and I sat in our bedroom reading glossy magazines, not talking for hours on end.

Dashiell spends some time upstairs writing analysts' notes about patients in Ben's study. I know this because at one point he calls down, 'Why is it so hard for an analyst to write notes about patients?' And Perdita replies, 'Hmm, don't know.' She's concentrating on her own work.

Strange that Dashiell is also an analyst, like Ben. And Schlap. It could be a sign, a symbol. Of what, I can't tell.

I haven't moved from the chair. I don't want to miss a second of these precious moments.

Perdita types at the kitchen table – on *my* laptop, hair falling round her face, shoulders hunched, that familiar line through her forehead, so exactly like mine. When she's deep in concentration, her tongue sticks out of the side of her mouth, which used to happen every time we'd revise. Now and then she talks to herself, 'Oh, for God's sake, *really?*' and, 'Risky, Justin,' and 'Way too bearish. Philistines.'

I talk back to her. Tell her variously, 'I love you,' 'I need you,' 'You have a mark on your onesie by your right thigh – it looks like toothpaste,' and 'I miss you.'

She lets out a great deal of her familiar sighs, the ones just like Sylvia's. I keep absolutely still in case I break this spell.

At one point, she goes for a pee. Feeling like a criminal, I scoot round to look at the laptop screen – two windows are open: an Excel spreadsheet with little boxes stuffed with strings of numbers and a report on 'East African bond viability and risk'. My sister's definitely not a bird wrangler. I try not to think about it.

After some time – it must be at least another twenty minutes, because the sun has done its usual disappearing act behind the cherry tree in the garden – the front door goes and young voices fill the hall. I freeze in case it's my kids, but Perdita's face breaks a smile as she turns an ear towards the sound.

'Because I don't want him there,' a girl with a posh voice is saying.

'Why not?'

A boy – is it Wills? – posher.

'Duh. Because it's my party and—'

'Our party, Soph.'

Another girl. Or it could be the same one? The voice sounds identical, though it's hardly likely she'd be interrupting herself.

Identical voices. Identical twins. Perdita's.

'Because it's *our* party, Wills,' continues one or other of the female voices. 'And Cal will be following Lydia around like a wet blanket and Billy told me Lydia doesn't like it. You're not supposed to know that, by the way – it's a secret.'

'Cal's my buddy,' says Wills. 'And it's not his fault Lydia's hot.'

'He's not coming.'

'Hashtag MeToo.' Wills flops into the kitchen heavy-footed, looking just like Stan, except that Wills is blond and wearing the uniform of UCS private school. He dives into a cupboard and pulls out a packet of Hula Hoops and begins to crunch them noisily at the breakfast table.

'Don't quote *Me Too* at us erroneously,' says the same female voice.

The girls traipse in after him and my breath catches in my throat. Perdita's twins. They're so like my girls, right down to the hair and the height. Same-same yet different. I can't tell them apart. They're in the uniform of Perdita's and my old school on Harley Street.

Wills says, 'Men have rights.'

One twin says, 'You're not a man. Yet.'

'I was last time I looked,' mumbles Wills.

Heat spreads across my scalp. My twin nieces and my nephew. At ghostly quantum private school. Ghostly quantum Tories. Ugh. I love them instantly.

'Hi, Mum,' says Soph, or maybe it's the other one. She dumps a bag on the table.

Perdita frowns. 'Cass, whatever's in that?'

Cass. Kass. How odd.

Cass turns the bag upside down and empties the contents.

'Ta da!'

Packet after packet of red, white and blue balloons.

'Jubileee!' she trills.

They all laugh.

'For our party!' the other twin chimes.

'Brilliant!' says Perdita.

Their party? Their *birthday* party? Of course! A jingoistic birthday bash. A neat reflection of Blythe and Sylvia's. My girls' party, in the real world, not this parallel one, will be entirely different, of course, in spite of Faaris' misgivings about the catering.

Wills crushes his empty packet of crisps in one hand and aims it into the open bin. 'Yesss!'

'We're ordering curry for dinner. Your dad forgot to go to Waitrose,' Perdita says.

'Accha, Thik Hai, maaaate,' says Wills in an offensive and generalised rendering of an Indian accent.

'Wills,' says Cass or Soph quickly. 'That's racist.'

'If I speak another *language* in an attempt at the correct accent, I'm *not* being racist. Would you say that if I was speaking French? No, you wouldn't.'

'That's different,' says the other twin.

'How? Anyway, Bahman in Year 9 is part of our crew.' He does a two-finger gang sign and pimp rolls to the fridge. I watch as his foot drags through Ben's abandoned fencing foil.

'Bahman's *Iranian*, stupid,' says one twin. 'And you added the word "mate" at the end, which is not as I understand it, another language.'

And the other twin says, 'It's the context, Wills. It's called cultural appropriation. Mum, Wills asked if Putin was a homosexual this morning for, like, no reason.'

'I think our little brother here might be transphobic too,' finishes her sister.

'What?' Wills says, smartly. 'I am *not*. What's for dinner? I'm starving.' He's practically standing in the fridge.

Someone groans. I think it's Soph.

'Haven't you been listening?'

The other twin says, 'That's what Mum's been talking about, idiot: *curry*.'

'Oh, yeah.'

Wills picks up his bag and leaves the room. The thump of his feet on the stairs. A door slams.

He's so like Stan, I think again, except for the hair, the uniform and the racism. I suddenly miss my own children very much but at the same time have no wish to see them. This is the first time I've ever felt this way. They'll be here soon, anyway. I won't be able to explain any of this. I look at my sister and make a decision.

Parker whines and licks my hand. I ruffle the top of his head.

'Something's wrong with Barley,' says Cass or Soph, pulling a laptop from her school bag and laying it beside a load of text-books on the table. She sits in the one spare seat. 'Is it normal for him to lick a chair?'

Perdita sighs. 'I think the spectrum of what's normal is broad when it comes to dogs; he's been doing it all day.'

'Maybe it has leftover sausage juice on it,' says the other twin, laying yet another computer and pile of books next to her sister's.

I'm too slow to get out of the way and she sits in my lap. Into and *through it*. I keep absolutely still, my body rigid. She's not on my knee – she's sitting *inside my legs*.

I tell myself to relax. The sensation of her on me, in me, is a whisper of a feeling, like a caress, a gentle energy pulsing up and down my body. It makes me wonder if she can feel it, too.

'Ugh. This chair leg's covered in Barley slobber.' My niece's head dips towards her screen.

I try to put my hands on her waist, but I look completely stupid, even to my own eyes, holding on to nothing.

I get to my feet, rising up through Cass or Soph, and make my way round the table to my sister. I hover over her, pretend to lay my head against her shoulder as she makes small talk to the girls. I imagine her voice vibrating against my skull from her back, gently lulling.

A poem. A new poem for my sister. It's:

> *You crease me*
> *The spine of my favourite book*
> *Sit on my hands for you*

I'm falling. A different kind of falling. Falling down a well. Through a hot and open mouth.

I fall with my head still on Perdita's shoulder, the three ghostly women beside me, or myself the ghost in their world, the silence punctuated only by the clicking of fingers on keyboards. I'm losing something and I don't give a damn.

Time passes. I'm not sure how long. Perhaps half an hour. The doorbell rings and footsteps race along the hall.

'First!'

It's Wills.

'Get out of the way, moron. I've got the cash from Pops.'

The clink of change and a new voice says, 'Thank you very much.'

The curry. It's six already. My kids, Ben, will be home soon, *worrying*.

The door slams. The rustling of plastic as feet run back along the hall to the kitchen.

I watch Perdita's family from my position at the table.

'Bhuna's mine!' says Cass, or Soph, dumping the bags on the worktop and ripping open the foil casings.

Wills is saying, 'Who ordered Peshwari naan? *Almonds*: hello? My EpiPen's out of date; you could have *killed* me.'

'We got it so you didn't hoff the lot.'

'I won't be "hoffing" any, whatever that means.'

'Exactly.'

Dashiell comes downstairs. I move out of the way to allow my sister's family to assemble at the table. They help themselves to the cartons of takeaway. One of the twins asks why everything has meat in it and Perdita has her mouth full while speaking. I love her for that.

This is my sister's normality. Her life passing in a pleasant, uncomplicated stream of this-then-that. What a privilege to bear witness. My hands long to rise and meet one another, to thank God properly for giving me this chance, but it's time to leave. I have no doubt my own family, once they arrive, will find this house empty. I have a plan: I'll be at Katherine's. And Perdita, well ...

I step back from the table, put my palm flat to the wall as I go to steady myself. Except the wall has other ideas and my hand goes right through it. I stare at my wrist, buried in the brickwork. I twist it one way and the other: can't feel a thing. I look at Perdita and her family one last time, the food disappearing with alarming speed. Wills is laughing at something Dashiell's doing with a pot of chutney. The girls are secretly feeding the dog under the table. Only Parker notices my departure.

I leave the car outside our house and take the tube back into town. I sit on the Northern Line and think about quantum physics and what it means to be alive, to be *real*.

I know nothing about anything. Absolutely nothing.

Things I Loved About My Sister: Part 11

This is the hardest one to write.

It was a hot summer, our eighteenth birthday fast approaching, our own party at the Bethnal Green Working Men's Club in just three days. Mum and Dad had done a ton of organising: the food, drink, the DJ, booked Victor/Victoria with her CND pubic hair for the cabaret. My sister and I had been responsible for the guest list, navigated disagreements around the presence of a few individuals, but on the whole, things had been harmonious. We'd just finished our A levels. It was all coming together. Life beckoned. We couldn't know exactly what the future held, but we could feel it right there at the tips of our fingers. We just had to reach out and grab it.

Perdita had chosen, inexplicably, to take photography A level along with her three science subjects. She'd spent the previous twelve months snapping trees and vegetation, as if no one had ever seen a wilting snowdrop or dead earthworm on a sodden path. She'd used her excellent vintage Leica, until it had broken irrevocably when her friend had come over and accidentally knocked it into a sinkful of water. The replacement camera she'd hastily been given had been cheap and took shiny, non-atmospheric snaps.

Her end-of-year project had been something involving the unstable nature of time. The concept was sound, but the execution lacked a certain something thanks to the poor lens quality. I'd allowed her to borrow my second-hand camera – not as good as the Leica, but far superior to her new cheap camera – to improve matters and had been nagging her to return it ever since. I needed it for the party, I told her, to capture our memories in all their chromatic splendour. She'd keep forgetting it, though – left it in the darkroom at school. It was so unlike her.

On the Wednesday, feeling guilty, she'd finally returned to Harley Street to pick my camera up while I stayed at home in my pyjamas, chatting on the house phone to friends.

Two hours and seventeen minutes later, we got the call. I'd been the one who answered the phone. Dad, still an actor at the time, had been out at an audition for a film, Mum had been throwing some pot. She and I had raced to UCH in a cab, but we'd been too late.

Dead at the scene, they told us. Mum had been the one to identify the body. I couldn't bear to see. I didn't want to witness her broken, damaged face.

The police had interviewed us later: no suspect, they'd said, they'd do their best to track the person down. We didn't care about that. We just wanted her back.

I slept in her room, in her bed, that night. The pillow smelled of her. I held on to her pyjamas and felt that I, too, had died.

Chapter 12

As soon as I'm out at Oxford Circus, I ring Katherine on the mobile she claims Ben bought for her.

'I'm coming to stay,' I say. 'I need your help. For tomorrow morning. It's very important.'

'Absolutely,' she says.

No questions. I'm grateful.

I text Ben explaining that I'm going to stay at a hotel – a lie, obviously – as I need space to think, and ask him to send my love to the kids and that:

NO ONE needs to worry

He calls immediately. I don't answer. I text back:

Which part of 'I need space' do you not understand?

I weave through Great Castle Street, past that strange pub that plays host to people who work in John Lewis drinking inside it, and cross onto Margaret Street. I feel light of foot and slightly high.

The moment feels oddly separate, unstitched from the patchwork of my life, and I wonder if I'm dreaming until Ben calls again, then again.

On the fourth go, I pick up. 'Yes?'

'Marns, why are you lying?'

'I beg your pardon?'

'I've just done Find Your iPhone. You're in Cavendish Square.'

'Find *My* iPhone. At least get the name right. And how dare you!'

Honestly, though, I don't care. I've got a plan. Ben isn't a part of it.

'You're going to stay at Katherine's, aren't you?'

'It's none of your business, but if you must know, yes.'

There's a crackling sound at the other end. Stan comes on the line.

'Mum?'

'Hey, darling!' I'm inappropriately cheery.

'Are you okay? Dad says you're going to stay with this woman who's, like, mad. How's she your friend? He said she wears this dress that's from the Middle Ages and she talks about stuff in a stupid accent.'

'Stanley, I'm going to stay with a very nice, very normal' – oh, the lies – 'new friend I met recently. She's a writer like me. She's from New Zealand.'

'When you coming home?'

'Soon, love. Tomorrow. Can you put Daddy back on?'

'Dad, Mum wants to talk to you again.' Stan sounds sad.

'Marns—'

'Ben, you complete Judas.' I end the call and switch off the phone.

Then I'm ringing Katherine's bell and she's answering and I'm explaining my plan and telling her that my kids want to meet her, which isn't true, and she's saying, 'Kids? Really? I never know what to do with kids,' and I'm slapping her on the back and saying in a loud voice that children aren't aliens, and we're upstairs drinking vodka and tonics and Kass is trying to sleep with me again. But I'm wound so tightly that I can't, and she's moving off to her bedroom in a sulk saying I've made her terribly sad, and shortly after that, I ask her where she thinks my penis has got to, and she looks at me like I'm crazy and snorts and says, 'You're even madder than I am,' and that puts *me* in a sulk. I fetch a pillow and some blankets and lie on her sofa. Soon after that, I'm asleep.

At 9.45 a.m. the next morning, Katherine and I, who have made a truce over coffee and biscotti from her cupboard, are actioning my plan. I have my 'Things I Loved About My Sister' notebook in the largest pocket of my dress. I'm ready. We're hiding round the corner on Queen Anne Street, a position from where we have a clear line of sight to the school. My mind is boggy from eight hours of restless tossing and turning on Kass' blue sofa.

The waiting is unbearable. I turn my phone on – eleven missed calls from Ben and an email from Veronica.

These are amazing! Twenty-five poems in my inbox! I can't wait to show them to The Others. I'm back in the office later today. Should have told you about my holiday. Margate's interesting. Good pizza. Hope Pantea didn't scare you.

V

x

I show the email to Katherine.

'Good work, Marnie.' She reaches down and squeezes the top of my thigh.

I want to text Veronica back and check about the laureate thing, but there isn't time.

An Uber taxi pulls up. Out jumps Perdita in a sharp black trouser suit. I take a breath in and hold it.

Katherine nudges me. 'That's her?'

'Yeah!' My heart does a little jump. 'You see her?'

'Well, obviously,' Katherine says. 'Natty ... shoes.'

Black suede kitten heels. My sister's hair is bigger than yesterday and blow-dried to perfection. She looks every bit the successful vulture capitalist and I wonder what on earth she thinks our school is hoping to learn from her, unless it's how to profit from another's misfortune.

I need to see how all this is going to work. Will she float along the corridors if we're existing in parallel worlds, endlessly crossing over?

'Do we both have our feet on the ground?' I look down. My feet do appear to be touching the floor.

Katherine is saying, 'Classy.'

'She always is. *Was.*'

Katherine and I walk right up behind her. It's heady being this close to Perds again. She mounts the grand pillared steps to the school doors. We follow. The distance between us diminishes and my feet lift up away from Earth and I'm floating several inches above ground. Katherine appears to be doing the same.

'Our feet! This is what happened in my house yesterday, but only when I was close to her,' I hiss. 'What does it mean?'

'I don't know,' Katherine hisses back.

Perdita rings the ceramic bell on the wall. There's an actual bell-ringing sound, which throws me a little because I can't remember what exactly I'd just decided about the physics of everything. She's busy smoothing the front panels on her trousers.

'It's because we're in parallel worlds,' I explain to Katherine.

'We are?' Katherine's eyes widen.

'Yep. She's not a ghost. Or reincarnated. She can't see us, but the bell has just rung for real. You or I could ring that bell, too, if Perdita wasn't nearby. Get it?'

'Not really.'

'Perdita and I can make contact with tangible things across our two universes, just not *at the same time*. Now, is the school receptionist going to look through the little camera lens and see us *all* standing here at the door, or just one of us? And if so, which one?'

'Ah,' says Katherine. 'I see.' She rubs my arm supportively.

Perdita waits in front of us, her trousers neatened.

I reach out to touch the edge of one pocket. 'Look!' I say to Katherine. 'My fingers go right through her!'

Perds fans herself and says, 'Hot flush *now*, for Pete's sake?'

'Hello?' A posh voice over the intercom. 'Oh, it's you!' says the voice.

I recognise it as belonging to Mrs Shaw. Mrs Shaw is the school receptionist and has been working the front desk since the Jurassic period.

'I'll come and let you in.'

Mrs Shaw opens one of the doors and peers out. She smiles when she sees Katherine and me, or Perdita, or all of us, I can't tell.

'Such a lovely surprise!'

She opens her arms as if we were long-lost friends. Either side of Mrs Shaw's face, Perdita and I lean in to kiss her cheek. My kiss goes right through Mrs Shaw's face. Perdita's doesn't. I hear her lips making a smacking sound on Mrs Shaw's cheek, which confuses me. Is it possible the school receptionist exists in both worlds simultaneously?

Perdita says, 'Sorry I'm late,' and I say, 'I think there might have been some mistake, Mrs Shaw,' at the same time.

To which Mrs Shaw replies, 'No matter! The girls are waiting for you in the main hall. Thrilled you're back,' and I still have no idea to whom she's speaking.

We follow Mrs Shaw down the arched corridor. It goes on for ages and smells faintly of Bunsen burners.

'Darling, it hasn't changed a bit!' squeals Katherine as we pass the library decorated in William Morris wallpaper.

It's the same print as the one in Schlap's waiting area, a funny coincidence. The Victorian wood and glass-fronted bookcases are presumably in the same place as the era in which Katherine attended – or imagined she'd attended. I'm becoming disoriented: Katherine is real, but also pretending to be Mansfield?

My crotch throbs. I might be about to be sick.

Perdita is ahead of us, chatting away as Mrs Shaw speeds along the terracotta stone floor. I can't hear what my sister's saying, and Mrs Shaw is walking with great intensity and not looking at Perdita in the slightest.

I'm feeling even more peculiar now: light-headed, flushing hot and cold. I turn to Katherine, who's grinning broadly at everything on which her eyes alight.

'Don't you feel it?' I whisper.

'Feel what?'

'The ... surrealness? Like we're seeing the world through a fisheye lens?'

'No. This is *heaven*.' And she skips ahead to catch up with Mrs Shaw and my sister.

The sound of girls' low chatter as we climb the grand staircase to the main hall.

'After you,' says Mrs Shaw.

Perdita pushes open the wooden swing doors into the

wood-panelled hall. The two of us – Katherine and I – pass through after her. It's smaller than I remember. Spaces from the past always seem bigger in my imagination than in reality. A phalanx of green-and-blue uniformed girls are sat facing away from us towards a dais, on which stands a single slender wooden lectern with a microphone attached.

Perdita thinks she's giving a speech. Or they're expecting *me* to get up and talk. My throat is parched.

A diminuendo as the girls spot Mrs Shaw bustling our little party up front, inviting us to sit in a cluster of empty chairs, one of which is occupied by a kindly looking woman around my age, clearly the latest principal because she's drowning in a black gown. Mrs Shaw bends to speak to her, after which the principal looks at us, smiles broadly, nods and mounts the dais. The hall falls silent.

'Girls,' says the principal over the mic. 'It is with great pleasure that I welcome an old pupil.'

My heart is thumping.

'This ex-student,' she continues, 'spent six happy years here, followed by a last term fraught with tragedy and grief. She's gone on to make a great success of her life, birthing three lovely children.'

At this there's a collective titter.

'Holding down a top-tier job and extending the arm of extreme generosity towards us, leaving a legacy in the name of her twin sister, taken from us long before her time.'

I don't have a top-tier job and I'm leaving them no such legacy; it's Ben who makes the money in our house and I'm certain he won't be gifting any of it to my old school. I look at Katherine. She smiles at me. She's about as much use here as a packet of rubber nails. I lean round to look at my sister. It must

276

be her who's to speak, but she's just staring straight ahead, the picture of equanimity.

Could it be me? *Someone*'s got to get up.

I float to the front edge of the dais and turn to face my audience. The girls applaud. Feeling more confident, I gesture for them to quieten. They're far more obedient than in my day.

'Thank you so much,' I say, voice wobbling. 'It's so wonderful to be back here, but I'm afraid there's been the most terrible mix-up.'

The girls' eyes aren't on me, though. They're on something, or someone, behind me.

'Thank you, everyone!' Perdita's voice amplified by the microphone.

I spin round. She's standing at the lectern holding a wad of speech cards. Her reading glasses are on.

'It's wonderful to be back here as a benefactor, rather than simply a parent. I'm looking at you, Sophie and Cass.'

Gentle laughter from the audience.

'This school is rich with my bittersweet memories. Each time I cross the threshold into the beautiful main hall, I must confront my past, but particularly today, for it marks the thirtieth anniversary of my sister's passing.'

Now hang on.

'As many of you will know, we lost her three days before our eighteenth birthday. It changed my life and the lives of my family forever. The school was incredibly supportive, providing me with an on-call counsellor and everything else I needed to hold things together.'

I trip off the end of the dais and fumble my way back to the seat beside Katherine, who takes my hand firmly in hers. I haven't *died*. We're *both* living. Our two worlds have squished, become entangled.

'Today, I don't wish to dwell on sad times' – Perdita's voice rolls across the hall, an unstoppable force against which I'm the immovable object – 'but instead celebrate the good things that came from such a tragic event: my family and I finding solace through therapy; learning that throwing ourselves into our working lives with courage and enthusiasm heals wounds; that nothing lasts forever, and that life – to use a cliché Marnie would have hated – is not a rehearsal.'

The sun goes behind a cloud through the high windows. Up on the dais, Perdita is smiling.

'My sister loved writing. Poetry. She was a keen fencer.'

My feet are disappearing through the floor. Literally, through the floor.

Ben is the fencer, not me. *Ben*.

'Marnie proudly announced to our family one night that she ranked fourteenth in the UK for the Under-16s,' Perdita is saying. 'A notable achievement until you learn that there were in fact only twenty-five fencers in that category at the time.'

Laughter.

I glance at Katherine again. She's calm, smiling, her chin tilted up. Her eyes contain a secret message.

Perdita says, 'Marnie was on the cusp of life, about to take on the thorny issue of a boyfriend – a budding musician, who even wrote a song for her and played it at her funeral. He's now a successful lawyer, of course.'

Another gale of laughter.

'She was in the middle of completing her A-level English dissertation: "A brief journey through feminism across the twentieth century: using the medium of written word and silver screen, beginning with the epoch-defining Katherine Mansfield, through Sylvia Plath, ending with the many supporting roles played by Blythe Danner in the movies of Woody Allen."'

At this, Perdita gives a little tinkling laugh, just like Mum's.

'And if you can understand that, you're a better woman than me.'

More chuckling.

'Anyone who knew my sister couldn't fail to recognise her in this work. Her favourite word was "interesting", and that's exactly what she always was, right to her core. She was also always so very into the idea of quantum entanglement, my sister. That we could all be living alternative versions of ourselves, existing in multiple universes at once. I like to imagine she's here with us now, listening in, having her own *interesting* thoughts.' Perdita looks around the room. 'So, if you're here – hi, Marns, you're welcome. This is for you.'

This is for me? No hello, Perds. And *you* are welcome.

The principal is getting to her feet.

'It leaves me only,' Perdita says, 'to finish with the most important moment. The reason I'm here today: I'm delighted to announce a new bequest, the Marnie Rose Bursary, for any girl who shows outstanding promise in poetry and creative writing. I invite you to come up here after I've left the stage and honour Marnie by reading her dissertation. And please, second seniors, join us on the roof terrace for drinks afterwards. Thank you.'

My sister and I take a deep breath at the same time.

The room is dark, or darker than it was a moment ago. I look behind me – 300 stony-faced blazered girls are clapping.

Now, Perdita is shaking the principal's hand. They're embracing. The principal is saying, 'Thank you.'

Several girls climb the stage. They stand behind the lectern to read my dissertation.

Sylvia Plath. *Blythe* Danner. Katherine Mansfield.

I might be suffocating.

There are no scientific reports to date, that I know of,

detailing someone's experience in a parallel universe, but that doesn't mean …

I shake my hand free of Katherine's, though her grip is strong. I float back up onto the dais and stand behind the lectern. *I* want to see my dissertation. *I* want to see what it is that I wrote.

But when I get there, there's no writing. There aren't even pages. There's silence. A silence which isn't words, or even an absence of words – it's nothing.

Far, far away, I hear the sound of one set of hands applauding and look up.

The room is empty save for Katherine, her hands meeting in a slow, rhythmic clap, as if she doesn't like the show she's watching.

Not far away in the door stand a concerned-looking Ben, Schlap in a grey wool suit, Mrs Shaw and the principal, who appears to have aged twenty years in the last five minutes.

Mrs Shaw is saying in a low voice, 'The two of them must have sneaked in somehow. Perhaps the front entrance was left ajar. I recognised her the moment I saw her. She hasn't changed a bit.'

I get a fleeting sense of pleasure that Mrs Shaw considers I look the same now as I did thirty years ago.

'Marnie,' says Ben gently. 'You need to step down from there. This is a school study day. There are students here. We need to leave now.'

'Ben,' I say, because he doesn't understand, no one does. 'There are many universes. Perds was here, *just now*, making a speech. I'm straddling multiple planes.'

Schlapoberstein is moving towards Katherine and saying, 'Come along, Mary. You really shouldn't be here.' He takes her by the elbow.

'I will not.' Katherine stands.

Why is she speaking in perfect Received Pronunciation?

'I will stay with Marnie. She needs help.' She waves at me with her one free hand, then reverts to her New Zealand accent. 'Don't listen to them, darling. You're doing just *dandy*.'

Ben has his arm around my shoulder now. How has he reached the dais so fast? He's coaxing me from the hall and down the stairs, his body curved away from me as if I'm a wild animal that might bite, all the while apologising to the principal, who's saying, 'Not a problem, Mr Hopkiss. I do hope she feels better soon.'

We make our way along the entrance hall. I smell those Bunsen burners again and wish that I was in a lesson in the fusty old chemistry lab. Seconds before we leave the building, I get a whooshing feeling and look up. I see a sign above a door that reads 'Fire Exit' in illuminated writing on a green background with a man running into nothingness.

Before anyone can do anything to stop me, I shake myself free of Ben's arm, grab Katherine and drag her sharp left through an archway and across the steps of the main staircase. We veer sideways again, dipping beneath another arch, through one door and out of another. I'm still able to find my way around this school with my eyes closed and soon I'm dragging us down what would have been the old servants' stairwell, so small and winding it almost doubles back on itself, into the basement. We fly along the low corridor to the caretaker's cubbyhole, me praying there isn't an actual caretaker in there, and through the small wooden door, which I slam behind us.

It's pitch-dark inside. We're both panting. I hear Ben and the principal calling my name from the floor above. My hand searches the wall to find the light switch. The orange neon strips flicker to life. We squint as our eyes adjust.

I think: this is me having a panic attack.

'No one's going to believe us.' I can hardly get the words out.

'No,' Katherine replies.

'Who the fuck *are* you?' I poke her hard in the chest with my finger. My heart feels like it's about to jump out of my chest.

Katherine's hand comes up to my face and she slaps me roundly on the cheek. It stings like mad and I feel myself instantly redden.

'You're hysterical,' she insists. 'You need to calm down.'

'*I* don't need to calm down!' I hiss frantically. '*You* need to calm down!' No, that's not right, 'where *are* we?'

'In a cupboard,' she says.

'No, which world?'

Several sets of footsteps descend the staircase directly above us.

'Have you ever worn masks in your world?' I ask her.

'*Masks?*'

'Because of a disease. A pandemic.'

'You mean the Spanish flu?'

'No, another one.'

'Of course not!'

I throw a glance around the room. The cubbyhole is exactly as I remember it: messy, sloping steeply at one end. A couple of wooden shelves run at hip height along the length of both sides, littered with bits: sandpaper, pencils, tools. Perdita and I used to hang out here at lunch with the caretaker, doing Ouija boards, smoking fags.

Perdita's in another world than ours. But what about the principal? And the schoolgirls I saw just now in the assembly hall?

'Did this room exist when you were at school here?' I ask.

'I can't remember.'

'I think you would remember if you'd actually gone here, *Katherine*.'

A speck of my saliva lands on her chin. She doesn't wipe it away but stands there looking at me.

Now, the voices are directly outside the room. Neither of us moves.

A sharp knocking at the door.

I grip her arm very hard. 'Tell me,' I say. 'Which world?'

'Marnie, please, you're hurting me.' It's her RP voice and it takes me by surprise. I let her go.

'Marnie?' sings Mrs Shaw.

Or maybe it's Mrs *Sure*. I can't remember if I've ever seen her name written down.

'We know you're in there, both of you.'

'We'll come out,' I call. 'If you promise to believe what I'm going to tell you.'

'For God's sake,' I hear Ben say quietly. Then much louder, 'Marns, please. Come out, sweetheart. We need to get you home.'

I blow my nose on a piece of kitchen roll off the shelf. The paper smells of turps.

'Mary.' Now it's Schlap. 'Stop this. Come out at once.'

Katherine nods at me, then at the door. I pull it open. We emerge blinking into the basement corridor.

Ben, Schlap, Mrs Shaw and the principal are assembled in a semicircle in front of us. It's like Katherine and I are foxes that have been cornered outside our den by a pack of hungry dogs.

Ben re-establishes his arm around my shoulder and leads me in a procession with the others up the stairs and back along the entrance hall until we pass through the front doors.

This is what happens in a quantum universe mix-up situation. This is probably what anyone labelled schizophrenic, anyone burdened with the term 'paranoid delusions' has experienced. They've been *elsewhere*. Everyone – but everyone – in the similar-to-yours-but-not-quite-your world believes you're stark raving mad and there's nothing you can do to persuade them otherwise.

And worse, if you then cross back into your own reality, which is what appears to have happened to me here now, you might as well just say you've been abducted by aliens.

It's overcast and cold on the street. It was high summer when I entered the school thirty minutes ago and I'm shivering in my oversized dress, which I now realise resembles a sack. When I look down, my feet seem different: smaller, narrower, like the memory of feet – the way the school hall looked to me when I saw it just now as an adult.

Ben's trying to hail a black cab. I watch one idle at the lights. There's an advert on its side for a financial retirement plan. *I* had a plan, though now I can't remember what it was. I listen for the cab's familiar diesel rumble, the ticking of the meter running, but everything's muted, as if I'm wrapped in cotton wool. I whistle with two fingers in my mouth to attract its attention and its indicator goes on.

Schlap is saying, 'Mary, go home, all right?'

Katherine-Mary nods her assent and moves off in the direction of Schlap's house. I wave after her.

'Why won't you stay here and tell them?' I call to her with fading desperation. 'Why won't you back me up?'

Or *are* you really her? I think in my head. Are you in fact, as Ben imagines, entirely mad?

'*Would you not like to try all sorts of lives – one is so very small?*' she answers, walking away with a wave of her hand.

'*But that is the satisfaction of writing,*' I say to myself as I watch her go, completing the Mansfield quote for her. '*One can imper-sonate so many people.*'

Ben ushers me into the cab, which has pulled up beside us. I sit at one end of the long rear seat, Ben puts himself next to me and Schlap folds down the one that faces us. Riding with his back to the direction of travel will make him queasy. What's weird is that I no longer feel inside myself at all but seem to be floating nearby.

Ben instructs the driver. 'St Michael's Street, St Albans, please.'

'We're going to Mum's? That's going to be expensive in one of these.'

Ben takes my hand and squeezes it.

Perhaps Katherine Mansfield – the real one, I mean – had it right: if I focus on my writing, make it my priority, I'll no longer need this elaborate conceit I call reality because I'll create it for myself on the page. Perhaps I must write a novel. A book could be the answer to everything.

I stare out of the window, watch London passing me by, giving way to the North Circular, a dual carriageway, then the M1. Perhaps it's a metaphor for getting old. I don't even know what I mean by that.

The whole way, there are no trampolines without nets in back gardens to look at. Schlap's face is set. There's no point in speaking, so I say nothing.

My mother and father are waiting for us as the taxi pulls into my parents' drive. Mum's wearing the DIET apron. The ties are straining around the middle: too many of Dad's baguettes, I think, which actually makes me laugh. Everyone stares at me, so I stop. Dad has his hands clenched, I notice.

Mum offers Schlap a once-over before taking me in her arms. 'My darling.'

'Your bed's waiting for you, love.' Dad pats me softly on the back. 'Let's get you in it.'

'Okay,' I say, but my voice is strangled.

'Oh, *look* at her,' Mum's saying.

Dad leads me upstairs. I'd imagined I'd resist any of my parents' more charitable behaviour, but it turns out I've gone all bovine and follow Dad willingly, head bowed. It feels as if we're travelling downwards, but that can't be right. I hear Ben quietly introducing Schlap to my parents.

Schlap is saying, 'I fear I'm largely responsible.'

'You?' Mum trills. 'Responsible?'

'For Marnie's cognitive bias,' Schlap says.

Mum's tone is sharp. 'Her *what*?'

Dad leads me along the landing and into my bedroom. The duvet is turned down, just like it used to be when we were ill as kids. There's a glass of water, a copy of *Private Eye* and a single freshly cut rose from the garden in a little vase.

Ben's voice rumbles below, bassier at a distance. 'Patricia, cognitive bias is when a person creates a subjective reality and tailors their behaviour according to that reality.'

This doesn't sound either temporary or harmless and little needles of fear begin to prick me beneath the armpits.

'I see,' says Mum, but I can tell that she really doesn't.

I do, though. I see entirely. There's no quantum realm. Not one that I could ever be aware of, anyway. I'm just plain old having a breakdown.

I imagine the grumblings of an audience having watched the film of my life in a cinema, making their way along the aisles, popcorn stuck to their shoes, let down by the anticlimactic nature of this conclusion. Or worse, Veronica, reading it as a manuscript, shaking her head: bad Marnie, poorly done, Marnie.

'And in what way are you responsible for her ... cognitive bias, Doctor Schlapoberstein?'

My bedroom door is wide open and I hear every word crystal clear as if I'm still in the hall with them.

Schlap explains that there's an eccentric sitting tenant called Mary Read, who believes herself to be Katherine Mansfield, living on the third floor of his house. He's tried on several occasions to have her removed, but some ancient tenancy rights prevent it. He says Mary dresses appropriately for the period and speaks in an Antipodean accent. He says if one weren't in a robust mental state, one might question if one had seen a ghost, perhaps. A reincarnation.

I'm no longer removing my clothing but am standing motionless in the centre of the room. Dad's hand has come to a halt in mid-air. I've been undressing right in front of him and haven't even noticed.

'And?' Mum snaps when Schlap has finished speaking.

'And Marnie told me several times that she'd come across Katherine Mansfield,' Schlap continues. 'But since I've recently suffered a stroke, my memory has been compromised. *Is* compromised. I'm afraid I dismissed her claims as a figment of her extremely fertile imagination. I believe that this dismissal was in part responsible for her recent episodes. I'm terribly sorry.'

There's a silence. I remove my jewellery – watch, earrings, ring – and slide them carefully onto the saucer beneath the vase with the rose. They chink as they touch the glass.

Mary Read. Schlap's sitting tenant. She didn't tell me that bit. I thought she was one of Schlap's patients, like me. I hate her suddenly.

Downstairs, the little group move off into the living room and their voices are lost.

287

I look at Dad. He's looking right back at me, eyebrows raised. He smiles, bless him.

'Get your pyjamas on,' he says. 'Don't listen to all that jazz.'

I want to tell him it's not jazz, it's talking, but I'm extremely tired now and all I want to do is sleep. I pull on a pair of greying and pilled brushed-cotton pyjamas and fall into bed. Dad starts fussing with the duvet.

I lie back on the pillow. There's a spider on the ceiling. It's tiny and moving slowly from one side of the room to the other. I think how vulnerable it is, but also how lucky to lead such a simple life. If that spider lost a sibling, it wouldn't have cognitive bias. It would take the loss for granted as part of its short spider life. Then it would get back to making webs and things.

On the shelf on the other side of the room, I spy one tall pink hardback in a land of short creased-spine paperbacks. I can read its title from here: *Penis Envy and Other Bad Feelings* by Mari Ruti. It was a Christmas present from my parents three years ago in response to a comment I made at dinner once about wishing I had a penis just for a day. I'd completely forgotten I had it. I haven't read it because I left it here at the house by accident.

I turn to Dad. 'Are the girls and Stan coming soon?'

'Yes, love.'

His voice is soothing.

'They'll come right by to say hello after school.'

'Cool.' I sigh and roll over to stare at the window.

I have a dream.

I'm on the flat roof at the top of Schlap's house. Not far in the distance, female laughter and the clink of glass against glass. I make my way to one edge of the building and look out in a southerly direction.

A block and a half away, my sister, sipping champagne on the roof terrace of our old school. She's relaxed and smiling, standing in a throng of teachers, the principal and her own twin daughters. A gaggle of other sixth-formers mill around with flutes of orange juice. The girls are, to a woman, carefree and happy. They're all young: pretty or gawky, or pretty *and* gawky, in stiff uniforms, skirts and blouses. I recall the scratch and itch of those clothes, the smell of the school scarves after weeks lying balled up in fusty lockers.

And then I remember the accident.

A motorbike, not a car. The driver in a black helmet coming at me at speed, wrists twisting at right angles, the handlebars moving towards the pavement, wheels skidding out from underneath him. He's in leathers, sliding like they do in films, engine over-revving, not stopping, not stopping. A horrible thumping noise, a hard, sudden impact at my knees and then the back of my breastbone. No breath left. My feet lifting high in the air, head flipping back and down at the road. I know I must look like a gymnast this far up and that something very, very bad is happening. The last thing I see: a man in a Hawaiian shirt standing on the curb, face contorted. He's shouting for help, his arms reaching to the sky as if he's praying.

I wake up sweating. It wasn't me. It was Perdita.

Flinty chips of panic mount sharply in my head, making connections with one another, thickening, then melting and setting hard in a block like toffee. Perds and I are mirrors of one another. Or we're the same person. Or we're both alive.

Mary Read. A sitting tenant.

Footsteps outside my bedroom door.

'Darling?'

It's Mum.

'Can I come in?'

She doesn't wait for me to say yes or no, just enters anyway without knocking. She tiptoes across the room with exaggerated care and sits at the end of the bed.

'Sweetheart, how are you feeling?'

The apron's off. She's wearing a wildly inappropriate teddy-shorts thing underneath, with thick ribbed green tights and a biker's bandana tied at the side of her neck.

Is she, though? Or is her outfit part of my cognitive bias?

'What time is it?' I sound groggy.

'Three in the afternoon. Daddy's going to make you a boiled egg.'

'That's nice.' I sit up. 'I'm not *ill*, Mum. I mean I am, but not in a flu sort of way. I'm just ...' The word hangs in the air.

'Don't think about it now,' Mum prompts. 'Dr Schlapoberstein has been waiting downstairs to talk to you for two hours. You know, darling ...'

She spins me round. I'm forced to look directly into her eyes. They're swimming with tears.

'I can't help thinking if you'd only used the Church instead of this awful analysis, we wouldn't be *in* this mess. Anyway.' She sniffs ostentatiously. 'He'd like to speak to you when you're ready.'

'Right.'

'And the vicar's on his way over.'

'What?' I throw the duvet off. I stand too quickly and feel dizzy and the edge of the mattress cuts uncomfortably into the backs of my knees. 'I'm not dying. I don't need the last rites.'

'Don't be silly. He's not coming for that.' Mum also rises to her feet.

I think about the times I hoped I'd discovered my faith, prayed even, over the last few days. I think about my talk with

Vicar Pete. What does it mean if I'm still not sure I'm a be-liever? How can I face him now?

Mum and I are standing opposite one another like two cow-boys in a western, except closer. It does feel as if we're about to duel.

I imagine my brain is a fogged window in a car. I imagine bringing my hand up and wiping back and forth so I can look at the view.

'I need ...' I manage finally. I don't know what I need. 'I think I need to talk. To you.'

'About what?' Mum's eyes open wide.

'About what?' Is she doing this deliberately? 'About Perdita. The fact that she's ... not here any more.'

Mum waits patiently for me to say more. But I'm still not entirely sure if Perdita truly is gone. I'm staring at Mum's stomach, my fists all curled up and pushing against my kidneys.

'Perhaps you think it was my fault,' I say. Heat spreads across my face. 'Perhaps,' I venture, 'you wish it had been me instead.'

My mother grabs my arm. 'Wish it had been *you*? Of *course* I don't, Marnie. And how could it possibly be your fault?'

'Because.' My jaw goes tight. 'You know I made Perds go back for the camera.'

Mum lets go of my arm and her body goes limp. I begin to wonder if this is yet another of my episodes.

'There hasn't been,' she says, emphasising each word, 'for one moment, not a *second*, when either your father or I con-sidered you responsible. And ...'

I wish she'd shut up now.

'... it's *you* who's never wanted to talk about Perdita.'

This is damned well not true, and she knows it, but she's nodding as if she thinks she has a point.

'For *years* we've been waiting for you to bring it up. It was hardest of all for you. But the counsellor at school told us to hold off till you were ready.' She lets air leak out of her mouth slowly. Her voice softens. 'If you'd like to talk about Perdita, Daddy and I would *love* that more than anything.'

'You spoke to the school counsellor?'

The world is a jagged, whoopy place.

'Of course we did,' she says. 'You were all we had left.'

A slash opens in front of me. Perhaps this is the portal to the other world: the one where Perdita lives. Or perhaps this is where all the bad stuff, all my noisy chattering, can be packed, giving me space to feel something real. In my head, I throw everything into the foggy no-man's-land, like old clothes into a suitcase, then shove it to one side, but it turns out it's inside my body, a maw in the pit of my stomach.

I get that same feeling, like I'm going to be sick.

A clump of something bad slides out of my mouth. It has the texture of vomit, but I stare at the bed where it's fallen and see nothing.

I'm aware that someone's letting out a long, ugly howl. It's probably Mum. I think how ridiculous it sounds and by the time I realise it's me, I don't care, because I've stopped doing it.

Feet are shuffling outside my bedroom door and people are asking if things are all right, and Mum's holding me tightly and saying, 'She's fine!' and 'Shush. There, there.'

I'm not sure I entirely trust her, which makes me angry, but the hugging feels nice. My body's shuddering and twitching.

Ben pokes his head round the door. 'May I come in?'

His hair is messy on one side as if he's been leaning on his arm and his mouth is fixed in a line.

Mum doesn't look up. 'Not now, Benjamin.'

I disengage myself from her embrace. 'I'm nearly fifty, Mum. Of course you can, Ben.'

'*Fine,*' Mum says, and leaves. I hear her whisper on the other side of the door, 'Tread carefully. She's *fragile.*'

Ben looks at me and rolls his eyes, which makes me giggle. He's letting me know he knows it's still me.

I stand by myself in the middle of the room. He maintains his distance, standing at the mantelpiece, possibly because he thinks I'm angry with him, possibly because he's angry with me.

Perhaps he's afraid of me, his partner, the experiencer of cognitive bias.

He picks up a framed photo of Perdita and me, taken on one of our many family holidays in the Lakes. We're about ten years old, hair blown back by the wind, the sun shining on our faces. We have buck teeth and long lashes and are smiling uncertainly into the camera.

'I remember exactly when that was taken,' I tell him. 'On a boat travelling across Windermere, in October '82.'

'Oh?' says Ben, as if he's never seen the photo before, as if I haven't told him about that trip a million times already. 'It's lovely.' He puts the photo down. 'Look, Marnie ...'

It's never good news when people start with 'look', followed by my name.

'I don't think you're crazy. I need you to know that. I do, however, think you'll agree that you would benefit from help that isn't solely Schlap.'

'Uh-huh.'

'And possibly some medication.'

My heart does an unpleasant leap.

'What kind?'

Ben wants to turn me into one of those drooling zombies in the institution where he works.

He raises his hands. 'Please. We'll find the right treatment.'

'*We.* You, you mean.'

293

'No. Us, together. This won't fix itself overnight.'

'It might.' I give him a protracted sigh.

Ben waits patiently for me to finish.

'It's ironic that you're a shrink and you've ended up with a nutter.'

He doesn't smile. 'It'll take time and careful thinking. To work out exactly what you need.'

'What I *need*,' I say, repeating my way into my conversation with Mum, except that this time I know where I'm going, 'is for you not to make me invisible.'

He has the temerity to look startled.

'You don't pay me enough *attention*. Ever considered that that's a factor' – I gesture to myself – 'in all this?'

He goes very still.

'What?' I say, but I know what.

I should grow up. I should take responsibility. Long ago, something awful happened in my life and it's not my fault, but it's not Ben's fault, either. I think about his stupid book, his annoying hair flicking, his constant cashew nut munching, his skill of actively not listening, and feel really, really sad.

'Everything's so simple for you,' I say.

Ben asks if I've ever considered that his keeping things simple is a choice he's made. I tell him that's the sort of response I would expect from a cis white male, and that 'choice' is a privilege. He asks me when I'm going to stop seeing myself as a victim, which is harsh given where I find myself at the moment, but I appreciate his honesty. At least he's not patronising me which means he probably doesn't think I'm *that* insane.

'Please don't leave,' I say.

'Leave the room, or leave the relationship?'

'Me!' I sob.

His mouth starts to twitch. 'Don't be stupid.'

I wipe my nose on my sleeve and look down at the carpet. It's brown and old but very clean. Dad finds hoovering relaxing.

'Ben. There's something I need to tell you.' My tongue has gone dry. 'I slept with Mary Read, the woman in Schlap's house.' Everything inside me seems to be drifting up towards my head. 'I mean, I thought she was Katherine Mansfield, but anyway.' My head is a helium balloon. 'That's what I did. I'm sorry.'

'I know.' He leans one elbow against the mantel. 'Mary told Schlap, who told me.' He raises his shoulders.

'You *know*? Why are you shrugging like that? Don't you care?' I look around to see if I can locate a clock.

'Of course I care. What are you doing?'

'Is this real?'

'Oh, Marns.'

'I just ... Why can't you help me out?'

'It's real. This is happening, sweetheart.'

That's twice he's used 'sweetheart' on me today. He never normally calls me that.

'What if I'm not mad, though?' I risk asking. 'What if I crossed into another dimension and returned?'

'Marnie.' He looks at me warningly.

'It could happen. Follow the science!' I don't know why I'm bothering. I think of something. 'I thought I had a cock,' I whisper.

'You ... what?'

'A penis. I grew one. I could feel it and everything. And I used it. On Katherine. Mary. Whatever her name is.'

Ben looks at his shoes for a long time.

'You know,' he says eventually, 'that's not that unusual, penis envy.'

'No,' I insist, glancing at the Mari Ruti book that I haven't yet read. 'You don't understand. It wasn't *envy*. It was real.'

'Marns. You need to understand I do this for a living. What you're telling me is another example of your cognitive episode.'

He licks his lips. I wonder if he's nervous.

I glance at his jeans. They're too wide at the ankle and there's a hole in one knee. I get that panicked feeling again.

'You know, when I saw Perdita in our home, she and Dashiell mentioned something called a "lockdown" and talked about a "sixth wave" and said they'd need to get their *masks* out again, as if there were some sort of deadly disease spreading across the planet.'

Ben frowns. 'Now that *does* sound a little crazy.'

'I know.'

It really does, when I say it in this room with my partner, in this world where we are, of course, disease-free and not in some sort of proto-dystopian quantum soup. Ben's right: I need help.

'When did we last have sex?' I say, after a moment.

'Huh?'

'Three months ago? More?'

Where has the person I used to be gone? I need to find her. Even a small piece would do. So I can trace my way home.

'I thought Mary was pulling Mansfield quotes out of her fanny.'

Ben starts laughing. Really properly laughing. And I realise with great certainty that everything will be okay between us.

'Oh, Marns.' He wipes the tears from his eyes and moves towards the door. 'I'm going to let Schlap in, all right? He's been outside for ages. He wants to apologise. I'll just be downstairs.'

'But I don't want to talk to anyone else now.'

'I think you should,' he says. 'I think it'll be helpful.'

I tell him I'm sorry again as he leaves.

I'm not sure I have the energy for another chat. Ben's

just said it's going to take time to fix me, so why the sudden urgency from everyone? I feel a bit like a carriage clock on the *Antiques Roadshow* with, in a break with tradition, *all* of the experts trooping in one after the other to do a valuation.

Where to put myself to receive Schlap? I settle on staying where I am: upright and smack in the middle of the room.

'Marnie?' Schlap respectfully remains out of sight behind the door.

'Come on in, then,' I say but nicely.

He makes his way to the faded armchair in the corner of the room, pulling his trousers out at the knees in his usual style as he drops to sit.

'So,' he begins.

'So,' I echo.

We stare at one another.

'I'm not imagining this, am I? Ben said this is real.'

This is a philosophical grey area I have no desire to visit, but it's important to check.

'Ben is correct.' He smiles.

'He told me you want to apologise, but there's no need. I heard what you said downstairs. It's not your fault. Let's face it, Mary wasn't the only thing I was making mistakes about.'

Schlap says, 'Hmm.'

He has mournful eyes. They remind me of Parker's.

'Death can be a lonely place,' he says. 'Shall I tell you something? Something that, to my mind, is a positive aspect to your ...' He looks uncomfortable.

'Breakdown?' I offer.

'Let's call it that if you feel okay with it. Each one of your imaginings was a figment, a symbol, Marnie, do you agree?' He pinches the bridge of his nose, as if he's Hercule Poirot. 'Simple manifestations of your repressed unconscious.'

'Well, perhaps not so much the *simple* part.'

'So, although subjectively your cognitive bias may seem to be a negative event in the overall timeline of your mental health, it could be turned on its head, could be celebrated. Do you see? Jung would argue your creations were art, on a par with the best poetry, painting and music.'

'Would he?'

'Indeed. Art exists outside what is real. Or "not real".' He makes air quotes with his fingers.

It's odd, him sitting in the chair and me standing in the middle of the room. Like a session gone awry. I scuff my feet against the carpet. Perhaps this is why Schlap does it. When life is too much, when he can't fathom the beyond-ness of things, scuffing his toes is the only action that tethers him to the Earth.

'You know, Mum says I'm the one who doesn't want to talk about Perdita, but that's not true.'

'Well, that's your mother's experience of events. That doesn't make you wrong. We both know the truth is subjective, just as life, *objectively* speaking, may not have a point.'

'But which of the events – as you call them – of these last few days was real, and which wasn't?'

He rises. 'Does it matter, in the end?'

'Yes.' The thought of it not mattering makes me want to stamp my feet.

'Only you can answer that question, my dear. But perhaps not today, eh? I truly am sorry for any part I played in this.'

'Will you have to retire?'

He meets my gaze. 'Possibly.'

'Can I still see you?' I sound awful. 'I'd still like to see you.'

He chuckles. 'I don't think I'd be able to charge you.'

'Even better.' I pause. 'I've been thinking I might try writing a novel,' I say.

'I look forwad to reading it one day.'

He gives me a hug, which feels unprofessional but lovely. After that, he walks out, closing the door behind him.

It's nice to be alone. I wander to the window and stare down at the back garden. Dad's snipping chives from a rectangular flowerpot with a pair of kitchen scissors.

I put my hand against the windowpane and am hit by that odd, yet familiar, melancholy. I tap my fingers against the glass. Dad looks up. He straightens, squints into the setting sun and gives a wave with the scissors.

'Boiled egg, five minutes!' he mouths.

I nod and rub my stomach with my hand.

Downstairs, the front door is opening. My children! My kids are entering the house, the sound of them robustly lip-smacking Mum and Ben, their feet thumping on the stairs.

There's a jumping sensation in my stomach. They might not know what to say to me, or worse, might be scared. What if—

'Hi, Mum.'

It's Stan, wearing his usual expression of benign indifference. He rolls across the room to kiss me vaguely on one shoulder.

'Those pyjamas are rank.'

'Thanks.'

Sweet, sweet smelly Stan. I could weep with happiness. I grab his hand. It feels reassuringly small.

'I'm fine, by the way, in case you were worried,' I tell him.

'I know.'

He shrugs, without looking at me, and walks away humming, parking himself on the side of the bed, where he takes out his phone and begins to text. I think about all of his friends, the secret world of Stan that I know nothing about.

'Mum?' The girls are standing side by side, trying hard to

act casual, and for a second, I can't tell which one of them has spoken.

'I'm so sorry,' I say.

'What for?' Sylvia asks kindly.

'I've not been a great mum recently. I think I just need ...' I'm telling everyone I love today what I need, but it isn't getting me anywhere. 'I'm so sorry about your party. Would you mind very much if we delayed it for a couple of months?'

'Course not.' Sylvia takes a step forward. 'S'totally fine.'

With relief I sit next to Stan on the bed.

'We love you, Mum,' says Blythe. She heads towards me, nuzzles the top of my head with her nose. 'Take all the time you need. We can look after Dad.'

This is the nicest thing that's happened so far today.

'I love you so much,' I say. 'You're all brilliant.'

'Well, I am,' says Stan, without looking up from his screen. 'The girls are shit.'

Dad calls up, 'Egg's ready!'

I'm absolutely starving. I grab the kids and we head downstairs so they can watch me eat.

Days pass – three of them, I think. It could be more. I'm mostly in pyjamas, reading childhood books in my bedroom or watching the telly, or eating gorgeous simple meals made by Dad. Sometimes I'm in the garden helping Mum with the azaleas. My relentless inner monologue becomes unusually quiet and I note with relief that I'm no longer making jokes in my head, no longer undermining myself.

People come and go, Ben and the kids mainly, but also Vicar Pete, who's here for moral support.

I manage to ping off an email to Veronica, briefly outlining what's happened but also checking if she ever made any mention of the laureateship regarding my work. She hadn't, of course. Goodness knows what it was she'd really said.

On one of the days, I receive a text from Katherine–Mary's number.

How are you, darling?

I stare at it for a long time, wondering whether or not to answer.

I'm okay. No thanks to you.

Seconds later, she replies.

I'm sorry. I have problems.

I gathered. You lied to me.

No. You saw what you wanted to see. Yes, I spend most of my time dressed in another woman's clothing, pretending to be her, but that isn't a crime.

Don't make jokes.

I'm deadly serious.

We had sex under false pretences. Didn't you know I was vulnerable?

We were both consenting adults. And we are ALL vulnerable.

I look at the wall for a moment.

What about my penis?

What about it?

Why did you encourage me to imagine I had one?

There's a long gap before she answers.

Marnie: it's a man's world.

I don't hear from her again.

As the days go by, I begin to feel my own more accepted definition of 'normal', by which I mean myself, but without cognitive bias. I become confident of the difference between when things happen objectively and when they're simply in my head. It's faintly amusing that everyone talks about my having had 'an episode', or 'a breakdown'. These terms are cold and banal, and far, far from the complex world, the colourful events, that I've experienced in the last ten days.

One thing I am sure of and that is that I don't think I'll ever be able to stem my constant over-thinking. I don't feel too bad about it. I attribute it to trauma. Schlap was right when he said I was depressed. But not in the classic sense: I have PTSD.

I attempt to read the *Penis Envy* book but give up on page ten. It's not that it's bad, just that I'd rather read Enid Blyton.

I spend a great deal of time writing lists about what happened in order, untangling things in my head. I *did* write my history dissertation around Katherine Mansfield, for example, but back at the school last week, when I started to make connections, stuff such as names like Blythe and Sylvia, that was simply a set of coincidences. I *did* do fencing and so does Ben. Another coincidence. Mad people look for connections where there are none.

But what about other events? What about Faaris telling me about Perdita Rose's payment for the party? What about the man I saw in Schlap's waiting room? The magically swapped paintings and my poems buried in Mum's planter? What about Perds? What about quantum entanglement? That's a real thing, not just something I invented in my head. For these I have no explanation, which is maddening in itself, though there's nothing more I can do about it now. Sometimes life is like that. That may seem a passive line to take, but honestly, it's more like acceptance. I feel Faaris would approve.

On the evening of what I estimate to be the fourth day at my parents' house, I sit in the armchair in my room alone, the photo of Perdita and me on the boat at Windermere in my hands.

The kids are downstairs with Ben. They've been here for hours. We had supper together around the kitchen table. Mum did a lot of belly laughing. Stan told a story about falling asleep on a 134 bus and waking up at the end of the line in Barnet. It was nice. Warm. Real.

I'm hoping to go home tomorrow. Everyone agrees this is a plan. Next week, I have an appointment with a psychiatrist, a woman with an unremarkable name. I'm confident her shoes will be ordinary. The following week I'm seeing someone else to begin a course of EMDR.

I look down at the photo. My fingers leave greasy prints on the glass.

It was a great holiday: the four of us travelling around the Lakes, the sun shining on the heather-red hills, Perds and I poking through the sunroof of Dad's car, arms in the air.

Schlap says my imaginings are to be celebrated. I want to imagine my sister. I want to conjure her here for me, now. For a person suffering from cognitive bias, knowingly conjuring up events might be risky, and the desire feels secret, shameful.

There's a soft knock. Someone's waiting in the doorway. She's framed against the lengthening shadows that fall across the landing. An actual physical need blossoms inside my chest.

Her gaze slides around the room. She's young, lissom as a streak of ribbon. She's in the clothes she wore on the last day I ever saw her alive; my pale blue Levi's 501s – she'd borrowed them without asking – the ones with the rips at the knees, a black-and-white striped top and Doc Martens. The police offered to give them back after the inquest, but I couldn't bear it. I'd always imagined they'd have had blood over one leg – they'd told me she'd smashed her knees – yet here they are, pristine and lovely, just as she is.

For a second she does nothing, but then her eyes lock with mine and I watch them widen and crease, and her whole face opens, and tears shine on her cheeks. I'm instantly up, flying out of the chair, and we're in one another's arms, and my arms go right around her, she's that tiny, and the room spins, and I *feel* her, *smell* her, her peachy shampoo, and I'm crying, as well. They're tears of happiness; sometimes it's hard to tell the difference.

Her skin is as warm as hot chocolate, the flesh of her arms below her top is smooth, taut. Her small, high breasts push against my chest. I squeeze so hard I risk suffocating us both.

'Marnie?'

There's a stutter in her voice, her lips on my head. That one word, my name. It vibrates at the side of my skull. I've never felt so alive.

We pull away, hold one another at arm's length. My eyes travel from her forehead to her nose, the smooth curve of her cheeks and mouth, the short chin with a hint of a dimple, the top lip that is wide and curved and points upwards into a smile. So few wrinkles. Did I ever look this perfect? I've never in all my life considered myself to be beautiful, but looking at my sister here, myself outside myself, I see that once I was. She smiles, uncertain. Her hand goes to her mouth.

'Have I got stuff on my face?'

'Nope. You look ...' Here I am, reflected in her pupils. I can't tell exactly what my face is doing, making the shape of a smile or frowning, but I know I'm full up on the inside and that Perdita feels the same. 'You're perfect.'

'Where are we, anyway?'

I love that she's casual. It's as if we've never been apart.

'Whose bedroom is this?'

'It's my bedroom in Mum and Dad's new house,' I say. 'They moved to St Albans.'

'St *Albans*?' she cries, and we both giggle. 'Look at you,' she says. 'How did you get so old?'

'Time's a cruel mistress.' I hug her again. 'That's what they told us – old people – when we were young, d'you remember? We never understood what they were talking about.'

She looks down at her legs. 'Sorry about the jeans. I'll wash them and give them back. Promise.'

'No need. Oh, Perds. It's *you*!'

'It's me!'

I love her so much I think I might pass out. I hold my palm open for her and she presses her own against it, and winds her fingers through mine tightly. Her hand is warm and dry and soft.

'Let's sit.' I settle us cross-legged on the floor, facing one another. I lean in and kiss her hair. 'There's not much time.'

It's dark now. I can just make out the sharp lines of the bed. It comes so fast, the failing light.

My sister's eyes are luminescent in the gloom. Her breath is sweet, minty. Her fingers smell of biscuits. I can deny her nothing.

Perdita bends towards me, our foreheads touching, the two of us like swans, like the shape of her non-existent, never-to-be-born daughters' imaginary birthday cake.

'Missed you,' she says. She puts her hand up to itch her cheek. 'Old carpets.' She lets out a sneeze, then a laugh.

'I don't have that.'

'Yeah.' She touches my nose. 'You got the creativity and no dust allergies.'

'But I got the eczema.' I want to melt into her. 'Tell me about yourself.'

She cocks her head and her hair falls across her eyes. She scrapes it back behind her neck. 'What d'you want to know?'

'Anything,' I say. 'Everything.'

She snorts. I think how like my girls she is.

'Okaaay.' She squints at the ceiling, 'Um. I still have our childhood collection of marbles, the ones with coloured swirls. Did you know that?'

I shake my head.

'They're in the attic along with the photo album with the red cover and all of our BAGA gymnastics cotton badges in a box.'

'Right.' This is brilliant. 'Remember why Mum never ironed those onto our leotards?'

'Children' – Perdita imitates Mum's voice – 'shouldn't be labelled.'

I pull my feet in further under my bottom. 'Go on.'

'Okay. That boy, Frankie Pullen in the other class.' She makes a groaning noise. 'I don't really fancy him. He's so *nice*, I can't bear to reject him. When he kissed me at a party, he stuck his tongue that far down my throat I thought I was going to puke.'

'I remember.'

'How can you remember that bit? I've only just told you.' She drops her voice to a whisper. 'He tried to finger me, Marns. It was like being stabbed in the fanny by a Twiglet.'

I try very hard not to laugh. 'Ouch.'

'Yeah.' She looks around the room again, at the bed, the armchair, the little table. 'You know, sometimes I think about what it would be like if you weren't around.'

'Do you?'

'I don't know why. You tell *me* something, now.'

'Okay.'

I tell her how I went snowboarding with friends on Millennium New Year's Eve in Andorra and broke my rib falling onto my own fist. I tell her I used to stare out of the open window in our old house in Kentish Town, play Kate Bush at top volume and will her to fly back in. I tell her I'm allergic to *something*: to oysters. And that I love Negronis and that Stan has terrible taste in music.

She says, 'What's a Negroni?' and asks me who Stan is.

I tell her silly stuff, like how I once went out with a young man I met at a friend's birthday party in a large room at the Great Eastern Hotel in Liverpool Street. He arrived at our floor in the lift and I dropped my glass when the lift doors opened to reveal him standing there, as if rendered dyspraxic by his beauty, when really, I was just very, very drunk. This story makes her laugh a lot.

I tell her I like the smell of grapefruit, and that I'm entering the perimenopause and it's seriously messing with my body and my mind.

She says, 'Define perimenopause.'

I'm mesmerised, dazzled by her. She is a series of blinding catseyes on a dark road marking the way home.

'I want to read you something,' I say.

307

'What is it?'

'A poem. For you.'

She crosses her legs the other way and looks pleased. 'Wow. No one's ever written anything for me before.'

'Oh, they will,' I tell her. Then I read her the poem:

> *You crease me,*
> *The spine of my favourite book.*
> *Sit on my hands for you*
> *While the sky flies away.*
> *Love your ugly face*
> *Live with my fingers in your mouth.*
> *Fit me*
> *Settle on me like a moth.*

She doesn't say anything. Just takes my hand and kisses it.

The sound of the TV floats up from downstairs. Stan's singing to the theme tune of *The A-Team*, repeated on some cable channel, before it suddenly switches to someone talking.

'Are you ready?' I say to Perdita.

'Ready,' she answers.

I kiss her forehead. 'It's time,' I tell her.

'Okaythenthat'sgreat,' she says.

It's Perds. That's who says it.

Said it.

My girls have inherited my sister's vernacular. It's a miracle.

Or epigenetics.

I wrap her in my embrace for the last time, breathe her smell. Neither of us can bring ourselves to move.

'Perds?'

'Yes?'

'When we were little, did we ever play a game in the car

while we were travelling on long journeys? It involved moving our hands and feet up to the top of the window. I remember we played it on our trips to the Lakes, mostly. Have I got that right?'

Her eyes are alight. 'Where the windows were always warm when we touched them? Yeah! In my head, the sun was always shining outside, but that can't have been the case, can it?'

I smile. 'That's how I remember it.'

'Cool.'

She looks pleased.

'Thank you.'

'Thank *you*.'

We bow to one another.

I put the photograph carefully back on the mantel.

I found those marbles, after she died. Just as she said, in the box in the attic with the certificates and the red photo album. I've still got them at home.

I head downstairs. The wool stair runner is prickly against the soles of my feet. The hall tiles, when I reach them, are icy. I pass the living room: the kids and Ben are sitting on the sofa with their backs to me in a line watching the *Ten O'Clock News*.

Directly ahead, in the kitchen, Mum and Dad are laughing. I approach cautiously and hover in the doorway. They stand at opposite ends of the long room throwing Dad's home-made bread to one another, a ritual in our home since we were children. Dad always told us it improved the rise after the kneading had been done, though in truth I think he just enjoyed watching us topple under the weight of the dough. A fine mist of flour hangs in the air – he has a dab of it on his cheek.

They see me and stop.

'All right, poppet?' says Dad.

'Yeah,' I say.

I take out my 'Things I Loved About My Sister' notebook and put it on the one patch of worktop not smeared in flour and rolling pins.

Outside, unseen by anyone else, I watch Perdita pass the kitchen window and disappear into the night.

'I've got something I'd like to read you,' I tell my parents.

'Of course.' Dad hurries to put the bread down.

Mum and he sit on stools around the breakfast bar, their faces lifted.

END

Acknowledgements

Thank you hugely to the following people without whom this book simply wouldn't exist. The wonderful team at Gollancz: Marcus Gipps, Brendan Durkin, Claire Ormsby-Potter, Will O'Mullane, Lucy Cameron, Claire Dean, Micaela Alcaino and Paul Hussey.

My agents at United, forever my safe space – thank you: Laura Macdougall, Olivia Davies, and Jen Thomas.

The Faber Academy 2018, the course on which I wrote this book. My tutor there, Richard Skinner, for his continued support and mentoring, as well as my entire class for their feedback and cheerleading. They are Charli Faux, Chloe Timms, Deborah Appleton, Hayley Dunning, Lorna Blackman, Nicole Johnston, Sarah Rutherford, Jane Peng, Alasdair Lawrence, Kate Reid, Ruth Geldard, Michelle Sagan and Lily Shahmoon. I cheer for them, too, on their writing journeys.

I'd also like to thank my ever-brilliant writing group here in North London: Roger Hyams, Albyn Leah Hall, Jessica Weetch, Megan Walsh, Sarah Flax, Pascale Harter and Anne Rabbit.

Thanks to my mum for reading several early drafts of this novel, and for her encouragement. And to Deborah Appleton, Nicole Johnson, and Emily Bruni for the same.

Thank you to John and Kit Stevenson, as ever, you have tolerated my commandeering of the living room coffee table to get this novel written.

Thank you to Queens College School, for teaching young women they will always have permission to strive to become whatever they want.

To Katherine Mansfield, for the inspiration and for allowing me to use your words. I hope you would approve.

Finally, I would like to acknowledge any young person who has lost their life to suicide, or who has left before their time for another reason. Fare forward and safe travels, wherever you may be.

Credits

Susannah Wise and Gollancz would like to thank everyone at Orion who worked on the publication of *Okay Then That's Great*.

Agent
Laura Macdougall
Olivia Davies

Editor
Marcus Gipps
Claire Ormsby-Potter
Áine Feeney

Copy-editor
Claire Dean

Proofreader
Bruno Vincent

Editorial Management
Jane Hughes
Charlie Panayiotou
Tamara Morriss
Claire Boyle

Audio
Paul Stark
Jake Alderson
Georgina Cutler

Contracts
Anne Goddard
Ellie Bowker
Humayra Ahmed

Design
Nick Shah
Joanna Ridley
Helen Ewing

Finance
Nick Gibson
Jasdip Nandra
Elizabeth Beaumont
Ibukun Ademefun

Afeera Ahmed

Sue Baker

Tom Costello

Inventory

Jo Jacobs

Dan Stevens

Marketing

Lucy Cameron

Production

Paul Hussey

Fiona McIntosh

Publicity

Will O'Mullane

Sales

Jen Wilson

Victoria Laws

Esther Waters

Frances Doyle

Ben Goddard

Jack Hallam

Anna Egelstaff

Inês Figueira

Barbara Ronan

Andrew Hally

Dominic Smith

Deborah Deyong

Lauren Buck

Maggy Park

Linda McGregor

Sinead White

Jemimah James

Rachael Jones

Jack Dennison

Nigel Andrews

Ian Williamson

Julia Benson

Declan Kyle

Robert Mackenzie

Megan Smith

Charlotte Clay

Rebecca Cobbold

Operations

Sharon Willis

Rights

Susan Howe

Krystyna Kujawinska

Jessica Purdue

Ayesha Kinley

Louise Henderson

6/8/22 CENT